THE THRILLER THAT WAS SUGGESTED BY THE HEAD OF THE KGB!

"During a meeting with Andropov, the KGB chief told Semyonov that 'for a couple of years, the CIA had a very important operation in the Soviet Union.' Andropov offered to put Semyonov in touch with KGB generals familiar with the case, 'if you're interested.'

" 'Of course I was interested,' Semyonov says. 'It was sensational!' "
Chicago Sun-Times

"[Semyonov] has been there. He knows the men involved. He's a friend of Mikhail Gorbachev and Gorbachev's wife Raisa is one of his biggest fans."
The London Daily Mail

"Semyonov is a dynamo—and an enigma who seems to become more mysterious with each facet revealed."
Publishers Weekly

TASS IS AUTHORIZED TO ANNOUNCE...

JULIAN SEMYONOV

Translated by Charles Buxton

AVON BOOKS · NEW YORK

Originally published in the U.S.S.R. in 1979 by *Druzhba Narodov* under the title *TASS Upolnomochen Zaiavit . . .*

AVON BOOKS
A division of
The Hearst Corporation
105 Madison Avenue
New York, New York 10016

First Avon Books Printing: August 1988

AVON TRADEMARK REG. U.S. PAT. OFF. AND IN OTHER COUNTRIES, MARCA
REGISTRADA, HECHO EN U.S.A.

Printed in the U.S.A.

K-R 10 9 8 7 6 5 4 3 2 1

NOTE TO THE READER

Julian Semyonov's novel is set internationally, partly in Moscow, partly in Africa, and there are some scenes in the U.S.A. Western readers usually have some trouble with Russian names and therefore a "cast list" follows on the next page. There is also a glossary at the end of the novel of words that occur in the text. These are marked with an * and can be looked up alphabetically.

CHARACTERS IN THE NOVEL

Nelson GREEN: American businessman, boss of Worlds
    Diamonds
Michael WELSH: Deputy director of the CIA
Harold WEEKLY: American businessman, Vice-President
    of the PLP Corporation.
Simon CHOU: American businessman of Chinese origin
Ho LIU BO: General, Deputy Minister of Foreign Trade
    in Peking

Dmitri Yurevich STEPANOV: Soviet journalist
Vitaly Vsevolodovich SLAVIN: KGB field officer
Konstantin Ivanovich KONSTANTINOV: Major-General,
    KGB
Pyotr Georgevich FYODOROV: Lieutenant-General, KGB

George GRISO: Prime Minister of Nagonia
Mario OGANO: General, leader of Nagonian nationalist
    rebels
Robert LAWRENCE: Representative of International Tele-
    phonic and CIA Station Officer, Lewisburg
John GLEBB: businessman resident in Lewisburg
Paul DICK: American journalist with the *Post*
General STAU: Chief of Police, Lewisburg
Pilar SUAREZ: Spanish woman, resident in Lewisburg
Donald GEE: American journalist with the *Star*
Eugene KUSANNI: American film director
Emma GLEBB: wife of John Glebb
LAO: Chinese secret agent in Lewisburg

Charles van ZEGER: Dutch businessman, resident in Moscow

Lida KONSTANTINOVA: wife of Konstantinov

Igor Vasilyevich DULOV: KGB officer, Lewisburg

Mikhail Mikhailovich PARAMONOV: garage foreman with Soviet firm Mezhsudremont

Adrei Andreyevich ZOTOV: marine engineer stationed in Lewisburg

Viktor Khrisanfovich KHRENOV: Russian emigré, resident in Lewisburg

Olga Viktorovna VINTER: research assistant, wife of Zotov

Leopold Nikiforovich SHARGIN: civil servant in the Ministry of Foreign Trade

Oleg Karpovich ARKHIPKIN: gardener at the Soviet Embassy, Lewisburg

Ivan Yakovlevich EREMIN: Deputy Head of Department, Ministry of Foreign Affairs

Ivan BAILLIEU: Russian emigré, resident in Lewisburg

Irina PROKHOROVA: woman friend of Slavin

Raisa Ismailovna NIYAZMETOVA: doctor, friend of Vinter

Sergei Dmitrievich DUBOV: research assistant, friend of Vinter

Galina Ivanovna POTAPENKO: accountant with a Soviet auto service firm, friend of Vinter

Lev Vasilyevich LUKIN: research worker, friend of Vinter

Olga VRONSKAYA: secretary, friend of Dubov

Vitaly VINTER: father of Olga Vinter

SIDORENKO: retired lieutenant-colonel, neighbour of Dubov

UKHOV and KARLOV: film directors at Mosfilm studios

Rimma NEUSTROYEVA: make-up artist at Mosfilm studios

LUNS, KARPOVICH, JACOBS: CIA officers under diplomatic cover, Moscow

PANOV, TRUKHIN, PROSKURIN, KONOVALOV, GMYRYA, GRECHAEV, ZHVANOV, GABUNIA, NIKODIMOV, DRONOV, GAVRIKOV, STRELTSOV: KGB Officers, Moscow.

1

Inside the Military-Industrial Complex

"You see, Michael," said Nelson Green thoughtfully, as he watched his grandchildren doing somersaults in the swimming-pool, which was lined with red tiles brought back from a posting in Turkey, "any sense-perception is reliable enough—*as a perception.* But beliefs based on perception are a different matter. A belief can be true or false . . . A lecture I once heard by Professor Mitchell sticks in my mind—you were still a boy then, a long way from Deputy Director of the CIA! Anyway, Mitchell said that if an oar dipped in water looks broken, then those sense-data are correct inasmuch as they are what the observer experiences. But if the observer goes on from this to say that the oar really *is* broken, then his belief will prove incorrect . . . In other words, my dear Michael, people's mistakes don't consist so much in errors of perception—perceive what you like, good luck to you!—as in their bad judgement . . ."

Nelson Green leaned back, squinting. His eyes were as small as droplets of water, almost hidden from sight under greying eyebrows. During meetings of the advisory board of his corporation, Worlds Diamonds, the secretaries could never work it out: was the old man really watching them, or had he fallen asleep with his eyes open?

"So my sensation that the strawberries we've just

been served have the fragrance of Texas—is *that* correct?''

"That's not a sensation, Michael, it's a judgement. And the answer is negative. The strawberries we just ate couldn't smell of Texas, it's still too cold there. They smell of Africa, and these days I have to bring them over from Lewisburg, not Nagonia, which is a pity. They cost forty-seven cents more in Lewisburg and the air journey is 192 kilometres further—which means extra fuel and that costs money."

"Don't tell me you're going broke?" said Welsh.

"Could be," Green rejoined. "As they say, it begins with a few cents, not millions of dollars."

"So . . ." Welsh paused. "Tell me, what influence do you have with the Pentagon these days?"

Green took a sip of jasmine tea.

"You mean as regards deliveries of strawberries using USAF air transports," he pretended to misunderstand. "I think I could work on them . . . But seriously, what do you mean? Got something specific in mind?"

"Yes. But it all hangs on the support of the Pentagon."

"No problem there. But the State Department—have you brought *them* on board yet?"

"Are you kidding?" Welsh replied. "And risk some fool go public on us! No, it's far too early for that. You know, I recently saw some medical reports. Our diplomats drink far too much these days. A survey carried out in three of our embassies showed that seventy per cent of the staff suffer from chronic liver complaints!"

"Don't dodge the question, Michael. You know very well that my own interests are not so far removed from those of our buddies in the State Department. Worlds Diamonds lost maybe three hundred million dollars in Nagonia, but they said good-bye to a couple of hundred thousand. And they naturally feel sore about it."

"Nelson, believe me, it's still too early to bring in the State Department. If it all goes according to plan—"

Nelson Green interrupted: "Don't argue with an old man. The Special Envoy is a business partner of mine. He'll say exactly what we write out for him in my office.

Take my advice, Michael, don't be a fool. Just give me
the outline of your plan, perhaps I can be of use to you,
even if only as an adviser . . ."

"Well, the outline will interest you. The first thing is,
we have an agent in Moscow. A very well-informed person. So we're not planning in the dark, we can consider
our moves, knowing in advance the possible counter-moves
from the Kremlin. Do you understand what that means?
We've never had an agent like this before, Nelson, and
that's why I'm so confident of success."

"Touch wood, all the same."

Welsh rapped his knuckles on his head: "Best ce-
dar," he said, and hurried on: "So the point is, since
we have such an agent we must strike as quickly as
possible. In the past we've always failed because of a
lack of *judgements*—all we've had to go on was pure
perception."

"That's neat," Green approved. "I love finish in everything, and the highest form of finish is the circle.
Now—what do you want me to take up with the Pentagon?"

"It's vital that the fleet should be deployed off the
shore of Nagonia on the day and hour when our operation begins. We need the Air Force to be ready to drop
in a commando unit. A thousand men, no more. The
Green Berets could do it with their eyes shut. That's
all."

"If I've got you right, it's only at the final stage that
you want to introduce the Navy and the Air Force? As a
deterrent, eh?"

"That's right."

"And the Special Envoy, who like I said I have a personal interest in, you'll bring him in straight away?"

"I'm not in favour of it, Nelson, but if you insist . . ."

"Thank you. And when is it to be?"

"In two or three weeks."

"What about agency finance for the operation?"

"You know the Company," said Welsh. "They're par-
anoid about disclosures."

"Maybe I should buy some shares in them and try a

takeover. This tendency to collaborate with the Soviets is getting very blatant. First the Vienna talks . . . then Salt 2 . . . So a thrust in Nagonia, I think, would be quite in order. Will you have some more strawberries?''

"With pleasure. Only I like the Nagonian ones better—just for the record . . .''

2

**An Exclusive Interview with George Griso,
Prime Minister of Nagonia**

George Griso looks tall in the photographs, but they are misleading. He is a short wiry man, but for all that he is strangely slow in his movements, and when he turns his head he does so carefully, as if he were afraid of seeing something terrible.

When I mentioned these observations to him, George Griso took his time to answer. When he did it was as though he had to conquer some mysterious and invisible weight.

"You guessed right," he said. "It's only a year since I learned to walk again. Any sharp movement still gives me pain, and I'm worried about having to go back into hospital. At the present time I couldn't afford to do that."

Then Griso told me the story of his injuries.

"During the armed struggle in Nagonia when the victory of the people was no longer in any doubt and we were advancing swiftly on the capital, Bishop Fernandez sent me a letter. In it he proposed a meeting between us in the village where I was born. He said that he was ready to go there alone, at any time, so as to try to reach agreement on a stage-by-stage transfer of power to us.

"We discussed this question at a meeting of the Political Committee. After all, Fernandez had previously adopted

5

a neutral position, a position not entirely worthy of a servant of Christ's Church, whose duty should be to take the side of the meek and humble. Nevertheless, I insisted on the meeting. It seemed to me that Fernandez must remember his childhood and the cup of humiliation which he too had been forced to drink because of the colour of his skin, before the missionaries took him off to school in Rome. My brother Julio collected a battalion of escorts and deployed them in the vicinity of the meeting-place. We realised of course, that the colonialists knew about the letter. Even if Fernandez was sincere in his desire to achieve peace, *they* could still try something.

"As it turned out, Fernandez was indeed sincere.

"However, a couple of hours before Julio's battalion reached my village through the bush, an army commando group was parachuted in. They rounded up all the villagers and asked which was the youngest child there. When the people pointed to a new-born baby called Rosita, the commandos took a bayonet and pierced the flesh of the child in the sight of everyone. Then they led half the villagers away into the bush, and warned the other half that if they breathed a word about anything that had happened, all seventy hostages would be killed.

" 'If anyone comes to the village,' they said, 'greet them as you would do normally, and let them do whatever they have come for. Then we will return your families safe and sound. But if you disobey this order and reveal that we were here, we will kill you all. You've seen for yourselves that we know how to do it. And don't worry about the baby, it's too small to feel the hurt . . .'

"Rosita's mother began to cry out that the child *could* feel everything, but the soldiers gagged her mouth and ran a short bayonet through her breast. Then they led the people off into the bush.

"When Julio emerged out of the forest, he didn't set up guard posts in the village because Fernandez had warned that the authorities could only guarantee the safety of our meeting if troops remained in their positions; otherwise they wouldn't let Fernandez through the road-blocks.

"You understand that my whole family, all of them,

even my distant relatives, were among the hostages. In their innocence the villagers supposed that if they fulfilled the colonialists' order—keep quiet and you will get your people back—they would save the lives of my children, mother and sister. What can you say? These were gentle, terrified people, and their oath of silence had been sealed by the blood of little Rosita and her mother.

"Yes, I know that you will compare our situation with your own experience of partisan actions in the war with Germany. But please remember this: by the 1940s the Russian people were literate, they read books, went to the cinema, so they could distinguish truth from falsehood. Your people had learned the hard lessons of patriotism, they had an experience of work and struggle behind them. But what could you expect of our people, who had never known what statehood is, who had never had control of their own country?

"To cut a long story short, Fernandez arrived, we met each other and everything went as planned. His proposals could, we decided, serve as a starting point for negotiations. We worked out a joint declaration—he and I, on our own. In fact, it was he who suggested this. And then the commandos crept quietly into the village. I wasn't armed—it had seemed only natural to trust the Bishop. After all, his condition was *peaceful* negotiations . . .

"The first one the soldiers tortured was Fernandez. All they wanted from him was the confession: 'I received money from the communists. In return they told me to call for an armed struggle and civil disobedience.' However Bishop Fernandez refused to bargain for his life. He bore himself with dignity, even when they put burning coals to the soles of his feet and stuck white-hot needles under his nails.

"Then the soldiers set about me. They bound me hand and foot and suspended me upside down from the branch of a tree. This torture is called the 'swallow.' It was as if I was a high diver caught in mid-leap from a cliff into the sea. However, I was physically very strong, and I could have lasted out the torture for a considerable time. When they realised this, they led over my mother, stripped her naked,

and said that they would burn her to death right there before
my very eyes, if I did not swear to give up the struggle, and
show them the way through the bush to our HQ. I couldn't
tell them that, you must understand it was impossible. So I
stayed silent. Then they threw my mother to the ground and
poured petrol over her. I cried out that every one of them
would pay with their life for this barbarity. I said that they
should kill *me* instead, by the most horrible means that they
could think of—after all, *I* was their enemy, not this old
woman. They replied that she had given birth to a cynical
bandit, if her son was prepared to let his mother be sacrificed
for his own lunatic ideas. They threw a lighted match onto
my mother. I began to thrash about and cry out, but my
mother begged me: 'Son, son, you'll bring yourself down.
Don't, don't!' ''

George Griso got up slowly from the table, went to the
cupboard, opened it and took out a bundle of photographs.

''Here you are,'' he said: ''Look, this is my mother. These
photos were taken when she was already quite old. When
she was young none of us even knew what a camera was.
The first time we ever saw a photograph was only ten years
ago. Have a look, while I make a telephone call . . .''

(Griso had no call to make. The truth was that he was
overcome by the emotion of his tale. And I confess that I,
too, could hardly bear to listen any more.)

Griso coughed. ''But I must finish the tale,'' he went on.
''It's very important to tell everything that there is to tell.
Perhaps then people in other countries will understand why
we fought for seven years, despite losing brothers, fathers
and mothers, and why we will go on fighting to the last. We
have suffered too much in the cause of freedom to give it up
easily and without a battle to the death.''

He lit a cigarette, sipped some water and continued:
''Then they led over my son Valerio. He too they undressed, or rather they didn't so much undress him as tear
his shirt off. It was a present I had given the boy, and he
was very proud of this shirt, sewn out of one of my wife's
old khaki skirts. Valerio was crying loudly, stretching out
his hands to me and begging over and over: 'Daddy, save
me! Daddy, save me!'

"Bishop Fernandez cursed the murderers. In reply, one of the commandos emptied a cartridge of bullets into him. Another of them smashed his rifle-butt into Valerio's face, poured petrol over his senseless body, and stooping down on one knee, set light to him with a flick of his cigarette lighter.

"Julio heard the gunfire and rushed into the village. The last thing which I remember was a gun aimed at my stomach. A soldier was tickling me with the barrel as if it were a blade of long grass, repeating all the time: 'Laugh, George, laugh! Go on, give us a laugh, you bastard!' And then he squeezed the trigger, and I woke up two months later in hospital. But within three months our guerrillas were in Nagonia. *That* is why I can't turn round quickly and find walking so difficult. It's sad, of course, to be an invalid at thirty-six, but I can shoot as well as ever and I still wield a pen effectively enough."

George Griso smiled broadly, but with the bitter, rather distant smile of someone who has been close to death.

"I am ready," he concluded, "to answer any questions you may have concerning the situation in our country—only let us leave it till next week. Today I'm flying off to the border, where Ogano has collected all his bandits. The question of our statehood, that is, our whole future, is about to be decided on the field of battle. Mario Ogano has the back-up of the CIA and Peking, and I don't think that there is any force that can stop him striking a military blow at us. A negotiated settlement, it seems, can be ruled out. Even so, I myself would be ready to treat with Ogano, even if that meant going unarmed just like before. I would go and talk with him without fear, because all he could do is kill me, and that isn't frightening—to die for your country. Forgive me for sounding heroic, but that's what I feel. To say anything else would be insincere."

Special Correspondent Dmitri Stepanov,
sent by telephone from Nagonia.

PS—to the editor: Please don't cut this report in the name of "sparing the readership" the horrors which Griso suf-

fered. Better than a hundred lines, emasculated and
smoothed out, don't print it at all. Flying home next Saturday. Regards to all. D.S.

The Ambassador finished reading. He put down the report. "Surely they wouldn't take the scissors to this?" he
asked Stepanov.

"Yes, I'm afraid they easily could, Aleksandr Aleksandrovich."

"How do you explain it?"

"Our national character. Maybe we're too soft, or
should I say 'tactful.' But that kind of tact is sometimes
worse than robbery. Look, I'll give you an example.
Have you ever seen the anti-alchoholism programmes
on TV?"

"No, somehow I never have."

"Well, I advise you to have a look. Instead of screening
something strong, say a Lipatov story like the 'Grey
Mouse' about a talent destroyed by drink, or a documentary about Mussorgsky's death, I remember once I saw a
hypnotist! Imagine—there the viewers are, probably expecting conjuring tricks from the man, only to be disap-
pointed. He's putting alchoholics to sleep in a clinic! Even
the fact that he's actually hypnotising them isn't *proved.*
In general, surely a harsh 'no' is better than an ambiguous
'maybe' . . ."

"Heaven knows . . . Propaganda is a form of politics,
and in politics harshness is a dangerous thing."

"You mean as regards foreign policy," said Stepanov.
"There I agree. But I'm talking about the principle of
cutting things because you're afraid of them. Anyway, I've
had my little gripe, that's enough . . . So what can we
expect, Aleksandr Aleksandrovich?"

"I'm afraid Griso is right. Ogano won't negotiate, because he has nothing to take to the talks. He's a puppet
manufactured by somebody else. All they need from him
is a coup. The only question is *when?* If only Griso had
six months' grace he wouldn't have to worry about Ogano,
or even a dozen Oganos. It's a sad story, this lack of time,

not just for the man but for the country . . . All the same, I can't make out the Americans at all. They're making fools of themselves with Ogano.''

The ambassador paused. ''You know,'' he went on, ''perhaps it's their mode of thinking that lets them down. They look at Ogano, and their solution is as simple as the mathematical statement 'a triangle is a figure with three sides' . . . Our philosophers would call it analytic, that is, the lowest form of thinking. And where does it get them? Our synthetic method is superior in that it always introduces something new about the object under study which moves the argument forward. 'A straight line is the shortest path between two points'—now *that's* a good example! Without a philosophical ABC the Americans can only commit blunder after blunder. They need a broader perspective, correct me if I'm wrong. Then they wouldn't be so keen to start a fight here. So your piece has a synthesis I like: you help to show *why* Griso will resist to the death. To state something *a priori* is to say nothing in our times. Victory goes to the side that informs its people best, and information has to come not only from the head, but also from the heart . . . When are you off to Moscow?''

''On Saturday,'' Stepanov said, ''but not for long, I'll get things sorted out there in three or four days.''

''Seeing the editor?''

''First thing.''

''Convey my regards to him. I'll drop him a line—just to back you up, Dmitri Yurevich.''

Top Secret

To the Kremlin, Moscow

The Government of the Republic of Nagonia requests you to afford us immediate economic aid. We are surrounded by states in which pro-Chinese and pro-American elements have spoken openly of an economic blockade. There exists a threat of direct military aggression. If we do not receive Soviet aid, the fate of our Revolution is sealed.

George Griso, Prime Minister

Top Secret

To Moscow

Acquaintance with the position on the ground here leads me to suggest that the three advisers who arrived with me will not be able to afford any real help, for colonialism has bequeathed to the country a complete absence of the necessary trained people. In Nagonia there are effectively no engineers, no doctors or agricultural experts, let alone any military officers. The incursions of reaction are hourly and ubiquitous. If we intend to give assistance to this country, in which forty per cent of the population suffer from tuberculosis, seventy per cent from trachoma, and ninety-eight per cent are illiterate, then we need here immediately at least 300-500 advisers. Not to be stationed in the Embassy, but to work in the port, to teach the farmers how to use tractors, to assist in the organisation of medical aid. Nonetheless, I must warn that there is nowhere to quarter the advisers because the former hotel-owners have put the sewage system out of action, while the electric power stations are idle, and the oil terminals empty.

A. Alyoshin, Ambassador of the USSR
to Nagonia

Top Secret

To Peking

The Russians have begun an airlift of advisers to Nagonia. Acting on our advice, General Mario Ogano has formally requested military aid from the US Embassy in Lewisburg. Our work on the preparation of a dockers' boycott on the unloading of Soviet deliveries continues, and we expect concrete results in the next few weeks. To sustain Colonel Ababe from the Nagonian Staff HQ, who is committed to our cause, we need a sum of $300,000.

> Du Lii, Ambassador of the People's
> Republic of China to Nagonia

To the Central Intelligence Agency of the USA

Preparations for "Operation Torch" are practically concluded. However, according to information received from reliable sources, we anticipate that the formation of regular military units in Nagonia may be completed significantly before our planned action. In this event, the conduct of the operation could encounter a series of difficulties of an organisational nature, that is, our commando force may be required, so too the introduction of special sub-units. Our sources also predict that in the near future the Russians will be despatching a large shipment of trucks and agricultural equipment to Nagonia. This will have an appreciable effect on our ability to preserve a position of economic instability in the country. Bearing in mind the strategic importance of "Operation Torch," please question agent "Mastermind" as to the scale of the forthcoming Russian deliveries. An answer would enable us to define precisely the nature and timing of our operation.

> Robert Lawrence, CIA Chief of Station
> Lewisburg

From a Speech by the US Special Envoy

"Social justice, democracy, law and order—these are the sole objectives of those patriots of Nagonia who, under the leadership of General Ogano, are presently being subjected to inhuman treatment by the Griso regime. My country has never interfered and is determined never to interfere in the internal affairs of other states. However, I am obliged to say in this august assembly that public opinion in the United States is following closely the course of events in this African country. At the same time, rumours being spread around in the press inside the Soviet bloc claiming that the USA is maintaining links with Peking in the organisation of sabotage against the present government of Nagonia, are devoid of any foundation whatsoever and are nothing but a slanderous invention . . .''

3

Tempo

45225 66167 85441 96551 81713

Konstantinov smiled to Panov, as the latter laid in front of him a table of figures.

"How many times in all have they transmitted to him this month?"

"It's quite incredible, this is the *fourth* time. But why are you so categorical that it's a 'him'? Surely it could be a 'her'?"

"If so, I'm sorry for her. The consequences will be identical. But there is a masculine feel to the figures—don't you think?"

"A masculine feel to the figures . . . An amusing idea. But you're right, Comrade General."

"So you think that without the code these radio messages will defy deciphering?" Konstantinov continued.

"Here, have a look." Panov placed on the table a sheet of paper covered in mysterious numbers, dots and commas.

"Rather like the early Italian Futurists," Konstantinov remarked. He stood up and went into his room. Today was his duty-day in Counter-Intelligence. It was Saturday, a chance to put in a little time with the paperwork, finish off everything that had piled up during the week.

On the table in the office there lay a red file. In it was the most recent coded telegram from Nagonia. It described how in the early hours of the morning two Soviet experts had been shot at by separatists from one of Ogano's groups. Both men had been taken to hospital in a serious condition.

Next to the red file lay a blue one. This was for specially important documents, and in it was a letter from the Soviet Embassy in Nagonia.

Slavin

"Fighting could break out at any moment," Stepanov repeated with conviction. "And it will be no joke."

"You think that Ogano will stop at nothing?" Slavin asked.

"He's got no alternative, Vitaly."

"His masters have."

"You're sure they have full control over his actions?"

"Absolutely," said Slavin.

"Well, I'm not so sure."

"Why?"

"In 1933," Stepanov explained, "the big business magnates believed that they could control the Führer. And what happened? Ogano is an African Hitler."

"Hitler had steel, copper, coal, But what about Ogano?"

"Nagonia is the key to the whole of Southern Africa. If this crook topples George Griso, his present masters will well and truly have to reckon with him."

"So why your lightning return to Moscow?" Slavin inquired.

"To deliver some film. If there is going to be any editing, it needs to be done quickly so as not to hold up the processing."

"Did the picture work out well?"

"I think so. Tomorrow I'm flying back."

"I envy you," said Slavin.

Stepanov grinned. "There speaks the old troubleshooter," he remarked, leaning back in his chair.

It was noisy that day in the restaurant of the House of Writers. For the first time that year the menu began with *okroshka**, and a rumour was going round that the management had agreed with the House Committee to begin taking deliveries of prawns and draught beer. So the animation among the regulars was quite marked—even feverish.

"I don't believe in any such agreement." Stepanov made a wry face and pushed the salad towards Slavin. "Pilsen lager or Rostov prawns—why deceive yourself? In life you might as well enjoy what you've got."

"Grumbling again?"

"No, just laying witness to a few home truths."

"You should put on the habit then, and have done with it," said Slavin. "Anyway, they say that monastic life is very good for the creativity."

"You really think so?" Stepanov grinned as he poured them both a vodka. "The monk's habit stands for self-restraint—but surely *any* restraint, even in the name of freedom, is a form of bondage."

"You can't argue with Engels here, Mitya, when he says that freedom is the recognition of necessity . . . The statement is cast in bronze, my dear—don't touch it!"

"So you're still taking me seriously?!"

"You should stop writing books—I'll maintain you, just for your idle table-talk!"

"I can't promise to oblige you. I think I'd die if I stopped writing, and life is too precious."

"Look, what if I order a glass of wine?"

"Fine—but wouldn't vodka be even better?"

"Intellectually, I agree, Mitya—it's just my organism won't take it! I only drink vodka when it's my official duty."

"So you're a disciplined hypocrite, eh?"

Slavin grinned. "Not at all. I'm a tennis player, Mitya, a tennis player."

"All right. By the way, Vitaly, is there any way to make you lose your temper?"

"None at all."

"In no circumstances?"

"Never been known."

"You're a very self-confident person."

"Confident, I would prefer to put it, Mitya—confident. But as regards restraint and freedom, I recently read a cunning little theory by a philosopher. A mediaeval philosopher, rather obscure—Bonald's his name . . . Anyway, according to Bonald, Man is born unfree, and the main cause of this is Nature, which is our main controller. Man can only become free if he exerts the maximum of effort towards his goal. True, eh . . . ? Bonald's conclusion is interesting, too. Be energetic, he says, join a trading or a builder's corporation and become free, thanks to the rights which that corporation has won itself. Serve your corporation—and you will make a fortune. Be Godly—and the Church will support you in all your enterprises! Make yourself rich *and* religious, and you will become a nobleman—and *that* gives the biggest privileges of all . . ."

"Sounds great. A theory for careerists!"

"You're a creeping pragmatist, Mitya. I can't understand for the life of me how you inspire the reading public with your books! . . . Anyway, I haven't quite finished—"

"What? More Bonald?"

"The new is the well-forgotten old. That means whenever I remember something, really I am reinterpreting something forgotten from the past. It's like co-authorship."

"Off you go again!"

"So, anyway . . . Bonald had a beautiful scheme. The crown of freedom is attained by the nobility, he said, but the nobility is also a defence barrier. Once you're a noble, gold and silver no longer matter to you. The nobility blocks the common plebs in their constant drive to accumulate wealth, it stops plutocracy gradually taking root. The title of nobleman is a reward for success, but it also commits you to self-discipline. It's a limit to accumulation, it *channels* this urge. Do you understand? Bonald had a curious way of warning society: if you destroy the nobility, he said, then there will be nothing to hold back the masses in their drive to accumulate wealth. Their goal will be riches, as an end in itself. And the result will be the creation of an aristocracy—an *aristocracy without nobility!*"

Stepanov was listening with interest, he had pushed away his *okroshka* bowl.

"Eat, Mitya! Go on, eat!" Slavin sighed. "A man of letters should always eat like a wolf."

"If a man of letters eats like a wolf, then it means he works for the propaganda bureau, reads aloud his own poems and short stories, and has packed up serious writing. You know, when I told our opposite numbers in Spain that we writers get paid for public appearances, that they send us on creative study-tours and give out free accommodation at artists' rest homes, they didn't believe me. 'It's all red propaganda,' they said, 'it can't be so!' So, anyway: a writer should suffer from ulcers, Vitaly, from a bad heart and piles! Only then can he appreciate the penitential pleasures of creativity."

"I was recently talking to an artist, a very interesting lad, an angry young man, launching into everything around him like a bull in a china shop. A restorer, works with icons . . . I was given one for my birthday, I should say, and I wanted to get it restored. So, the artist came along, had a look, sighed a bit, took it home and did the job brilliantly. I said thanks to him, and asked why he didn't make a living out of it. But he balked at that: 'You can't paint icons,' he barked, 'if you don't believe in God.' What do you think of that?"

"He's talking rubbish, your restorer. Icons were our Renaissance, they're our great painting. That's how one should look at them—as our national school of art. Religious belief is not half as relevant here. At that time the idea of the nation was a consuming passion for artists because we were under Tartar occupation. By the way, that's what made the Russian monasteries so important. They're different from monasteries in other countries because of their exceptional role in preserving Russian culture."

"Be careful you don't sink into nationalist mysticism, won't you?" Slavin grinned again. "Hey, who is that girl?"

Stepanov turned round. A tall woman with large eyes was standing by the bar smoking a cigarette and drinking coffee from a small cup decorated with the initials of the House of Writers in gold.

"I don't know."

"She's beautiful, eh?"

"Very."

"How old, d'you think?"

These days young people are ageless. It's only us fifty-year-olds who are obvious, with our bald heads, pot-bellies and tired eyes. But these—"

"You're jealous?"

"Yes."

"I'm not. I'm proud of my age. To live half a century is worth a medal, I'd say . . . Anyway, what's the difference between our monasteries and other countries'?"

"Well, there's distance. In Italy one monastery is only a maximum of fifty kilometres away from the next one. Ours are separated by thousands of kilometres, but they still managed to preserve the essence of the same national idea, some special condition of the spirit."

"And you always got top marks in Marxism?!"

"Always."

"So did I. But I can't agree with you here."

"Why not?"

"*Condition of the spirit* is far too woolly. Condition of what class? What region? The army? The civil service? The peasantry? One can't just generalise like that. Do you mean the spirit of the rebel Pugachov*, or the Empress Catherine, or Pushkin's Grinyov? Nationalism always serves the interest of some particular group, Mitya—the group that's in control!"

"We're coming back to the problem of monasticism. *Control* is really the same as *restraint* and on the level of society they're a precondition of any State system."

"But I am not arguing with you! I only want to ask— what kind of State? Monarchy has fallen—and I don't only mean ours—because of its own weaknesses, though it too was a kind of government. Our freedom was born on the ruins of the age-old idea of the State with its nationalistic exclusiveness—remember what a rough ride foreigners got here in those days, eh! And our icons, as you said, were the product of absolute peace and purity of idea—created in a period of invasion and crisis, like so many masterpieces. War engenders brilliant poster art, whereas philosophy needs distance, it can't be born under cannon-fire. War is the desire to survive, to fight another day, while peace is living and having time to think. And thought is the basis of individuality, it creates the personality. Quite simply, the Russia of Rublyov and Theophanes the Greek* gave the world more individuality than all our following centuries put together! That's the paradox! And it's ridiculous to ask Nature to spread things evenly. You know, I look at our film industry today, at how it *demands* masterpieces—quick, quick! But that's stupid, isn't it? When cinema was new, it produced Chaplin, Eisenstein, Clair, the Vasilyevs, Dovzhenko, Hitchcock. But now it's boringly normal—it's just like television, Mitya! We'll have to wait for a new accumulation of unknown quantities to create a *new* revolution in the cinema. And then, remember, even in its heyday cinema created only twenty, perhaps thirty masterpieces. But now it's an industry, a production line, a plan! How can you expect a production line to create the qualities of the Renaissance?! Even so, step back a bit and have a look—we still have our stars! Godard, Kurosawa, Kramer, Fellini, Tarkovsky, Peter Ustinov, Antonioni, Abuladze, Nikita Mikalkov—isn't that enough? You couldn't ask for more, could you, we don't deserve it!''

"What are you arguing about? I confess, I'm lost."

"You can't understand because you're too introverted. Hang on, who's that old man?"

"Old Minya, you mean? He's the porter here."

"He looks just like Christ."

"He is, himself. Though he used to bet on the horses."

"So don't you despair—the path to holiness lies through sin . . . Will you treat me to an ice-cream?"

"I will." Stepanov turned round, searching with his eyes for Bellochka the waitress. At that moment the administrator looked into the room—a small lounge converted from a verandah.

"Is a Comrade Slavin here?" he asked. "He is urgently wanted on the telephone."

"Ice-cream is off today," said Slavin. "Thanks and all the best, Mitya."

Konstantinov

Konstantinov looked apologetic as Slavin entered the room. His question was almost a statement: "Annoyed I hauled you in?"

"Of course."

"Don't be angry. Here, have a look at this." He handed Slavin the letter from Lewisburg. "It's just arrived."

"A report, I suppose, on the forthcoming landing of travellers from outer space in the vicinity of a military installation?" Slavin grinned as he took out his spectacles. "New data on the cooling of the sun . . . ?"

"For someone as devoted as you to the planetary dimension, I'm afraid that the communication will offer little interest . . ."

Slavin quickly read the letter and raised his eyes. The crown of his high-domed head crumpled into a mass of wrinkles, as it always did at critical moments when it was necessary to make a quick decision.

He looked questioningly at Konstantinov.

"I'll read it aloud," said the latter. "Do you mind if I read it again out loud?"

Konstantinov slowly put on his thick-framed spectacles. His face, strangely enough, became even younger as he did so. (When they made him a general, the veterans had joked: "Forty-five is too young to be a general these days, you're still a boy. It was only in *our* time that they handed out stars to thirty-year-olds.") He began to read:

"Last December two Americans, one of them called John, were in a room at the Lewisburg Hilton with a Russian. They were talking about how to work together and exchange information about some 'neighbour.' The Russian was a well-fed bastard, and he speaks Portuguese and English too fucking well for his own good. I know the danger I am putting myself in by writing this letter, but I couldn't keep silent any longer.''

Konstantinov glanced at Slavin, and there was a flicker of laughter in his eyes. ''Well,'' he concluded, ''any comments, Vitaly Vsevolodovich?''

''It's written by a Russian, that's obvious.''

''What makes it so obvious?''

''Just the way it reads . . .''

''So you think that the CIA, if they wanted to start playing games with us, couldn't get a little linguistic advice on vernacular expressions?''

Slavin smiled: ''Who from? The editors of *Dahl's Dictionary* avoid all suspicious contacts. They're afraid of the police. Did you know that each new volume of the new dictionary is fetching 100 roubles on the black market? . . . But why are you in such a cheerful mood?''

''Is it noticeable?''

''Very.''

''I'm pleased because I've decided to take a risk.''

''What sort of risk?''

Konstantinov reached for a sheet of paper. In bold writing he drew a number one on it, then circled the figure.

''Let's begin at the beginning,'' he looked up at Slavin, and paused momentarily. ''. . . Radio messages are being transmitted to an unidentified agent in Moscow. They are arriving regularly, and in recent days with particular frequency. It can be assumed that the transmissions will prove impossible to decode. So the suppositions of our friend Panov will remain suppositions and nothing more. We can't read the messages. However, let us ask ourselves: what is the hottest flash-point in the world at the present moment?''

''Nagonia, I suppose?''

''Right. Now let us assume that this letter is not a trick, not an attempt to compromise one of our people working in Lewisburg, and put to ourselves a second question: where is the CIA strongest in Africa?''

''Right there in Lewisburg.''

Konstantinov repeated: ''In Lewisburg, absolutely correct. And how many kilometres is Lewisburg from the border with "Nagonia?"

"About seventy."

"Right."

Konstantinov wrote on his sheet of paper the number two, and circled it with a still bolder line.

"Now let's look at a third point," he said. "Let's assume that the steadily accelerating feverishness of radio transmissions from the CIA's European HQ is connected with the aggravation of the situation in Nagonia. Let's assume that, right?"

"OK," Slavin agreed.

"That means, if we decide to take a chance and consider the possibility that the CIA is interested not so much in Lewisburg as its 'neighbour' Nagonia, then couldn't they be cooking up some serious trouble there?"

"I'll go along with that general assumption. But I agree that the hypothesis does have its risks."

"Fine. We'll take a chance and develop the idea that the CIA is preparing something in Nagonia, and that is why they're pestering their agent in Moscow so regularly. Remember, once upon a time there were ballistic missiles installed in Nagonia with nuclear warheads, aimed at you and me. Now they are there no more. The loss of Nagonia was a devastating blow for the Americans. My guess is that they would try anything to get it back."

Konstantinov looked hard at Slavin, waiting for some reaction. In his eyes there was no longer even a hint of a smile.

"That means we have to ask," said Slavin, "what exactly *are* they up to in Nagonia?"

"I would start by asking: what level is the CIA agent? What is his level if the CIA have brought him into play as part of their foreign policy activities? Because you should understand how serious this 'African blow' could be. It is yet another attempt to set the American people against us, to stymie detente, create a new crisis, put the world on the brink of catastrophe. Who is to gain from this? The Americans? No. Us? Even less. The warlords of the arms industry? Yes. The CIA? Undoubtedly. If we accept such a hypothesis, that means the author of the letter from Lewisburg is right. It means the CIA could be beginning a new operation of their own. So—did they indeed recruit one of our people in the Hilton? And does this person have access to secret documents? If so, where?''

Konstantinov drew a cigar out of the breast-pocket of his jacket, peeled off the cellophane slowly and with relish. He lit the cigar and took a long, bitter-sweet drag.

"Consequently,'' he concluded, ''we have to decide how we can best catch the spy. When he's collecting information? Or transmitting it? Is there a spy-ring involved, or is the agent working independently?''

"Perhaps it would be worth beginning with a check-up on our own staff in Lewisburg?'' Slavin suggested.

"Well, if we assume there's a *ring*, we'll also have to check people who have worked there in the past, and then weed out those who don't have access to classified documents. And we must concentrate on people who are in the know—both here and over in Nagonia.''

"But the radio transmissions are coming to *Moscow*,'' Slavin pointed out. "What is the sense in sending radio messages here, Konstantin Ivanovich, if their agent is in Lewisburg?''

"So you rule out the ring version? What if the CIA is receiving its information in Lewisburg, and then asking for confirmation from its person in Moscow? Would you deny *that* possibility?''

"No,'' replied Slavin thoughtfully. "I wouldn't discount it.''

Konstantinov reached for the telephone and dialled the number of Lieutenant-General Fyodorov.

"Pyotr Georgevich,'' he said, ''I'm discussing with Slavin the last radio message we received. And the letter. The letter is interesting. I could give you a report on Monday . . . Good. We'll be waiting.''

Konstantinov replaced the receiver.

"P.G. is on his way now from the *dacha**. Round up your people and we'll prepare some ideas. We have the basis for a criminal investigation. Clear it with the prosecutor's office. That's all for now.''

Konstantinov

Over breakfast Konstantinov's wife Lida looked at him with a questioning and slightly hurt expression. She had heard him telephone Slavin and arrange a 7.45 A.M. assignation on the tennis court.

Noticing the way his wife stood up from the table, Konstantinov smiled at her fondly, slightly ironically. He had a basic sense of what she was thinking (a sense which could be annoying, he said to himself, but at least it forced couples to treat each other with respect and to avoid slipping into a deadening marital routine).

Lida put the coffee on the table, pushed some cheese towards her husband.

"Would you like a biscuit? We've got some wholemeal ones . . ."

"No thank you! How many calories is it they've got? Too many, anyway. And it wouldn't be fair on you if I developed a paunch at such an early age."

"Early?" Lida smiled. "What do you think will happen to humanity when the average lifetime of a person approaches two hundred years?"

Konstantinov finished his coffee and pushed away the cup. Lida too understood her partner: he was on his way. After twenty years together one recognised a person not by their words so much as the build-up to them.

For his part, Konstantinov also realised that she was about to rise. He stretched out his hand and touched her fingers.

"Don't worry, I haven't forgotten about that book," he said. "I've got some comments on it. Do you want to note them down, or will you remember them?"

"What, you've actually managed to finish it?!"

"Of course. Look, Lidushka, the manuscript is worthless. It's a tired piece of writing, and as a famous critic once remarked, any literature has a right to exist—except *boring* literature."

"That's first principles, Kostya. But I wanted you to help me find a way of *explaining* my rejection of it."

"Do you *have* the right to reject it?"

"What?" exclaimed Lida. "Of course I do."

"That's very bad, that 'of course.' I confess I'm afraid of that kind of editorial omnipotence. What if your author goes out and hangs himself? Or if you've missed a genius?"

"But we both looked at the manuscript."

"I'm a dilettante," Konstantinov objected. "Just a reader."

"The most difficult profession, by the way. And then, today's readers are much more honest than certain of our critics. The critics spend all their energy trying to guess who to praise and who to kick in the face. But people don't rely on guesswork in the library reading-rooms or the bookstores . . ."

"It's a bad situation."

"Kostya my love, I know better than you how bad it is. *That's* why I asked you to read the book."

Konstantinov shrugged his shoulders. "The book is a collection of cliches," he said, "not literature. The bad factory director and the good party organiser, the innovator whom they gagged at first and who in the end gets a medal, the one drunkard in the whole of the workshop . . . Why do people have to *lie* so? If there was only one drunkard in every factory shop, I'd be placing lighted candles in the church! The desire to please—*whoever* you are trying to please—is a form of insincerity. And then public opinion suddenly realises what is going on, and everyone starts shouting: 'Where have all the whitewashers sprung from?' After all, did anyone *force* your author to write lies? No, he's just elbowing his way forward to get a bite of the literary pie—I call it a form of speculation! I'm right, aren't I? Real literature is when a person pours out their soul, and then you don't notice the labour put into it. But here we have a strange kind of mish-mash: the author is part-dramatist, part-debater, part-storyteller, part-orator. And in each of these professions you can apply only one description to him—he's mediocre. In our century of the information explosion you can't afford to be egocentric: the very air is saturated with ideas. Or at least you have to be an egocentric genius."

"Did you flick through the other reviews of the manuscript?"

"I read them, so what? The patrons of the arts will have their fine articles in the papers, but the book will still be pulped for lack of buyers! And that's only half the problem; the main thing is that this leads to a kind of devaluation of literature, which is alarming. That is how it seems to me, in any case."

"Do you know what would happen if I delivered that judgement, Kostya? It would be called a hatchet job . . ."

"Yes . . . but why should literature be turned into a kind of parliament: 'You scratch my back, and I'll scratch yours, in coalition we're stronger.' That's wrong, it means that the literary process is just eating itself up."

"I'd make a lot of enemies if I wrote so harshly."

"Well, you have to know how to defend your position. I wouldn't compromise. Any more questions?" he smiled. "Otherwise I'm off to lose to Slavin."

Slavin was five minutes late. When he arrived Konstantinov was already warming up, knocking tennis balls against the wall.

"Punctuality," he remarked, "is the courtesy of kings, Vitaly Vsevolodovich."

"Well," Slavin rejoined, "I'm not a king, Konstantin Ivanovich, I'm only a colonel so I am permitted to be late . . . Anyway, there was a traffic jam on Kutuzovsky Prospekt."

While they were changing over on court, Slavin continued thoughtfully; "You know what that jam made me think of?"

"Trying to distract me so that you can beat me to love?"

"How did you guess? No, I was really thinking how the speed of our century changes people's psychology. At one time the police used to react instantaneously to the slightest infringement of the speed limit, as quickly as a matador! But now they wave drivers on: 'Move up! Move up!' even allowing them into the centre lane, *anything* so long as there is no jam, that is, a loss of time. I like that very much. What do you think?"

"During rush hour," Konstantinov replied, "they wave you on, but just try breaking the speed limit in the middle of the day, their matador reactions are the same as ever! That transformation in our psychology is still an eternity and five hundred years away. You serve!"

"And so I'll sum up."

Konstantinov put his glasses in his pocket, and leaning back in his chair, glanced around the group of agents he had summoned to the conference: Slavin, Gmyrya, Trukhin, Proskurin, Konovalov.

"The task of uncovering the spy," he began, "will proceed in the following directions. First, Proskurin's department will establish which government organisations are connected with supplies to Nagonia of agricultural machinery, hospital and power-station equipment. Second, Konovalov's team will keep a watch on all known CIA agents in the US Embassy. All their contacts, the routes of their journeys should be analysed in the light of the data we receive from Proskurin. Third, Slavin will hand over command of his department to Gmyrya, and himself fly out to Lewisburg. Slavin's job will be to clarify the situation on the border with Nagonia, to establish how strong Ogano is, and to identify the author of the letter. After that—"

"With luck . . ." Slavin interposed.

"After that," Konstantinov went on as if he hadn't heard, "provided that Slavin is convinced that we are dealing with a genuine person and not a plant, he will show our anonymous correspondent photographs of members of the Soviet mission."

"Did you know that a room in the Hilton costs forty dollars a night?" said Slavin. "And that I've got to stay there—*got to,* because if this isn't all a trick, then I think our correspondent works in the Hilton, most likely in the café or restaurant."

"That's pure speculation," Konstantinov remarked.

"If so, then our lab deals in speculation," Slavin rejoined. They sent me their analysis of the letter. It had traces of butter on it and the smell of cheap cheese . . ."

"But what if it just happened to be composed over breakfast?" inquired Konstantinov, "in one of the hotel rooms?"

Slavin grinned: "Then it would smell of strawberry jam," he said triumphantly. "Hiltons rarely serve cheese for breakfast, and besides, if it was our friends from the CIA who concocted this business, surely they would have ordered ham and eggs! Cheap cheese is more like a McDonald's, they're dotted all round the world now."

Konstantinov and Slavin arrived at Sheremetevo Airport in the middle of the night. There was the scent of wormwood in the air. It felt as though any moment the hum of cicadas would be heard.

"Shall we have some coffee?" Konstantinov suggested.

"Good idea."

They sat down at a small table. The airport was almost empty. Two waitresses were talking idly about how it was too early in the year for the beaches round Riga, it was still rainy there and the water too cold—although the sand only took a day to warm up, it was so soft and nice to walk on, and the smell of the pine trees was quite fantastic! The Baltic gave a better tan than the Black Sea, it lasted longer . . . Konstantinov glanced at Slavin and smiled. Leaning towards his companion, he whispered: "It's funny, you and I have got another game of tennis ahead of us. Only this time there can't be a loser, we've *both* got to win . . ."

Slavin looked at him. "With telegrams," he hazarded, "instead of tennis balls?"

"Exactly. And don't get angry as you always do, if at some stage I stubbornly hold out against some course of action you request."

"In other words, if you *forbid* it," Slavin corrected him. "But I shall take offence all the same."

The waitress put the coffee in front of them.

"Where are you flying to?" she inquired.

"Bulgaria," replied Slavin, "The sea is already warm there."

"But there's not much sand," the waitress objected,

"and warm sand is more important than the sea, it warms your body up for the whole winter . . . Last year I was on holiday in Rumania. It was nice, of course, but the sand wasn't much good, just pebbles . . .''

Konstantinov followed her with his eyes, and shook his head. "You have to admit," he began thoughtfully, "time is an astonishing thing, Vitaly Vsevolodovich . . . How peaceful this moment feels!"

"The warm sand of the beaches and the smell of pines," Slavin repeated. "It's a beautiful picture, but what's *time* got to do with it? I don't see the link."

"I can explain if you like."

"Please do."

"Sixty years ago two things would have been impossible . . . No, not even sixty. Even *thirty* years ago it would have been unlikely: first a waitress setting off abroad on holiday, and second, the Cheka* as an instrument of detente."

"You mean," Slavin tried to follow the other's train of thought, "—you mean that thirty years ago we were tied up chasing bandits and trying to get rid of the Vlasov* and Bandera* terrorist gangs?"

"I thought you said you didn't see the link . . . That's exactly what I meant. And today you are flying to Lewisburg, to catch a spy involved in a conspiracy against tranquillity—they say, don't they, that the sand in Lewisburg is baking hot, only palms instead of pines . . . I have this constant feeling of pride," Konstantinov continued. "We began from nothing, and now, in defending our own security, we can be of assistance to little Nagonia. If we can stop the shooting from breaking out there, the age-old tranquillity will remain, just sea and sand—"

There was a crackle over the tannoy. The announcer's voice was thick, as if tired.

"Passengers flying to Lewisburg are requested to proceed to the boarding gate."

Slavin rose from the table. "Spoken by a blond of twenty-seven," he surmised, "with blue eyes and a birthmark on her cheek . . .''

"And there's peacefulness in her voice," Konstantinov

continued, "though the mole is probably on her cheek, and her eyes are green."

Slavin

Slavin's colleague in Lewisburg was young, about thirty-five. His name was Igor Vasilevich Dulov, and he pronounced the surname with a drawn-out vowel sound—D*oo*lov . . .

"In fact, as yet nobody at all has really asked me for help," Dulov intoned, glancing occasionally at Slavin's pointed cranium. They were walking along the seashore under a white-hot sun which burned down mercilessly, quite blinding them. "Once the commandant's wife came to me. Thought she was being followed."

"Superstition! Don't they know, all you have to do to be safe is make the sign of the cross!" Slavin joked.

"Anyway, we checked."

"Of course. I hope it wasn't Dulles following her?"

Dulov frowned. "Dulles?" he echoed.

"You know, Alan Dulles."

Dulov laughed. He laughed without constraint, cocking his head to one side rather like a goldfinch about to burst into song. His eyes, too, were like a finch's—small, piercing black, and slightly bulging.

"Then there was Paramonov," Dulov went on. "With him it all came out only after he returned to Moscow. A court summons arrived at the Embassy, but the trail was already cold."

"You went to court?"

"Yes. From there they pushed me over to the local traffic police. But the police denied all knowledge of the incident. You know the sort of thing: 'We don't know anything, we can't remember anybody . . .' "

"Didn't Paramonov himself say anything about the affair?"

"Not a word to anyone."

"What was he employed as?"

"Garage mechanic. By all accounts, a fine mechanic.

He put a Fiat carburettor in Zotov's Volga and now it goes like a rocket, 150 km.p.h. and a whisper.''

"What?" Slavin was suddenly lost. "Why a whisper?"

"Quietly, I mean, effortlessly."

"Sorry, I wasn't thinking," Slavin agreed, and then continued: "But what about the local CIA? How much do you know about them? Have they been snooping around any of our people?"

"There *is* one interesting character here. John Glebb. A businessman, so to speak. Zotov sees him quite often."

"Who?"

"Andrei Andreyevich Zotov, a marine engineer. I told you before. I warned him that Glebb was possibly connected with intelligence, but he only laughed. 'That's *your* job,' he said, 'to see the CIA in anyone and everyone.' "

"He was right to laugh. But what kind of a man is he? Have you got anything on him?"

"No," Dulov replied. "He's a plain speaker, a man who's not afraid to complain—but I'm convinced he's honest."

"What does he complain about?"

"The same things as all of us—only a bit louder! About our slipshod habits, our security-mania, our laziness, the overstaffing, the bureaucracy."

"An idealist, then?" Slavin smiled, remembering his conversation with Dmitri Stepanov.

"Something wrong in that?"

"No, how could there be?" Slavin was surprised.

"By the way, who deals with the timing of our deliveries to Nagonia?"

"Zotov again. Ships bringing supplies to Nagonia have to be loaded and unloaded here in Lewisburg for the whole trip. In Nagonia itself there is nothing. The ports were to all intents and purposes dismantled by the colonialists."

"Has Zotov been here long?"

"In his third year. The last seven months he has been on his own. His wife went back to Moscow. Recently Zotov was there himself."

"Why did his wife leave? Couldn't she stand the climate?"

"No, that wasn't the problem. Something went wrong between them, I think."

"Would it be possible to pin-point on what flight Zotov returned to Lewisburg?

"Nothing simpler. There are two flights a week, Friday and Tuesday."

"Why not Tuesday and Friday?" Slavin was curious. He loved to set logical tests, they helped him to gauge a person's reactions. With some people you could explain things for hours, getting as little response as from a block of wood. With others, a glance at their eyes was enough to see that they understood.

"Because Friday is a better starting point," replied Dulov. "After all, it leads straight into the weekend."

"Which reminds me, I suppose you have some tennis courts?"

"In the Hilton."

"Where exactly? I don't think I noticed them."

"In the basement," said Dulov. "There's air-conditioning, and the surface is excellent."

"Do you play yourself?"

"No, I'm only a fan."

"Who do you support, then?"

"These days the Polish Consul, but I used to support Zotov's wife. She plays an excellent game . . ."

"Tell me, has Zotov been friends with Glebb a long time?"

"Oh, yes. They met about three months after Zotov arrived. So I suppose they've known each other two and a half years at least. Glebb invariably attends our receptions. Lots of our people know him."

"Does Zotov speak English?"

"Yes. And Spanish and Portuguese. He's an educated fellow."

"You seem to like him," Slavin observed.

Dulov understood that the comment wasn't just casual. Nonetheless, he moved his head to one side in his characteristic bird-like way and looked hard at Slavin with his beady eyes.

"Yes, I do," he replied.

"Thanks—for not hedging your bets and saying you've got nothing on him. Good man . . . Is Zotov a drinker?"

"No. But he can take his drink."

"So, he *is* a drinker?"

"No, he can take his drink," Dulov insisted stubbornly. "He can drink heavily, but he never gets drunk. He's not one of your lone boozers. I'm only judging by what he does at receptions."

"Any affairs with other women since his wife went away?"

"I think that you have been incorrectly informed about Zotov, Vitaly Vsevolodovich."

"*You're* the only one who has told me about him, Igor. I didn't know anything at all about Zotov before. How does he spend his free time?"

"Travels around the country. He has picked up an interesting collection of books."

"Is it easy to buy Russian books here?"

"Used to be, but not now. Everyone has realised that in Moscow you can't find anything interesting, so they do their shopping here. Zotov has a lot of art books—some on local African art, too."

"By the way, is there a museum in town? Is it easy to buy books on African art?"

"There's no museum. The art books are published in Paris or London. But wouldn't you like to have a chat with Zotov yourself?"

"Definitely. The only thing is—not straight away, all right?"

"Fine. You know best, Vitaly Vsevolodovich."

"Now, Igor . . . ," Slavin continued, "Is there anyone you know who has met a Russian emigré in the Hilton? You know, been approached by someone—offering, say, vodka, souvenirs, records . . ."

"The Hilton has a total of about six white staff, the rest are Africans. I know the barman, he's a white—a Frenchman called Jacob. He's a spy, the son of a bitch, he can be bought by anyone who has the money. But very charming with it. Then there's the white maître d'hotel Lyndon Williams . . . More I can't say, I'm afraid."

"Do *you* speak to Glebb at embassy gatherings?"

"Of course I do."

"When is our next cocktail party or reception?"

"On Saturday."

"We must make sure that they send an invitation to Glebb."

"Fine. Will *you* ask about it?"

"What for?" Slavin exclaimed, "No—I'm just here out of sentimentality, a desire for some real action. You know, I was a war correspondent at the front . . . No, you take care of it, all right? And introduce me to Glebb."

"But he knows who I am," Dulov objected.

"So what? That's fine."

"Fine maybe, but surely he'll guess your present profession. It could be used to start a scandal in the local press . . ."

"If they were to leave our people alone—whether at home, or here, abroad—then I wouldn't need to make trips like this," Slavin replied harshly. "*They* are the ones who start it, sneaking around affairs that come within the sphere of our national security. Let them leave our people alone," he repeated, "and then we'll stay put in Moscow."

"Shall I explain it to Glebb just like that?" Dulov smiled.

"Well, why beat about the bush?! Even in our business, not everything needs to be concealed . . ."

"Whatever you say."

"By the way, Paramonov never attended the receptions, did he?"

"No, Vitaly Vsevolodovich, after all, he wasn't a diplomat!"

"So we can exclude that possibility?"

"Absolutely," Dulov said with certainty. Then he sighed: "Especially since, with our financial estimates, every last bottle has to be accounted for!"

Slavin's questions, it should be said, were not to the liking of Dulov. Put point-blank, without any preamble, they obviously had an ulterior motive. The younger man did not know this motive, and could hardly help feeling uncomfortable.

However, Slavin liked Dulov's answers. He liked people who could defend their own point of view regardless of whether—and here even tone of voice could give the game away—it would be more tactful to offer answers in line with the questioner's expectations, especially a questioner of Slavin's own rank and calling . . .

To Centre

What do you know about Paramonov? Has he informed anyone about the fact of his detention by the Lewisburg police? If so, whom? Does Centre possess any data on Russian emigrés in Lewisburg? According to my information, there are about forty here.

Slavin

To Slavin

Data on the Russian emigré community is negligible, since there is no emigré club in Lewisburg. Uncorroborated evidence suggests that a certain Khrenov, forenames Viktor Kuzmich (Kirillovich) lives in Lewisburg. Khrenov is a former Vlasovite* and participant in the battles for Vrocslav (Breslau). Exact place of residence unknown, but according to three-year-old information he used to rent a room in a hotel near the station. Also known that at one time in Kiel Khrenov used to live off his winnings at the snooker table, and went by the nickname "Off Two Sides Into The Pocket." Since we have no evidence as to whether he joined Vlasov voluntarily or under pressure, you should exercise maximum care when planning a meeting with him. No information on his contacts with other security services, but we know that while in Kiel he took part in several robberies.

Centre

Konstantinov

Proskurin laid out on Konstantinov's large, dark brown walnut desk ten sheets of paper. On them there were written the names of ministries and departments connected in one way or another with exports to Nagonia.

Konstantinov glanced over the sheets and asked, somewhat irritably: "Can't you get anything more concrete?"

Proskurin shrugged his shoulders: "I've set our sights roughly. But the circle is shrinking. There are only a few people left."

"How many of them have access to classified documents?"

"Twelve."

"Is that preliminary data prepared?"

"Yes."

"Any warning signals you can see?"

"I haven't got anything on any of them."

"Well, good then!" Konstantinov cried. "We shouldn't 'have anything on' good Soviet people! Either there are facts, or there's nothing."

"I'm using all the present criteria."

"Fine. As for the criteria, they're permanent. Where is the material on these people?"

"Trukhin is typing it out again."

"When will he finish?"

"By lunch-time, I think."

Konstantinov glowered at Proskurin. "When will he finish, I repeat?"

"By 14.00 hours."

"Thank you."

There was a ring on one of the telephones on the desk, Konstantinov unerringly guessed which one, and picked up the receiver: "Hello. Yes. Good morning. Well? Come over straight away."

He hung up, stared thoughtfully at the telephone for a moment, then turned back to Proskurin: "Does Paramonov appear in your list?"

"The one Vitaly Vsevolodovich spoke about?"

"Exactly."

"Yes, he does."

"And is he in the inner circle?"

"No. You said yourself that the agent would most likely be sending political material."

"True. But Paramonov could be a messenger for the information. Where does he work now?"

"In a Mezhsudremont."

"What's his job?"

"Garage foreman."

"What *is* this Mezhsudremont?"

"I haven't got that far yet."

"Can you give me an approximate answer, then?"

Proskurin shrugged his shoulders: "I'd prefer not to. I know your attitude to approximate answers."

"You're right, in general. Please try to find out quickly. Since we had the message from Slavin, the observation teams have picked up alarm signals on Paramonov, they're doing a report for me at the moment. Can you find out in a quarter of an hour?"

"I'll try. But it would be safer to say half an hour."

"Good. But can you also find out, please, whether Paramonov helps any of his bosses with his car—as a private job, as they say. Is there anyone he's changed a carburettor for, or looked at the coils? Do you understand? Slavin picked this angle up, it's up to us to analyse it thoroughly. In half an hour, as we said?"

From the file:

"Surname—Paramonov. Forenames—Mikhail Mikhailovich. Born—1929. Nationality—Russian. Family Status—Married. No relatives abroad . . .

"Subject came out of office Mezhsudremont at 12:47 A.M." paused by bus stop, looking around as pretended to tie shoelace. Waiting until all passengers had boarded bus, subject jumped in last, just before doors closed. After riding two stops, got off, checked again, stopped by window of store Mineral Waters. Slipped inside just as assistant put up notice saying "Gone to Lunch." No contact with anyone except shop assistant, drank only a glass of mineral water. Boarding bus without checking, returned to Mezhsudremont and spent rest of day in garage, repainting in a silver colour Zhiguli* car, licence number plate 72-21.''

Konstantinov raised his eyes to Colonel Konovalov. Apparently the other had been waiting for this glance, for he immediately took a second sheet of paper out of the file. The sheet was typed with almost no margins. Konovalov held it out to the General.

Konstantinov buried himself in the reports:

''Surname—Tsizin. Forenames—Grigory Grigorevich. Profession—shop assistant of store Mineral Waters, in the Sverdlov District Food Trading Organisation. Born—1935. Nationality—Russian. Non-party. Family Status—Married, relatives abroad on mother's side. Convicted in court on a charge of negligence at work, sentenced to one year of corrective labour at his place of work.''

''Where do Tsizin's relatives live?'' Konstantinov inquired. It wasn't that he imagined that Konovalov could give him an answer—he'd had too little time. It was really more of a hint, done in a tactful way so as to avoid giving offence.

However, Konovalov—a greying, rotund man who sat in a slightly bent forward position—made a magician's gesture and produced yet another piece of paper:

''His uncle,'' he began reading: ''Surname—Tsizin, Forenames—Mark Fyodorovich, lives in Ottawa, works as a porter in a slaughter-house. His aunt is Tsizina, Anna Genrikhovna, a cleaner in a hotel.''

''How did they land up there?''

''After the war. Driven out by the Hun.''

''Only a war veteran could use that word,'' Konstantinov noted to himself. ''Today we would express it otherwise: driven out by the 'fascists.' And in that linguistic trifle there resides one huge difference of meaning.''

''One more item of information, Comrade General,'' Konovalov went on.

''How have you managed so quickly? You've had so little time.''

''Ah, Konstantin Ivanovich . . . That's why they are pushing me out onto my pension. They say I drive the young ones too hard.''

"We'll retire together," Konstantinov promised. He took the report. Its very first line stopped him in his tracks.

"Zhiguli licence number plate 72-21," it read, "belongs to citizen Vinter, Olga Viktorovna, born 1942, nationality—Jewish, non-party, no children, husband—Zotov Andrei Andreyevich, works in Lewisburg."

Konstantinov rose abruptly from behind his desk. Opening the safe, he went through the papers left by Proskurin and laid one of them to the side. Stooping over it, he took a drag on his cigar, realised it had gone out, and lit it again so absent-mindedly that the flame burned the leaves all the way up its left side . . .

"Have you got anything more on Vinter?" he asked Konovalov.

"Nothing at all, Comrade General."

"Thank you, Trofim Pavlovich."

"May I have permission to go now?"

"Yes, you may. We'll have to keep an eye on Vinter."

The grounds for this were the following: senior scientific worker Olga Viktorovna Vinter was employed in a planning institute where she had access to secret documents, some of them connected with the situation in Nagonia. Her candidate's thesis had been devoted to the problem of the penetration of international monopolies on the African continent.

"And, if it's not too much trouble," Konstantinov asked, "try to dig me out her dissertation."

In half an hour Proskurin was in his office.

Konstantinov glanced at him over his spectacles.

"Mezhsudremont deals with arrangements for the repair of Soviet merchant ships on international routes. They have business contacts with East and West Germany, Great Britain, Yugoslavia and France. The director is a man called Erokhin. Doesn't have a car for private use, but the deputy director, Yevgeny Nikiforovich Shargin, who deals with African destinations, has a Volga. Paramonov looks after it, does all the running repairs. He obtained some new tyres for it, with special treads I understand."

"Is that all?" Konstantinov asked.

"No, there's more. Although Shargin doesn't have ac-

cess to secret information, he is a regular visitor at the
Ministry of Foreign Trade. His brother, Leopold Nikiforovich Shargin, works there on purchases of foreign technology. The brother has flown to Lewisburg on three
occasions. Among his negotiating partners was John
Glebb—the fellow you're interested in."

"We," Konstantinov corrected him. *"We* are interested
in him. Yourself included. I think we had better intensify
our surveillance on Paramonov. Investigate Tsizin too.
Who can do that?"

"I would suggest Grechaev."

"Why him?"

"Do you have any objections?" Proskurin countered.

"No . . . Well then, let him have a look at Tsizin. But
you understand, it must be done with maximum sensitivity
and precision."

"Very well."

"Does Olga Vinter come into the inner circle?" Konstantinov went on.

"Yes. But I intend to exclude her from consideration.
She's a mouthy, assertive woman, but in the opinion of
everyone who knows her, an outstandingly good person."

"And what about her husband?"

"Her husband my people haven't had time to work on."

"You see, her husband is Zotov. He's stationed in Lewisburg. And he handles, among other things, the question
of deliveries to Nagonia."

"So that's it . . . ," Proskurin said slowly. "You mean,
it's a ring of them Zotov—Vinter—Paramonov?"

"Zotov at that end, Vinter here, with Paramonov as a
courier to pass information?" Konstantinov elaborated the
idea. "Is that how you visualise the ring?"

"Theoretically, it is quite possible . . . ," Proskurin
replied, "elegant even, I would say . . . But Streltsov has
already had a good look at Vinter, spoken with her friends,
and they all insist with one voice: she is a good person.
Could she really mask herself so cleverly, eh? On the other
hand, if it's a ring, she has to act a role, or rather . . ."

Konstantinov listened to Proskurin thoughtfully, rolling
a pencil between his fingers as he did so.

"Does Vinter still play tennis?" he asked. "Slavin said that it was a frequent pastime of hers in Lewisburg. A tennis court is a fine place to meet the most varied assortment of people . . ."

"We haven't established anything as regards tennis, Konstantin Ivanovich."

"It wouldn't be too much trouble to do so, eh? And also—where does she play? In what club—Spartak, TsSKA*, Dinamo? I'm curious about her partners."

Within two hours Proskurin brought back the information that Olga Vinter played at the courts at TsSKA. Among her partners were a deputy head of management at the Foreign Affairs Ministry, a general from the engineering directorate, a senior Gosplan official, and Leopold Shargin from the Ministry of Foreign Trade.

To Slavin

Give us anything you have on Olga Vinter, Zotov's wife— her contacts, interests, moral character. Discover whom she played tennis with and where. Did she have any regular partners, and if so who exactly? Who helped her collect the material for her thesis?

Centre

To Centre

According to the evidence of people who knew Vinter, she was particularly interested in US commercial penetration in Africa. She gathered the material for her dissertation in the Library of Congress, also in the Press Centre attached to the US Embassy. Who precisely helped her at the Press Centre we haven't yet been able to establish. No regular tennis partners. Several times she played at the Hilton with the wife of the British consul, Caroline Tizzle. Mrs. Tizzle is approximately thirty years old, daughter of General Hamelord, who worked as a liaison officer between M16 and the CIA in 1949-51. She also played with

Robert Lawrence, the local representative of International
Telephonic. The general opinion is that Vinter went back
to Moscow after an affair with a man called Dubov, a
Candidate of Economic Sciences whose posting to Lewisburg ended a year and a half ago.

Slavin

To Slavin

Establish the full name Robert Lawrence, his age and any
distinctive physical characteristics. What more do you
know about Caroline Tizzle?

Centre

To Centre

Caroline Tizzle is well-known for her radical opinions.
She speaks very critically about the situation in the West,
writes articles for the left-wing press about Africa, and
has published two pamphlets on the Ian Smith regime and
one commentary on covert CIA operations in England.
Western diplomats shun her. According to information received from reliable sources, she is not connected with
the intelligence services. The data on Lawrence I am in
the process of establishing.

Slavin

To Centre

Olga Vinter's tennis partner at the Hilton, American Robert William Lawrence, was born in 1920 and came to Lewisburg a month after the overthrow of colonialism in
Nagonia. Worked in Chile, also as representative of International Telephonic.

Slavin

To Slavin

According to our information, Robert William Lawrence, born 1922, married, two children, resident in New York, is provisionally identified as the CIA's Station Officer in Lewisburg. Find out who his contacts are. How many times did he play tennis with Vinter? Was any other Russian present there during their games together? If so, what topics were raised in conversation? What were the relations like between Vinter and Lawrence?

Centre

To Centre

Request your permission to meet Lawrence.

Slavin

To Slavin

Avoid contact with Lawrence.

Centre

To Centre

I consider it imperative to meet Lawrence.

Slavin

To Slavin

We repeat: avoid contact with Lawrence. Elucidate the character of the relations between Lawrence and John Glebb.

Centre

To Centre

Glebb and Lawrence swim every morning in pool at the
Hilton. Their relations are very friendly. Lawrence uses a
private room at the hotel. According to the waiters, the
apartments used by the CIA are situated on the fifteenth
floor.

Slavin

4

Slavin

The Soviet Embassy gardener Arkhipkin woke early, about five in the morning. Soon to retire, he was serving out his last months in Lewisburg, and counting the days until he returned home.

Arkhipkin was out in the garden well before any of the diplomats arrived for work. The Ambassador and Chargé d'Affaires who lived in the Embassy Residence were still asleep. It was quiet in the grounds. The sun piercing the fierce and opulent greenery was pale to the point of colourlessness, and the grass had that peculiar shade which is possible only in Africa.

At six o'clock there would be a change of police guard at the Embassy entrance, the gardener knew. Often he would hear the murmur of an unhurried conversation, sometimes snatches of a quiet song—especially when the weather promised a breeze to relieve this stifling heat, for it was as if the guards had an inbuilt barometer.

The police jeep drove up and three young men sprang out of the front, adjusted their machine-guns, exchanged laughing greetings and were soon talking softly with the men they were to replace. It was at this moment that Arkhipkin heard, somewhere right next to him, a hoarse whisper in his own Russian language: *"Muzhchina, da pomogi zhe!"* ("Man, help!")

A strangeness of expression and accent in this utterance so surprised Arkhipkin that he automatically crouched down warily beside the fence. Looking round, he saw a man trying to reach up to its top—the fence was wrought-iron in an ornate Spanish colonial style with sharp spear-headed railings. A small parcel with a stone tied to it for ballast was balanced precariously on the railing.

"Pomogi zhe!" the man called again, tremulously, standing there in the street and glancing towards the policemen. Arkhipkin saw that they had noticed him.

Then one of the police shouted something at the man behind the fence and they all ran towards him. The jeep jerked into motion. Arkhipkin lifted the parcel off the railings with his rake and propelled it into the grounds of the Embassy. The man gave a grateful smile and dived into an alleyway as narrow as a country lane—two cyclists would have had difficulty passing in it. The jeep's brakes screamed.

There was a burst of machine-gun fire. Arkhipkin, clutching the parcel to his chest, almost ran into the Embassy. He heard one more burst of fire, then silence . . .

Slavin scanned again the slip of paper in the parcel:

"I sent you a letter about how the Americans won over that bloody traitor of ours in the Hilton. I sent it by post, but whether it arrived, I know not. Since then I've seen the Americans in the hotel again, but not the Russian. I want you to understand why I'm telling you this. I'm an old man, and the war destroyed my life. Since then I've knocked about in different countries and wept tears of regret on many a hotel pillow—*but why him?* With his smug face, so young and healthy? If my letter didn't get to you, watch out, because the Americans have got one of your people."

"What *was* this letter he sent?" asked Dulov.

"After the war he must have worked in Germany," said Slavin, not replying to the other's question. "See how he writes *gotel**. Only Russians who've lived some time in Germany use that word."

"But Ukrainians say *gotel*," Dulov objected.

"True. But Russian residents in Germany say it to a man. I worked with people who were transferred back from there at the end of the war, so I know. Well, and where is the gardener?"

Arkhipkin came sideways into the room, pausing by the door as though—so it seemed to Slavin—he was about to salute and click his heels.

"An ex-sergeant-major, most likely," he thought to himself. "One can tell them a mile off."

"Sit down, Oleg Karpovich," he began. "Shall we have some tea?"

"Thank you, I won't refuse a cup."

"He's an Ivanovo man," Dulov put in, "you know what tea drinkers they are . . ."

"But I thought the most famous drinkers came from Shuya," said Slavin. "Isn't that so, Oleg Karpovich?"

"The Shuya people more than Ivanovo, true," agreed Arkhipkin. "Ten to fifteen cups at a go . . ."

"Really? Fifteen cups!" Slavin was comically interested. "Is it possible?"

"Put on the *samovar** and we'll see," Arkhipkin was forced to smile. The tension in him, obvious at the start of the conversation, was less visible now.

"Anyway, what's the difference?" Slavin mused. "The towns are so close . . . But, for example, I can tell a man from Ryazan from someone from Kursk, easily."

"Well, that's obvious," Arkhipkin agreed. "A Kursk man is a Southerner, with dark eyes, whereas the Ryazan man is closer to us, blonder . . ."

"And the man who threw the parcel over, what region do you think *he* came from?"

"I didn't have time to look at him properly."

"Did he have dark eyes?"

"Sorry, I didn't see. And then, when they began to shoot, my God, everything just went out of my head! Those machine-guns . . . shooting from the waist, just like in the war . . ."

"You actually saw the policemen shooting?"

"Yes, I think so."

"Let's go into the garden and find where you were standing when it happened. It might help you to remember, eh?"

"Let's go," agreed Arkhipkin, glancing painfully at Dulov. "Only, I can't remember anything, I was so frightened I couldn't even get a word out."

They quickly identified the spot where the unknown man had thrown the packet over. Arkhipkin nodded towards the railings: "That's where it was stuck."

Slavin stood underneath the fence. From here he could see the narrow alley, sloping downhill.

"And when they began to fire, did the man zigzag to avoid the bullets?"

"No, only when he jumped on the bicycle."

"Ah! So he had a bicycle standing there?"

"Yes, it was leaning against the wall. A woman's bike."

"The alley turns into the street. Which way did he go, right or left?"

"Left, of course. Down the hill—it would make a quicker getaway."

"But where does the street lead?"

"I don't know, I rarely go out of the Embassy. Not knowing the language here, you can easily get lost . . ."

"The street leads to the railway station," explained Dulov. "It comes out into an avenue where there are trams and lots of cars, you'd never catch him there."

"You're sure they didn't kill him?" asked Slavin.

Dulov interposed: "When I heard the shots, I ran out of my flat onto the balcony, and I could see it all. The man obviously escaped because when they ran down the alley, there was nobody in front of them. And when they got to the bottom of it, there was no shooting either. Obviously he ran into one of the courtyards along the street, there are enough to choose from."

"Did you check?"

"Yes, we did. But if they'd got him, they would have said so on the radio anyway. They wouldn't have missed the chance of smearing us." Dulov was certain. "He *must* have got away."

"Was he grey-haired?" asked Slavin.

"You don't see, I just can't remember," said Arkhipkin. "Partly grey, or it could have been bleached by the sun . . ."

"What was he wearing?"

"A suit, of course."

"All right—but what colour? Old or new? Did he have a tie? Or not?"

"That's the trouble, it's gone clean out of my head," Arkhipkin groaned.

"Did he have any scars on his face?"

"No scars. But he was missing a finger. Or maybe even two fingers—that I did notice."

"Well, that's important! So . . . did he say anything to you?"

"No, he didn't say anything, that is, he just whispered something like—*muzhchina,* help me . . ."

"What? *Muzhchina?*"

"Either *Muzhchina* or *chelovek**, I think, but I couldn't say exactly."

"If he said *chelovek,* that means he's a Ukrainian," Dulov remarked.

"Not necessarily," Slavin objected. "I've got a friend, one hundred per cent Russian, from Voronezh, who usually addresses a friend as *chelovek* or *cheloveche* . . . But whatwas his voice like? Rough? Hoarse? Or just normal?"

"Hoarse, that's what it was exactly, hoarse . . ."

"And you can't remember any other details about him?"

"Sorry, no. You don't want me to mislead you by pretending, do you?"

Slavin returned to his office and spread out his books and information on Lewisburg. He was looking for bars with snooker tables, especially around the railway station. He found four—the *Sporting Kids, Naples, Casa Blanca* and *Las Vegas.*

He called in the gardener once more:

"Oleg Karpovich, by the way, can you play snooker?"

"Badly. I've mucked about with the drivers, only once or twice, for fun . . ."

"Well, it's your lucky day. You're going to have a game with me."

"But there's no table here at the Embassy. Or are you joking?"

"I don't mean in the Embassy. You and I are going out on the town."

"The only place you can play snooker is in the bars, and the rules are, we aren't allowed in there."

"Oh well, with the two of us it won't be so frightening," Slavin winked at Arkhipkin. "What do you say, Oleg Karpovich?"

"If we have to, then we have to," the other replied, rather heavily.

"Now look," Slavin continued, "we'll be looking for your man—whom I'll call 'Fingerless' from now on. But it's possible we may meet *another* Russian, I'll point him out to you. I want you to go up and have a chat with him, OK?"

"He's not a Soviet citizen, is he?" Arkhipkin guessed.

"An emigré. Served under Vlasov," replied Slavin.

"A bastard like that! I can't talk to him, I'd rather strangle him! Did you know, I fought the Vlasovites at Breslau, they're not humans, they're animals . . ."

"If we find 'Fingerless' straight off, then everything is all right, but if we have to search him out by stealth, then I'm afraid you'll have to talk to this Vlasovite, whether he fought opposite us at Vrocslav or not. In any case, you can't judge every emigré the same, Oleg Karpovich. For every one of them who sold himself to the Germans and went with Vlasov of his own free will, there are a hundred other ones who were forced. I understand completely and you're right—it's impossible to justify it, but emigrés are all very different kinds of people."

"You're very reasonable, it's only I have a heart as well as a mind. I didn't tell you, the Vlasovites killed my younger brother at Vrocslav."

In the *Sporting Kids* it was noisy and crowded. The players had a lot of swagger but less skill. Betting was weak, around three dollars a game, and "Fingerless" was nowhere to be seen. Arkhipkin lost three games in a row to Slavin. His hand shook noticeably as he struck the ball, and in between play he chalked his cue relentlessly and peered around the bar with an anxious expression.

A waiter brought them beer on a tray, running skilfully through the tables. Slavin asked him:

"We're looking for Khenov—any idea when he'll be here?"

"He doesn't play here any more, sir. You'll find him at the *Las Vegas* or the *Hong Kong*. Usually the *Hong Kong*. The Chinese have put in some beautiful tables. The best players all go there now, and they say bets are up to two hundred dollars a time . . ."

In the *Las Vegas* Slavin and Arkhipkin hung around near the tables for a while. The play was good. Silence reigned in the hall. Slavin motioned his companion to the bar and ordered highballs. Arkhipkin's hand was still shaking, and he downed the cocktail with undisguised distaste as he looked around him.

"Come on now!" Slavin smiled, "Look what strong arms you have. What have you got to be afraid of?"

"I'm just not used to it," the other replied. "I'm a country person, I don't like the low life, it goes against my nature."

"You know the word 'orders'?"

"Yes, but I still feel out of my element."

Slavin turned to the barman: "When do your best players play here?"

"We have only one genuinely good player at the moment, sir—Mr. Khrenov, whom they call 'Off Two Sides Into The Pocket.' A class player."

"But surely he plays at the *Hong Kong*?"

"Yes, sir. But he does play here too, fairly often. Recently, though, he's begun going to the *Hong Kong*."

"Why? Better tables?"

"No, sir. The food's cheaper. The prices there are incredibly low, the Chinese import everything. We can't do anything about it, they're determined to make us go bust! It's true, alcohol costs the same there, the Belgians ship it in. We're being forced to lower the prices on cocktails or we'll simply go down the drain . . ."

In the *Hong Kong* the barman pointed out Khrenov

straight away. Their quarry played with obvious mastery, unhurriedly, his sleeves rolled up to his elbows, keeping up a continuous barrage of comments directed at his opponent, speaking in English with a dreadful accent: "Aim! Aim better, John! Relax, relax, or you'll miss your chance! Got your money ready? Or do you have to go and ask your wife for it?"

Slavin sat down at the bar where he could see Khrenov in the mirror.

"Have a good look at him," he whispered to Arkhipkin. "In a moment you can go and ask him for a game."

"Oh God!" Arkhipkin groaned. "My stomach is already turned upside down . . . Can I have a glass of something for courage?"

"Another highball?"

"No thanks, I'd rather have vodka."

"The vodka is rubbish here. Smirnoff, it's sickly sweet. Would you like some whisky?"

"Fine. I'll have 100 grams."

Slavin ordered a double whisky. Arkhipkin downed it, grunted, climbed off his stool and set off towards the table where there could be seen playing the man they nicknamed "Off Two Sides Into The Pocket."

"Listen" he called to Khrenov in Russian, "Want a game? For five roubles . . . I mean, dollars?"

Khrenov swung round sharply, took a step backwards, his hand instinctively fishing through his pockets for a cigarette.

"Who are you?" he asked gruffly.

"A gardener."

"Where from?"

"The Embassy."

"So you're a Red?"

"What else? Yes, if you say so, a Red."

"How did you know me?"

"I don't. The barman just said you were Russian, so I came over, I can't speak the language here . . ."

"Wait, I'll just finish this off."

Khrenov turned to the snooker table and five shots later the game was over. He played professionally, and from his vantage-point at the bar Slavin could see that earlier he had been merely showing off, leading on his partner and giving him a chance. Stuffing his winnings of twenty-five dollars into a shirt pocket, Khrenov said to Arkhipkin:

"Do you play well? Or shall we talk? It's the first time I've seen a Red, I've not met one since the war."

"Done something naughty, then? We're not hard to find if you're not avoiding us."

"True," replied Khrenov. His hard eyes swept over Arkhipkin's face. "Let's go and sit down at a table. Have a drink on me."

They went over to a corner table near the window. Slavin had to swivel in his seat to see them.

Khrenov ordered two vodkas—the small forty-gramme measures they served here. Arkhipkin stared at his glass.

"You'd like a proper drink? Wait, I'll order another. They don't understand drinking here—sipping at it, it's unnatural . . ."

"Listen where is that fellow—"

"Who?"

"Er, what d'you call him—"

"Kolka?"

"No . . . ," Arkhipkin fished uncertainly, wiggling his fingers in front of Khrenov's face.

"Vanka, you mean? 'Fingerless'?"

"Yes, that's it!"

"In the hotel as usual. He's working shifts, twelve hours on the trot. But why do you want him?"

"I need to speak to him. He was on the radio."

"What did they say about him? That he was a criminal, about Vlasov and so on?"

"No. His sister is looking for him."

"Go on! What, his sister?! How on earth did she track him down?"

"On the radio they have a programme, you come on and say, 'I'm looking for my brother, he's so and so,' and so on. But what is Vanka's surname?"

"Look—" Khrenov seemed preoccupied and didn't answer, "But what if someone *did* give themselves up, how much time would they have to serve?"

"Depends on what for—"

"You don't understand, comrade gardener, we've been *baptized*, Vanka and me, we're *baptized.*"

"What?"

"Let me tell you. When the Germans took us from the camp, we were all scared and almost dead with hunger. They took us to a village, gave each man a rifle and drew up the men they had identified as Commissars in a line in front of us. One of the German officers, Hans, came up to each man in turn, dug his pistol into the back of his neck, and said: 'Fire.' It was a question of either shoot or be shot. And as soon as you fired and the Commissar slumped over dead, the Germans took away your rifle and said: 'You're free now, go where you like.' We were baptized in blood, where could we go? So that's how the word came about . . . There you are, comrade communist . . ."

"Tell me how I can get hold of this man with the missing fingers. Do you know his address?"

"There is a lot I know, gardener, but I need a little more to make me tell. We're too educated for that. Maybe Vanka doesn't have any sister, and it's the NKVD* who sent you."

"Why would the NKVD need him?"

"The NKVD needs everybody, gardener. Don't you try to confuse me. Where are you from yourself?"

"Ivanovo."

"Then we're neighbours. Vologda."

"From the town?"

"No. A village called Pryaniki. Ravines all around, gloomy forest and streams flowing at the bottom. When you step out of the cabin in the morning—silence . . . And the woodpecker's rat-a-tat-tat. Try to find a woodpecker here, it's nothing but cockatoos! . . . What's your name?"

"Oleg Karpovich. And yours?"

"Victor Khrisanfovich. I'm not short of cash, I've got a decent room here, but still there's a pain in my heart. I dream of going home . . . But that means twenty-five years inside, and I'm fifty-three already . . . When would I ever get out? That's the thing."

"They don't give you twenty-five years now. Fifteen, more like."

"Well fifteen. That's no weekend either. I'd be sixty-eight when I walked out. Who needs an old man? Not my family. The opposite—it would be disgrace for my brothers and sisters, they probably still live in Pryaniki. Now I'm 'reported missing,' but if I return, then what? They'll send me to Siberia, and who can blame them? I've only myself to blame, so here I am, playing snooker in the company of thieves."

"Listen, just tell me his name . . ."

"Don't push me! Until I have a word with him, I can't say anything. By the way, do you think there really is a village called Pryaniki near Vologda? I could have chosen any name . . . You see, Karpich, we're *educated*, life taught us that, so we don't even trust our own selves . . . Come back here in a week's time if you want to know. Maybe he'll agree, but I wouldn't bet on it. There are only one or two of us here, we Russians protect one another, we have no secrets from each other. 'Fingerless,' as you call him, is a cagey old soul, avoids strangers like the plague, lives alone . . . Well, shall we have another?"

Superintendent of the Criminal Police General Stau was handed a tape of the conversation between the two foreigners by the owner of the *Hong Kong*, Mr. Chou Nu. It was a precautionary measure, heaven knows what for, but all the bars in Lewisburg had been fitted with the necessary technology.

Stau immediately telephoned John Glebb.

"John, would you be interested in a Russian working in one of our hotels?"

"If he worked in the Ministry of Foreign Affairs, yes I would," Glebb laughed. "But they're just lackeys here, haven't risen any higher, and what's the use of a lackey? What's his name?"

"I haven't tried to find out. They call him 'Fingerless'—we don't know anything more than that."

"OK, let's meet tomorrow and have a think."

"One of the Russians was the gardener at the Embassy."

"Really? That makes it more interesting. What's it all about?"

" 'Fingerless' has a sister who is looking for him, the gardener said they broadcast a message from her on the radio."

"Quite possible. They have a programme like that . . ."

"The gardener was at the *Hong Kong* with a man called Slavin. Just in case it's useful, I've established that Slavin is staying at the Hilton Hotel."

"In the Hilton?" Glebb repeated after a pause. "Well, thank you, Stau. Give me a day, I'll be back in touch."

Plunging into the air-conditioned coolness of the Hilton's vestibule, Slavin suddenly felt the sweat on his body. His shirt was damp and the cream hadn't saved his face from burning after his walk along the beach.

He went to the desk, asked for the key to his room, bought all the newspapers and turned towards the lift. Then he heard his name called. He turned round. At the bar there stood a fat, untidily dressed man, and beside him— the sunburnt, grey-haired, strikingly handsome figure of John Glebb, his face smiling and exuding friendliness.

"Hello, Ivan!" The fat man called again, spluttering beer onto his khaki-coloured shirt. "Don't tell me you don't recognise me, old chap?!"

5

Konstantinov

Top Secret

To Major-General K.I. Konstantinov

In reply to your query, we can report that yesterday from 21.00 to 21.30 hours, at the time of the radio transmission from the CIA HQ in Athens to the USSR, of the persons listed by you only Olga Vinter was at home, and therefore could hypothetically have received the coded transmission.

Major Sukhanov

Top Secret

To Major-General K.I. Konstantinov

In reply to your query we can report that the transmissions from the CIA's Intelligence HQ in Athens could only be picked up on a extra-powerful radio, such as a Phillips, Panasonic or Sony. However, a definite answer can only be given in concrete instances after examination of the particular piece of equipment or of its instructions and technical specification.

Captain Sharipov

Top Secret

To Major-General K.I. Konstantinov

The evidence we have received from interviewing acquaintances of Vinter and Shargin confirms that both possess a high-capacity radio, the 1976 model Panasonic Deluxe.

Captain Grechaev

By the evening of the same day, Konovalov's section responsible for surveillance of CIA workers identified by counter-intelligence had ascertained that on the previous night Second Secretary at the US Embassy Luns left his flat on Leninsky Prospekt by car and after misleading the officers assigned to follow him, was lost to sight momentarily at 23.40 hours as he turned off the Mozhaisk Highway into Victory Park.

"Once in the park, Luns drove down a narrow roadway," Konovalov's report continued, "then stopped the car for a few seconds, got out, tapped his foot against the tyres, lit a cigarette and drove off again. He made no contact with anybody. From Victory Park he drove at high speed to the Embassy, where he stayed till 3 A.M., and then returned home—again through Victory Park, but without slowing down or stopping. This time, however, a man who had been sitting on a bench in the rain came out of the park, and proceeded along the route taken by Luns. As the buses and trolley buses were no longer running at that hour, the man proceeded home on foot. We have confirmed his details: name—Roman Grigorevich Shebeko; address—1812 Street; occupation—retired lieutenant-general . . ."

To Centre

Please send information on an emigré aged about fifty years, missing two fingers from the left hand, blonde, suspected of having lived several years in Germany. Possibly Ukrainian. Check all Khrenov's contacts at his former addresses, in case the other man was there too. Would it be possible to find out from management records at the Hilton the names of all Russians working in their African hotels?

Slavin

To Slavin

No success in finding "Fingerless" among Khrenov's contacts in Kiel. However, Khrenov was friendly with a defector, Mikhail Isaevich Portnov, a Soviet engineer on business in Kiel to purchase machinery. Portnov hanged himself after leaving a note bitterly condemning those who had persuaded him not to return home. It was directly after this episode that Khrenov went to Africa, seemingly he was deeply shocked by the death of his friend. Will do our best to establish the names of persons of Russian origin working in the Hilton chain. When meeting Khrenov next time, please exercise maximum caution.

Centre

Department head General Fyodorov listened carefully to Konstantinov's report. Then he remarked:

"I visualize the beginning of an operation like doing repairs in a flat. Everything is calm and quiet, but cracks have appeared on one of the walls, so it's decided that the paint needs another coat. And then the builders bring in their materials, the floor is spread with newspaper, and they begin to break and bust everything, and you think: farewell to peace . . ."

"You were lucky they spread your floor with newspaper," Konstantinov observed. "*Model* builders you had, it seems! Ours took it in their head to walk about the parquet floor in hob-nailed boots . . ."

"Yes, quite," Fyodorov sighed. "Gone are the days of

the craftsman. I put it down to the last war, when our womenfolk, poor souls, took over the factories, old grandmothers and boys of thirteen.''

''I remember we slept on the workshop floor,'' Konstantinov smiled. ''You couldn't even walk home, you were so tired, and anyway there were the bombs. We hung up hammocks and slept there. We were so used to the hum of the machinery, it was a comfort even—at that time the most terrifying thing was silence . . .''

''Absolutely,'' said Pyotr Georgevich after a pause. ''The terrifying thing was silence . . . They annihilated twenty million people, and with that perished a whole generation of craftsmen. And what is a craftsman? Someone above all, with *meticulousness*, an intensive, careful meticulousness. So if we get to the essence of the problem, these hob-nailed boots marching over the parquet floor are quite understandable, alas! Tragic but understandable. Want some tea? Or coffee?''

''Coffee.''

''It's not bad for your heart?''

''I suspect that anything, even the most trifling crisis we deal with, from the point of view of stress is worse than a cup of coffee,'' said Konstantinov

''Quite true,'' said Fyodorov, ''but that position demobilises the argument, don't you think.''

''*Demobilises?* To work constantly under arms is also stress. I don't see how I can be *demobilised.*''

''You're as bad as Slavin,'' Fyodorov laughed, ''—pedantic and cunning.''

''No,'' Konstantinov rejoined heatedly. ''I can't agree. There's no one in the world as cunning as Slavin.''

When the secretary had brought in two cups of coffee and a plate of *sooshki**, Pyotr Georgevich brought out a sheet of paper and began to sketch a figure on it.

''Can you see?'' he asked.

''Yes.''

''Then correct me if necessary.''

''No, it's not necessary.''

''All right, no flattery now. So—it seems your enquiries, especially since Slavin's telegram, have centred on Paramonov, eh?''

"That's right."

"Then you began to look at Olga Vinter. And she turns out to be the wife of Zotov. Yes?''

"Exactly."

"By the way, I asked Slavin what he thought about re-calling Zotov from Lewisburg. No answer yet. I guess that he means he doesn't think he has grounds to request this. No one is going to like it if we make such a request without the facts to back it up.''

"What about Zotov's friendship with Glebb?'' Konstantinov objected.

"What of it? Even the ambassador shakes Glebb's hand at receptions. There's no evidence he's a CIA agent, it's all conjecture, he's just a businessman who's well disposed towards us . . . But let's move on. What combinations are possible here? Paramonov, while detained by the police, is recruited by the Americans, because of something. But what? Slavin doesn't have a theory yet, so we're as good as guessing with coffee grounds. Anyway, how would Paramonov's recruitment benefit our CIA comrades? He doesn't have access to information of a political kind. What use is he to them? The CIA doesn't need his type.''

"Transmission of information.''

"OK. Between whom?''

"One can imagine a combination like this. Zotov in Lewisburg identifying the problems. Vinter here working on them, she sees secret material, she knows a lot. And Paramonov as the message-boy.''

"Can I make a slight correction? What about Zotov on the ground, with Shargin as the main source of operational information, and Vinter to check it? At her institute she gets material from practically all the ministries. Paramonov, I agree, is for transmission of information. Is *that* possible?''

"Yes." Konstaninov considered his reply, and then went on: "And so is a third hypothesis. Vinter has a multitude of tennis partners. They're all exceptionally well-informed people. So it's there, on the tennis court, that she puts feelers out on the complicated political issues, with Shargin to work in detail on the questions she refers to him. Paramonov is again the transmitter.''

''But transmitting how? Where? To whom? Not to General Shebeko surely . . ?''

''No, all *he's* doing is writing his memoirs—and it isn't going well, I understand,'' Konstantinov remarked. ''Many people naively assume that writing is an easy business . . . The old man is an insomniac, we've checked. He walks every night in Victory Park.''

''Where was Paramonov when Luns was driving there?''

''At home.''

''Vinter?''

''We don't know.''

''Shargin?''

''Having dinner in a restaurant with his brother.''

''And where were they all at the time of the most recent transmission from the intelligence centre?''

''Shargin was at work—consequently, *he* couldn't have received it. Paramonov was at home, but Gmyrya has established that Paramonov sold his Panasonic two months ago through a secondhand shop on the Sadovaya. Vinter was at home.''

''We must write out a time chart showing who was where at the time of each transmission. I used one during my tussle with Canaris and 'Papa Muller*,' with excellent results . . . What kind of radio does Vinter have?''

''A Panasonic.''

''By the way, we must ask Slavin about these Panasonics—who bought them, where, when and for how much. It looks as though they all got them in the same shop, but if it was in different shops, that's even more interesting.''

''We'll get onto that immediately.''

''How many other suspects do we have now in our 'inner circle'?'' asked Fyodorov.

''Yesterday evening another five people dropped out—they're out of town. Two more have left government service and are studying for doctorates. The rest are clean as a whistle.''

''Sounds good. But can you be sure?''

"That's the results of our checking."

Pyotr Georgevich pushed his empty teacup to one side, and as he did so, Konstantinov guessed the cause of irritation.

He was not mistaken.

"Why on earth is Slavin being so slow? Why doesn't he let us know what his theory is?"

"Well, he himself must be on tenter-hooks. But he can't rush, can't afford to—and that's the nub of it! He knows that the moment he shows our photographs to the person who wrote the letter, all our guessing is over. He knows very well how desperately we are waiting for his news, Pyotr Georgevich."

An aide put his head round the door.

"Comrade General, Panov has some urgent information."

"Is he on the phone?"

"You asked us not to put anyone through, so he's here in person."

"Let him come in."

Panov placed on the table six sheets of paper.

"Three at once, Comrade General! Never heard of such a thing."[1]

"Aha!" said Fyodorov, evidently intrigued by the information: "Time to beg a cigar off you, Konstantin Ivanovich. This intensity of work can only happen on the eve of real *events* . . ."

[1] The radiogram from the CIA intelligence centre in Europe read as follows:

"Dear friend, The information which you gave us has been of inestimable value to our cause. Our chief has been acquainted with your point of view and with the material you sent. We will carry out your request and send you what you require without delay at the time of our next secret operation. The meeting places are the same as before. Please speed up the reading of the documents in your possession, and convey to us your opinion as to whether an increase in Russian aid to Nagonia is possible in the event of a major crisis there. Your opinion and the views of colleagues on the same level as you would be extremely valuable to us. Your friends, 'D' and 'L.' "

This message proved impossible to decode in Moscow. (Author's note)

Lieutenant-General Fyodorov had joined the Cheka when he was twenty-one, a young radio engineer who had volunteered to go off to the Spanish Civil War, and who fought there with a legendary band of counter-intelligence agents, learning his craft from Grigory Siroyezhkin. When the war with Germany began, he joined the struggle against the Abwehr* and the Gestapo. Hundreds of Hitler's agents were caught and rendered harmless by Fyodorov's section. Next there was the struggle with the bourgeois nationalists ending in the rout of Bandera, the exposure of covert fascist hangers-on, and the fight with Dulles to force the handover to justice of Nazi executioners who had fled overseas in the search of new masters. Then began his work against spies sent into action by American intelligence.

Decisive and with a razor-sharp intellect, Fyodorov now as always spoke calmly and thoughtfully.

"Do you still play tennis?" he asked Konstantinov.

"When I have time."

"Well, find time, eh? Have a look at Vinter yourself. In the end, you know, a report is one thing, but the person themself is another. Get a proper idea of what she is like. And another thing: this business is complicated, extra-complicated, I would say. So I think that you should bring that famous meticulousness of yours to bear on the details of it, or on what *appear* to be details. After all, a spy case is foreign policy, it requires exceptional care and thoroughness."

6

Slavin

"No, Ivan, a hundred times no!" the fat, untidy man in khaki who had called out to Slavin repeated, with that almost pedantic stubbornness of one who is never without a drink in front of him. "It was by your own hand you all perished! It was you and your Stalin who constantly threatened Europe with aggression. What was there left for us to do?"

"You just repeat the same thing, as though you'd learned it by heart," Slavin took a gulp of beer and glanced at Glebb as if expecting support.

"Mr. Slavin is right," Glebb agreed promptly. "Truman was a bad guy, Paul. And he did actually hate the Reds, what's the point in denying it?"

Paul gave no sign of even having heard Glebb. He ordered another glass of beer, placed a hand on Slavin's shoulder, and—winking somehow with both eyes at once, as if he were conducting two conversations simultaneously and playing some trick in both of them—pronounced very gloomily and slowly: "Ivan, Ivan, don't you remember in April 1945, how we walked around Dresden the whole night together and talked about the future, and how triumphant we were later in Nuremburg when they dragged those Nazi swine into the dock? Don't you remember?"

"Of course I do. I remember you didn't only use to wink, but at that time you were still suffering from shell-shock, and you used to jerk your neck. You were really cruel with yourself, laughing at yourself so that nobody else could do so first. And you never drank, not even beer, and you were in love with a girl with a Nazi past.''

''The shell-shock went, but I'm the unlucky kind of guy whom everybody laughs at anyway, and like all born losers I get terribly offended—so offended, Ivan, that it gives me heartburn. These days I can't make jokes at myself, that's the privilege of the strong. I start drinking from early morning—and I find it the greatest bliss in the world! As for the girl with the Nazi past, you were right to take against her, she had a son by me and then ran off with an ex-inmate of Dachau. Now she poses as a victim of fascism, claims state benefit, and runs a committee in Dusseldorf for the humane treatment of animals. She set it up, by the way, after you Soviets launched that dog Laika of yours up into space. Well, that's *me*. What about you? What have you been doing since Nuremburg?''

''Living, Paul, living. How would you both like to come up to my room? I've got Russian vodka, caviar and black *sukhari** with salt.''

''With pleasure,'' Glebb agreed at once. ''There's nothing better than Russian vodka—our whisky is shit by comparison.''

''Government servants always run down their own,'' remarked Paul Dick—for thirty years a correspondent for various provincial newspapers, a Pulitzer prize-winner, an ace reporter of legendary bravery; thirty years ago—slim, handsome, athletic; and today—extinct, burnt out, old.

When they were in the lift, Paul stood aloof and to one side as Glebb described to Slavin the corruption and depravity of the Lewisburg regime, and the arrogance of the multinationals as they grasped into every corner of the land. Finally he could contain himself no longer: *''All* government servants,'' he repeated, ''if they're not covert ones, run down their country, it makes them more popular with foreigners. I find your comments, John, cheap and tasteless.''

"In a moment he'll say I'm a secret member of the Communist Party," Glebb sighed, "or a CIA agent and the chief of the local mafia."

"As far as the local mafia is concerned, I say nothing, because I have no evidence, but in Hong Kong you *did* have some interests, so they say. You're not in the CIA because Dulles filled the Agency with high-fliers with a left-wing background—like Marcuse. And you're not in the Party, nor even a sympathiser, because you fought in Vietnam."

Glebb ushered Slavin and Paul Dick into the lift, covering the eyehole in its door with the palm of his hand so that it didn't shut too quickly—they were moody and unpredictable, these hotel lifts. As the three of them walked down the quiet air-conditioned corridor with its durable green carpet, he remarked: "Whatever anyone says, here we are, able to say what we like to each other, however harsh or aggressive it might be. Isn't that what freedom's all about?

"Exactly," said Slavin, "I quite agree."

"Words don't make freedom," said Paul. "And you and your people, Ivan, have gone so far from it that meetings like this are the exception when they could have been the rule. It hurts me, really hurts me, d'you understand?"

Slavin opened the door to his room.

"So we've lost our freedom, is that what you say?" he replied. "And when Churchill made his speech at Fulton, when he called on the West to join forces against Russia, and the grass hadn't even had time to grow over the bomb sites—was *that* nothing to do with it?"

"But what was he supposed to do? Fulton was Churchill's last chance to preserve the glory of the British Empire, by setting us against you. What he wanted above all was the role of conciliator—England's age-old role. But you were stupid enough to get carried away. And when our own cretins mucked up everything and the whole world echoed with gunfire again, it was Churchill who called for talks between us as one-time allies—so he did get his conciliation, a victory for British prestige . . ."

"But what did *you* do to help us understand Churchill? We were new then to this kind of politics, Paul," Slavin replied, reaching into the refrigerator for a bottle of vodka and a tin of caviar. "In 1946 when Churchill made his Fulton speech, my country wasn't yet thirty years old, and you Americans had only recognised us for thirteen of them. Did *you* help us to understand Churchill? No, all you did was howl: Down with the Reds!"

"You had violated Potsdam."

"How?" Slavin asked with unexpected harshness. "Facts, please!"

"What facts! It was obvious, Ivan, the whole drift of events was obvious! At that time you could have rolled into either Paris or Rome—Thorez and Togliatti* were there waiting for you."

"Could have or *did?* It was you, Paul, who began to interfere in Poland, Hungary, Czechoslovakia, threatening people with your superior power while we kept silent. We kept silent for a long time, Paul, and pulled our belts in tighter—we were hungry, we were building up our country from the ruins. It's dishonest to accuse us of aggression when we had only one aim—to pull our people out of the dug-outs. But you began to bankrupt us through the arms race. Your strategy was to stop us putting resources into peaceful production, to starve us out. And we were forced to take counter-measures. Yes, harsh ones sometimes. So *who* violated Potsdam, the agreement of the Big Three, signed by Truman and Attlee? Who called for its revision? Us or you?"

"Your people often even deny that there *were* any 'harsh measures,' " Glebb remarked, studying the vodka from the ice-compartment as it poured thickly into the three glasses. "They say it was all provocation."

"Who?"

"Your Embassy staff, the engineers and trade people."

"How do you know them?"

"He's from the Trade Mission," Paul sniggered, "selling his country, and while he's about it, radio equipment."

"I'm proud that I have so many Russian friends," said

Glebb. "They're great guys, the only trouble is that as soon as you mention anything controversial, they start talking like *Pravda.*"

"And rightly," said Slavin, and continued quickly: "Cheers, Paul, I'm glad to see you. If you're here, that means something exciting is going to happen."

"We're off to Nagonia soon to cover the fall of Griso," Paul answered. He threw back his vodka into a throat which, so it seemed to Slavin, was as fiery red as the furnace of a coal stove.

"You shouldn't confuse wishes with reality," said Glebb. "To bring down Griso, you need people and money, and his opponents have neither."

"You liar," Paul said dismissively. "They have the money, and they have the people."

"That means, you know more than me," Glebb shrugged his shoulders and indicated with his eyes towards the bottle.

"He wants Paul to get drunk as quickly as possible," Slavin realised, "and to start talking rubbish, so that I'll think *everything* he says is fantasy."

He poured another round of vodka.

"To the great Russian people!" Glebb proposed the toast: "That we should learn to understand and trust one another! In the final analysis, we live in the same world, under the same sky, with the same ocean lying between us—which we can and should build a bridge across."

"I'm for," agreed Slavin, clinking glasses with Glebb. He gulped down his vodka, rose and walked across the room to the telephone: "What's the number for service here?"

"Dial fifteen," Glebb replied. "That's if you want to order a sandwich or peanuts. They have great peanuts here, they're fried with salt—delicious and very cheap, a beautiful snack."

"And if I wanted to provide some food for a guest?"

"Then dial twenty-two, that's the hotel restaurant. The cooking's good here, but it's all fairly expensive."

"Hello, this is room number 607. Good evening. What

could you recommend us for dinner? There are three of us. Caviar? Thank you, we already have some Russian. Fish? What? *Asau*?"

Paul Dick stretched out a hand towards the vodka bottle and momentarily lost his balance. Glebb looked at Slavin and shook his head from side to side: "That's too expensive," he whispered. "Leave it, ask for *merlusa*—it's decently priced and very tasty."

"*Merlusa*, please, some salad and coffee. Yes, thank you. Ice-cream?" Slavin put his hand over the receiver. "Is their ice-cream expensive?"

"Like yours—very cheap," Glebb laughed. "But not half as good."

"And three ice-creams. Yes, fruit-flavoured. Thank you. We'll expect you."

Paul successfully poured himself some vodka, again gulped back the whole glass, and looked soberly at Slavin and Glebb.

"You know, kids," he said, "what I dream of? I dream of contracting cancer. The tests would have to show that I had cancer. But I wouldn't be in any pain, not yet. It's very important that I shouldn't be in pain. Then I'd really *have a party.* I'd have a party until I dropped dead, the kind of party I've never been able to have because of this goddam work, the kind of party which everybody dreams of: a party without the fear of a hangover the next day. It would be a real holiday, a complete release . . ."

"Oh, go to hell!" said Slavin, and again splashed vodka into the three glasses. "That's a frightful picture you've painted! I'd want to get quickly drunk and forget it. But why aren't you drinking, Mr. Glebb?"

"I am! What d'you mean—I'm drinking like a horse!"

"You're just a trickster, Glebb," Slavin said to himself, "—whereas a horse is an intelligent creature. If you were intelligent, you wouldn't watch me drink so intently or seize on the signs of drunkenness so eagerly. Don't worry, I'll give you what you want, but don't push it, don't hurry me. It's true time is money, but you're just too *obvious.* More haste less speed, isn't that what they say? You should have a drink yourself, relax, doze off in the chair—then everything would be fine, and I'd really believe your story that you work in the Trade Mission selling radio equipment and—what else was it—your country, I think Paul said . . .''

Wearily opening his eyes with their leaden-coloured eyelids, Paul leaned dangerously towards Slavin:

"Even here, you're the ones to blame, Ivan. Even here in Africa, you're to blame for everything. We're only moving in to stop you going in first."

"Would it suit you," Slavin poured another glass for himself and Glebb, spilling drops on Paul's trousers in the process (I won't apologise, he said to himself, I'll make it look really drunk—in this heat it gets to you quickly), "if the Maoists moved into Nagonia? Would it suit you if *they* stuck their pistol at the underbelly of poor old Europe? Would she be able to stand up to it, that fine old lady? . . . Or can you see that threat, and do you want to help Europe?"

"The Chinese are insects, Ivan. Locusts. They're weak, no threat to us or you."

"That's not the way to talk about a great nation, Paul," Slavin cut him short. "That's not worthy of you. The Chinese are fine, good-hearted, intelligent people."

"Come on, let's drink to women," said Glebb. "To hell with you and your politics!"

"In a moment he'll suggest we call up a woman," Slavin realised. "He'll order whisky and call a woman. Or he'll say that he knows a good striptease here."

"I support you," he said. "In this age of the rat-race, only woman remains as a symbol of stability, that is, beauty."

"That's not bad," Paul grinned. "Sell it to me, Ivan. *Beauty as a symbol of stability.* Ten dollars? Fifteen then. Imagine the report I could write for the swine back home. 'Beauty—as a symbol of stability. These were my thoughts as the helicopter carried me deep into the jungle, towards the sea shore and six-foot high Mr. Ogano, orator and soldier, who promises to give back to the people of Nagonia the freedom that has been trampled underfoot by Griso's Kremlin marionettes . . .' Not bad, eh?"

"Not bad. Fifteen dollars then. Or take me with you to Ogano."

"The KGB would throw you into jail," Paul replied. "Ogano's your enemy, therefore you've no right to talk to him. Don't forget I know about you, Ivan, I'm old and therefore wise."

"Enough points scored, you guys," said Glebb.

"I think our dinner's coming at last. Listen—there's a noise in the corridor."

"I can't hear any damn noise in the corridor," said Slavin. "You've just got audio-hallucinations."

There was a knock at the door.

"Yes," the three men answered in chorus—two in English, one in Russian.

A black waiter stood on the threshold of the doorway, his hands on a trolley laid with plates of fish. And so, Slavin's wild idea—that the waiter would be white, and definitely Russian—was destined to remain a wild idea and nothing more.

Paul Dick picked at the *merlusa* with his fork, tried it, and spat: "Africans can't cook," he said. "When they threw out the French and the Belgians, the world's number one gourmets, they condemned themselves to slavery at the hands of our McDonald's—hamburgers, coffee and cheese sandwiches. Very convenient and, more important, cheap enough for anyone."

"Cheese sandwiches," Slavin repeated to himself. "Very cheap, the McDonald's bars . . . What section of the Hilton would 'Fingerless' work in? In the restaurant? But they wouldn't feed their own waiters in the hotel—this isn't Russia! So why shouldn't he eat in a McDonald's?

"By the way, are there any McDonald's in Lewisburg yet?" he asked, offering Glebb the salad. "The restaurant here will definitely be the ruin of me, and one can always do with a snack in the middle of the day."

"Of course, there are," Glebb replied, glancing regretfully at the empty vodka bottle, "but they don't allow them in the city centre. They're creeping up to the Presidential Palace from the slums. McDonald's are clever, they've put snooker halls next to the snack bars. That's where the blacks spend their leisure time—snooker is ten times cheaper than the movies . . ."

"And television?"

"You're mad! You think people here could afford a TV?" Glebb glanced again at the empty bottle. Paul finally noticed the glance, rose, went over to the telephone, and dialled fifteen. (Drunk, drunk, but he still remembers the number, Slavin noted, especially if it's to do with a bottle!)

"Two bottles of whisky," he said, "to room Number—"

"607," Glebb prompted him.

"To 607. Put them on the bill to room Number 905, Paul Dick. As quickly as you can!"

"Why does he show off his memory?" Slavin pondered slowly, nodding at Glebb who was describing how McDonald's had done a deal with a subsidiary of Nestlé's to sell coffee. "A normal person would never have memorized my number and remembered it as long as you, or have listened to me and Paul talking at the same time like that. Khrenov said 'Fingerless' worked twelve-hour shifts. I must find out how long the waiters work here. But why've I fixed on a *waiter* so surely? And why has Glebb fixed on *me?* Because he definitely has. Surely he couldn't know about our meeting with Khrenov—that would be too quick, even if he *is* CIA and has contacts with the local police. No, I'm just scaring myself, they *couldn't* have told him yet."

"Mr. Slavin, are you planning to write about the situation in Lewisburg?" asked Glebb.

"I must confess, I'm more interested in Nagonia."

"So why don't you go there? Or do you support your official line that Lewisburg is the HQ of the conspiracy?"

"I support it, of course. I don't disassociate myself from Moscow. Anyway, I have a colleague based there . . ."

"Ah! Mr Stepanov? We read his articles here—and his books too. Many people are angry with him. He's too harsh on us . . ."

"Disprove him, then. If he's lying, disprove it. But don't just get angry, that's undemocratic."

"Stepanov writes well, even if he's lying," said Paul, and he decanted the rest of the vodka into his glass. "Journalism and literature—they're *both* a lie. The more talented a lie, the closer it is to the truth. You have to lie plausibly—then it's art. You have to know how to describe your life inventively, not boringly like people really live. Only then can you become a Tolstoy or a Hemingway."

"Who?" Glebb asked, "Hemingway? But he's dead, isn't he?"

"And Tolstoy's moved from Minnesota to Miami and now goes fishing in the Gulf of Mexico," Paul said sarcastically. "Although," he continued, looking at Slavin, "Hemingway really is forgotten in the US. If he'd been born in the last century, then it would be another matter, but he's our contemporary. We knew him, we drank with him, and the girls told us how bad he was in bed, and his servants gave interviews about his greed . . . The twentieth century can't have classics, because of the power of the mass media. In Tolstoy's time there was gossip, but today everything takes shape in banner headlines in the newspaper columns. Don't believe all the shit we print, go there and see for yourself, make yourself an authority! And then there's the telephone . . . Communication has become *ridiculously* easy. Try in the old days to call up Yasnaya Polyana and interview Tolstoy. Like hell! You'd have had to go in person, asking permission first. And that bound you, drew a line between him and us . . . But today it's just a telephone call: "Count, could you make a quick comment on *War and Peace? . . .* "

"Time," Slavin agreed. "That's true, Paul. Very pessimistic, but true. So it works out that we are depriving ourselves of classics? The twentieth century wants to disappear into history without classics to its name? Don't we know what we are doing?"

"But we *do* know."

"Is it that our cultural level is too high? Everyone being literate, and so there is too much fashion for this and that? Too many individual tastes?"

"More like antipathies. As for culture, you're only partly right, you're projecting the level in Russia onto the rest of the world. That's a mistake."

"Friends, isn't this the time to turn our minds to women?" Glebb at last broke in. "Of course, I know that you're both great intellectuals and cultured people—but I hope you're not sexless. Or would Mr. Slavin be afraid of the consequences? As far as I understand, your people are forbidden this kind of, er, contact . . ."

"Now we have the 'birds,' " said Slavin to himself. "All according to plan. Old as the world, but it works, damn it! Well, let's see his talent!" He turned to Glebb.

"For your people too," he observed, "I've heard, *this kind of contact* is not exactly recommended."

Glebb glanced into Slavin's eyes. His face darkened momentarily, but this was just one half-second. Then he went over to the telephone, flopped into a chair next to it, took out of his hip pocket a worn-looking notebook, and turned straight to a page. At that moment he looked up and saw Slavin observing him. Without pausing he shut the book again and began to dig about in it. His expression was like Father Christmas making up a party game which would end in presents for all concerned.

"What would you like—white or black?" he asked, still leafing through the book.

"I'm colour-blind," Slavin replied.

Paul Dick burst out laughing.

"Oh, how cunning you are, Mr. Slavin!" exclaimed Glebb, "—always avoiding a direct answer . . ."

"Direct answers are for when you're in court."

"You know a lot about courts?"

"Naturally."

Paul said: "More than you, John. He sat through the whole Nuremberg trial. From start to finish."

"That was politics, Paul. What I mean is that when I ask Mr. Slavin about women, he answers just like a diplomat—neither yes nor no, always keeping himself clear as regards the rules . . ."

"What rules?" asked Slavin. "What rules do you mean?"

Glebb was saved by the entrance of the waiter from the bar, carrying bottles of whisky and a bowl of ice. Slavin saw that the American could not wriggle out of it: really, how could a simple businessman explain his knowledge of intelligence service *rules?*

Paul downed his glass at once, and poured out whisky for Slavin and Glebb.

"Just coming," Glebb called, dialling a number. "One minute, Paul."

He waited as the phone rang and rang at the other end, then disconnected and dialled a second number.

"Your girls are already distributed round the rooms in this hotel, undressing in the bathrooms," said Paul. "To hell with them, the whores!"

"Oh, don't be so unkind," Glebb protested, "and such a cynic! It's just that you've been so unlucky, Paul, never to have had a true woman friend, but only strumpets."

"The best woman friend is a shameless strumpet. Then you don't have to talk to her about Brahms or pretend that you like Stravinsky."

"Hello, Pilar," said Glebb. He had finally got through. "I'm having a chat with two very interesting acquaintances. Would you like to join us? Why? You disappoint me, Pilar. No, please . . . I beg you, eh? That's a good girl! Room Number 607. We'll be waiting for you."

Pilar turned out to be a beauty indeed—a tall, slender Spanish woman with huge round eyes and a smile that was charm itself. She greeted Paul and Slavin pleasantly, kissing Glebb in a chaste and kindly manner on the temple. Pilar clearly felt at home in hotel rooms. She immediately turned on the radio to the hotel's own jazz programme, choosing the right button instinctively. Then she took the glass of whisky offered to her by Slavin, and took a tiny sip. Noticing his glance, she explained:

"Don't be cross. After all, I'm Spanish. We drink wine, and never get drunk on it—only on interesting acquaintances!"

"Now I must get into conversation with her," Slavin

thought quickly, shivering slightly from the strain, ''and offer her that interesting acquaintance . . .''

During all these hours and days since the first discussion in Konstantinov's office, he had proceeded on the assumption that the Russian who sent the letter was probably one of those wretched emigrés eking out a miserable existence in the slave conditions of the hotel industry. In the Hilton at least the pay would be decent.

However, during all this long conversation, it had not occurred to Slavin that a critical decision would have to be made by him so suddenly. Nonetheless, clearly the old law about the transition from *quantity* (by which he meant his manoeuvrings and guesses) to *quality* (or action), had led him to a step which at first glance seemed strange, but in essence—in the present circumstances—was the only rational one.

''Just a minute,'' he said, rising, ''I'll be back.''

''What's happened?'' Glebb leaned forward.

''Oh, nothing much.''

He went downstairs to the restaurant and, rather unsteadily, approached the Maître d'Hotel.

''Excuse me, could you tell me whether any of your waiters,'' he asked, ''is from England or Germany? Of course, from Russia would be better, but obviously that would be hoping too much, wouldn't it?''

''But what's the matter, sir? Couldn't perhaps someone French help you? Our barman is French . . .''

''It's for something special . . . I'm entertaining a friend, she doesn't drink whisky, only cocktails, Russian cocktails . . .''

''Wait, wait! We have someone called Belyu, working in the basement. I think he was born in Eastern Europe . . . When our black servants were on strike, we put him on room service . . . One minute, sir . . .''

The Maître d'Hotel picked up the receiver and dialled three. He asked: ''Luis, could you tell me, has Belyu left work yet? One of our guests wants to speak to him from room . . .''

''607,'' Slavin said, trying to relax and get rid of some of that terrible tension.

"Room 607. All right, Luis. And when does his shift begin? Eight? Thanks."

The Maître hung up.

"Belyu starts work again at eight o'clock tomorrow morning, sir. I'm very sorry . . ."

"Then could I ask you to send me upstairs a bottle of champagne?"

"What sort? Sweet? Or some *Brut?*"

"It's all the same—only Russian."

"But with an American label, if you don't mind, sir. The Reds make *Brut* for the States."

"It's a pity about the label . . ."

"I'll try to have a look in the cellar, sir. The Russians have changed their labels, now they call their champagne something different—so as not to offend the French. I'll go down to the cellar myself, sir."

"Thank you, that's very kind of you . . . And please, send upstairs a bottle of Russian vodka."

"Yes, sir. Smirnoff?"

"No, Russian."

"Stolichnaya or Kazachok?"

"Kazachok? Never heard of it. Maybe you mean Kubanskaya?"

"You're obviously an expert, sir, on Russian vodka. Yes, Kubanskaya. I'll send you a boy in ten minutes."

"Now I must think of an excuse for a little drive," Slavin thought hurriedly as he rose in the lift to his room. "I'll begin flirting with Pilar and offer to take her home. And then I'll drop in at the Embassy and get the photographs. At eight o'clock I can meet Belyu here. My god, it *was* him who wrote the letter! I'll ask Moscow tonight what they know about him. With any luck, they'll know something—even the tiniest thing will do! And if Belyu speaks Russian, and if it was him who wrote to us, and *if* he recognises among the photos the man whom the Americans recruited in the room—then tomorrow I can fly back to Moscow with my mission completed . . ."

7

Konstantinov

The meeting with MID* department head, Eremin, was set for twelve noon in the Novoarbatsky Restaurant.

Several years previously, Konstantinov had examined Ivan Yakovlevich for his candidate's thesis. The subject of the thesis was the "National Liberation Movement on the African Continent and the Actions of the NATO Countries." It was in his capacity as an expert in international law that Konstantinov had interviewed Eremin, and with customary scrupulousness he set him forty-seven questions for verbal answer. For Konstantinov technicalities did not exist, and he had grown to expect the same precision in everything from those around him. From this point the two men became good friends. Eremin postponed his interview for a month, but passed it brilliantly—without dropping a single mark.

Konstantinov arrived at the restaurant ten minutes early. He ordered two bowls of bouillon with *parozhki**, enquired as to the waiter's opinion of the cutlets Kiev-style that day, and ordered a double-strength black coffee.

"And to drink?" asked the waiter. "Cognac? Or perhaps a vodka—we have Posolskaya."

"For drink we'll have mineral water—Borzhomi," replied Konstantinov.

The waiter was clearly offended. Shrugging his shoulders, he straightened the tablecloth so roughly that Konstantinov had to grab hold of his glass to save it from falling and breaking.

Eremin was five minutes late.

"Sorry, Konstantin Ivanovich, I miscalculated the time. I decided to mix business with pleasure, and came by foot."

"According to diplomatic protocol, five minutes' lateness is permissible," smiled Konstantinov. "And forty minutes, I think, will be enough—both for our little conversation, and for dinner. I've ordered bouillon."

"You're a genius," said Eremin, "a kind genius. Well—tell me, what's the complication?"

"Nothing definite. I just wanted to sit and talk with you in person. Over the telephone's not the same, I can't see your eyes. You and Slavin are sly old foxes, both of you. I think I understand you best from your silences."

"Is that a compliment?"

"Undoubtedly. Cunning is a necessary gradient of the mind, it is opposed to corruption and mendacity. You know, I recently specially re-read a chapter in an interesting book from the last century. It's called *On the Art of Military Stratagems.*

Eremin laughed: "There is a similar book, published in Paris in 1839, called *The Elegance of Diplomatic Stratagems.*

"So it's a compliment?"

"I guess so. Well, tell, me, how can I be of use to you?"

"You see, Ivan Yakovlevich, the thing is this: according to our most recent information, there is going to be bloodshed in Nagonia soon."

"Your information suggests the show of force isn't purely a demonstration, a test of strength?"

"My information says that they're preparing a bloodbath. What about yours?"

"We don't think that they will go as far as open aggression. I agree that the hawks have chosen Africa as a new field of combat. But they aren't ready for a serious fight, memories of Vietnam are still too fresh. It'll just be a propaganda ballyhoo, a storm in a teacup, probably no more. They want a bargaining counter for the disarmament talks, so they're rocking the boat—dragging us to the edge of a crisis, right to the edge.''

''My impression is you're wrong.''

''Is that your own personal opinion?''

''Yes. But it's based on facts.''

''The bouillon is superb. Only it needs a little bit of salt.''

''You salt-eaters! You know it gives you blood-pressure?''

''That's me!'' sighed Eremin. ''My blood pressure jumps up and down all the time . . . The soup is delicious, they do it well, the chaps here . . . I'm surprised, really, that you should feel so strongly about the probability of aggression. Let's weigh it up. Ogano boasts of his friendship with Lewisburg. But Lewisburg is not half as monolithic as it might appear. Though the pro-American groupings are strong there, the government is not united. By no means all the members of the Cabinet are in solidarity with the idea of unconditional support for Ogano— he's far too odious a figure for that. And then there's the newly awakened national self-consciousness. People don't want to get drawn into cross-currents of US politics. The Americans mess around too much, making fools of themselves with their loudness and their mercenary interests at a time when the world is more conscious than ever of the concept of national *dignity*.''

''Lewisburg's Minister of Defence, nonetheless, has declared his support for Ogano . . .''

''Yes, but he also refused to hand over to him a consignment of guns purchased in Israel.''

''What does Ogano want more guns for? He already gets them direct from the States and Peking.''

''For *rapprochement*. He asked Lewisburg for arms so as to tie his neighbours in with his cause. But they refused. It's a symptom. I think that the President, too, understands the complexity of the position. That's why he made his offer to Griso and Ogano to mediate in the conflict.''

''And?''

"Ogano is still saying no, but I reckon that in the end he'll have to enter the talks."

"But what will his programme be? He doesn't have a constructive programme, does he? All he wants is a fight . . ."

"He's being worn down, Konstantin Ivanovich. He'll have to come round in the end."

"With his masters' permission?"

"Peking, of course, will categorically oppose negotiations with Griso. Peking's interest is in an open confrontation. But Washington, it seems to me, is anxious about how it will turn out. Of course, the monopolies are putting on the pressure, they've lost their market, their interests are obvious. But it's risky for them to decide now on a fight, especially since our position is completely clear: we'll help Nagonia, because we have a treaty with it."

"This morning I looked at the speeches of the US Special Envoy . . ."

"What do you expect from him, Konstantin Ivanovich? He's Nelson Green's man, his job is to say what Green wants him to. But above him there is the government and administration, and they are not half so united as it might seem."

"In this case I was thinking by analogy, like British Law . . . The speeches of American diplomats were just the same before the outbreak of war in Vietnam. They have worked out a crisis scenario which is precise—even, I would say, elegant. You should remember, Ivan Yakovlevich, that in the African arena the hawks are pushing Europe. They have great hopes of dragging in their NATO partners."

"But the *arm-twisting* is too obvious, Konstantin Ivanovich. Europe is too wise, politicians know here that you don't start a fight in your own back yard. Because it won't be water from the Yangtze that they take to put out the flames, and the Mississippi's rather far away too."

"Which of the business tycoons in Lewisburg do your people rate highest? I mean the Western traders."

"The Germans are doing fine, clever chaps. Hansen is very big—they're in railways. Kirghoff and Boltz are in textiles, automobiles, cement. Of the Americans, perhaps the best are Chickers, Land and Saucer—they represent Rockefeller, they're practically all-embracing.''

"And Lawrence?''

"I don't think I remember him.''

"International Telephonic,'' Konstantinov prompted.

"Oh yes, I *have* heard of him! There were some rumours about him, that there's someone behind him, some shady connections . . .''

"And Glebb? Do you know anyone with that surname?''

"I think he's suspected of links with the CIA . . . His business is just a cover.''

"Or could it be the opposite?'' Konstantinov grinned.

"True. That's quite possible too.''

"Tell me please, Ivan Yakovlevich, would a leak of information—on the Nagonian question—really hurt us?''

"I don't dare think of it!''

"Unfortunately, *I* have to.''

"The signs point that way?''

"Yes.''

"Incontrovertibly?''

"We're working on them.''

"That's bad.''

"Not good, I agree.''

"I'd say very bad, Konstantin Ivanovich.''

"We're letting the enemy gauge our possible responses?''

"Exactly.''

"But still, you reckon they're not looking for a showdown?''

"I reckon not.''

"Well, *I* think they are. And they'll start it—if we don't stop them. Outwit them, in other words. Tell me, do the scientific-research institutes process a lot of papers from MID?''

"A lot. A whole lot. What do you expect—science depends on information, and if you keep it on hard rations, you'll get nowhere. But couldn't this be a provocation? Can you be sure it isn't a mistake?''

"We can't be sure. That's what we're looking at right now . . ."

Konstantinov drove Eremin back to the Ministry, then dropped in to his own office to look at the latest telegrams. Finally, he set off for the tennis courts. Trukhin had arranged a game for him with Vinter.

"I'm still an apprentice to the art of tennis," said Konstantinov. "So don't be too hard on me, will you? You're used to strong opposition, I expect?"

"Not really," Olga smiled, and her face changed at once, became younger. "The barber learns his art on an orphan's head."

"What's that? An orphan's head? Where does that come from?"

"An Afghan proverb . . . Shall I start, or do you want to practise your serve?"

"I'm ready for anything. Only please try not to humiliate me!"

"Don't worry, I'm completely uncompetitive. I play because I find a game puts you in trim for the week. It works you up *vkhurst**".

"Vkhurst?" Konstantinov echoed.

"Don't you remember? 'One eternal sonata, learned with zest'."

"Mandelshtam?"

"Where do you work?"

"I'm a lawyer."

"Then you amaze me. These days it's only physicists who know poetry. Humanities graduates, in my experience, prefer more simple conversation. Well, shall we start?"

"Good luck!"

Olga Vinter was indeed a fine player. It sometimes happens that a person who is strong in some field where he can, so to speak, wallow in success, is fond of showing off his talent. This can break or humiliate an opponent, causing envy, ill-will, or in a word, irritation. The opposite type is more rare—the kind of person whose ability makes him more open and accommodating. These people are happy to share their knowledge with others, it gives them obvious joy, especially when they can see the results of their generosity. To be with such people is not only pleasant, it is enriching. Any kind of *giving* inevitably has a boomerang effect: awakening talent in someone else, you get back one hundred times more, through different facets, and from this variety of facets, your talent becomes richer, sparkling in all shades of colour—for talent, if it is genuine, is always many-hued, only mediocrity is unambiguous.

Olga Vinter gave Konstantinov a chance, playing carefully, but without that absurd aggressiveness often found in the amateur game and for some reason considered essential and even inevitable.

"I didn't push you too hard?" she enquired after the first game. "Do slow me down if you want."

"No, on the contrary, you're too easy on me."

"I don't know how to be easy—on myself or others," Olga replied. "It can be offensive—in love, in sport, or professionally."

"I noticed that theme in your thesis—"

"My thesis was yesterday," said Olga, and her face became very young again. "No, really, I'm not boasting, it's just that as soon as something is done and finished, you see distinctly all its gaps and weaknesses."

"I didn't notice any gaps, you painted a very full picture."

"It's not difficult to do that when you've lived two years in a country. It infuriates me that our institutes don't give young researchers a chance not just to visit somewhere for two weeks—that's useless!—but to actually *live* there, to get a real feel for the society. Then you'd get results . . ."

"But it would cost a bit, probably, for the government— I mean in foreign currency."

"Nonsense! You could work in a library as a cleaner. Of course, you wouldn't earn enough to buy a car or a hi-fi—but enough for a flat, a coffee and a cheese sandwich. And you'd experience the charms of the Western world not just from the sidelines, but from inside. The 'Voice of America' works brilliantly for the same reasons. Before, they were so boastful, now they're more clever, they've learned self-criticism, they take their own society to task. Anyway, don't let me get angry—or I'll take it out on you on court!''

One of the reasons why Konstantinov was a good cónversationalist was that he could listen. In fact, he didn't just listen, he lived the words of the person he was talking to, his eyes expressing constant and intelligent interest— an interest far more effective as a stimulus to communication than any verbal posturing.

"But why did you concentrate on the multinational companies in Lewisburg?'' Konstantinov asked, when they were sitting in his trusty Zhiguli. "The American firms there are mainly solo outfits, aren't they?''

"I covered that in the first part of the thesis,'' Olga replied. "Yes, they are creating a base there, manning it, digging in. Whereas we spread ourselves too thinly, we're generous, scared to offend, unwilling to demand guarantees. We're trusting, whereas Uncle Sam drives a hard bargain and never gives a cent without getting a contract in return. He knows how to count his money. First *he* settles in, then the multinational gangsters arrive.''

In advising Konstantinov to take on personally the meeting with Vinter—which had become a top priority— Fyodorov was also conscious of another aim, one which only those concerned with the continuity of cadres would understand.

Fyodorov knew very well, of course, that various points of view were current in the security apparatus as to the role of a high-ranking commander in any given operation. Some considered that a general had no need to occupy himself with details, that there were plenty of well-qualified officers or promising young Chekists* to delegate to. Any of them could have done what Konstantinov was doing on the tennis court.

And yet, in every concrete situation Fyodorov considered that it was vital to find the right combination of two ideas—*leadership* of an operation, and direct *participation* in it. A precise sense of how to combine these two was essential to a strategy of relations within the collective.

"Peter the Great built ships," Fyodorov used to say. "So why shouldn't generals take part in an operation? If not, tell me by what bureaucratic code of demarcation this is excluded from their job description! And once in action, young officers can see them, and learn: *nataska** is a good word, Turgenev used it. Can we afford to reject it?"

"I may be going to Lewisburg . . ." Konstantinov continued. "Would you be able to advise me—what to see, whom to call on?"

"Of course. What's your business there?"

"We unload some of our exports to Nagonia at their ports. They're way behind schedule, and we may have to take legal action."

"It won't work. The ports have been taken over by the Americans." Olga's interest had quickened. "I suspect that they may have mafia connections. It looks very much like it. The bars, the McDonald's for example, serve the Americans directly, there are lots of them all round the harbour and airport. Zotov once told me that the Sicilian mafia rules because it controls the ports and airports . . ."

"Zotov? Who's that?"

"He's a man whom I loved. He was . . . Well anyway, he's a very good and intelligent person. You should speak to him, he's got a clear head, a very generous and kind person."

"Were you in Lewisburg as part of your research?"

"No, I was there with my husband—with Zotov. Could you drop me in the centre—if you have time?"

"With pleasure. I guess your thesis makes you one of the youngest Doctors of Science?"

"Well? Bread alone will not fill a person."

"Why anger the Gods?"

"In general I agree, it's not worth it."

"But who else, apart from yourself naturally, should I see before I leave?" Konstantinov persisted. "Who is there in Moscow on Zotov's level?"

"There is no one else like Zotov," Olga replied. "Nor is there likely to be."

"Has he completed his thesis?"

"No, he's not an academic, he's worked all his life. But

he could give any Doctor of Science a hundred marks' start, and still beat him! That's how well he feels and knows Africa. But he's very outspoken, and not everyone likes that.''

"Depends what he's outspoken about . . .''

"His ideas,'' Olga grinned.

"All the same, it depends what ideas.''

"It would take a long time to explain. You don't know Lewisburg . . .''

"And what foreigners would it be worth talking to?''

"The people in their MID are rather boring . . . Probably the Ministry of Education . . . They have a lot of young staff, with bolder ideas.''

"What about the business community? There must be Germans and Americans who have worked there for years, and know the position. I mean the tycoons, who make serious deals and so must have contacts with serious lawyers.''

"Germans?'' Vinter repeated. "I don't know any Germans there.''

"There's Kirkhoff, Boltz, Hansen . . .''

"True, I've heard the names, but they never really interested me.''

"Well, which Americans? Saucer, Lawrence, Chickers, Glebb, Lansdom?''

Vinter stared at Konstantinov with a perplexed expression: "And you're asking *me* for help?! You're already well prepared for this trip! All those names are serious Americans, I know them . . . Chickers and Glebb are good fun, only our people call them CIA. But I put that down to a relapse into spy mania.''

"Why?''

"Well, you see . . . In my opinion, a spy has got to be, above all, an intelligent person. But Glebb openly flatters us, sighing about what a beautiful country the Soviet Union is, how amazing we are. All that nonsense. I never believe people who praise you to your face.''

"Surely it's worse, if they abuse you to your face.''

"No, better. When they flatter you, you feel a complete fool, you don't know what to say.''

"You say he's stupid. But he embarrasses you, and consequently you behave in an abnormal fashion. And when a person behaves abnormally, then they end up saying or doing the wrong thing."

"All right. Don't worry about Glebb . . . Write down his number . . . I'll talk to my friend, maybe he'll be able to tell you something."

Back in his office, Konstantinov went straight to the pile of new correspondence. Among the papers was a telegram marked urgent from Slavin. It read:

Do you have any information on a man called Beliu, approximately sixty years of age, assumed Russian origin, works as a loader in the electrical department of the Hilton Hotel. Also John Gregory Glebb, born Cincinatti, served in Vietnam, before that worked in Hong Kong, recalled after scandal over shipments of narcotics?

Konstantinov turned to his secretary: "Has a reply been sent to Lewisburg?" he asked.

"We've drawn a blank on his first question, Konstantin Ivanovich."

"So there's nothing at all?"

"Absolutely nothing."

"Belyu, Baillieu . . . We must look at Bellow. Belof, if it's a Russian German. Belu, if it's Ukrainian. Bellow, of course. Have you looked at all the variants?"

"No, not that widely."

"Well, get someone to. Immediately. And what about the second point?"

"We have four Glebbs on file, all connected with the CIA. Richard Paul Glebb, born 1937, has never worked in Hong Kong. Then—"

"Slavin's only interested in Glebbs who've worked in Hong Kong."

"Then there are two: John and Peter. But Peter didn't serve in Vietnam. So that leaves John Glebb. As regards the scandal which he was implicated in, all we have is a reference in *China Analysis* and the *Far Eastern Economic Review.* Apparently in 1966 a man called Glebb was held by British police at Hong Kong airport when they nabbed some of Lao's people with a suitcase of heroin valued at one million dollars.''

"A suitcase-full would be worth three million, minimum. And what else?''

"That was the first report on the incident. Later reports don't mention Glebb at all.''

"When was he in Vietnam?''

"At the beginning of '67.''

Konstantinov laughed: "So Vietnam was for him like what the Eastern Front was for German convicts. The comparison fits, I think! Have you sent off the stuff to Lewisburg?''

"I was waiting for you, Konstantin Ivanovich.''

"No need. Get them to send it off at once. What's the time difference between us and Lewisburg? Three hours? That means it's now seven o'clock there?''

Konstantinov was wrong. The time difference with Lewisburg was different, and time there was moving fast.

8

Glebb

Glebb awoke with a start, as though someone had hit him.
Closing his eyes again, he tried unsuccessfully to work out
why he had woken, in such a cold sweat, with a sensation
of clammy horror. It was amazing what rubbish you could
dream in this hot weather. But when he shut his eyes, all
that swam to the surface was three black figures—six, zero,
seven. They stood before him so distinct and close that he
involuntarily rubbed his eyes. Opening them again, Glebb
stretched, glanced at the clock, and saw that it was ten
minutes to six. He swung a well-conditioned body out of
bed, padded with sweaty feet across the glazed tile floor
to the telephone. As he picked up the receiver, he noted
how his hand shook. It was some time before he heard the
receiver lifted at the other end of the line.

"Robert," he whispered in a scarcely audible voice,
"Come straight over to the swimming pool. No, I can't
wait. I want to have a swim straight away. You've got it?
Straight away."

He put down the phone and looked again at the clock.
It said seven minutes past six. Glebb dressed, splashed
cold water over his face, and jumped in his car. Ten minutes later he was in the Hilton swimming-pool.

Robert Lawrence, the CIA's regional representative, sat
sleepily in a chaise longue, his face creased, his eyelids
heavy and with the characteristic bluish tint of a chronic
kidney sufferer.

"What's up?" he enquired sleepily. "I was working till the early hours. What's gone wrong?"

"I don't know. Maybe it's nothing—yet. Yesterday I was with Paul, we met the Russian whom Stau told me about. It went off fine. But suddenly I thought—why is he staying in Room 607?"

"Because there weren't any other rooms . . . The season has begun, remember, the tourists are already arriving."

"But why did he choose the room where we recruited 'Mastermind'?" Glebb asked quietly, moving closer to Lawrence.

"Because that room is specially furnished for Russians . . . Is *that* why you woke me up?"

"Not only that, boss. Do you remember who it was that day who served us? Who brought up the food? The niggers were on strike, weren't they? I'm sure it was a *white* man who served us, none of us knew him. One of his fingers was missing. And the Russians have begun asking after a man with a missing finger who works at the Hilton."

"You've gone mad."

"I haven't gone mad. I'm just scared. That Slavin, he has the eyes of a devil, and he's no fool!"

"So the rest of the Russians, I suppose, are idiots?"

"No—but you *do* understand what I'm worried about?"

"Well, let's suppose he *is* from their counter-intelligence. As an assumption. So what? If they have indeed tumbled 'Mastermind', then Centre long ago saw through our game. After all, he meets our men regularly in Moscow. Could he be planted by the KGB? Hardly. His information is from firsthand sources, it's the genuine article—that's why our people are making such a fuss of him."

"Boss, would you like me to go and check who it was that served us in Room 607? You always criticize me for not having the right airs and graces, and because I don't speak French. But I have the sixth sense of a professional gambler. And I can sense something, boss, I can sense it!"

"Who will you find to tell you who laid the table?"

"I'll find someone. Remember, they asked us to collect information on the strike leaders?"

"No, actually I don't."

"Well, *I* remember."

Glebb hurried up to the lobby, asked for the number of the Maître d'Hotel, and was directed to the manager on the basement floor. Ten minutes later he was back at the pool. Lawrence was swimming in the green water. His movements were measured, smooth, feminine.

"Come out, boss! Quickly!" Glebb called, standing on the edge of the pool, and continued: "We were served by a man called Ivan Belyu. A refugee from Lvov, missing two fingers from the left hand. It's *him* Slavin is looking for!"

Lawrence sprang out of the pool with a litheness that belied his complexion. Swinging a bath-robe around him, he muttered worriedly: "Who has our files on displaced persons? Why should a Frenchman have such a passport? It looks like a mix-up, don't you think?"

"I'd like nothing better, boss!"

They went up to the fifteenth floor to room 1500, a suite which had been occupied by the CIA for the last two years as its Lewisburg base. There they woke Waltz, the station anchorman and records officer. Without washing, Waltz went straight to the card index and found an entry which read as follows:

Ivan Baillieu, previous name Ivan Byely. Born 1925, Ukrainian, home town—Zhitomir. Joined the Germans during the War, afterwards remained in Belgium, later driven by high inflation to Tunis where worked as a stevedore in the docks, then moved to Lewisburg. Has relatives in Zhitomir, but doesn't write for fear of causing them unpleasantness. An embittered man who says that his life is ruined, blaming the Americans for everything because we persuaded him not to return to Russia. No known contact with the Embassy. Drinks heavily.

"Well?" said Lawrence. "What do we do? Shall we ask Langley?"

Glebb did not answer. He was dialling 607. At the other end, the telephone rang and rang: Slavin was not in his room. Glancing meaningfully at Lawrence, Glebb dialled a second number.

"Stau, good morning," he said, automatically lowering his voice as though speaking to an agent from a telephone box. "Could you help me out? Find out what time Mr. Slavin arrived at the Russian Embassy . . . He's balding, heavily built, dark eyes, quick in his movements. I think he went there about four o'clock this morning . . . Stay there, I'll phone you again in a minute."

His back still to Lawrence, Glebb dialled Pilar's number.

"*Guapeña*, sorry to phone so early. When did our friend leave you?"

"He took me home, John, then we chatted for about five minutes in the car . . . He refused to come in, asked to see me today. At eight o'clock."

"When did he leave? That's what interests me."

"About three, maybe—"

Glebb didn't wait for her to finish the sentence. Slamming down the receiver, he rang back to General Stau.

"John," Stau said, "There was a man at the Embassy, apparently quite similar to your Mr. Slavin."

"When did he leave?" Glebb interrupted.

"You didn't ask about that."

"Find out right away. And ask the police on sentry duty at the Russian Embassy—what did the man look like who was hanging around the fence there? What interests me above all is: were any of his fingers missing?"

Lawrence put a coffee percolator on the electric hob mounted in the bar counter, and wiped his face with a sweaty hand.

"What shall we do?" he asked.

"Octavio has gone to see Ogano. Pereira is dropping arms into Nagonia. There's nobody from my commando group at hand, boss."

"But why should we need one of them?"

"Why do you think? Surely you don't want to try to talk to this Baillieu about the superiority of our society over totalitarianism! Where's Slavin—that's the point."

"Wait a minute, John. I don't understand why you're spouting all this rash talk, or why I'm listening to it. After all, what can this Baillieu tell him?"

"He can't tell him anything, boss. But he can point his finger at a photograph of 'Mastermind,' that's what! And then we're done for, me and you. And we could hardly complain. We'd have failed to protect the most valuable agent we ever had! An agent who has contacts at the very top!"

The phone rang. Glebb noticed how Lawrence winced slightly.

"Hello again," said Glebb. He was sure it was Stau, and he was not mistaken.

"Slavin left the Embassy a moment ago, John."

"You're not following him?"

"You gave us no orders. You said that we should wait today. He seemed fine."

"Thank you, Stau, you've really helped me out. Could you find me the address of an Ivan Baillieu? My guess is, Slavin's on his way to him now."

"Date of birth? Place of birth?"

"He came here from the north, about ten years ago. Works now in the Hilton. He's *one of them*, do you understand? Slavin has gone off to see him—we've got to stop him."

"Should we send some men over there? If, of course, we can find his address."

"Only on the word from me. Got it? For the moment, don't do anything—it'll only scare off the game. Only when I say, Stau, have you got that? I'll hang on now, I really need the address . . ."

"What 'game' do you have in mind, John?" enquired Lawrence.

"An interesting little ploy, I think, boss. I want to get Slavin arrested—as a Russian spy and a terrorist. That would help us in a number of ways. In fact, the advantages would be almost too many to count, especially on the eve of 'Operation Torch.' ''

At eight o'clock that morning Glebb found Slavin in the hotel basement, sitting in front of the locked door of the workshop and spinning a tennis racket in his hands.

"Vit!" he called. "Good morning! It's nice to see you. What are you doing here?"

"Come to tighten my strings," Slavin replied. "Good morning, John. By the way, do you play?"

"Tennis is a game for aristocrats, Vit. I'm a working-class lad myself, my dad was a docker. I'm a boxer—I love a fight, especially with a good opponent."

"Me too. We could borrow some gloves, if they have any here, and work out a bit in the ring. Only I bet there aren't any gloves. There isn't even anyone to do my racket strings. They told me there would be a handiman here in the basement—they said he can turn his hand to anything."

"Who's that?"

"Heaven knows."

"Where is he?"

"God knows . . . I've noticed, people don't value time here. It seems your lessons go unheeded."

"You think *we* know how to value time, Vit! That's just propaganda. We're maybe a tiny bit superior to the locals here, but even so . . . OK, when your racket's been finished, come upstairs, we'll have a coffee before you go looking for a partner."

"Zotov's getting me one."

"Who?"

"He's one of our engineers."

"I know a lot of your engineers. What was his name, again?"

"Andrei Zotov."

"No," Glebb shook his head. "I don't know Zotov. Though maybe he was introduced to me under a different surname?"

Investigation No. 1 (Trukhin, Grechaev)

Grechaev had quite an interview on his hands. He had been sent to see Tsizin, the boss of the Mineral Waters shop where Paramonov went every day, apparently, always at precisely the same time, after checking to see whether he was being followed. Or so the surveillance team had reported.

"Yes, yes, yes!" cried Tsizin fussily—a short, sweating man. "And don't look so innocent as though you've come to inspect the boiler or count the empties. As a worker in the service sector, I've learned vigilance the hard way, mate! Let's have it straight: I've been shopped, haven't I? Who was it? I bet it's Prikhodko—writing one of his usual treaties on how I'm melting down empty bottles into German silver. Or was it Drynov that shopped me? I suppose he said I was selling Borzhomi* bottle tops on the side, I've got an arrangement with Sharudinov . . . Do you want to see my overheads? And I *don't* sell fresh water instead of Essentuki any more. Our clientele's too educated now, everyone's worrying about cyrrhosis . . ."

"Please, there's no need to go into all that—" Grechaev finally interposed. He had run through in advance all his possible roles in this encounter. "I'm not from OBKhSS*, you know."

"So where *are* you from? From the pregnancy clinic? Or Mosfilm*?"

"That's it! The Film Production Department," Grechaev answered. He had decided to use his old acquaintance with Assistant Producer Kharin, a school friend who was thrown out of the Bauman Art College for unbridled drunkenness and a tendency to scandalous behaviour in public. (Or that was how the Komsomol* meeting formulated it—a "tendency," rather than "scandalous behaviour" itself. They had softened the sentence, not wanting to spoil the lad's life.)

Now it was Tsizin's turn to be surprised. Like any service worker, he nurtured a particular interest in cultural figures.

"Really?" he said, "Do you have the relevant identification?"

"No—it's not the same as being from OBKhSS . . . What do I need one for? I'm just an assistant to the producer—Bobrovsky, have you heard of him?"

"Tolya?" Tsizin shrugged his shoulders. "What d'you mean, heard of him? He comes in literally every week, usually buys Slavyanovskaya. Strictly an under-the-counter arrangement—I suppose it's wrong really, but the intestines of even one artist are dearer to me than all the sufferings of the alcoholic element."

In reality, Bobrovsky had twice bought water from Tsizin, exchanging a total of perhaps three casual phrases with the man. But this was enough for the shop manager—an opportunist quite satisfied with the fact of the meeting, and ready to dress it up as an old friendship.

"So, look, we would like to make a request of you . . ."

"Please go on."

"We'd like you to help us to organize a film-take."

"In the shop?"

"Yes. It's an interesting episode, or scenario. If you like, we'll send it to you."

"Will you film me personally?"

"Oh, yes."

"No, really?"

(Oh, human conceit! Why does it always fasten itself on to the film producer? Why this need to *imprint* oneself for eternity?)

"Really. At least, Bobrovsky wants to."

"So why didn't he come himself? Tell him I'll have some Naftusya in a few days. It's like nectar, almost too good to drink! No hangovers, it washes the liver and the kidneys clean, literally like washing powder."

"What are your first names?"

"Grigory Grigorevich. Call me Grisha."

"Yes, yes, that's just like my boss said . . . Well, Grigory Grigorevich, we would like to organize a film-take here. We'll need a hidden camera."

"A hidden one? Is that how Grisha works?"

"Grisha who?"

"Chukray*. Puts down his contraption and pretends he's photographing little birds. But really he's looking at a young lad necking with a girl . . ."

"That's right."

"Well, nothing could be easier! We'll drill a hole in the door," Tsizin turned around. "My storeroom is back there. You can set up your equipment, I'll string along the customers . . . Only, hang on, you won't see my face! Who is going to recognize me from behind?"

"Don't worry, we'll use two cameras. The customers will think we're filming you, while we're shooting from two angles."

"And you'll show the back angle in the cinema, and the front one with my part will be thrown in the rubbish. I know that number, don't I?"

"Well, you have a word yourself with Bobrovsky about that, if you don't believe me."

"As if I don't know that these days it's the No. 5 who makes the decisions, not the No. 1! I don't know what rung you are on the ladder in Mosfilm, what an Assistant is, and whether it's higher than an Aide, but it's not worth arguing about—whatever *you* put on his desk is what will go in the film. Same with us, isn't it? For a start, the Director of the Rayprodtorg* would never invite me into his office. He's like the Pope, you can't take your request to *him*, you have to suck up to his *secretary!* But her kidneys and intestinal system function like clockwork, so Naftusya is no use there! Luckily, she dreams of string tights, and the head of *that* section is one of my ulcer men, so I hold back a Slavyanovskaya and Vitautas for him—and there's your tights and an order for new empties . . . But you know, it's not *me* that these bottles are for, are they? They're for your workers, aren't they? All right, I get my twenty-five kopecks too, but what a terrible effort! Tsizin takes home twenty-five kopecks for his good services to ulcer victims. So they will be nicer people and not drink the blood of the people during the working day, if I just stew them in Smirnovskaya! So who am I working for really? My own gain, or the communal good? You could just tell them to get lost, couldn't you? 'No Essentuki today, complain as much as you like, what's it to me?' And *that's* permitted, if you say *that*—no bother at all! Oh well, what can you do, why wind yourself up all the time . . .''

"Do you need to get permission from anyone for the filming, Grigory Grigorevich?''

"If you want to screw up the film—ask for permission. You know the story about how some man came to God and asked him to make his neighbour Ivan's cow kick the bucket. You don't? Well, he went and asked God: 'It's just a trifle,' he said, 'but it'd be so nice . . .' Anyway, what'll happen is that every shop manager in town will try to spoil my chance, burying his boss's secretary in presents, if only she asks the director to make the film in *their* shop. We're all human, after all, we all want to get into the great Soviet cinema!''

"Yes, but we'll be filming in the afternoon, and you're especially busy at lunch hour . . .''

"So what? I'll get hold of Auntie Vera, she's a pensioner. I'll give her some fruit juice and get her to ladle it out on a tressle table outside the window! Then there's another—''

The door banged noisily behind Grechaev's back. He turned round. On the threshold stood Paramonov, staring fixedly at Tsizin. The shopkeeper smiled and made a strange, hardly noticeable sign with his hand, asking the while: "What do you want?''

"Er . . . No, it's . . . I just wanted to ask, have they delivered the Sairme yet by any chance?''

"Drop in a bit later. It hasn't come in yet, but it'll be here by five.''

Grechaev looked up at the shop window. Right there in front of his eyes stood seven bottles of Sairme.

"So, there you are," Tsizin was saying. "And don't go to the Raypischchetorg*, for heaven's sake, or you'll be sucked into the intrigues. I'll tell you what—run over to the top man, in the district trading office. He's a young fellow but with a good head on his shoulders, he'll do everything you want. Just say you need to film at Tsizin's shop and nowhere else will do.''

''So he's an ulcer man too?''

Tsizin didn't follow: ''What? No, he's a perfectly healthy young—''

''So why would he do anything, just for Tsizin?''

''Because it'll be *you* asking, and anyone with any sense would do a favour for a worker in the arts . . .''

''But what if those bottles in the window contained ordinary water?'' asked Konstantinov, looking up from Grechaev's report. ''Dummies, I mean?''

The head of the group, Colonel Trukhin, replied: ''They could be dummy bottles. But why should Paramonov go to Tsizin for Sairme when I checked and his own works canteen sells it anyway?''

''Anything more from your tailers?''

''Paramonov walked up and down the street for seventeen minutes, looking at his watch. Then he went into telephone booth number 7319, and called exchange number 244, probably to speak to Leopold Nikiforovich Shargin—''

''Probably?''

''The telephone dial was hidden by his back, and he put his fingers in front of it, so our officers couldn't see the other numbers . . . But Paramonov doesn't know anyone in the Sadovaya Sennaya telephone district except for Shargin.''

''I accept your first assumption: most likely he really was calling Shargin, but I don't accept the second. But what if he was phoning a contact you haven't yet identified? Is *that* possible?''

''Yes, but with one proviso.''

''What's that?''

''That Paramonov himself is the agent receiving the CIA's messages. That *he's* the link person in the network.''

''What happened next?''

''Paramonov went back to Tsizin, who poured him a glass of water which Paramonov drank. But he didn't pay

for it, or even say thanks and goodbye. He just ran out to
the bus stop, jumped on a bus, and seven minutes later
was back in the garage.''

''And then?''

''And then he continued his work repairing Olga Vinter's car.''

''Have a look at Shargin. Have you found out yet what
documents he gets from the secret archive?''

''Yes. He sees all the ones Langley would be interested
in.''

At that moment Shargin was standing on the crossroads
of Arbat and Smolenskaya by the exit from the *Gastronom** shop. He was clearly in a state of some agita-
tion. Peering intently at the traffic, he at last caught
sight of a car with a diplomatic number plate. He
stepped down from the pavement into the road and
waved in greeting to the man sitting at its wheel. The
car braked, and the two men spoke together for several
minutes. However, the subject of their conversation was
inaudible, because Shargin was leaning on the door and
speaking through the open window.

Next, Paramonov drove up—in Olga Vinter's car. He
parked the Zhiguli beside the diplomatic car. Shargin got
in, and drove to Preobrazhenskaya street, Block 7, picked
up two girls, set off to the Rus Restaurant, and from there
to Paramonov's bachelor flat where they spent the night . . .

Konstantinov

''Shargin was talking to Van Zeger, the representative of
Trade Corporation, a business partner of his,'' said Proskurin.

''A partner, eh? Do we know anything to make us suspicious of him?''

''He's an ordinary businessman. We don't think he's
connected with the secret services.''

''And what about the girls who were with Paramonov
and Shargin?''

''Boilerwomen, both of them.''

Konstantinov placed his spectacles on the end of his nose, and looked at the lieutenant-colonel questioningly.

"Boilerwomen," the other repeated. "One graduated in textiles at technical institute, the other—in food industry. Both are from Rostov, came to Moscow to look for work here—there's such a shortage of workers, they'd give the devil himself a temporary residence permit and a bed in a hostel. So these two girls got a one-room flat together. Twenty-four hours on duty—forty-eight hours off—on the town!"

"So whom do they go around with?" Konstantinov inquired.

"They've only just been identified, Konstantin Ivanovich, we're looking into them now."

"This case is beginning to expand out in all directions, don't you think? Like a snowball. And that's bad, eh?"

"What can we do about it? They're the facts. And facts are obstinate things."

"You've got a good memory," Konstantinov remarked. "Nonetheless, despite the facts, I don't like the way the case is spreading out. People aren't like snow. A *human snowball* is a horrible concept, don't you think?"

As soon as Proskurin, having finished his report and agreed a plan of action, had left the office, Konstantinov rang Olga Vinter.

"Hello, champion," he said. "Your pupil speaking. I'm afraid I'll be late on court tomorrow—my Zhiguli is playing up, and getting a service will mean wasting a whole day. I don't know any good mechanics . . ."

"Oh, well, *I* do. Only he won't charge you anything if you tell him I sent you. Buy him some vodka, he loves Pshenichnaya, or even better—gin. Have you got a pencil handy?"

"I'm ready."

"His name is Mikhail Mikhalovich Paramonov. Only don't say on the telephone that it's to do with car repairs . . ."

"Poor old thing. He's afraid, is he?" Konstantinov laughed.

"It's his generation. They're a bit barmy, aren't they—frightened of everything."

"By the way, did you speak to your fellow African students?"

"No luck so far. They don't seem to want to talk—probably hoarding their ideas for articles, the mean bastards! By the way, do you listen to the 'enemy voices'?"

"Sometimes."

"Yesterday London transmitted an interesting commentary on Nagonia. You can bet your bottom dollar they're planning an invasion, just like the Congo, the statements are almost exactly the same."

"Let them invade, we'll come to their aid. After all, we have a treaty with Nagonia," said Konstantinov. His words were an exact reply to the question which the CIA had put to their agent in the last coded transmission.

At the other end of the line there was a silence.

"Are you there, Olga?"

"It's all right. I was just lighting up."

"You don't smoke, do you?"

"Just begun."

"When?"

"Today . . . OK, phone Paramonov. I'll tell him to expect you. And make sure you come tomorrow, I like talking to you."

"Same here."

"Don't take it as a compliment, I think you're far too harsh! If I was to write what you said—that they can invade if they like, and we'll come to Nagonia's aid—I'd get my head bitten off."

"By whom?"

"My bosses."

"Why?"

"They'd say it was too hard-line. That I'm not the government, and that our enemies are just waiting for declarations like that . . ."

"But why do they need to wait, when it's all spelt

out in the treaty, and the treaty was published in the papers? . . .''

"They'd object that the treaty will be broken off as soon as the coup takes place. Then we have no way of sending help, it'd be an infringement of international law . . .''

"Untrue," said Konstantinov, thinking furiously whether he should continue this conversation or stop and prepare more carefully for the next time, perhaps during tomorrow's tennis game. "Untrue," he repeated, "because they can only topple the lawful government of Nagonia with the help of forces from outside the country. *That* is a gross infringement of international law. Anyway—thanks for Paramonov!''

Paramonov shook hands with Konstantinov, then followed him out into the garage forecourt, inspected the Zhiguli, lifted its bonnet, and fiddled with some wires.

"Olga said you had a serious fault . . . But one of your leads is worn through, that's why it's losing power. If you ever go abroad, buy a Bosch set. It's very useful, the bourgeoisie sure know how to make a mechanic's life easier.''

"That they do," agreed Konstantinov. "Do you have a pair of spectacles by any chance? I can't see properly what's in there, I left mine at work . . .''

"My glasses are in the office," Paramonov replied. "I don't use them any more, I wear lenses . . .''

"What?''

"Contact lenses—I bought them abroad. Cost half my wages, but I've had no bother since.'' And he laughed—a full unrestrained laugh. Konstantinov caught the odour of vodka.

"Shall we have a drink in your canteen, or go to the café?'' he asked the mechanic.

"Sorry, old comrade, I'm afraid there's no drink on the premises. We have a rule against it here. The firm's director is a slave-driver. He has high blood pressure, and he doesn't drink himself—a bloody lance-corporal, not a person! If you ever have a serious problem, come again and I'll help. For Olga's sake, I'd pull burning chestnuts from the fire. She said to me you're going to Lewisburg?''

"Yes. Can I take a message? Or bring you back something?''

"Well . . . But what's your line of business?''

"Law.''

"How do you mean?''

"My trip is to ratify Shargin's deliveries.''

"You know Leopold?''

"By name only . . .''

"A saint. A real *Mtsyri**. No, I asked why you were going because . . . perhaps you could help. You see, I've saved half what I need to buy a Zhiguli, now I need the other half. Really, I need to work another couple of years 'outside the cordon.' Leopold promised to help but, you see, he's only a small fry, just an economist—whereas I can see from your face, *you* are more important!''

"How do you mean—*you can see?*''

"Hard to explain. It's just a second sense . . .''

"Did you come back from abroad a long time ago?''

"No, recently.''

"An interesting country?''

"All right. Well, let's see what's good . . . For a start, you can buy radio gear at reduced price—it comes straight from Hong Kong. The clothes and fabrics are not bad either. But the shoes are rubbish—they say Spain's the place to buy cheap shoes, apparently there a good pair of boots only cost ten bucks.'' Paramonov closed the bonnet.

"That's all,'' he said. "You can drive without worries. But buy some Bosch leads all the same, and save yourself trouble in the future.''

"Thanks for the advice. Do you have any cold water here?''

"There's mineral water in the buffet.''

"What kind? I only take Slavyanovskaya—an ulcer, you know.''

"God knows what they have. Whatever's been delivered. Give my regards to Olga, just tell her not to overdo it. I'm afraid she's a bit of a roadhog . . .''

"I'll tell her. Was it *you* who taught her to drive?"

"No."

"Her husband?"

"No, he was against it. Worried she might have an accident—they cause a terrible stink about it over there, not like us."

Konstantinov took a bottle of gin out of his briefcase, and held it out to Paramonov: "Thank you, Mikhail Mikhailovich."

"No, really," the driver protested. However, after looking carefully at the bottle, he took it.

"I think I've met Zotov," Konstantinov remarked as he got into the car. "He limps slightly, doesn't he?"

"Yes."

"A good fellow?"

"A shit. Olga did the right thing when she left him."

"Why?"

"He's a miserable bastard. If one thing's not wrong, he'll complain about something else. In the end I refused to look at his car. He was always moaning, checking on you as though you were cheating or something. Sniffing around like a bloody policeman! . . . Just because some people can't hold their drink . . . For others, I think, it sharpens the wits, and the work goes better . . ."

"But I don't think he was ever a teetotaller himself."

"No. But I wouldn't pull the wool over your eyes, he hardly drinks—or only a small glass if at all. True, he could knock back a litre, but not in one go and not to enjoy it. Over there you all live in each other's pocket, there are no secrets, everyone knows each other's business . . ."

"Well, not quite all, I'm sure," Konstantinov snorted, as he turned the key in the car's ignition. "Nobody can fully know another's business. A person can't even know himself fully. Thanks again. See you."

To Slavin

Find a way of visiting the local police station where Paramonov was taken. Try to discover the reason for his detention.

Centre

9

Slavin

Slavin understood everything when the three policemen pushed past him, led by the hotel doorman, and opened the door of the room where Baillieu worked—a stuffy, windowless room, with the pipes of the hotel air-conditioning system overhead. On the joiner's bench a vice was fixed, with tools spread out on a leather apron. From the way they were scattered about, you could guess at once a Russian worked here. It was that special kind—an *inspired* disorder, the kind only one of our craftsmen can create as he works away oblivious of the time, and then suddenly remembers something, glances at the clock—it's already late!—and drops everything and is off . . . A German or American puts his tools away ten minutes before the end of the day, the time is fixed in his brain, he doesn't work a minute longer than he has to, for time is dollars, it costs money.

"Where is our handyman?" Slavin enquired of the doorman. "I was told that he's the only one who can help me with my racket."

"He's been murdered," the other replied, but one of the policemen gave him such a fierce glance that he coughed, turned away from Slavin, went into the corner and sat down on a stool.

"Stand up," said the same policeman to the doorman. "And don't touch anything with your hands."

Slavin went back to his room, opened the door onto the balcony, lowered himself into the chaise-longue, and stretched out gingerly.

"I'm afraid I underestimated you, Glebb," he thought. "It's a blow, yes, a serious blow that you've scored on me. True, by the same token I now know for sure that it was you who recruited one of our men in the room, that's definite now. Which means that Baillieu was telling the truth. But now *nobody* can point a finger at one of those photographs lying in my pocket."

Slavin went into the bathroom and burned the photographs which he had collected from the Embassy the night before. After rubbing the ash in his hands, he washed it away down the sink, then sprayed the room with an aerosol to get rid of the smell of burnt paper, and went back to the balcony.

"What is needed now is some neat, well-checked disinformation," Slavin finally decided: "I have to soothe Glebb's fears, otherwise I'll never carry out this mission, everything will go up in smoke, and we'll never catch the spy. And there is only one person who can help me right now—Paul Dick. Through Paul, I must convince Glebb that my actions in the restaurant last night were an accident, a drunken accident, that I didn't see Baillieu and never could have. I must convince him that his alarm at what I said was unfounded. I can do this if I let Paul in on a *part* of the truth. And Paul will realise that Glebb is from the CIA, and that too will be to my advantage, for the future."

The bar was empty apart from Paul Dick—morose, crumpled, his hands shaking as he drank.

"Alcoholism is a social disease, Ivan," he sighed. "At least that theory lets me start drinking every morning! Care for a gulp yourself?"

"Coffee, please. I want to have a go on court. Listen, why do you keep calling me Ivan?"

"As far as I'm concerned, all you Russians are Ivans. It's great to use one name for a whole nation. We should all be called John, it's a pity we aren't."

"Why do you say that?"

"Because we're so divided, each for himself, and we have no common purpose. But you're a monolith, and whatever they tell you to do, you do it."

"You should re-read Tolstoy or Dostoyevsky, Paul. It's wrong to see a nation as a kind of flock of sheep who never question their orders. Read Russian literature."

"Literature tells lies. It just throws a blur on reality. Read Dickens, and you would think that the British were the most sentimental nation on earth. But in Dickens' time they were tying Indian sepoys to cannons and blasting them to pieces. Maupassant wrote the truth about the French— remember how one of his fellows pushed away another's hand and let him drown, so he could save his fishing net instead! And we're always talking about French elegance, French style . . . The French are the most mercenary people in the world . . . And then you have Goethe with his *Sufferings of Young Werther*—while in the concentration camp at Maidanek his fellow-countrymen burned people alive . . ."

Paul turned to the waiter who was standing behind him, bending over their table slightly: "A Bloody Mary," he said, "for me. And for the gentleman—a coffee."

The waiter bowed and withdrew. Paul Dick lit a cigarette, and suddenly coughed so hard that his eyes sprang out of his head and his face turned purple.

"Why are you destroying yourself, Paul?" Slavin asked.

"I'm already destroyed, Ivan. I'm just lingering a little over my departure."

"Then wait a while more before you go. It's too early still. Life is bloody interesting . . ."

"Uhu . . . D'you know what killed Steinbeck? It was Hemingway who killed him. Yes, yes. He was tortured by envy of Hemingway—not his books, I mean, but his life. That's why Steinbeck went to Vietnam, somehow to get even with Ernie. He wanted the glory of being a war correspondent, he was tormented by it. There was no Spain now, no Republic to defend, so off he went to Asia to where the shooting was, hoping that the thrill of danger would take his mind off things. Envy destroyed me, too, I used to envy *everyone*, d'you understand? It kills you . . ."

"Would you like me to give you a story?"

"Go ahead."

"Give me your word that you won't reveal me as your source?"

The waiter brought the coffee and a glass of vodka with tomato juice. Paul Dick downed the glass. Immediately drops of sweat broke out on his forehead.

"OK. Now I can talk to you! Hey there, sonny, bring me another Bloody Mary, only this time make sure it has a little more ice . . . Well, go on. I give you my word."

"Tonight a man was killed because of me."

"Go to hell!"

"It's too far."

"Well then—tell me what it's about."

"Do you remember when I went down to the restaurant last night? I was going to offer you a Russian cocktail."

"No, frankly I don't. But it doesn't matter. Go on.

"Well, I found out that a Slav of some kind, with a Franco-American surname, worked here in the basement. And today he's dead—murdered because your secret service found out I was asking about him."

"Don't talk rubbish!"

"Show me otherwise."

"How do I know he wasn't an agent *of yours?*"

"If he was," Slavin grinned, "that would have been fine. If he was *our* man, he'd have known a lot of useful secrets—things like how to make the air-conditioning work in your Hilton . . ."

"What's his surname?"

"Baillieu. Ivan Baillieu. And if you talk to Glebb about it, please don't quote me—OK?"

"Why? Do I notice symptoms of the Russian disease—spy paranoia?"

"You know us well . . . But just remember—the moment you ask him about Baillieu, Glebb'll say: 'When did Slavin find out about it?' I don't mean at once, it could be within thirty minutes, casually—but he'll definitely ask."

"You want to bet?"

"A bottle of vodka."

"Done! I'll give you a ring."

"Or drop in, that's better. Are you having lunch later?"

"I don't know yet."

"Let's go to a McDonald's, somewhere on the outskirts. It would be interesting to look at the people . . ."

"Good, let's meet in the hall. Two o'clock—is that OK?"

The girl in the car hire firm finally found a Fiat. Slavin hadn't wanted a Ford (too expensive, guzzling twenty litres a minute) or even a Mercedes. He guessed he'd feel more at home in a Fiat, no need to get used to it or learn its ways. Say what you will, the Fiat was father to the Zhiguli, all you had to do was get in and put your foot down . . .

Before leaving for town, Slavin spoke to the garage mechanic: "I've never driven in Africa before," he said. "Give me a few tips—how can I be sure of avoiding the local cops?"

"They're no trouble at all, sir. Of course, if you get drunk, they'll take away your licence. Being a white, you could expect to pay about a hundred dollars—it's a kind of police tax here—and they'll give you a good working over too. They haven't yet learned to accept bribes politely."

"What else should a white driver know?"

"Nothing else, I think, sir. If you're taking a girl home at night, and you want to mess around with her, don't let her take her clothes off. The girls here have got clever, as soon as they're undressed, they start shouting they're being robbed. To hush up a scandal like that would cost at least three hundred bucks . . ."

"Thanks, I'll remember," Slavin promised. "Nothing else to be afraid of?"

"Nothing. Oh, do you wear glasses?"

"Yes."

"Don't forget to take them with you. Have you noticed how many of us wear glasses? Our eyesight is useless, they say our grandmothers and grandfathers didn't eat properly, lack of vitamins and so on. The police just love it when they catch a driver whose eyes aren't up to scratch. Not that the fines are that bad—only about twenty dollars, for you that's nothing. But for us there's nothing worse than a fine.''

"I hate them too," thought Slavin to himself. "Well, thank you, friend mechanic. Now I must act. Let's just hope Paul doesn't get too drunk . . . I don't think he'll betray me to Glebb. Or he shouldn't. But if he does, well, there's nothing I can do about it, the action will just speed up even more. And there's no doubt about it—our 'duel' has begun, and begun with Glebb on the attack. All the same, he shouldn't have gone looking for me in the basement, he shouldn't have gloated quite so obviously about his victory.''

Slavin came out on a wide promenade which ran along the sea shore. He tested the Fiat's controls. The brakes were prompt and firm.

He glanced in the mirror. A black Mercedes was following him, four men inside.

"Well then," he thought, "Let's have a little race, lads! . . . But you're barking up the wrong tree. You should have chucked Glebb and his gang out of town—then I wouldn't have to be here at all. I wouldn't be looking for Ivan Baillieu, and I wouldn't be here charging around town finding out things I need to know. And I will find them out, I promise you, one way or another!''

As the Fiat came alongside a petrol station, Slavin suddenly braked and turned in with a squeal and screech of tyres. The Mercedes was too late to turn off the road. It swept past Slavin and stopped a little way up the road, beside a newspaper kiosk.

The doors of the car, however, remained shut. It was clear that it had not occurred to the Lewisburg police that Slavin might turn back in the opposite direction. Only when he asked the attendant to fill up his car, and the latter had opened his tank and turned on the pump, did a tall young man climb out of the Mercedes, walk over to the kiosk and buy a newspaper.

"Please, check the air if you can," Slavin asked, fastening his seat belt down.

"It's fine," said the attendant, glancing at the wheels.

"I asked you to check, not just look at them. And can you rock the wheels and see that the bolts are properly fixed." Slavin held out a dollar, and the man in a quick movement took the note and like an acrobat squatted suddenly down on his heels.

"Hey there!" warned Slavin, laughingly, as the car began to shake wildly. "I didn't ask you to turn it over!"

"Everything's all right, sir. I just wanted to check properly," the attendant replied. "The pressure in your right front tube is too high, it could blow. I'll let it down to 190, you have 240 at the moment."

Slavin waited until the traffic lights turned green ahead up the road, releasing an accelerating stream of cars. He jammed the car into gear, tore out of the garage and turned back in the direction from which he had come. The men in the Mercedes looked aghast; the oncoming traffic was too dense for them to do a U-turn and follow. Slavin turned into a side-street and parked in the courtyard of a small hotel. He went into the bar and ordered coffee. Only half an hour later did he return to his car, confirming as he drove off, that there was nobody on his tail. They had lost him.

"You've only yourselves to blame," Slavin mentally chided his would-be minders. "No one but yourselves . . . So don't be cross with me, will you? I didn't take any liberties, all I did was turn back . . . Next time stop your car *behind* me, why did you get in front? When you're following somebody, you can't afford to be so naive."

Slavin had already broken the law five times when a policeman finally stopped him. The heat was unbelievable, the car white-hot, the asphalt melting like ice on the river on your last fishing trip at the beginning of spring. Slavin remembered how well the pike used to bite at this time of year on the upper reaches of the Volga. Only on the Volga you'd feel the cold and a scent of freshly laundered linen, whereas here you could hardly breathe at all, and your feet were burning through the soles of your shoes—damn this equatorial climate!

"What speed were you driving at, sir?" the policeman asked, with a half-salute. He too was sweating hard.

"I think I may have been over the limit," Slavin replied.

"I'm glad you admit it straight away. Your driving licence, please."

Slavin patted his pockets. "Strike me dead. I've forgotten it . . ."

"The death penalty has been abolished in our republic," the policeman replied drily.

" 'Execute or pardon?', that was the question they used to ask the Tsar. *Our* police would respond immediately to the expression," Slavin thought mechanically. "The capacity to forgive is part of our national character. Dostoyevsky was right, absolutely right."

"Well, what should I do?"

"Come with me to the station, sir. I'll have to check your identity."

This was what Slavin had been aiming for.

In the station he spent half an hour sitting in a dark corridor. The air-conditioning was out of order and the stuffiness unbearable. An elderly policeman whom Slavin judged to be the duty reception officer, struggled heroically against drowsiness.

"Do you always have to wait so long here?" Slavin asked.

"Just relax," the old man replied. "At least it's out of the sun."

"But there's no air."

"Air is everywhere," the old man rejoined, "Even in the sea, so my grandson tells me, there is air too."

"But if I ask the officer to hurry up with my case," asked Slavin, "will he be angry with me?"

"He won't be angry, because he can't do anything anyway: the doctor is at lunch."

"I don't need a doctor, it wasn't an accident."

"Everyone who comes in here has to see the doctor, sir, to check whether you're drunk, or you can't see properly, or whether you took too many sleeping pills last night . . ."

The doctor turned out to be a young African woman. She examined Slavin in a businesslike fashion, though her posture and movements were athletic—as though her body were fitted with hinges allowing a special elasticity. The surgery, where she directed Slavin to sit, was even more stuffy than the corridor because its two small windows were covered with thick black blinds.

"Have you been drinking?" the doctor enquired. "How much? When?"

"Yesterday I had some whisky."

"At what time was that?"

"In the afternoon."

The doctor glanced at her watch.

"If it was after two, then the analysis may show an excess of alcohol, and I will be forced to take away your licence."

"You or the police officer?"

"We are one and the same."

"I'm curious . . . What else could you take a licence away for?"

"For use of drugs, or a serious heart condition, or a bad squint . . . Please give me your finger . . ."

Five minutes later, the doctor came back out of the laboratory, nodding her head sympathetically.

"It seems you did have your whisky before two o'clock, there's no trace of alcohol. Sit down in the corner, close your left eye, and read me out the letters on the board, please."

"I can't see without my glasses."

"But you're not wearing your glasses. What right do you have to drive a car without them?"

"Please don't be angry."

"I'm not angry—it's the law," the doctor cut him short, the sharpness of her words contrasting harshly with the balanced poise which Slavin had so marvelled at. "The law has no feelings, even if those who carry it out *also* have a heart inside."

"How much did she fleece Paramonov for—if my guess

is right?'' Slavin wondered. "He could have panicked, thinking that they would take away his licence, rushing from place to place all over Lewisburg that night, trying to collect the bribe money. It all seems to tally, let's pray it happened this way. We know that he borrowed fifty dollars from Nikishkin, and seventy-five dollars the same night from Proklov. He only had to add twenty-five dollars of his own, and 150 dollars would have been quite enough to persuade even the most unfeeling officer of the law—with a human heart inside . . .''

To Centre

Please find out about Paramonov's eyes? Does he suffer from astigmatism? Does he wear glasses? If he does, how badly is his vision affected? In Lewisburg this can result in loss of a car licence.

Slavin

To Slavin

Your theory is correct. Paramonov is ruled out.

Centre

<u>10</u>

Dearest Love,

The old saying that distance makes the heart grow fonder seems less and less like the truth to me the longer you are away. It's sad, because any step back from adoration of a person is a tiny crack which water gets into, and in winter the frost strikes and the water turns to ice. Which in turn breaks up the monolith—sooner or later.

I'm not trying to say I want to leave you, of course. Quite the contrary. If you look at it logically, then I have nothing to leave, for love isn't marriage, you don't have to break it off, it comes to an end by itself.

Anyway.

I'm writing in the knowledge that I shouldn't write this way. It's hard on you. But I find justification—or at least a defence!—in the fact that you like to hear the truth. That's what you've always said—that I should never hide from you what I feel.

Yesterday I went to the Moskva River. Heavens, what a lot of people! And all of them young, beautiful, long-legged—Ilf's* description I think. That was his phrase—"I want to be young, slim, and to ride on a bicycle." I suppose that is the kind of sentence you should write on your death bed, and not like me—after going swimming. But I felt so frightened there, I could just *see time*. The

boys and girls of twenty or thereabouts—there are so many
of them, they're all so beautiful! At thirty-two I felt like
an old woman . . . But that wasn't what frightened me. It
was when I found a place on the beach next to a fat woman
of about forty. Her children were next to her, two girls
and a boy, and she didn't feel like she was an old woman
at all—she was a *matron* in the traditional style, and she
wasn't afraid of her wrinkles, her stomach, or anything—
because her children were beside her.

Anyway.

Young people today chat you up without subtlety, invite
you back to their "pad" to listen to music, and aren't in
the least offended if you refuse. One young man, true,
began to read me Gumilyov. He read well, but his fingers
were terribly thin—I see fingers like that everyday in the
X-ray theatre, for some reason we have a kind of bone
tuberculosis going around, it's very strange.

Every day I wake up and think that you've gone out
jogging, and my first thought is to jump up and get things
going in the kitchen. But then I remember . . . No, I don't
remember—rather it *hits* me . . . And that's wrong too.
Nothing hits me, I'm just crushed by the knowledge that
you're not beside me. And so, quite calmly—with you not
here to tell me off!—I light a cigarette and remember Al-
exei Tolstoy: "To inhale on an empty stomach is a quin-
tessentially Russian habit." Only a truly great actor or
writer could make a one-line diagnosis like that!

I'm very quickly getting out of the habit of having you
around. Habit is our second nature, they say. Why *second?* Our first nature is an assortment of habits. Second
nature, if it exists at all, is self-discipline.

Oh yes, I went to a great concert. Young people in styl-
ish black velvet suits singing traditional Russian folk-
songs. I was almost in tears. Folk costumes are of course
tremendous, but they're like decoration now, and maybe
not so much decoration as museum exhibits. And that's
no use to anyone. But to sing Russian harmonies in smart
modern clothes—surely that helps to preserve those an-
cient songs for our own generation.

Yesterday Konstantin Ivanovich telephoned and said that you're doing fine and that you'll soon be back. I said I'd been listening to their radio, and that he was lying, that you *weren't* doing fine, and that you *won't* soon be home. He burst out laughing, and I decided that I was just winding myself up. Just like a silly woman. Hysterical as usual. So don't take it into your head to throw me over because I send you such miserable letters—you won't find any better, we're all exactly the same, only some of us can keep up appearances for longer.

Whereas you men are all different. Not only different, but you each have your own bad side, your own good features, your own sort of jealousy. We can't attain that.

I met Nadya Stepanova. Did you know that they were divorced? A strange woman. You shouldn't call a man your husband and then speak like that about him. It reflects worse on you than it does on him. Anyway, it's hard to hurt Stepanov now. After all, he publishes books, he's a man of letters and not subject to the normal codes of conduct like us sinners. He is judged by different criteria. Wouldn't you agree?

You know, I often remember how we first met. You were so shy, you didn't know how to approach me, and I liked that terribly. And I saw how cross you were with all the seaside Romeos asking me for a match, or please what's the time now. I remember how nicely you laughed when I asked you: ''I suppose you want matches too?'' Do you know how we girls fall in love? You must! Much more whole-heartedly than all of you! Added to that, we all know Pushkin's words—''The less we love a woman, the more attractive she finds us''—but it doesn't help, you only have to talk a few minutes on the beach with another woman, and we immediately throw a tantrum. But we are more cunning than you—naive, I know, but cunning nonetheless—and so we begin to flirt outrageously with any passing idiot, and then you—I mean you more intelligent ones—lose interest in us. And we *know* that that will be the result, but still we make the same stupid mistake. And because of this impotent cunning we are castigated as sluts and whores.

You know, I thought just now—how nice, how beautiful it is with you! No obligations except one—to love one another. My dear Comrade Slavin, do you realise how much your friend Irina loves you? No, you do not realise, dear Comrade Slavin, not one little bit! And she is going to spoil this letter because of it, and have to start another one—the official revision where everything will be "tip-top." Or do I have to?

I kiss you, my love. Since you are twenty-two years older than me, I nourish the hope that in eight years' time, when you go on your pension (is that what you military people call it?), I will always have you beside me. Although I won't. I couldn't keep you in the X-ray cabinet, could I? So it won't ever work "all the time." But every morning and night—definitely.

Anyway.

But even then you'll always be leaving me. Because it's obvious that you literally cannot live without partings. So, I must console myself with the exquisitely tender expectation of happiness—of that moment when you will return.

from Irina Prokhorova,
who loves Vitaly Vsevolodovich Slavin

To Centre

Since the murder of Baillieu, Khrenov has disappeared from Lewisburg. I found his address, but the landlady of the hotel told me he had taken his things and bought a plane ticket. To where, she didn't know. We can presume that he has fled in fear of CIA reprisals.

Slavin

To Slavin

Can you use your sources to ascertain the fate of a freight consignment, registered No. 642, sent by land from

Lewisburg to Nagonia? It's very overdue, and the cargo is still undelivered.

Centre

To Centre

According to information received from sources close to Ogano's press office, cargo No. 642 was seized at the end of last week. Ogano has revealed that he knew in advance when the lorries would be setting out from Lewisburg. He has stated that from now on all convoys with loads for Nagonia will be intercepted by his "Green Berets." Who gave him the relevant information is unclear, but the Lewisburg authorities would know the date of departure and route of the convoys. All this comes under our transport people, according to the agreement signed with the Ministry of Transport here.

Slavin

To Slavin

Which of our staff is responsible for the routes and timing of transport convoys to Nagonia?

Centre

To Centre

The consignments timetable is controlled by Zotov. The routes were arranged by an official at External Trade Organisation by the name of Shargin, during a trip to Lewisburg in April this year.

Slavin

To Slavin

We are looking into Shargin. What else can you tell us about him?

Centre

To Centre

The general opinion of Shargin is positive. The only proviso concerns his tendency to heavy drinking. It has been noticed that he tends to be anxious in the company of women. As regards the high-capacity Panasonic radio, Shargin bought one direct from a businessman called Gregorio Amaral for $512. However, when he left Lewisburg, Shargin also declared at customs a Minox camera—the latest version, the smallest camera available here—and a German dictaphone costing $125. The Trade Mission's accounts department here tells me that Shargin received a sum of $650 for a daily subsistence allowance and his apartment was paid for by his employers.

Slavin

To Slavin

Please find out whether a businessman from Trade Corporation called Van Zeger was in Lewisburg at the same time as Shargin.

Centre

To Centre

No businessman called Van Zeger is recorded as having visited Lewisburg.

Slavin

To Slavin

Please find out whether Trade Corporation has an office in Lewisburg.

Centre

To Centre

There is no office of Trade Corporation in Lewisburg.

Slavin

11

Investigation No. 2 (Zhvanov, Gmyrya)

When Sub-Lieutenant Zhvanov picked up Paramonov, the latter had already glanced about him, checking the reflection in a window of a food store to see if there was anyone following, and had then darted into Tsizin's shop, Mineral Waters.

Zhvanov knew from previous days that Paramonov would not dally long at the counter, and so he followed straight in behind him, and observed how Tsizin poured his customer a glass of water from a Vitautas bottle, standing not on the counter in front of him, but in the refrigerator behind.

Paramonov drank the water in one gulp. His face froze for a moment, then blood rushed into his cheeks. He put five kopecks on the plate, turned and went out of the shop.

Zhvanov managed to grab the glass before Tsizin's hand could reach it. He sniffed the rim—it smelt of alcohol.

"Give us some out of the bottle," Zhvanov said. "Do us a favour!"

Tsizin took fifty roubles from his pocket, held it out to Zhvanov.

"Please! Give us a break, chief!"

"What's *that* for? I don't need your money, thanks," Zhvanov said angrily, "just pour me a drink. What, d'you think I would shop you?"

"Please wait, don't shout!" Tsizin switched to a whisper.

"Hang on . . . I thought that you were . . . one of . . . I'll pour you one right away, mate, with pleasure . . ."

He retrieved the bottle from the fridge, but as he opened the cork the bottle slipped from his hands and broke into pieces on the floor. Straight away Tsizin took a second bottle, this time carefully opening it over the basin. Now he went onto the attack: "What do you want? Pour *what?* You thought I sold vodka here, eh? Well prove it then! It's a bloody lie—and I'll do you for it!"

He continued to holler at Zhvanov as three old women came into the shop.

"He's trying to extort money from me! Told me, he did, to pour him some vodka, but where do I have vodka here? It's a provocation—and I won't have it! The new Constitution says you can go to court for this. Look what a smart fellow he is, with his beard and all, a real Diogenes—I *don't* think . . ."

Paramonov's wife was visited by Colonel Gmyrya. After listening to his questions, she sighed, and then replied so quietly that it was hardly audible: "I don't quite understand you. Has something happened to him?"

"No, nothing at all. But it will be better, both for him and for you, if you tell me the truth."

"Well, he has a glass of spirit now and again," the woman answered, even more softly, and her unhealthy, puffed-up face spread into a strange grimace. "When it's a holiday, or a birthday party . . ."

Gmyrya leaned back in his chair. He looked around the room, saw its ascetic tidiness, the table polished and shining, the divan spread with a white coverlet, the bright-coloured geraniums on the window-sill. He sighed to himself and went on:

"You must forgive me, but you are not telling me the truth. It's no use. Because an alcoholic is not someone who sleeps on park benches, it's someone who has a glass of vodka every day before lunch and dinner. And then begins to drink before breakfast. And for his wife it's even worse if she ever once had the luck to work abroad, because she now has to move heaven and earth just to feed the family on macaroni, and to keep up appearances—just so long as nobody discovers her tragedy, just so there's no scandal. Where is the Sony system you brought back? He sold it, didn't he, for two thousand, because he didn't have enough money for vodka. Where's your camera? Also gone to the second-hand shop. Another thing gone on vodka, Klavdia Nikitichna, isn't that so? Where's the money put aside for the Zhiguli? In six months he squandered the lot—quietly, without any scandals, like a good family man! Half a litre a day, and that's five roubles, and ten roubles on Saturdays and Sundays, and his wages are 180 a month, his wife doesn't work, and his daughter needs help too towards her college grant—isn't that so?''

The woman burst into tears. She cried soundlessly, pitifully, and there was something terrible about her large shapeless figure and the childlike and inconsolable tears which she did not even try to wipe away. Obviously she had plenty of occasions to cry.

''He's just a bloody slob,'' she whispered. ''An alcoholic—I wish he'd kill himself with it, it's the ruination of him! Every day—every bloody day . . . If it was only five roubles! Then we would have bought the car. You know we dreamed of taking the whole family to the South—that was when Marinochka was still living with us. But she got married because of him, she was still a little girl, and now she's stuck away from us with her in-laws. He drinks off five roubles during the day, then another five in the evening, and at the weekend, if he hasn't got a job on the side, he drinks twenty, starting first thing in the morning. And if I say anything, it's 'shut up' . . . I tell him he's a tyrant, that they'll find him out anyway, no good'll ever come of it, he'll never be sent anywhere abroad again. But what's happened now?''

''Nothing yet. Were you with him when the police took him in?''

The woman threw up her hands.

''Where? What police?''

''In Lewisburg, just before you left . . .''

''Was that the time he didn't come back one night, then? And then he had to borrow some more money, isn't it?''

"Whom did he borrow from?"

"The Yevsyukovs, and someone else, he said it was for presents and souvenirs. Then he went and sold the tape-recorder, at half its cost, for these same souvenirs. And he used to have a go at me if I bought vegetables."

"Did he meet Shargin in Lewisburg?"

"Curly haired, is he? Wears scent? Yes, over there. Took him everywhere in the car, to all the businessmen, to the beach. That's another fine one! All friendly and 'tra-la-la' to your face, but let you once turn your back, and he'll drag you through the mud."

"Could you show me your camera please Klavdia Nikitichna . . ."

"What! Don't you know, he took *that* to the second-hand shop as well. And it was a fantastic camera.

"Wasn't there a miniature one too?"

"A Minox? No, we didn't buy that one. You can't get the film here, so we decided against it . . ."

"When did he start drinking?"

"It was when he took over as boss in the garage," the woman replied with conviction. "Before that, when he was a mechanic, he had to move himself too much, so he didn't drink. But once he took off those overalls and put on a smart blue tunic, and began to deal with the clients— *then* it started. One day with one client, the next day— another. But he's honest, you understand. Don't think he takes money on the side, he'd rather give away something of his own than let anyone down."

"And when did his eyes begin to deteriorate?"

"At the same time. He drinks on an empty stomach, it rots your insides, the bloody stuff! Some get ulcers, others have heart trouble, and my fool husband's eyesight went. And you wouldn't know the lengths he went to, just to conceal it! 'That's it,' he used to say. 'If they find out about this, my career's finished, they'll never let a blind man go abroad.' In the end he got some contact lenses. He says that now the medical commissions are not so tough any more, they'll let him go . . . So he's off raving it up again, with a vengeance . . ."

"Did you try to see a doctor?"

"What? Where would I have seen a doctor?" the woman suddenly exploded with bitterness. "In the Embassy or something. So I go in and say my husband is a drunkard, eh? I'd be on the first flight home. And be out to work here—and then try to wash the stain off your character! If I could have done it quietly, I would have spoken to somebody, but not like that. Better to shut up and hope . . ."

"For what?"

"For him to get an ulcer. Or for his kidneys to go. Sidorov there drank so much, they had to cut out a kidney, and what a turn for the better it was in his family! Now he doesn't take even a drop, they've got a garden allotment, his wife saved enough to mend her raccoon-fur coat, and they're buying a three-room flat in Chertanovo . . . Well, what can you say? People aren't afraid of the comeback these days, so they drink. Their life is full, wherever you work, you don't get paid less than a hundred and fifty roubles . . . Compare when we were young, eh?"

"Yes, in our time it was different," agreed Gmyrya. "But where is the radio? He bought a big radio, didn't he?"

"Sold it! Our radio used to be able to pick up anything. We bought it at half-price, he put in a carburettor for some businessman—he can do things so that the engine saves fuel. Well, the businessman gave it to him for free. And was it a radio, such a radio! . . ."

"And who else did he put a carburettor in for, Klavdia Nikitichna? Did Glebb, an American businessman, ask him as well?"

"No, and he wouldn't have done it, he steers well clear of Americans, my husband. They explained to us what sort of people they are, always trying to catch you out with provocations when you least expect it. And that's worse even than vodka, we know that."

"In this case vodka's worse," Gmyrya said and stood up. "Much worse, believe me . . ."

"Hello, my name is Lieutenant-Colonel Proskurin, forenames—Mikhail Ivanovich. I'd like to have a word with you regarding the time you were working in Lewisburg."

"Please come in, Ivan Mikhailovich," Paramonov answered, his face expressing elaborate concern.

"Actually, it's Mikhail Ivanovich, but I won't be offended if you find it easier the other way round."

"Sorry, names always get me mixed up."

"Well, that's not a terrible catastrophe, is it? Tell me, when you were in Lewisburg, did you meet an American called Glebb?"

"Am I suspected of something? Is this an interrogation?"

"No. I have no right to interrogate you, because there is no accusation against you, for one, and we are not calling you as a witness, for second. This is just a chat, and you have the right to refuse to answer my questions . . ."

"I don't remember a Glebb, honest to God, I don't remember him!"

"Here, have a look at his photograph."

Paramonov took the small photograph, and held it close to his eyes: "It's so little," he said, squinting hard. "How are you supposed to see properly?"

"Your eyes—how do you manage to drive?"

Paramonov's head rocked back. He went pale.

"When I drive, I wear contact lenses."

"I'm only interested in one thing: after you were detained by the Lewisburg police, did anyone come to the station to bail you out?"

"No! I wasn't guilty of anything! I was sober! I wasn't on bail, I promise!"

"So on that day you really hadn't had anything to drink?"

"Not a drop!"

"And the day before?"

"Also not a drop."

"Come on, now!"

"I swear, not a drop! I hardly drink at all!"

From the desperate way in which Paramonov lied, Proskurin realised finally that he was not their man. A dishonest, irresponsible man, a drunkard, but he had nothing to do with the CIA, almost certainly nothing . . .

"I gave them money," Paramonov said quietly, painfully. "They forced me to bribe them, said that I shouldn't be driving without glasses . . ."

"How much did you give them?"

"A hundred and seventy-five. I only had fifty, so I borrowed off friends, and then the policeman wiped out the medical report . . ."

"You don't remember the name of the doctor?"

"How would I be able to do that? A good-looking woman. As it happens, she wore glasses too . . ."

"And no foreigner offered you any help?"

"I would have said about that in any case. Can't you understand my position?" Paramonov begged. "To have my licence taken away in Africa—my career would have been finished!"

"How?"

"My work," Paramonov explained. "Without a car, I'd never get anywhere on time! And in the heat over there, you can't go on foot! The distances are enormous. I would have let down the collective. They expected me to be efficient—go here, go there, and so on."

"More than anything, they expected honesty from you, that's a fact. We've checked, and we found out that if you had told us honestly what happened, our legal people would have informed the Lewisburg authorities that you had passed our medical commission, which is part of the international convention. And so you *were* allowed to drive a car, and nobody had the right to accuse you of anything . . . You should have had more respect for yourself—and more important, for the job you were doing . . . Instead you bribed them—what good does *that* do for your career?"

"Are you going to tell all this to Mezhsudremont?" Paramonov asked, almost inaudibly.

"I'm afraid that I do not have the right, the constitutional right, to inform them. Otherwise I would, I probably would."

Slavin

"Good morning, Andrei Andreyevich."

"Good morning," replied Zotov.

"I would like you to help me work out one or two things about the situation here. My name is Slavin—Vitaly Vsevolodovich."

"Then it's not me you need."

"Everyone says that you have the best feel for the situation—especially in connection with Nagonia, our shipments, their timing . . ."

"You can read about all of that in our reports. But what's the point? . . . Write what you like, it won't budge the cargoes one inch."

"Why?"

"Because we're making a serious mistake."

"That's possible," Slavin agreed. "Only in the given instance it would be useful to know why: *Where* are we going wrong, and *how* can we remedy our mistakes? The position in Nagonia surely deserves it."

"To remedy them is very simple. The port authorities have borrowed five million off us. It's nothing, of course, compared to what we throw away, but by the standards here, it's money. But we are too ashamed to ask for it back. We should say, if you can't return the debt, then at least treat us properly, handle our Nagonian boats, let them go first and don't keep them waiting three days on the berth. But we're too soft, we're afraid they might take it badly and get offended. And then all the papers will slam us and—"

"But fear of giving offence is a testimony of strength, Andrei Andreyevich, isn't that so?"

"True. But how will we look one another in the eyes if they crush Nagonia? And you know, there are people there, people who can work, who are already saying that we Russians make big promises which we can't keep, that our goods arrive late and meanwhile the country is burning. How are we going to face it?"

"It's bad. Very bad."

"And they tell me here that I'm mean and a grumbler.

I'm not mean, it's just that I go down to the port more often than the others. I talk to lots of different people and I can see their opinion of us—they think they can wind us round their little finger.''

"Well then, could you tell me how we can best write this up, OK? But I have to go to lunch at two o'clock with a friend—an American colleague, we haven't seen each other since Nuremburg . . .''

"Dick?''

"Yes. You know him?''

"The friend of a friend. A thinking newspaperman, I gather. Pity he's drinking himself to death.''

"I'll come back up about four o'clock, all right?''

"No, I'm busy at four. Make it around nine.''

"In my room?''

"Where are you staying?''

"In the Hilton. Room No. 607.''

"Sixth floor?''

"Yes. You turn right along the corridor.''

"I know. Good, I'll be there at nine.''

Paul Dick sat down beside Slavin, swearing as he did so: "You've dragged me into a real filthy business, Ivan,'' he growled. "Which McDonald's shall we go to?''

"Let's try the one near where Baillieu lived.''

He lived in the *bidonville*, the McDonald's there is a dump. I've already checked it out.''

"I'd like to have a quick look around, too.''

"Let me into the secret, Ivan. What do you know about this Baillieu?'' Paul Dick pushed eight dollars towards Slavin. "Take it, buy yourself a drink. I couldn't wait, I've had one.''

"What's this?''

"Don't play the fool, I lost the bet. You sussed out John better than me. He really *did* ask about you, just as you said. Go on, tell me, what do you know about all this?''

"Nothing. I'm just going on guesswork. It seems Baillieu rented a room somewhere near the station.''

"The port. Noisy just the same. Cranes outside the window working day and night. Go on.''

"It seems that he had Russian books in his flat—"

"Ukrainian. And postcards, a lot of old postcards . . ."

"And there was stale cheese lying on the table, and half a *baton* of bread, no?"

"The cheese was very stale, and there was no baton, only crackers . . . So you've been in his room?"

"If I had been, Paul, they would have already called me for questioning. What was the murder weapon? A pistol with a silencer?"

"No. They killed him with a marksman's rifle, from on top of a harbour crane, through the window. His hobby was embroidery, you know. His room was full of napkins, teacloths, embroidered strips. Hens and cockerels. Listen, what do you know about him? It wasn't for nothing you wanted to find him, Ivan . . ."

"What sort of books did he have, Paul?"

"I can't remember . . . No, I did write them down in my pad, of course, but I left it in my room . . . Poetry. Mainly poetry."

"A room as small as a closet, cranes outside the window, napkins embroidered with cockerels, books of poetry . . ."

"You classify the facts very elegantly. You used not to be able to do that. I remember at Nuremberg all you wanted was pure information. The years have given you more freedom, I see, Ivan. You can put facts and ideas together without looking over your shoulder."

"Thanks for the compliment. Were there a lot of police?"

"Two cars."

"Press?"

"They let them in later, after the search."

"What were they looking for?"

"God knows. They hinted that he could have been an agent of yours."

"Hints are for the girls, in this game you need hard evidence."

"So what? You can make it up, can't you?"

"What do you mean?"

"I mean that he lived near the harbour, and the harbour

is full of your ships carrying goods for Nagonia. A campaign is just starting here against that—so Baillieu was the man who looked through his binoculars and passed the information.''

Slavin laughed heartily.

''Why not?'' Paul demanded, and went on: ''The important thing is to cause a stink, someone else can clear it up. In the final analysis, the one that is covered in shit will always be seen as the guilty party—he's the one who has to wash it off.''

In the McDonald's near the port, two blocks from the third-class hotel where Baillieu had lived, it was hot and stuffy. Slavin was amazed by the number of flies—fat bluebottles which circled slowly around like overloaded Junkers, and with the same tiresome humming.

''Let's have some coffee,'' he suggested. ''And go somewhere in the open air to eat, all right?''

''No. Look here, you positively knew that Baillieu, didn't you, Ivan? He was your spy . . .''

''Paul, we don't need to keep a spy here, honestly. We have said openly that if they invade Nagonia, we will help Griso with all the means at our disposal. Our cards are face up, no secrets. In general, there are few secrets in the world today. You can compute any action or reaction, you only have to use your head a bit.''

''In that case, compute what my President is up to. What's *his* policy?''

''Do you have an opinion of your own?''

''Yeah. He's too sincere. And that's a dangerous quality for a leader, who is supposed to be flexible.''

''If that's true, I can sleep peacefully. But, in my opinion, the situation is quite different. Your war industry donated a lot of money to the President's pre-election campaign. As a respectable citizen, he has to pay his creditors back. How? Only increased military production can give them the cash straight away. So—start production of the neutron bomb! Here's ten billion for you—and one debt is cleared! But they wouldn't let him start full production of the neutron bomb—it was too risky, and every

American politician with any common sense was against it. They're like us, they understand that our peoples—however they try to prevent us—will somehow become friends. That is an actual historical process, a perspective we believe in. When it didn't work with the bomb, your boss tried it on with the peaceful sectors of industry, to get money from *them* so as to pay back the military-industrial complex, and in that way to save some face. And he agreed to peaceful negotiations with us. But as we all know, not everyone in Congress supports this. And so, he fell between two stools. But he *has* to make a choice, events will force him, the Americans themselves will demand it.''

"That's not far off. But I'm more right than you, because he *could* find a third path, one dictated by *calculation.* But he won't do it . . .''

A black waiter approached the table, and served them coffee in cardboard cups. As he did so, he said to Paul: "I saw you today, sir.''

"Yeah? I didn't see *you.* ''

"You did, sir. You were coming out of the flat where Ivan was killed.''

"Ivan, what Ivan?'' Paul was taken aback.

"Baillieu. He was Russian, you know,'' said the waiter.

"I'm Russian too,'' said Slavin.

"Oh, sorry sir, I wouldn't have supposed you were Russian. I thought you were English . . .''

Slavin reached for a packet of *Yava.* He drew out a cigarette, but did not light it. Really, he didn't smoke at all, sometimes he just put a cigarette in his mouth, and that was rare.

"Listen, why did he live here? What would a Russian come to Lewisburg for? Did he ever say anything to you about it?''

"No. He only sang when he was the worse for drink.''

"Was he always the worse for drink?''

"No. He began to drink more heavily when the Russian ships started coming here. Your sailors often drop in here to have a beer. Baillieu always used to sit over there, in the corner of the bar where it's dark, just looking at them. And when they left, he'd begin to drink, and then he'd sing his songs. But nobody interfered with him, no, we let him sing. We only chucked him out if he began snivelling and crying . . .''

"They let him sing," Paul Dick repeated. "That was very humane of you, to let him sing! It'll be noted down in heaven. Give me some whisky on the rocks, please."

"We have Spanish whisky, sir. 'Dick' whisky it's called, Americans usually don't like it."

"My countrymen are cretins, don't pay any attention to them. Don't tell them it's 'Dick,' just pour it out boldly and shove it under their noses! Only knock the bottom of the glass so that the whisky splashes up a bit."

"Thank you for the advice, sir, I'll try. Would you like to play snooker, perhaps? We have a very decent table, and heavy balls."

"Listen," asked Slavin. "Did this Baillieu ever—even just once—sing his songs when the Russian sailors were in the bar?"

"Yes, he sang them once sir, crying all the time, and they gave him some postcards . . .''

"When was this?" asked Slavin.

"I think it was in December, sir, but I couldn't say exactly. But I remember that after that time he always looked rather frightened, as though he was waiting for something."

Slavin placed some postcards in front of the barman: "You can have these—in memory of him. Only don't let them kill you with a sniper's rifle."

"Thank you for the present, sir, only I'd better not take it. The police are going round asking for everyone who knew Baillieu. They've taken all the postmen into the station to check through their books for letters and telegrams addressed to him. Anything could happen, sir, so I'll thank you but no—we've learned here not to trust our own shadow . . .''

"In December, the first Russian ships arrived here," Slavin mentally summed up. "And our Ivan saw real Russians for the first time since the War. And he wrote us a letter. And for a long time couldn't make up his mind to send it. It's all so clear and simple! And then, obviously,

Glebb worked him out, like I did, and eliminated him. And now only he and he alone, John Glebb, can point his finger at the photograph of the person whom they recruited."

Slavin stopped the Fiat outside a small Polynesian restaurant with tables arranged out on the shore under the shade of wide wicker umbrellas. Paul Dick was first to clamber out. Immediately, he broke out in sweat.

"Hang on!" said Slavin. "Turn round and admire the Mercedes behind me. They've really got me on a lead. And memorise the number—it's unique, and I guarantee that you won't find it in the records of the local traffic police."

"Stop it, Vit!" Paul Dick finally called Slavin by his real name. "You really shouldn't be so suspicious!"

"When we go back into town, have a look—it'll be a blue Ford tailing us. And don't bother to argue with me, because the bet will be double the one I won this morning."

"That means that Glebb is one of *them,*" said Paul in a low voice.

"Did *I* tell you that?"

"Don't take me for an old fool, OK?"

Konstantinov

General Fyodorov passed a file bulging with documents[1] to Konstantinov. The latter looked carefully down the columns of figures and concluded thoughtfully: "We're still in complete darkness. Nothing interesting to report, only that Vinter has suddenly decided to go to Pitsunda for a week."

"Her annual holiday?"

"No. Unpaid leave."

"Is that normal procedure in her institute?"

"We'll ask."

"Can you do so now?"

"If you let me telephone Proskurin."

"Can I phone him myself?" smiled Pyotr George-vich, "—or does he only take orders from his direct superior?"

Ten minutes later, Proskurin confirmed that senior scientific staff at the institute where Vinter worked were permitted to take unpaid leave. He also reported that early that morning Shargin had flown down to Odessa—not on leave, but on business for his organisation. His task was to carry out a spot check on the loading of cargoes bound for Nagonia.

"Well, come on then," said Fyodorov. "Let's sum up the progress so far. First: Paramonov is ruled out, he's clean."

"I would call him No. 2, Pyotr Georgevich. I would call Ivan Baillieu No. 1. Our department in Novorossisk has interviewed some sailors—in December it was mostly ships from there that went to Lewisburg—two of whom, when interviewed, confirmed that they were in the McDonald's and remembered Baillieu. He sang *Rushnichok* and *Polyushko-Polye** for them, and asked whether he could come out to their boat and climb up the storm ladder. He wanted to go home, he said, and he didn't

1. The text of the un-decoded radio message from the CIA to its agent in Moscow read as follows:

"Dear friend, Thank you for your communication. It was extremely interesting, and we have conveyed your information not only to our chief, but also to the government. We are interested in what action from our side could prevent Moscow from giving immediate military assistance to Nagonia in the event of any developments in that country. Your anxiety about an investigation into your own or your friends' activities, seems to us the effect of over-exhaustion. We would advise you to go away and rest for a few days, preferably to the sea. In your next transmission, please send us the results of your medical tests. We will consult with leading specialists and if necessary send you the right medicine. Nonetheless, we will think over your suggestion regarding the cover operation. Maybe your idea should be carried out a little later? Or do you insist on the immediate implementation of this move? We send greetings from your friend 'P.' She has invested part of your fees in shares in United Fruit & Trade Corporation. Wishing you all the best, your friends 'D' and 'L' (Author's note) give a damn if he had to go to court and they threw him in prison . . .''

''How old was he when the war began?''

''Eighteen. He ran off with the Germans. Slavin says he was one of the 'baptised.' ''

''That means our agent is working here in Moscow. Any hopes that this is just a provocation—radio transmissions into the void—have to be put aside once and for all. Wouldn't you agree?''

''I'm afraid so.''

''Shargin? Or Vinter?''

''None of the others seems to fit into the pattern of our suspicions.''

''The 'others' means how many?''

''Everyone concerned with Nagonia. Six people.''

''Do you want to ask for approval to go through their records?''

''No, I couldn't justify that. It wouldn't be well received—by you, more than anyone.''

''What a cunning piece of understatement is hidden in that phrase—it wouldn't be 'well received,' eh?''

''All the same, I do need you to sanction our work on Vinter and Shargin. As for Zotov, I'm waiting for a telegram from Slavin in Lewisburg later today. It should be here by midnight.''

''Go home, and wait for it there.''

''Yes, and I can do some work while I wait, Pyotr Georgevich. They've dug me out some material on the scandal involving Glebb. I rather think that this is the end of the string which we have to grab hold of, if we're going to pull in all the rest.''

''Good. I won't go to bed before one. Call me if there is anything important.''

''Gmyrya will fly out after Shargin and have a look at him down there. And I'll go down to Pitsunda after Vinter, maybe the day after tomorrow—if you agree.''

''To Pitsunda, you say,'' Pyotr Georgevich frowned. For a moment he sat motionless, then he took up one of the files laid out neatly on the desk. He leafed through the papers, picked out one of them, and passed it to Konstantinov, remarking: "Just as well I remembered."

The document contained the information that US Embassy Press Attaché Luns, identified by counter-intelligence as a CIA officer, was flying to Pitsunda—on the same day and flight as Olga Vinter!

"Well, well!" said Konstantinov, returning the document. "I think it's all clear now. Gmyrya can thank me for his free excursion to Odessa, I hope he gets a good sun-tan and enjoys his swim. He won't have any work to do."

"No, I wouldn't say that . . ."

"You think it's still worth checking down there?"

"Naturally. And send someone with the Press Attaché. But why are Luns and Vinter travelling in the same plane? Surely they'd take more care with their agent—if she *is* their agent? Or is it a coincidence?"

Further checks confirmed that a ticket in the name of Olga Vinter had, indeed, been bought on the same flight as that on which Luns was travelling. However, Vinter was not on the plane, nobody handed in her ticket, nor did she appear in Pitsunda that day, the next day, or any time subsequently. Meanwhile her home telephone rang unanswered, despite regular calls to the number every two hours.

Konstantinov asked Proskurin: "Did your people go to see her at her work?"

"We didn't want to set the alarm bells ringing, by asking unnecessary questions. After all, she's very sociable, on good terms with everybody. Anyone can see her that wants to . . ."

"What about her father's house?"

"She's not there," Proskurin grinned. "My colleagues reported that 'her physical presence has not been established.' "

"You've looked at the block where she lives, asked around for her?"

"Nobody knows anything. The flat is locked."

"So in a word, you've lost Vinter?"

"Yes. You could say that."

"What *else* can you say?"

"There isn't much else, I suppose."

"Direct your people to organise a search for Vinter. Leave no stone unturned. You're right—we don't want to sound the alarm by causing unnecessary commotion. But we *must* find her—immediately and without fail. So, let's go through all her contacts. You said that she is quite unusually sociable . . . Which of her closest friends, her old friends, could we trust?"

"In what sense?"

"Good question," Konstantinov observed approvingly. "Yes, we are obliged to trust everyone, unless proved otherwise. But I meant only one thing—whom could we trust not to say even a word about talking to us?"

"Doctor Raisa Ismailovna Niyazmetova. That's her closest woman friend. But she doesn't have a telephone, and she's not at work. She's on a sick note, we've already checked."

"Well, let your people have a word with her. Politely and very tactfully."

Investigation No. 3

Konstantinov's handwriting was neat, and he wrote quickly. However, he preferred—especially in recent years—not to write, but to type straight onto his portable typewriter, judging that the printed word differed significantly from the written. Furthermore, while preparing his thesis for publication (the theme was non-secret—"Political Manoeuvres of Nazi Germany on the Eve of Franco's Rebellion"), he had been amazed to discover that a typewritten page differed incredibly from one printed on a press—so much so that they could seem like two completely different texts. He drew the conclusion that anyone concerned to convey their ideas fully—the highest expression of an idea being its printed form—should look carefully at the paper and even the type that was used for printing: whichever way you looked at it, *form* meant *content*. And then he remembered his father's friend—for whom the printer's type and paper were a source of such pleasure that Konstantinov thought at first he was putting it on. Only much later did he realise what a highly developed sense of beauty the old man possessed.

Konstantinov asked his secretary not to put any calls through or to let any visitors into his office—unless, of course, there should be a breakthrough with Panov in the decoding department, or with Trukhin (looking for Vinter), or if a telegram arrived from Slavin (yesterday's one had added little to the total picture, in it Slavin merely reported that he was investigating the Zotov theory and asked again for any information on Glebb to be sent as quickly as possible).

Having worked with Slavin for ten years, Konstantinov understood his sense of urgency. In Slavin's place, Konstantinov would have done the same. After Glebb had eliminated the one and only witness who could have identified the CIA's agent in Moscow, only a knockout punch would do. They had to force Glebb himself to reveal the name of the traitor. A lead on this had only emerged after Slavin had fixed on Paul Dick's phrase about the Hong Kong mafia, which Glebb had so elaborately tried to erase with a dozen different phrases of his own.

Konstantinov worked till late. Five files of documents and assorted newspaper cuttings passed under his scrupulous gaze, as he extracted names, nicknames and dates from the texts.

The following picture built up before his eyes: On 12 December, 1966, at Hong Kong airport, Customs Officer Bench ordered a second search of luggage belonging to Mr. Lao, official of the banking corporation Lim Limited, and to Miss Carmen Fernandez, both of whom were departing on a flight to San Francisco.

Escorting Mr. Lao and Miss Fernandez to the departure gate was the Vice-President of the Hong Kong branch of USAI, Mr. D.G. Glebb. Mr. Glebb suggested to Customs Officer Bench that he retract his instructions to search the luggage, because, in Glebb's words, ''Mr. Lao is a close friend of mine, a trusted friend of the US, and Miss Fernandez is also an official of the Board of Directors of the American jewellery firm Cook & Sons.''

Bench replied that he in no way challenged Glebb's confidence in Mr. Lao and Miss Fernandez, but that he could not retract his order because this would place him in a difficult position in front of his junior officers.

Glebb then persuaded Bench to step into one of the side rooms, where the Vice-President of USAI revealed that he was also CIA Station Officer in Hong Kong. Although on the next day Bench refused to confirm this part of his statement under oath, during the incident that erupted in the airport five minutes afterwards he repeated it out loud, and it was recorded by *Chronicle* reporter Donald Gee on dictaphone. Indeed, it was on the basis of this tape that Gee published his sensational story.

Despite Glebb's protests, the suitcase was opened. Inside it, the customs officers discovered a false bottom, containing heroin valued at three million dollars—a sum unheard of in smuggling cases at that time.

With ten minutes of the search, Mr. Lao's lawyer was at the airport. Mr. Do Tsili stated that the suitcase opened by the customs authorities did not belong to Mr. Lao.

One of Mr. Lao's three secretaries, Mr. Zhui, twenty years old, confessed that the suitcase was *his* property. He gave no other evidence and was immediately arrested.

As Mr. Zhui was being led to the police car in handcuffs, *Chronicle* correspondent Mr. Donald Gee heard Mr. Lao's second secretary say to the arrested man: ''Tomorrow you'll be out on bail—just make sure you behave yourself.''

However, on the way to prison the police car was ambushed. It was riddled with bullets, and Mr. Zhui was taken to hospital, but found dead on arrival.

After the publication of this article in the *Chronicle* and *Eastern Review*, reporter Donald Gee was accused of defamation and libel, for, as officially stated by the American Consul, at the time of the incident Mr. Glebb was at an opening of an exhibition of Iraqi ceramics. Mr. Bench now refused to confirm the presence of Mr. Glebb at the time of the scandal.

When the case was heard, Donald Gee handed over his tape to the court. On it several voices were clearly heard. Furthermore, Donald Gee produced photographs of three women wanted by Interpol to answer charges of involvement in the heroin business. One of them was as identical to Miss Carmen Fernandez as two drops of water are to each other. According to records at Interpol, this woman went under several names—including Maria, Rosita Lopez, Pilar, and Carmen Garcia.

After this Glebb disappeared from Hong Kong without appearing as plaintiff in the lower court. Miss Fernandez disappeared too.

Donald Gee was recalled from Hong Kong and posted to Thailand. There he became the victim of a terrorist assault which left him seven months in hospital. Afterwards, he returned to New York, but his newspaper refused to renew his contract. Donald Gee accused the CIA of instigating the attack on him. The libel court would not hear Mr. Gee's case, ruling that he could not provide sufficient docmentary evidence for his accusations.

Mr. Gee pledged to invest all the money he possessed in the investigation, which he would conduct himself, so as to collect the necessary proof.

The latest mention of the "Case of Donald Gee" related to January, 1970.

In 1976, a Donald Gee began to send back reports from Nagonia as a correspondent for an extreme right-wing newspaper called the *Star*.

To Centre

Thank you for the information on Glebb, Fernandez and Gee. Would it be possible to put these facts at the disposal of Dmitri Stepanov—the writer and journalist? He has worked on Hong Kong, narcotics and how the CIA and Mao's people are involved in the drugs business.

Slavin

"I think you'll have to fly to Nagonia, immediately. It'll be for a couple of days, no more," said Fyodorov, after he had listened to Konstantinov's early morning report. "But I want to give your mission a slightly different emphasis. First, I want you to have a thorough look yourself at whether the launching sites for ballistic missiles aimed at us are capable of being repaired—I mean the ones which the Americans had when the colonialists were in power. And second, talk to Stepanov: we've got to get to the bottom of Mr. Glebb—including of course the 'Hong Kong angle.' "

Konstantinov departed for Nagonia on a night flight. He arrived early the next morning and spoke to Stepanov during that day. His return ticket was bought for nine o'clock in the evening.

Konstantinov gave Stepanov a succinct, compressed account of the essence of the problem. He concluded: "Glebb. Lao. The Hong Kong angle. Narcotics, the CIA, the Chinese secret service . . . Can *you* help us sort all this out?"

"D'you think Lao was Peking's man in Hong Kong?"

"It seems so."

"That is not an answer, Konstantin Ivanovich. Either 'yes' or 'no'."

"But we don't know. That's why I flew over to see you, Dmitri Yurevich, with this request. But at the moment the one who interests us most of all is Glebb."

Just how much of a threat does he pose to our country's interests here, in Nagonia?"

"A very serious threat. It seems not beyond the bounds of possibility that he may be a link in a chain connecting the CIA with an agent in Moscow."

"A spy in Moscow? A Russsian?"

"We don't know. Not yet, anyway."

"The theme of treachery interests me," said Stepanov. "How do you see it, by the way?"

"An anomaly," Konstantinov replied with conviction. "More than that, it seems to me that treachery is a kind of pathological condition, alien to a normal person."

"Aren't you simplifying the problem a bit, Konstantin Ivanovich?"

"The opposite, I'm complicating it, Dmitri Yurevich. But I'm only expressing my own point of view—why kowtow to others?"

"It's only that I'm not very good at taking photographs with a secret camera, or prowling around on the rooftops," Stepanov smiled.

"You have a rather amateurish idea of what we do in counter-intelligence," Konstantinov returned the grin. "The State Security organs are concerned with matters of state, and that means that our main weapon is our heads—rather than any acrobatic talents . . ."

"So how can I help you?"

"It's a tricky business, Dmitri Yurevich, and you'll forgive us if we take a rather protective attitude towards your good self—our country needs your books and films. So be careful, all right? The essence of it all is that there is an American journalist working here in Nagonia, called Donald Gee . . ."

12

Tempo

To the Central Intelligence Agency

Top Secret

"Operation Torch" has entered its final stage. All preparations have been completed. It is vital that you confirm with the Pentagon the delivery of helicopters to Ogano's group at the earliest opportunity.

The stages of the plan are:

On Day X (Saturday or Sunday—to hamper any appeal to the UN), three companies of paratroopers from Ogano's group, dressed in the uniform of the Nagonian people's militia, land by helicopter in the suburb of Saveiro. Here there will be waiting for them twenty armoured cars and fifteen light tanks, redeployed out of the jungle (Point B has already been equipped for the storage of fuel).

The tanks and armoured cars with the paratroopers then proceed to occupy the Presidential Palace. In the event of Griso refusing voluntarily to hand over power to the democratic majority, they take the necessary action as determined by the military situation.

The seizure of the Palace must be completed by 8:30 A.M., that is, thirty minutes before Nagonian TV goes on the air.

At 9:00 A.M. a group of parachutists bursts into the Television and Radio Centre, and broadcast a tape with a prerecorded message from General Ogano to viewers and listeners around the country.

I attach the text of Ogano's message.

CIA Station Officer Robert Lawrence

Top Secret

Draft text of Message by General Ogano to the People of Nagonia.

Dear fellow Nagonians! Brothers and Sisters! Children and Elders! In these critical moments I speak to you in words of respect, pride and love!

I congratulate you in your liberation from foreign oppression, and I am proud that you have found the strength to break the chains and say "No!" to the new slavery imposed on you by the clique headed by the dangerous adventurist George Griso—who, I can now inform you, was torn to pieces earlier this morning by crowds of angry Nagonian citizens who broke into his luxuriously furnished palace.

The State of Siege which has been declared in the country will be lifted as soon as we can put an end to economic chaos, destruction and terror. We declare with passionate and revolutionary determination: the nation will annihilate anyone who stands up against freedom and independence, or who tries to resist the will of the majority.

I take on myself responsibility for the immediate execution without trial of every person who raises their hand against the sacred cause of national freedom.

I declare in the name of the Emergency Assembly of the Nation, which was created tonight and which has taken on itself the functions of the overthrown government of traitors—that all treaties concluded by the Griso clique are to be considered broken off from this moment.

In the name of the Emergency Assembly of the Nation, I appeal for urgent military and economic assistance from all those who hold dear the cause of peace, independence and freedom.

Thank you for your attention.

Text drafted by CIA Deputy Station Officer J. Glebb

To CIA Station Officer Robert Lawrence

The Director has looked at the material prepared by the Department of Strategic Planning, and has made a number of critical comments which must be taken into account in the preparation of the final plan to be presented to the appropriate highest authorities.

The Director hopes that all the necessary corrections will be carried out in the next three or four days, it being highly likely that the date of the start of "Operation Torch" will be brought forward—possibly, to the second Sunday of this month.

The Director's notes must be destroyed immediately after reading.

CIA Deputy Director Michael Welsh

To CIA Station Team—Robert Lawrence, John Glebb (Copy to Ministry of Defence, Pentagon)

Top Secret, destroy after reading.

We enclose information received from "Mastermind" in Moscow via the latest secret drop operation at location "Park":

"In June–July the despatch is planned of six ships registered at the port of Odessa. The ships will leave Murmansk at twenty-four-hour intervals, in convoys of four, beginning on Friday. Naval escort of the ships is not envisaged."

CIA Deputy Director Michael Welsh

Konstantinov

On his return from Nagonia, Konstantinov was met at the aerodrome by Colonel Konovalov. There, on the tarmac beside the plane, he heard the news: "While you were away, Konstantin Ivanovich, we found Vinter," Konovalov said. "Only she's dead. Her funeral takes place today."

Konstantinov couldn't quite understand "*Whose* funeral? *Vinter's?* What the hell d'you mean?!"

In half an hour he was in his office, to a reception committee waiting for him.

"Inflamation of the lungs," Proskurin reported. "She had been coughing recently, but she still kept playing tennis. She had a temperature, took a lot of aspirin, tried to throw off the sickness, thinking it was nothing. She collapsed at Dubov's. It was from there they took her to the hospital."

"Who the hell is Dubov?"

"Her friend, a Candidate of Sciences . . ."

"What do you know about him?"

"We haven't looked at him yet . . ."

"So that's the rub, eh? A woman of thirty, in the bloom of health . . . But how come nobody at her work knew about this yesterday?"

"Dubov telephoned yesterday evening. Today is the funeral, he's inviting all her friends . . ."

"Can you send anyone?"

"What for?"

"Doesn't her death surprise you a little?"

"Not really. Apparently, there's a kind of lung epidemic rampant at the moment. Captain Streltsov checked at the medical training institute . . ."

That evening Proskurin reported that he had found a colleague to go to the funeral—a man who had studied with Gleb Grachev, Vinter's friend. So they had found a way in. Grachev himself invited the man, telephoning Dubov in advance to warn him.

Dubov replied that everyone was welcome who wanted

to remember "dear Olechka," the doors of the house were "open to all."

"Well, and what was it like?" Konstantinov enquired, afterwards.

"Her father was there about half an hour, he could hardly stand upright. Then Dubov called an ambulance and they took him away—poor old man, she was his only daughter . . . Everyone spoke very well of her, very warmly . . . Dubov cried, said that he could now say openly that he was burying the person he loved most in the world, and that he would never love another like her. He put an engagement ring on her finger—when they were beside the grave . . ."

"Have they telegrammed Zotov?"

"Not as far as I know."

"Why?"

"Well, in practical terms they were divorced, weren't they . . . ?"

"When did she fall sick?"

"Dubov's neighbour said that she collapsed during the evening. Dubov gave her some hot presses, made a mustard bath, put her feet in warm water. He was in a terrible state, the old chap said, but he did everything he could. And in the morning they called the ambulance, but it was too late, there was nothing they could do . . ."

"I just can't understand," Konstantinov repeated. "Not one single word of it. The neighbour, Dubov—have a look at them both, will you?"

Panov came in. He reported that over the last few days—that is, since Vinter's death—no radio transmissions had been picked up from the CIA Intelligence Centre.

"So that means, it was *her* receiving them?" Konstantinov asked thoughtfully, glancing at Proskurin.

"There's nobody else who could have."

"You're that sure?" Konstantinov shook his head, reached for a cigar, and began to unwrap the cellophane slowly. "Call everyone in, let's discuss the situation."

* * *

However, at 7.15 the next morning, precisely as it had before, the CIA's Athens Intelligence Centre sent a short radio message[1] to its agent in Moscow.

"So . . . That means it's *not* Vinter?" Konstantinov asked Proskurin and Panov. He had immediately called them into his office.

"Maybe they don't yet know she's dead," Proskurin objected.

"Maybe . . . Tell me, what was Vinter doing these last few days? Whom did she meet? What did she talk to them about?"

"Raisa Niyazmetova says that Vinter was at her flat the day before she died. It was a normal meeting for the two of them, nothing significant, chit-chat, that's all."

"Can you make anything of it?" Konstantinov asked.

"I can't, nothing at all. You know what—" he turned to Proskurin, "why don't *I* go and see Niyazmetova? I knew Vinter, maybe I can pick up something more concrete from her. But please warn her I'll be coming—the quicker the better . . ."

His visit to Niyazmetova had to be postponed, however: Konstantinov, Proskurin and Konovalov were suddenly summoned to a meeting with Lieutenant General Fyodorov. Their superior's face was so pale, it looked almost blue. He was sitting behind his desk, his hands stretched out in front of him, gripping an array of coloured pencils. His knuckles, fingers and nails were icy and bluish too.

"It won't be a revelation for any of you," Fyodorov began, "—if I take the liberty of reminding you that no intelligence work can be carried out for one whole year in the form of a *radio* monologue. There must be a feedback, even if we have not the slightest idea about the form it takes. There is a *dialogue*, whose intensity, we have confirmed, depends on the tension deepening at the present

---

1. The text of the undecoded CIA telegram went as follows:
   "Today we read your control signal. The meeting will take place in the agreed place at the usual time. Your friends 'D' and 'L.' "
                                                              (Author's note)

time on the African Continent, and specifically—in Nagonia. The conclusion is obvious: the source is a well-informed person, who is passing information to his masters on a wide range of questions. Consequently, every successful exchange in this dialogue represents a corresponding damage to our cause.

"We cannot establish the content of the transmissions. We *will* do so eventually—but the longer it takes, the greater the price we will pay to remedy the situation. So that's the position. Now, I want to pass on to you the special communication which I have just received from my superiors."

Fyodorov opened a red file, coughed, and slowly—almost as if dictating—read out:

"Today at 5:00 A.M. the cargo ship *Gleb Uspensky* was blown up as it approached the shores of Lewisburg with a cargo for Nagonia. The ship was registered at the port of Odessa. It had put to sea from Murmansk, carrying on board agricultural equipment, lorries and medical goods. Three members of the crew died in the explosion."

Fyodorov looked in turn at the three Chekists sitting in front of him. Again he rubbed his fingers, as if warming them: "It occurs to me that this action is a case of the CIA acting off its own bat. The US Government would not sanction such a shameless act—in the final analysis, they know that the situation is such that it could never be covered up."

Fyodorov was silent for a moment. Then, very quietly, holding himself back, he concluded: "It also occurs to me that if Felix Edmundovich* had received a message about the sinking of this ship, he would immediately have offered his resignation! Is that clear?! Because it is us who are to blame. Us! Slavin dilly-dallies philosophising in Lewisburg, you colour in your charts here in Moscow—and, meanwhile the spy is destroying people, equipment! If *you* can't find him—just say so, we'll put *others* onto it!"

"Slavin has carried out orders scrupulously. I am willing to offer my resignation immediately," Konstantinov said quietly.

Fyodorov took his hands off the table: "As regards resignations, first do what you have been instructed to do, General. That's all. You may go."

Slavin

At the cocktail party at the Soviet Embassy, Glebb took Zotov to one side and handed him a small book in a battered-looking cover.

"This was bloody difficult to find, it turns out," he explained. "I had to ask Washington. In the end, the Russian publishers Kamkin helped."

"Thank you. How long can I keep it?"

"You can have it for good."

"Go on! No, will a week be all right?"

"Fine. D'you want to copy it on the Xerox?"

"Our Xerox is bloody awful, but I'll have to do a photocopy anyway."

The book was about African folklore. As a bibliophile, Zotov could not resist glancing through it to find the date of publication: 1897.

"Thanks, John," he said again, "I'm indebted to you, really."

"It's I who am indebted to you, Andrew."

"Me? Why?"

"For your friendship."

"Friendship excludes the idea of debt, John—anyway, that's how we Russians see it. Debts belong to the world of business."

"By the way, on business, I wonder whether you could help me?"

"How?"

"I would like to see your trade representative."

"I'll fix it up. What about?"

"Nagonia."

"What connection do you have with Nagonia?"

"Just the same as you—I'm thinking about the country's future. My government has expressed concern about your deliveries of equipment there. And I know about it because one of the things my firm is working on is how to put your equipment out of action!''

"It's a waste of time, all that, John. Do you really want to have another Vietnam?''

"We don't, no. But you do, Andrew. Don't think that I support my government—there aren't too many wise heads in it, I'm afraid. But some of them do have a bit of grey matter: we won't get involved in Nagonia, it's you who are getting stuck there. You signed a treaty with Griso, you've pledged to help him, so what would hold you back from sending military aid?''

"I would send it.''

"You would—but *you're* not the government. Would your people support that?''

"No question about it.''

"Well, that's spoken like a man . . . When will you have a word with your boss?''

"Ring tomorrow, about three, OK?''

"Fine. And please say hello from me to your charming wife, Andrew.''

"Thanks.''

"When do you expect her back?''

"As soon as she finishes her business in Moscow.''

Shaking hands, the two men moved apart. Like any cocktail party, this one, organised in honour of the arrival in Lewisburg of a Soviet orchestra, was a form of diplomatic work: here meetings were set up, problems were touched on that held an interest for one side, if not always the other, and there took place an exchange of information—in carefully chosen and regulated doses.

After speaking to Zotov, Glebb exchanged a few friendly phrases with the Soviet Cultural Attaché, registered his enthusiasm with the conductor of the orchestra, and came up beside Slavin.

"When the mountain will not move towards Mohammed, then Buddha calls a conference of the non-aligned!'' he joked, embracing Slavin affectionately. "Hello, Vit my old friend, where have you been all this time?''

"Where have *you* been? I just try to go on working.''

"Ah! Work, bloody work!''

"Come on! It's not so bloody, is it?"

"I mean the strain, not our high aims, Vit."

"That's what I meant too—that the strain is not so bad. But I confess it's a different matter for my Fiat, trying to get away from the curious eyes. The people here are very suspicious, don't you think?"

"They follow you all the time?" Glebb sighed in commiseration. "Nothing you can do about it, just get used to it. They even follow me into the toilet. Pilar is expecting us tonight for spaghetti. D'you like spaghetti?"

"I love it—if there's a lot of meat with it. A rather intelligent French actress once defined for me very precisely the difference between a dinner in Moscow, and a dinner in the West. 'In Moscow,' she said, 'the shop-windows are a disgrace, nothing interesting in them at all, but wherever you are invited, there's smoked sturgeon, ham and caviar—whereas with us the shop windows are full to bursting, but when we invite you home, it's biscuits and a cup of tea.' Not bad, eh?"

Glebb laughed: "Not bad. Wicked but fair. The spaghetti won't only be with cheese, I'll tell Pilar to splash out on some meat . . . Will you come on your own, or d'you want me to snatch you away from under the noses of the local sleuths?"

"Snatch me if you please! That would be very kind."

"Good. First I'll fetch your partner, then I'll come up for you."

"My partner is at home in Moscow, John."

"I was talking about Paul."

"Ah, so he's my partner now? You must congratulate me—to have Paul Dick as a partner is truly an honour."

"He amazed me, talking on and on about that unfortunate Russian . . ."

"What Russian?"

"The one who was mending your racket."

"Ah, Baillieu. Was he really Russian?"

"Yes. And his name was the same as what Paul calls you—Ivan."

"Has his death been reported in the papers yet?"

"I don't think they will cover it for a while. My friends

in the local FBI say it's too early. There's too little evidence, and besides, they're convinced the case is too delicate for immediate comment.''

"If you find out anything new, will you tell me?''

"You want to write about the fate of a wretched refugee?''

"If his fate is interesting, why not? Of course I do.''

"By the way, did you read Mr. Ogano's statement?''

"He makes far too many statements. Which one precisely?''

"Today's. Some of our guys got through to him. He tore strips off them, the 'imperialist press' and so on . . .''

Slavin grinned: "By the way, does he play ping-pong?''

Glebb didn't immediately understand. He leaned forward—it was a habitual motion—towards the other: "Ping-pong? Why? What do you mean?''

"I mean diplomacy,'' Slavin replied. "Don't you remember?''

"Oh—Dr. Kissinger's games! It's hard to talk to you—you're too competent for a journalist, Vit!''

"An incompetent journalist is a contradiction in terms, John. So what did Mr. Ogano say?''

"He said that neither your advisers nor your deliveries to Nagonia will save Griso from collapse. He said that it would all be decided in the next three or four months.''

"He has said that before, I think!''

"He has. Only he never mentioned a date before!''

"That means they have set a precise date,'' Slavin said to himself. "Otherwise he wouldn't give away those three or four months. But the action will really begin much earlier.''

Returning home, Glebb went straight into his study, pulled down the Venetian blinds, turned on some music, and took out of his pocket a small dictaphone—a microphone mounted in a watch, a very convenient little thing. He plugged it into a special recorder and began to play back the tape. Zotov's phrases—"Our Xerox is bloody awful, but I'll have to do a photocopy,'' "Thanks, John, I'm indebted to you, really,'' "I'll fix it up,'' "I would send it,'' "No question about it,'' and "Ring tomorrow, about three. OK?'' he copied onto a new, super-sensitive tape, and put it into his safe.

After changing his clothes he drove to Pilar's house, gave her a second micro-dictaphone, and said:.

"Guapeña, your job is to kiss Zotov, call him 'my dear' and to guide the conversation so he says the following words—'I'm tired,' 'I can't go on,' and 'To hell with it all!' You have three hours to work on the scenario. Will you manage? Think it all over carefully because the recorder only has a forty-minute tape, understand? And let Alicia put more meat than usual in the spaghetti—that Slavin is used to getting what he likes. We'll spoil him for the time being, all right?''

Investigation No. 4

After talking to Konstantinov on the telephone from the Odessa department, Gmyrya went to the Aeroflot office and bought a ticket on the evening flight.

"Even a mangy sheep has one good tuft of wool, as they say," he muttered to himself as he took his bathing trunks out of his suitcase. "To come down to Odessa and not have a swim would be stupid. Especially since they've ruled out Shargin, thank God. So I've no worries, it's an unexpected *vacance.* "

Gmyrya was very fond of that French word. It was what he always called his hunting trips: *vacances*—just that. However, during all his time in counter-intelligence, and he had worked here for twenty-five years out of his forty-seven, he had never once had a real *vacance.* The summer season held no fascination for Gmyrya, so the usual tragedies with *putyovki** were unknown to him. He took one week at the start of the duck season at the end of August, two weeks for wild boar (that was in November), and if they allowed him a spring break, he went off to Akhtyri for the end of April—to shoot the northern geese.

Gmyrya knew how to measure his time, hunting had taught him how to calculate it exactly. So when he had finished talking to Moscow, he went into a café: he would have a small bar of processed cheese, a cup of coffee and a milk-shake, then go to the bus station and catch a ride to the beach, find out how to get from the beach to the airport ("why ask the lads in the department if I don't have to, and feel tied down, here's to freedom!"), give in his briefcase at the cloakroom, swim to his heart's content, and return to Moscow nicely warmed by the sun . . .

As he turned into the bar, Gmyrya collided into Shargin. Looking pre-occupied, Shargin ushered the younger man in first, then held out his hand to Van Zeger from Trade Corporation. Finally, he followed himself—Leopold Nikiforovich, no less!

The bar was empty, the hotel's guests having scattered about their business, the holiday-makers gone to sunbathe on the beach. Shargin sat with Van Zeger by a window, next to a palm which, as if in revenge for having been removed from Africa, grew only straight upwards—another half a metre and it would hit the ceiling.

"Why is Van Zeger here?" Gmyrya wondered. "I thought Shargin came down on his own."

Meanwhile the two men were talking softly at their table, in English.

"That's not like a gentleman," Shargin was saying. "You cannot, surely, be jilting me at the altar, Charles . . ."

"What do you mean?" Van Zeger was lost momentarily.

Shargin's English was so formal, his observation of grammatical rules so punctilious, that he was, in truth, often hard to understand.

"I mean that in the future I may not be able to help you like I have before."

"That's very bad, Leo. It will be bad for you and for us."

"Then keep to your promise."

"Do you think that it only depends on me?"

"But you represent your office's interests here, don't you?"

"I try to do so, Leo, but it doesn't depend entirely on me, does it? I'm not as all-powerful as it might seem at first glance. The money and glamour is just a sham. The worse things are in head office, the more luxurious the cars they send me here, the bigger the expense account to wine and dine my counterparts.''

''That's your affair, how many people you entertain. But I count on the minimum of good sense from your bosses. If they blurt this out in public, then I'm finished, do you understand? I know what I'm talking about, Charles.''

Shargin turned, took out some money, walked over to the counter and paid.

Van Zeger did not follow him.

''Come on, let's go,'' said Shargin, ''we've got things to do . . .''

Gmyrya took a taxi to the KGB office, telephoned Konstantinov again, and recounted to him, almost word for word, the strange dialogue which he had overheard. He then asked for authorisation to take suitable action.

To Centre

Shargin and Van Zeger spent the whole night in Shargin's room, composing a kind of special memorandum. They booked three calls—to London, Marseilles and the Hague—but the lines were busy and they did not get through.

Gmyrya

To Gmyrya

Return to Moscow. Shargin is in the clear.

Centre

(The report which Shargin had locked himself up in his hotel room in Odessa to compose, described how Van Zeger had received preliminary approval for the purchase of crude oil—an unofficial, purely informal approval—and had sent a telex to the directors of his firm. They in turn had immediately informed the Press about it, quoting a price which in no way suited the Soviet trading organisation. The official responsible for this price was none other than Shargin—although he had been given permission to convey to Van Zeger the Soviet side's preliminary agreement by the deputy director of the organisation. So, during the conversation in the bar witnessed by Gmyrya, Shargin was not just upset about a trifle, but by his trading partner's fit of irresponsibility . . .)

Konstantinov

"Raisa Ismailovna," said Konstantinov, as he was led into the small flat, with carpets hanging on the walls, "—I have a request to make of you."

"Please go on," Niyazmetova readily agreed, "—only I don't know who you are. They phoned and told me that a general would be coming, but they didn't explain why."

"I would like to hope that our conversation will remain a secret. From everyone—even your family, your closest friends?"

"Will you accept my word of honour?" the woman said softly, and her glance strayed involuntarily to a photograph on the wall. It was a picture of herself and a man, her former husband—they had divorced three years earlier, after he ran off with another woman. She had nothing to hold him with, for after an operation for an extra-uterine pregnancy Niyazmetova was unable to have children.

"Certainly, I will accept your word of honour," replied Konstantinov. "I don't know whether you know this story . . . When Kropotkin died, his widow wrote a letter to Lenin, saying that since all the anarchists were now locked up in prison, there was nobody to accompany the funeral cortege of the Prince and revolutionary. Could Lenin let out the anarchists for the funeral? So Lenin called in Dzerzhinsky, and after talking with him, the latter went to the Butyrka*, asked them to line up all the anarchists, went up to each prisoner in turn and took their word of honour that they would return to prison after Kropotkin's funeral. And they all came back. Every last one of them. So . . . Since I am from the KGB, which is the successor to the Cheka, so to speak, it goes without saying that I am trained to accept a word of honour."

"Did they really all come back?" the woman asked softly. "Amazing. Why don't they tell that story in the history books?"

"They do. I read about it in a book," Konstantinov replied.

"Well, I give you my word," Niyazmetova said. "The more since my uncle, Sharip Shakirovich, worked in the Cheka."

"I know. So anyway, Raisa Ismailovna, what I'm interested in is anything you can tell me about Olga Vinter."

"Olga?!" Niyazmetova was taken aback, and tears sprang immediately to her eyes. "What do you mean? It's all so sad, God, so sad! . . . Why are you interested, especially now—in Olga of all people?"

"When was the last time she visited you here?"

"I don't remember . . . About five days ago. Or four. But why?"

"Was she on her own?"

"No. With Serezha."

"What Serezha?"

"How do you mean—'what Serezha'? With Dubov. They came at about two o'clock, with some champagne. Serezha had found some *brut* somewhere—*Abrau Dyurso*, the driest of the dry. They sat around a bit, we chatted, then they left . . ."

"How was Olga feeling?"

"Fine. That's the terrible thing! If she had been ill . . . By the way, a young man came here earlier, asked all about Olga."

"Can you try to remember what happened that evening?"

"Nothing, really."

"How long were they here?"

"An hour, no more."

"You must have spoken about something."

"Of course . . ."

"But you can't remember, is that it?"

"You remember words when they're said in a crisis situation, but . . . Sorry, what's your name?"

"Didn't I introduce myself? Konstantin Ivanovich."

"Well, Konstantin Ivanovich, you will agree it's difficult to describe to a third party a talk with a friend, just a casual talk . . . Olga put on the cassette, she knows—" Niyazmetova began to cry again, "—she *knew* all my cassettes, because she gave me loads of them herself. She used to bring them back from Lewisburg. She put on Demis Roussos—he's a lovely singer, don't you think?"

"I'm afraid I haven't heard him."

"He's very popular now—completely uninhibited, soulful, kind of wounded, gives everything to his singing—like Victor Jara . . . Anyway, Olga put on Roussos. She was sitting next to Serezha, and she asked him whether he remembered the song. He said he didn't, so Olga said, 'You idiot, this is *our* song.' He seemed at a loss and just looked at her, and she burst out laughing. She had a wonderful laugh, so infectious that even a dead man would have smiled. Then she said: 'Don't you remember, they used to play this song all the time, when we were in our luxury suite?' But he still didn't understand—'What luxury suite?' he asked. Olga seemed to find that even more hilarious. 'In the Hilton!' she cried, laughing. 'In the Hilton!' Suddenly, he got up, knocking the champagne glasses over on her dress—it was a wonderful dress, a pleated skirt with a jersey top, very light, that's the fashion now. He was upset, took her by the hand and led her off into the bathroom. When they came back they were quieter, in a funny sort of mood . . . I asked Olga to tell us about the room, but she looked at Serezha, made an effort to smile and said: 'Another time.' Then she went silent, never said another word all evening . . . That was all that happened in sixty minutes."

Konstantinov asked quietly, "You don't remember which great writer it was who said that *talent is detail?*"

"Chekhov, I think."

"No, Chekhov said something different, he wrote that 'brevity is the sister of talent.' " Konstantinov sighed. "It would be good if our writers adopted that motto . . . No, it was Turgenev who wrote that about detail."

"But he could also have tried on Chekhov's maxim—all Turgenev's novels are very short!"

"True," agreed Konstantinov. (He was deliberately slowing down the pace of the conversation, trying to give the woman time to compose herself.) "That's true, of course. Read Turgenev again, I don't mean his novels, but his letters. Remember how elaborately he described the song of a nightingale? You could call it poetry in prose, he found words for every phrase of the nightingale's song in every district in the province of Kursk—amazing!"

"You know, Olga is a morning person," Niyazmetova said thoughtfully, and again stopped short. "I mean *was* . . . *was* a morning person . . ."

"I don't understand."

"I was thinking laterally from nightingales," Niyazmetova explained. "There are morning people, and evening people. Morning people are always smiling, even if they feel bad, they've a kind of fear of affecting people with their bad temper. But evening people make a show of their mood, like in a display window. I can't understand why you should be interested in Olga—I know that the Cheka always has a good reason for being interested in people."

"You said a moment ago that Dubov stood up suddenly and knocked over the table . . . Could you try to remember again what Olga said immediately before that?"

"She said 'our luxury suite,' and he didn't understand. And when she said about the Hilton, he stood up and overturned it—" Niyazmetova suddenly broke off. Tiny wrinkles bunched on her forehead, as they do with people who love the sun and get a tan very quickly.

"Could you tell me, please, Raisa Ismailovna, if you will excuse the question, whether their relationship began when they were both still in Lewisburg?"

"I'm glad you said 'relationship,' rather than when they started 'going out,' like everyone says these days. It's very vulgar, don't you think? I never asked about that, Konstantin Ivanovich . . . And she didn't say. Despite her open manner, she was quite a private person when it came to her personal life. But I think it all began there."

"Was she going to marry Dubov?"

"Hard to say. I don't know. I only remember that once

she confessed to me: 'Serezha doesn't like children.' After that she didn't see him for three weeks, stayed in my flat. I don't have a telephone, you see, so it's hard to find someone here, you can hide away to your heart's content . . ."

"Who else could she hide out with?"

"Galya Potapenko, that's a friend of ours . . . Or with . . . No, I think that's all."

"Did Vinter supervise any graduates at the institute, Raisa Ismailovna?"

"That sounds very cold—Vinter . . . For me she will always be Olyenka . . . As regards graduates, she must have had some, anyone studying for a doctorate would do."

"Yes, I know . . ."

"What, are you doing a doctorate yourself?"

"No, but I have graduates. Actually, I am a Doctor of Jurisprudence."

"I would never have thought it!"

"Why?"

"I don't know."

Galina Ivanovna Potapenko was a senior accountant at the Russian Auto Service combine. The telephone on her desk never stopped ringing. Konstantinov tried several times to start a conversation, but he could make no headway at all. Involuntarily, he looked at his watch—he had been here five minutes already and Potapenko was still discussing the construction of a car service base in Bronnitsi. They wanted it ready for the Olympics—service facilities would be needed on all main roads in the Russian Federation. With tens of thousands of foreign cars arriving, one would have to be fully armed . . .

"Galina Ivanovna," Konstantinov whispered, "I have absolutely no time . . ."

The woman nodded, cupped the receiver with her hand: "We'll go out into the passage, wait a moment . . ."

Konstantinov had decided not to summon Potapenko to the KGB. He judged, firstly, that an interview in his office would have a totally different atmosphere, the woman would be anxious. It wasn't for nothing that good doctors usually preferred to go out on visits. Studies showed that patients felt more secure and relaxed on their own ground. Secondly, Konstantinov suspected that he did not have quite enough facts to justify an interrogation. In fact, it wasn't one at all, just an inquiry.

"Well, let's go outside, we can have a smoke," said Potapenko, hanging up at last. "There'll be no peace in here."

In the corridor they found a place on a divan beside the window. Potapenko lit a Soviet Marlborough, clasped a knee with her left hand (almost like a beach pose, Konstantinov thought). She turned to Konstantinov:

"Raya phoned me, Konstantin Ivanovich," she began. "She asked me to help you, so here I am, ready. You have my word of honour."

"Thank you. So I can assume that you know what I'm interested in."

"Yes. It's all very strange."

"What exactly? Why strange?"

"Well, you see, that day Olga came to see me too. Her eyes were sore, she looked worn-out, I'd never seen her like that. I don't even know whether it's right to say . . . Anyway, she asked me to get some earrings valued. Diamonds with emeralds, very beautiful . . ."

"Why didn't she take them to the jewellers herself?"

"Because a month ago I bought some earrings as a wedding present for my sister, and went to Grigory Markovich to have them valued. He's an old chap, started work in Tsarist times."

"Couldn't she have asked you for his address?"

"He doesn't take orders from just anyone. He's retired, you see, not working officially. He only does jobs for people he knows—they're so suspicious, these old jewellers . . . But what is interesting is that later I found a note in the box, under the mounting, saying *serezhki ot Serezhi* ("earrings from Serezha"). So that means Dubov gave them to her."

"That was when?"

"After they left Raya, about three hours later. Olga left the earrings, said she would pick them up before her flight."

"Where are these earrings now?"

"At home . . . I was going to take them to her father . . . But it's terrible, they say he's very bad, can hardly breathe."

"Olga didn't say anything to you?"

"What about exactly?"

"Well, about why she looked so bad. Or why it was important to have a present from a friend valued?"

"Some things you just don't ask, Konstantin Ivanovich, even with a woman friend."

"But we men tell our friends everything—our real friends, that is."

"That's why we love you. So anyway, Grigory Markovich valued the earrings. They cost five to seven thousand roubles. He also thinks they are not Soviet-made."

"Where *were* they made, then?"

"He thinks it's Belgian work. The diamonds, apparently, are African—the Belgians used to own all the diamond mines there, didn't they?"

"Are you friends with Dubov, too?"

"How can I say . . . To be quite honest, I don't go for him. Though he's clever, and talented too—according to Olga. And he doesn't drink. Still, he's not quite my type."

"Why?"

"I don't know. He's just not, that's all. I didn't even go to the funeral. I knew there'd be a *performance,* I hate that sort of thing. One should try to bear it, stoically . . ."

"Where did Olga go when she left you?"

"I don't know . . . She phoned somewhere, asked about prospectuses and reference books . . . I don't remember. I think she phoned someone called Lev."

Proskurin listened to Konstantinov's report, then opened the file and flicked through its pages: "There's only one of her friends called Lev," he concluded. "Lukin, Lev Vasilyevich Lukin."

"Can I ask you, then, to have a word with him. Straight away, OK? And one other thing . . . We're beginning to get a picture of Dubov, a strange sort of picture . . . Where is he?"

"I've begun looking for him, Konstantin Ivanovich, but he seems to have disappeared without trace."

"Dead, too?" Konstantinov grinned, without amusement. "Find him by evening."

"Comrade Lukin, my name is Proskurin, I'm from the KGB*. Good afternoon."

Lukin ushered Proskurin into the flat. The large living-room was lined with shelves, all crammed with books, dictionaries, reference guides. Lukin worked in the international department of the Bureau for Technical Information.

"Don't worry about the mess," he said. "It's only surface-deep. I'm at your service, Comrade Proskurin."

"Thank you, I have a question to ask you."

"Please go ahead."

"I want to find out, Comrade Lukin, what Olga Viktorovna Vinter asked you about, the last time that you saw her?"

"Olga asked me for a Prospectus for the Hilton hotels. But what's wrong?"

"Comrade Lukin, *I* will ask the questions."

"Please go ahead."

"What sort of a prospectus is this?"

"A description of the hotels, restaurants, bars, the costs of rooms, addresses, telephone and telex numbers."

"Where did you get it?"

"From Italy, I think. Or from Great Britain. Maybe it was London . . . Yes, I think it was from London."

"Can you remember whether there is a description of the Lewisburg Hilton in the book?"

"Of course. I think that's the one that Olga was interested in."

"Why?"

"I don't know. She had a look at the prospectus, then stopped on the page where the Lewisburg Hilton is. Then she ran through the pages some more and smoothed them out—she knows how careful I am with my books . . ."

"Where *is* this manual?"

"Olga took it away with her."

"Promising to return it?"

"Yes. At the funeral I saw it in the room at Sergey's."

"Did she ask you for the manual straight off, or was it in the course of conversation?"

"No. As she came in the front door, she said—'Lev, give me the Hilton prospectus.' So I gave it to her. But what's happened, Comrade Proskurin?"

"You didn't notice anything strange in Vinter's behaviour?"

"Who? Oh, Olga? No. Only she looked terrible, as though she hadn't slept at all. But nothing particularly strange . . ."

The jeweller Abramov was allotted to Konovalov.

Konovalov gazed thoughtfully at the jeweller's shining pate as he wrote his statement, carefully, forming each letter:

"I Abramov Ignaty Vasilyevich, being called as an expert witness, do testify the following in respect of the questions put to me. The diamond earrings, set in gold on a platinum base, are a unique example of the jeweller's art. It is quite obvious that they were not made in the USSR, because the gold and platinum both contain clear traces of silver, which is forbidden here as a deviation from quality standards. The earrings are most likely to have been made in Belgium or Holland, though one cannot rule out the possibility that they are the work of the New York firm of Cook & Sons—judging by the box, velvet and plastic mounting. It is also possible that the earrings were made by the French subidiary of Cook & Sons now called Toulouse Loire. The price of the earrings is approximately five to seven thousand roubles. One can presume that in freely convertible currency these items would fetch from two to three thousand dollars."

"And why are you so sure about the particular firm of Cook & Sons, Ignaty Vasilyevich?" asked Colonel Konovalov, when he had re-read the statement once more. "Could you not be mistaken here?"

"Jewellers are like sappers: the first big mistake we

make is also our last . . . The stones here look as though they're watering, with a pale blue glint, and the edges are hand-polished with a little machine over-working. Who else does work like this, besides Cook? It's *us* who neglect our customers and make no effort to win their permanent allegiance. But over there, they *have* to win it, they live by the market and not by political education meetings. I hope you're not offended at my boldness, I'm just used to saying what I think—especially after the decisions of the historic 20th Congress*.''

''Where are there branches of Cook & Sons, could you tell us by any chance?''

''What d'you mean—*where?* Cook's rule the world, they have offices in every country. We're not talking about a seedstall, this is diamonds!''

''Though as it happens the seed trade also makes millions.''

''What, millions?! Compared to this, that's worth about as much as a sneeze in outer space! Poverty and bankruptcy! Diamonds can cost *ten thousand* million. Aren't we all used to the necessary deceptions when you deal with precious stones? Why make someone nervous over the price of their present? Better say nothing! A diamond means prestige—and nobody has yet been able to put a price-tag on prestige, have they?''

''Not yet,'' agreed Konovalov. ''But could you tell me please, do earrings like this fall into the category of official presents?''

''Ha, ha! Official presents—*that* means a Parker pen! You obviously don't have the *savoir faire* abroad. But I do! An official present is a notebook, a pack of presentation matchboxes, or at the very best a book on the architecture of Polynesia! You think the bourgeoisie is generous? They're mean—meaner than our meanest financial inspector! Cook's aren't for business, you give Cook's once in your life—a wedding present, to your daughter at her coming of age, to a lover. Forget about business when Cook's are involved!''

Konovalov smiled, ''Thank you, Comrade Abramov.''

To Slavin

Find out if you can whether Dubov took a room in the Hilton, and if he did, which one? Was it regular? What did it cost? How did he pay—by cheque or cash? Find out too where the firm Cook & Sons had its office. Who is the Managing Director? Is there a catalogue of jewellery items made in Belgium? Can you find the names of people who bought diamond earrings with emeralds around a year ago, at a cost of two to three thousand dollars?

Centre

Konovalov's unit had brought together all the information on Dubov. One of the things that Konstantinov wanted to clarify was why Dubov, after his return from Lewisburg, had turned down the offer of a doctorate.

"He didn't just turn it down, Comrade General," said Konovalov, well-primed after the previous night's researches: "In fact, it's rather a funny situation. First he was offered a post as department head, at a salary of 350 roubles a month. He refused. That was odd, because he persistently and in the most exact manner told his friends that he was short of money. Then he refused a place to study at the Academy. He waited for three months till a job came up as Senior Research Officer in the department of the Coordinating Institute which deals with all the secret material on Africa. The salary is 200 roubles, no bonuses."

"What benefits could he get in the Coordinating Institute? More chance to travel, promotion possibilities?"

"Not at all. They guaranteed him travel when he was offered head of department—practically anywhere in the world. They also promised him incentives if he decided to write a thesis. Whereas the chance of promotion in the Coordinating Institute is quite small, only if he does a thesis . . ."

"Has he started one yet?"

"No. We've checked, and he hasn't even mentioned it."

"Do they like his work?"

"Yes, they do. They say he's disciplined, works away quietly. He's very reliable with classified documents."

"What kind of radio does he have at home, by the way?"

"He's not in Moscow, Konstantin Ivanovich . . . We haven't been into his flat. We don't yet have permission."

"We must think how to find out about his radio."

"I'll work on it, Comrade General."

"When will you finish?"

"I'll give you a plan of action later today . . ."

At five o'clock Proskurin arrived.

"Where's Dubov?" asked Konstantinov.

"I'm doing everything I can to find him."

"Well in that case, I must warn you, don't break the law!"

Konstantinov opened a file with top priority telegrams: "Tell me," he continued, "who in our inner circle of suspects knew about our exports to Nagonia?"

"I'll have to look at the file, and see who's the main *figurant*—"

"What?" Konstantinov frowned. "That's a strange term. *Figurant,* according to Barkhudarov, means *ballet dancer.* But you mean suspect, I suppose?"

"That was what they used to say, Comrade General. *Figurant* is the word that expresses most truthfully the sense invested in it."

Konstantinov rejoined thoughtfully: "A word is inanimate, it can neither lie nor tell the truth—as I think Socrates once said. Truth or falsehood flow from combinations of words, placed together to create what we call a 'point of view' . . ."

(Konstantinov had two educations. In the autumn of 1954, he was working as a lathe-operator in Zaporozhe, when he was called up through the Komsomol and assigned to the KGB. He later completed a correspondence course at the law institute and then, while working on his dissertation, passed the exams for the philological faculty, his subject being nineteenth-century English Literature. Konstantinov's father—a border guard who died in the defence of Brest in 1941, was by profession a Russian Language teacher; that was probably why his son was so very pernickety about the precise expression of ideas. One of his favourite books was the classic work *Slovo o Slovakh** by the Leningrad linguist Lev Uspensky. The old scholar's stubborn fight for the purity of Russian language always inspired Konstantinov.)

"I've got to look at the material on our suspects. But why did the deliveries to Nagonia come up?" Proskurin asked in puzzlement.

"Because of Slavin's telegram. But I can help you: only one person in Lewisburg knows about the deliveries—Zotov."

"Considering his relationship with his wife—friendship and peaceful coexistence," Proskurin grinned, "—here in Moscow Vinter probably knew about them too."

"Yes, so we can assume. Well, who else?"

An hour and a half later Proskurin reported that there was only one other person who by virtue of his job would receive this information—Sergei Dmitrievich Dubov.

Top Secret

To Major-General Konstantinov

In answer to your request, I can report that an air ticket to Adler was issued four days ago at the Aeroflot Office in the Metropol Hotel in the name of Sergei Dmitrievich Dubov.

Lieutenant-Colonel Zykov

13

Donald Gee turned out to be a tall man with youthful looks and a shock of grey hair. A crimson scar ran across his forehead, and the journalistic world for that reason nicknamed him Gee Harvey Skortzeny—tagging the Christian names of Kennedy's murderer onto the surname of Mussolini's abductor.*

Gee had arranged to meet Stepanov in the hotel vestibule—the air-conditioning in his own room wasn't working. In fact, it wasn't working anywhere, for the colonialists had dismantled the system, despite offers of big money if they would only teach the local officials how to deal with the not overcomplicated machinery. The one place in the hotel where you could actually breathe was the hall. Here there was a draught, as all the doors were left open all day, and a breeze wafted in fresher air from the ocean, especially in the evenings.

"I'm Dmitri Stepanov, from Moscow. Thank you for finding the time to see me."

"I'm interested to meet you. To be honest, this is the first time I have ever spoken to a Russian face to face. You have some business to discuss with me?"

"Yes."

"Well, please go on, Mr. Stepanov."

"I'm interested in your epic struggle with Glebb."

Donald Gee's expression froze. He reached quickly for a packet of Chesterfields and offered Stepanov a crumpled

178

cigarette. Drawing deeply on his own, he retracted his massive head into a set of rather birdlike shoulders, and replied:

"I would prefer not to talk about that subject."

"Have you given up?"

"Not only given up. I've signed an unconditional surrender."

"Because you didn't have enough facts?"

"Not only because of that."

"You see, I have travelled around Asia quite a lot . . . I have some information on Mr. Lao's banking interests."

"Obtained legally, or through your secret service?"

"If my secret service had given them to me, I would hardly be able to publish a book about Mr. Lao—no secret service in the world likes its information to get into print. You chose the wrong end to unravel this case, Mr. Gee. You should have begun with the man who gave the orders to kill Lao's secretary."

"The killers were never found."

"Are you sure they really looked?"

"They went through the motions anyway. But what you say is quite credible in Hong Kong, of course . . . Have you been there?"

"No."

"If you're interested in the problem of world drug addiction, I advise you to go."

"I've tried. They won't give me a visa. Freedom of movement doesn't quite extend to Reds. Your people are only pursuing their own interests when they make such a fuss about it . . . Does the name Shantz mean anything to you?"

"Wilhelm Shantz, a German from Munich?"

"Yes."

"He worked there with Glebb."

"You know his story?"

"No. He's an old man, speaks English well, distributes American publications."

"Did you know he was a captain in the SS?"

"Is that one of your propaganda ploys?"

"We printed a facsimile of his execution orders in the papers, Mr. Gee. He's on the war criminals list."

"Then demand his extradition."

"We've done so three times. Anyway, he was involved in a terrorist group in Hong Kong. I think he trained your attackers too, did Shantz. He knows the ropes—he worked with Skortzeny."

"How d'you know *that?*"

"Skortzeny told me."

"What's the use of bringing all these new people into my case, Mr. Stepanov?"

"It helps a lot. After all, the majority of Americans hate Nazism. If you can show that Glebb covered up Shantz, then they'll see your case in a completely different light. I'm prepared to give you my stuff on Shantz. But you've got to tell me why you signed your unconditional surrender."

"You want to write about it?"

"That depends on you."

"I don't want you to write about it."

"Afraid of losing your job?"

"My life, you mean. The job is only half of it—I already learned how to wash dishes when I tried to get Glebb. This time they'll just shoot me . . ."

"Fine. What, then, if I write the story with different names and places?"

"It will cost you fifty thousand dollars, Mr. Stepanov."

"I get paid twelve dollars a day here, Mr. Gee. Considering I'll be here about a month, I may not be able to give you all of that . . ."

"I get you." Gee's face lost some of its previous tension. "You see, partner, I sold all my information on Glebb. Down to the last line. For ten thousand. When they sent me the letter and said that they'd kidnap my sister and kill my mother, I realised that they meant it. They meant it, d'you understand? So what do I do? Pack off my sister to your country? I haven't got the money, the tickets aren't cheap. Anyway, I love America—and I don't like your system at all."

"Just as *I* don't like *yours.*"

"I know. Many of my colleagues have read your books."

"And you?"

"No. I don't read anything, Mr. Stepanov. I don't believe *anything* that I see on the printed page. I know too much about how it's put together. I write what is demanded of me. I'm holding down a job, Mr. Stepanov. The *Star* bought me, and I'm pretty sure it was at the instigation of our Mr. Glebb . . ."

"No, he's not big enough for that, Mr. Gee. His bosses, more likely."

Gee shook his head, and grinned: "How much per cent d'you think Glebb transferred to his bosses' account from the profits of the heroin operation? Three per cent—no more. Those people are careful, they know how much to take. It's better, isn't it, a steady income, a little at a time, than all at once and blow the whole operation."

"What do you mean by *all at once?*"

"The rake-off was simple: from every successful operation Glebb got five per cent, for his cover. Out of five per cent he gave three to his bosses."

"Then why is he sitting in Lewisburg playing the fiddle to somebody else's star part, pretending to be a businessman—when he could kiss goodbye to the whole damn thing and retire to a well-earned rest in Miami? . . ."

"Because he went and blew all his money in Nagonia, Mr. Stepanov. Ten per cent of all the shares in the hotels here belonged to him. But he never had time to cash in his millions—the revolution came. And he has to get back his money, can't you see?"

"Do you have facts?"

"The facts are over there, in Lisbon and Paris. And in Berne—they have wonderful reference material there, if you have money to pay for it. Glebb couldn't keep the money in his own account, in our country the Treasury's fiscal system is far more efficient than the FBI . . ."

"Doesn't he realise that it's unrealistic—to get back Nagonia?"

"I think it's very realistic."

"It won't work."

Gee shook his head: "It'll work."

"You're sure that he lost *all* his heroin profits in Nagonia?"

"All of them," replied Gee, and something flickered in his eyes, then immediately went out. He turned, scanned the occupants of the vestibule with a hunted look, and again reached for his crumpled packet of cigarettes.

"But surely you would very much prefer him not to get back his money, Donald?" Stepanov asked quietly. "You don't want him to bring it off here, do you? I mean, to bring off the coup that would put those millions back in his pocket, so he can return in triumph to the States?"

"I don't want it at all, but even more than that, I don't want him to shoot my family."

"Yes, but there are people to do that for him . . ."

"No. Glebb knows how to do it all himself."

"What, fear of witnesses?"

Gee shrugged his shoulders again: "Why fear? He's not afraid. He can take them out when he wants to. It's just he likes that kind of work. D'you understand? He's a real green beret, his ideal is brute force. What you said about Shantz is exactly my idea of Glebb. I wouldn't be surprised if he had a portrait of Hitler on his wall at home—not now I wouldn't anyway."

"Can you tell me the names of the people that you've spoken to about Glebb?"

"I told you. I've sold all my papers—down to the last one. I want to stay alive. So that's it . . . Do you understand?"

"Yes, I do. Now, listen to what I want to propose. In several months' time I will be in the States. You give me some names of people who don't like Nazis. I will carry out my investigation. I'm owed some money there for a book, I can use it for a search of my own—all quite separate from your case."

"I thought you didn't get paid royalties outside the Soviet Union, I read that they take the money away from you."

"You shouldn't believe what you read in the papers," Stepanov laughed. "Though in this case they are more or less correct."

"Brave words, when you're talking to a right-wing journalist like me, Mr. Stepanov."

"You mean, a journalist working on a right-wing *newspaper*, Mr. Gee . . . That is surely not quite the same thing."

"Tell me why you—you personally—hate fascism so much? Of course, I know you lost ten million—"

"Twenty."

"Really?"

"Really. As for me personally . . . Well . . . When seven of your brothers and sisters—all of them under ten years old—are popped off by these Shantzes, and then these same Shantzes start publishing pretty books in Hong Kong about democracy and justice—"

"I don't touch alcohol, Mr. Stepanov," Gee broke in. "But if you can make something stick on Glebb, with hard facts, damn it, I'll drink a glass of Madeira to your success. Try to talk to his first wife. Sometimes she lives at home, but that's not often. She spends more and more time in a mental clinic—though I hear she's perfectly sane. Nobody will believe her, of course, but she can give you the facts. Her name is Emma Shantz. Her father is the same Wilhelm whom you described to me so eloquently and in such detail. Only remember: Emma was born in May 1945—and that fact is very important if you want to understand whom she loves or hates."

Slavin

"People have become nicer," Slavin repeated with conviction, as he hung his jacket over the back of a chair. "Just think—the most popular song back home now is a song about a friendly crocodile called Genya. In the old days they used to frighten children with crocodiles."

"Go and take a swim in the river here, there are plenty of friendly Genyas there, I can tell you!" Zotov replied. "No, it's not a question of niceness, just popularisation of science for the mass audience. I mean, look, a programme like the 'World of Animals.' They look so nice on the screen, these same crocodiles, you're sorry for the poor things . . . People have become sentimental, I'll agree with you on that. But as regards being soft or *kinder,* if you don't mind I'll stick to my own opinion. Humankind is making a mistake, Vitaly Vsevolodich . . . Do you lend money?"

"Yes."

"And do people always give it back to you?"

"Hm . . . Some do."

"Some do. But do you realise what happened in the last century if a man didn't repay his debts? If it came out in public, he'd go to the next room, and 'bang'—a bullet in his heart! But mention a debt now, and they say: 'Mean bastard, he can wait, it doesn't matter.' Or think of our meetings where we look at someone's character. Thank God, it's not so heavy these days—but look at what they used to do! Talk about washing dirty linen in public, it was more like the Spanish Inquisition! No, no, humankind is eaten up with bitterness, Vitaly Vsevolodovich, it has forgotten grief, it lives like a communal kitchen, it all but pisses in the neighbours' teapot . . ."

"Feeling homesick?"

"Homesick?" Zotov shrugged his shoulders. "If I had a home—maybe."

"But they told me—"

"See! There you are—*they told you.* And you said we're getting nicer! The truth lies somewhere near what St. Paul said. Do you remember? 'The Jews ask for signs, the Greeks for wisdom.' Now, that's true. Some people want miracles, others—knowledge. Some set store on luck, others—on ability. But *nobody* wants to make kindness a religion, look what happened to Tolstoy when he tried. I think he was closest to the truth . . ."

"Would you like a drink?"

"Yes, please."

"Only I haven't got any vodka left."

"Can't stand it anyway. But I adore whisky."

"Glebb says he hates whisky, and loves vodka."

"He's lying. He can't stand vodka, look carefully at him when he drinks it."

"Actually, I don't think he drinks much at all. At least, he always makes sure to stay sober."

"Listen, Glebb, listen," said Slavin to himself. He was sure by now that every slightest sound in his room was being recorded on tape. "Listen to what I say, I'd so much love to see you really drunk!"

"Anything to have with it?" Zotov asked.

"Only soda. Oh yes, I've also got some biscuits some-where. Want some?"

"Yes, I'm famished."

"Shall we go and have a bite?"

"Let's go to my place, eh? My aunt sent some sausage, beautiful dry sausage and *sulguni**. Do you like *sulguni?*

"Not half! All right. Thank you, with pleasure. But can we wait for a call first? A friend promised to ring and take me to Pilar's. Only I don't really feel like going . . ."

"An interesting girl, that. Sharp as a scalpel. Com-pletely masculine type of mind, despite her other charms. An amazingly *rational* person."

"Actually, rationality is a concept I agree with. It's rea-son that gives us knowledge. It's reason that unifies all our strange and wonderful opinions. An opinion is an opinion, even several opinions can't be joined into a concept. And a concept is a step on the ladder to knowledge, it puts together reason out of opinions, brings in imagination as well, consciousness and memory. Pilar has a wonderful memory, don't you think, Andrei Andreyevich? And she's had no lack of experience in life, eh?"

"Don't try to arrange her in pigeon-holes—logic is use-less when you want to analyse a person. A person is by nature illogical."

"Do you say that because of your wife?" asked Slavin softly.

Zotov took a drink of whisky, sniffed the biscuits, broke off a piece, and munched it lazily. "No. As it happens, everything there is logical," he said thoughtfully. "A dif-ference in age, difference in temperament, difference in interests, and, well, my own idiocy."

"Is it worth scattering your ashes on your head like this?"

"No. But repentance is one thing, the statement of tact is another. Since you raised the subject, I can assume you've heard whispers from all quarters, all of them against Olga, and that's not fair. She's cleverer than me, talented, naturally creative, that is, a thinker. And of course—she's beautiful. But I wanted to force her into my own image. And I ruined everything. There's no point making excuses—about how I worried about her, how I went mad wondering how she was feeling, who was with her, would she get hurt, what would everyone think? Either you accept the individuality of the person you're with, accept it completely, and then miraculously you can become one with them, or you don't. There is no third way, it's pointless to delude yourself."

"Have you asked to be recalled?"

"The opposite. I'm on the list for a cooperative flat at home, I've got one more year to wait. But we share our book collection—neither of us can live without it, let alone work. Anyway, where could I cart my albums on African painting, they weigh half a ton. And it hurts me to see Olga, and she knows that. Not that it's easy for her either, I think . . ."

"She hasn't remarried yet?"

"No—and she won't."

"Why do you say that?"

"Well, that isn't my or your business."

"I'm sorry."

"That's all right. I don't think you meant to pry . . . I used to cut short conversations like this, but there's no sense now . . . I feel like TASS—putting out official statements in a vain attempt to rectify the slander directed at her." He smiled awkwardly, and put down the glass. "Pour me some more, eh? It would be good to be an alcoholic—no worries, get as drunk as you like . . ."

"Why do you dislike drinkers so much?"

"My father drank himself to death. He was an amazingly gifted man, but he never made use of his talent. Actually, he was a kind of Greek . . ."

"What?" Slavin was lost. "Why a Greek?"

"Well, like a Greek, I mean. He didn't believe anything

said by anyone close to him. The Greeks, you remember, only trusted foreigners . . . They even distrusted their own Pythagoras—'Yes, he's a genius, of course, but only because he learned it from foreigners.' My father was a philosopher. And a philosopher is a person who studies nature, everything else is quackery. And so he found out everything he wanted to—and then took to drink. My God, a little knowledge is a dangerous thing, oh how dangerous! You remember when they asked Pythagoras what he did in life?''

"I remember. 'I don't *do* anything, I am a philosopher.' ''

"Well that was my father . . . At first he enjoyed the world as a spectacle, then he got disillusioned, and oh so tired. He didn't believe in himself or the people around him and he began to hurt inside, God bless him . . . Well then, it looks like your friend isn't going to ring, eh?''

"Let's give him five minutes grace, all right? He's a great guy.''

"They're all great guys,'' Zotov laughed. "Only how does that great guy Glebb get his information on our deliveries to Nagonia? I'm the only one who knows about them here—nobody else . . .''

Slavin hurriedly trod on Zotov's foot, but the latter waved his hand in annoyance. "They're not taping you, you know, why would they need to? You're not the ambassador, then it would be a different matter, they'd have installed some equipment . . .''

When he heard Zotov's final words, John Glebb rose abruptly from the table and began to pace up and down his office, with a soldier's even, rapid strides. Then he rewound and played the tape again, copying it onto a high-quality cassette for his official report. Finally, he stuffed the original tape into his pocket and went in to Robert Lawrence.

"The deed is done, boss,'' he said. *"Now* I can feel easy about 'Torch.' ''

"Well done. D'you want to let me into the details, or maybe you don't need my brain here?''

"Thanks to my *details,''* Glebb replied, taking offence

and not trying to conceal it, "You will receive congratulations from the Admiral and a medal, whereas all I will get is two weeks holiday."

"During which you will recruit yet another 'Mastermind,' so that eventually I get another medal, and you—another holiday," Lawrence laughed.

"There'll never be another 'Mastermind' like the one we have now, boss, believe me! There never will be. While we've got him, you and I are in the riding saddle, we can do anything we want, we're the focus of attention. Why, the President himself knows our names, we're safe from any backstabbing, no one can touch us. 'Mastermind' is Langley's big white hope, he's our passport to success. *I* think he's panicking unnecessarily, nobody can decode our messages. He's just tired, they'll let him have a rest when we finish with Griso . . . Anyway, my *details* tell me that Zotov has stumbled onto 'Mastermind' without realising it: he's got a limited outlook, typical of one of their apostles. But he spoke to Slavin about the deliveries which 'Mastermind' told us about. That means within a couple of hours Moscow will know about it, and they'll be looking for the information leak. And we are organising a leak. Right here. That'll be the ploy we promised 'Mastermind.'

"How will that help? What will it cost?"

"It'll cost nothing, just a couple of cocktails, nothing more. How do we do it? That's *my* affair—you look after the political direction, leave the tactics of close-up fighting to me. How will it help? It'll give us victory. First, the Russians will get proof that Zotov is our agent. Second, they'll get this information in such a way that we can accuse Mr. Slavin of spying. So get ready for a break-in here, the robbers will take a list of our 'friends' from your safe—one of them, obviously, being Zotov's. Third, the accusations of espionage and terrorism will force Lewisburg to expel the majority of Russians working here, so cutting the deliveries to Nagonia in half. The other half Ogano's guerilla unit can destroy. And fourth, once this campaign has started, especially when Stau has arrested Slavin, there'll be no observers left here, and if there are, they'll want to be super-careful. And on the eve of 'Torch' that'll be very useful, less noise.''

"Would you like a drink, John?''

"I'm not going to get drunk until the day they phone from Nagonia and say they're sending a helicopter to take me personally to visit Ogano's palace.''

"Touch wood . . .''

"I do that all the time—day and night—boss.''

"When will you stop shoving that in my face—your *boss?* How many times have I asked you to call me by my first name?''

"I'm a masochist, boss, self-abasement gives me pleasure.''

"How are you thinking of passing them the information on Zotov?''

Glebb threw his hands behind his head, stretched, and laughed for some private reason: "I rely on some opportunity cropping up, boss. And then, I harbour malice, you know, I never forgive an offence. I never forgive anyone.''

Lawrence studied Glebb carefully from under his thick grey eyebrows.

"Harbouring malice is a bad trait,'' he said, thoughtfully. "Especially in our profession, John. An agent should love his opponent tenderly, only *then* can he get close enough to smother him.''

Investigaton No. 6

Stepanov had met Hollywood director Eugene Kusanni three years before, during a festival in San Sebastian. Kusanni was there to show a documentary film about South Vietnam, while Stepanov, who had just returned from the partisans in Laos and Vietnam, was a member of the jury.

Stepanov liked the documentary: the American had shot his film with a precise and measured style, without "tricks.'' His forte was montage, owing something to two very different masters. On the one hand, there was the Jacobetti of *Dog's Life,* on the other Roman Carmen. Kusanni tried to link the incompatible: a woman giving birth under a barrage by Phantom bombers—and a lesson in a school of modern dance. The execution of a Vietnamese youth—and a lecture about black holes in space, given to a group of mesmerized students by a long-haired professor with childlike eyes, radiating kindness. A partisan concert—and the drug addicts of Berkeley.

Stepanov was introduced to Kusanni in the *Iberia*— a bar where all the cinema set used to gather, along with various idlers come to gaze at the celebrities.

"It doesn't hurt that they'll take me for a ride," said Kusanni. "You can bet on that. It just hurts that the top prize will go to Eusebio, and he's a fascist, a bastard, an arse-licker for their Generalissimo."

"You mean the film about Santiago de Compastello?" asked Stepanov.

"Yes. It's good film, it's just a shame it's made by a butcher who once led the Blue Division!"

"But that film isn't good enough for first prize!"

Eugene burst out laughing: "Is that your personal point of view? Or the opinion of a member of the jury?"

"Take it easy," Stepanov grinned.

On the next day, after various meetings in the lobbies, Stepanov realised that Eugene was right: the festival's organisers had worked over his colleagues, the members of the jury. Eusebio was already being described as the eventual winner. Every day the newspapers carried interviews with him and tame critics wrote their ecstatic essays.

But Spain is a country like no other. Stepanov had once joked in Tbilisi: "You Georgians are really no different from Basques, or the Spanish in general—what goes down best with all of you is a well-uttered toast and a banquet."

Stepanov got together all the newspapermen he knew. "Friends," he said, "I am not gunning for the Russian, but an American. This American, as it happens, is not rich, this is his first picture, he's not a member of the Communist Party, he's just an honest guy. I would like you to look at his film and write what you really think about it."

Next he met the festival director—one evening, in his

own room. Stepanov had learned that the Spanish prized
decorum above all: if you were a member of the jury, you
had to take not just a room, but a whole suite, and the
refrigerator must be crammed not with bottles of beer, but
real whisky, gin and bottles of Rosado from Navarre—
Hemingway's favourite and since then a fashion among
foreigners. Having created this code of decorum, the
Spanish then fell for its magic themselves—"it's funny,"
said Stepanov to himself, "but true."

When the two men were sipping their wine—Spaniards
are the most non-drinking nation in the world—Stepanov
began: "My dear friend, this conversation will be completely confidential . . ."

"I know what it is about already," said the festival director. "You support Kusanni. I have my people in the
newspapers, their information reaches me immediately.
You can't win, Señor Stepanoff, San Sebastian always
wants to be purer than the Pope himself. I know it's strange
to compare Washington with the Vatican, but all the same,
it's true. Our people are more pro-American than the
Americans themselves, they won't risk giving the prize to
an anti-establishment film, even if the director's an American!"

"You're wrong," Stepanov said, after considering this.
"Kusanni's opinions are genuinely pro-American. Believe
me, in a year or two he'll get the US national prize."

"The USA doesn't have a national prize for documen-
taries, the Oscars are only for feature films . . . And then—
I'm not quite convinced that the Vietnam war will be over
in a couple of years."

"It'll be over sooner than that, believe me. I've just
spent six months there, so I know what I'm talking about."

"I would like to believe you. I value your opinion, and
I would like always to be your friend and get to know your
country, not just as Señor Stepanoff. But please don't put
me in a difficult position. I cannot support you, there is
too much involved here. Eusebio will get the gold medal,
that question is already decided."

"It will be difficult for me to prepare public opinion in
Moscow," Stepanov said quietly, lighting a cigarette,

"when our Moscow festival comes round, and when you bring us your own pictures. When a Spaniard wins the prize in San Sebastian, that's one thing, but when he is honoured in Moscow, that's completely different."

"Moscow wouldn't give Eusebio anything. After all, one of his films was about the veterans of the Blue Division."

"Berlanga fought in the war. He too was a soldier in the Blue Division, but we all praised his *Executioner.*"

The festival director sighed: "Señor Stepanoff, it is one thing to be a soldier, quite another to glorify that war through the medium of art. Fine—if I send you three films by young documentarists, do you guarantee me a gold and a bronze medal?"

Stepanov shook his head: "No, despite all our faults and eccentricities, the prizes at the festival are there to be won, not promised in advance . . ."

The director moved towards Stepanov, beckoned him to lean over, and whispered in the Russian's ear: "I don't believe you . . ."

Then he rose and began to pace up and down the suite taken by the festival organisers for Stepanov. Glancing into the bathroom, he enquired the price of the room, supplying the answer to his own question, that it was bound to be more than fifty dollars. Finally, he returned to his place, and pronounced: "I guarantee your American the special press award—"

"Too little."

"You're mad! It'll cost me blood! Do you think it is easy to persuade the bureaucrats in the Ministry of Information and Tourism? I have to find the right *moves,* you know, and that is not so simple!"

"Since you should really give Eugene the gold, but you're afraid of Washington's reaction, give him the silver—that makes a little sense, at least. Everyone will understand why you could not do him full justice. Whereas if you give him the special press prize, then there'll be protests everywhere—not in Spain, of course—about Franco's censorship."

"Shhh!" the director jumped up from his chair again.

"Señor Stepanoff! Is that necessary? The Generalissimo is the father of all Spanish people, and we have no arbitrary censorship."

"All right, all right," Stepanov yielded. "I'm just telling you what the papers will say abroad, and I don't mean in my own country. The French will be the first. They are very sympathetic to the Vietnamese, ever since they got out of there just in time . . ."

In short, Eugene was awarded the bronze medal, which opened the way to a successful career in cinema. For the Americans are as much impressed by a reputation as the Spanish, but in their case the best thing is recognition abroad. Like any great nation, they look askance on prophets in their own country.

From that time, whenever Stepanov went to the States, Eugene—if he was at home, in San Francisco—would drop everything and nip over to Washington, where he would help Stepanov hassle for his visas (the authorities were never keen to let him visit the East Coast or the South), often travelling with Stepanov or lending him his car and the keys to his bachelor flat in Greenwich Village.

Twice Eugene visited Russia. Each of the two men knew the other's position—Stepanov being a Communist, Eugene a Republican sympathiser. Certain things they forebore to argue about, there was no sense, neither could convince the other. But they firmly believed that they could rely absolutely on each other, especially where it concerned something which could help bring their two peoples closer together.

So it was to Eugene Kusanni that Dmitri Stepanov sent a telegram from Nagonia.

"Mrs. Glebb, the doctor said I could speak to you for half an hour."

"Oh! What progress! That means I'm completely normal, everything's OK! Soon I'll be let home again . . ."

The woman laughed a strange, throaty chuckle, a bit like a laying hen.

"Mrs. Glebb, I wanted to speak to you about John . . ."

"It was him who put me here, so that I couldn't say anything to the FBI's bloodhounds. How did you manage to get in here? He pays the doctors big money, you know, for them to tell everyone I'm mad and to stop the Federal agents from touching me . . ." The woman leaned towards Eugene. "I beg you, just one drag, eh? A tiny little one . . ."

"You smoke heroin?"

"Shhh . . . Anything I can. I dream about that one drag . . ., long, dry, burning . . . Save me, please!"

"I haven't got anything with me, Mrs. Glebb . . . Not on me, at the moment . . . Do you understand? Look . . . If you can tell me what I want to know, maybe I could help you."

"You're lying . . . They'll never let you in again. They only let me talk once a year. John wants to know how much I still remember . . . One FBI man came to see me and left me a pinch of stuff. After that they stopped me seeing anyone for a year . . ."

"What was his name?"

"What's *your* name?"

"Eugene Kusanni, I'm a film director."

The woman laughed again, with her strange dry chuckle. "Then I'm Greta Garbo. Though no, she grew old too quietly for me! Take me like Marilyn Monroe—that's closer."

"Here is my driving licence, Mrs. Glebb."

"Ha! The other man showed me his licence, too! D'you think I believed him?"

"Did he tell you where he was from?"

"No. Just that his name was Robert Shaw. From the FBI, like I told you. I think he actually said so. No, that's right, he said: 'I'm Robert Shaw from the FBI.' "

"Did he ask you about that scandal in Hong Kong?"

"No. He just asked how Pilar was able to fly to Peking, and where she got her diplomatic passport. You see, they can't touch diplomats, those poor bloodhounds, they follow the scent and then bang! Their head hits against a bronze plate which says 'Diplomat.' And then he asked where John took her after Hong Kong . . ."

"Who is Pilar?"

"A tart. A dirty stinking tart."

"Where does she live?"

"What d'you mean—where? Where *he* is. He drags her round with him. He pimps her out, and then washes her off in the bathroom. He pimped her out to those poor boys in Berlin, when he gave them money—through her. And she supports Mao, she's some kind of revolutionary. She told him whom to shoot. And he told her who his friends were . . . Or rather, my father's friends . . . Daddy had to knock off some of these old crooks, so John helped him . . . You don't believe me, do you? Don't stare at me, I'm only mad you know . . . D'you know, I can do anything. Will you really bring me a little stuff, eh? Pilar always gave me something to smoke, she's really quite cute . . ."

"Was she the one who introduced you to heroin?"

"No. That was John. He had some goods and he didn't know what the quality was, asked me to try it . . . I should have slapped him in the face! I remember he just looked into my eyes as I took a drag, looked so hard . . . That was the way my brother looked at rabbits when he was amputating their paws . . . With a little saw . . . They screamed, you know, they really screamed! Oh, you should have heard how they screamed, those red-eyed little rabbits . . . But Daddy said I shouldn't interfere with Zepp, Daddy said that the path to science always lay through cruelty . . . But Zepp got fed up with science and got into politics instead. Politics is a science, isn't it? Politics is when you saw off rabbits' paws without anaesthetic."

"Where is he, your brother Zepp?"

"John helped him to become secretary of the New German Party, now he defends the interests of Germans. I'm a German, you know, we're all Germans, even Glebb is half-German, only he hates it when you tell him. But one of his relations worked with Hitler in the Reichsbank. Such a civilized man, so quiet, all he knew how to do was to count—gold crowns from Auschwitz, rings from Dachau . . ." The woman laughed again. "If you want to scare Glebb, ask him how his Uncle Siegfried is . . . Tell him you want to look for Siegfried Shantz, because of your family who were burned up in the ovens . . . Only watch out for your life: John never forgives anyone where questions like that are concerned. He never forgave me, that's why I'm here . . .''

"And did you tell Robert Shaw all this?''

"He was a fool, that Shaw. Just like a typewriter—always scratching away with his pen, always trying to confuse me . . . No, I don't think he's even heard of a country called Germany, or that Germans live there. When I found John's letters in my father's papers I realised that we were from the same family, and asked John about it. That's when it all began . . . Before that I was a different person . . . I was in the business . . . I knew how much was going to whom, and when, I knew whom they were going to hit, where and how, I was *somebody* . . . David Hugh— that was John's helper, they got rid of him later—said I would be the new Mata Hari . . .''

"And where is Hugh now?''

"Dunno. In Munich, I think. What's it got to do with me? Listen, can you take your clothes off? How much time did they say you could have with me? I love to make love . . .''

The woman stood up and threw off her gown. Eugene saw the bruises on her shoulders, her wrinkled, yellowish skin.

"You can't now,'' he said hurriedly. "They'll be here in a minute, we haven't got enough time.''

"But I don't need long. Come on, please! . . . Let me look at you, I beg you . . .

"I'll come again tomorrow OK? I'll be here at two o'clock.''

"They won't let you see me again. They never let anyone see me twice . . .''

"OK, put on your gown, we'll talk a bit more, and then we'll make love.''

"Her will is paralysed,'' Eugene said to himself as he watched Emma obediently pick up her gown and pull it over her yellow, angular shoulders. "It's always the same—

first heroin, then this horror . . . What benefit is all this to Stepanov? Nobody will ever believe me.''

"And where is Uncle Siegfried now?'' he continued.

"I pray to God for him to die, then I wouldn't be so ashamed to be alive . . .'' She began to laugh again. "To be alive—I *think* I'm alive, aren't I? . . . Yes, I'm alive,'' she repeated, with more conviction in her voice, "—because I can breathe, eat, drink, piss and shit. No, that's existence, not life. Life is something else. I used to be alive when John was there. When he left there was the powder, and when that was gone then it began to be like this: eat, drink, piss, shit . . .''

"But where is your brother Zepp?'' Eugene went on, conscious that his monotonous questions were irritating the woman. But he couldn't work out how better to talk to her, her reactions were so unpredictable. "Is he dead too?''

"Oh, no! Zepp sends upright Germans off to Africa to defend freedom. He makes speeches on the border, rounds up his friends in Munich. Surely you know Zepp Shantz, don't you?''

"Does he really live in Munich?''

"What? D'you think I'm making all this up? You're like Shaw! You're just another bloody bloodhound! He didn't believe me either! And I'm telling the truth!''

The woman began to shout louder and louder. The door opened and two men in white coats came in, looked reproachfully at Eugene, and led Emma away, still shrieking. His ears echoed for a long time afterwards with her despairing cry: "What, d'you think I'm mad?''

Stepanov telephoned his newspaper contacts in Munich. They gave him the address of Zepp Shantz's New German Party straight away, without even consulting the files . . .

Investigation No. 7

To Slavin

Find out everything you can about Dubov. The nature of his relationship with Vinter. Is there any record of meetings between him and Lawrence or Glebb—even accidental ones?

Centre

To Centre

I am unable to confirm the fact of any meeting between Dubov and Glebb or Lawrence. According to uncorroborated evidence, Dubov once accompanied Vinter to the tennis court when she was playing with Lawrence, but we do not know whether the two men knew each other. Dubov avoided contact with Americans, spent most of his time in the Embassy, the Trade Mission, or at home. He only made one three-day trip around the country in his own car. His standard of behaviour was irreproachable. He hardly drinks, he's a man of few words, reserved in character, with an outstanding capacity for political and economic analysis. However, Zotov related one fact which put me on my guard—from the moral/ethical point of view. In the first few months after they met, one day after Olga Vinter had hurt her foot, Zotov didn't have a car and asked Dubov to take her in to the hospital. Dubov took Olga, but later asked Zotov for five dollars, apparently to cover the high price of petrol. I went back over Dubov's route: if Zotov had called a taxi, the journey would have cost him two dollars thirty-five cents. If we take this shopkeeper mentality further, then the return trip would have cost four dollars seventy cents. So, in fact, Dubov made a profit of thirty cents. From the purely operational angle the story is trivial, but perhaps it gives the basis for a second look at Dubov's moral character. I should underline that despite this, all our people here testify with one voice to his neatness, self discipline, politeness—indeed there is no mention of a single fault.

Slavin

Top Secret

To Major-General Konstantinov

In response to your repeated request, I can state that Dubov, Sergei Dmitrievich, flew yesterday to Adler on flight 852.

Lieutenant-Colonel Zykov

From the file on "White Man":

Note: "White Man" was the code-name given to Dubov by the Abkhasian* Chekists, because he arrived at the Black Sea in a lightweight white suit, white shirt and white bow-tie. His shoes, by contrast, were black, heavy, and blunt-toed—an old-fashioned American style:

Booking in at holiday block *Mayak*, Room 212, "White Man" went down to breakfast at 8.47 hrs. He was placed at a table with two women, one of whom, a brunette, aged around twenty-three, left the café accompanied by him at 9.17 hrs.
  "White Man" proposed that *"Brunette"* come with him to his room, to which *Brunette* agreed.
  They spent fifty-two minutes in "White Man's" room, came out in swimming costumes and set off for the beach. There they swam and sunbathed until 12.49 hrs., after which they had lunch together in the same café. They were at lunch from 13.05 hrs. to 13.51 hrs. Then they went to "White Man's" room where they stayed until 16.10 hrs., after which they returned to the beach. They came in at 18.26 hrs., went to dinner, sitting at the same table as in the morning. "White Man" ordered a bottle of wine with the meal, label—*Tibaani*. Afterwards he asked "Brunette" to go for a walk with him. They met nobody, but proceeded out of the grounds of the *Pitsunda* holiday-home. Near the post office "White Man" left "Brunette" for a moment and, after changing three roubles into fifteen kopeck coins, telephoned a Moscow number and spoke to

a man called Viktor Lvovich. The only phrases of this that were audible outside the booth were: "We must hold on," and that he himself "would like to go with her, but everyone must do their duty to society." "White Man" urged Viktor Lvovich not to get up for a few more days, saying he would be back from "a business trip" in a week. After this conversation, "White Man" asked "Brunette" to go to the bar with him, where they danced until twelve o'clock, afterwards returning to his room where they stayed the night.

Gabunia

The Moscow number which Dubov had phoned belonged to Viktor Lvovich Vinter.

"Brunette" turned out to be Olga Vronskaya, twenty-two years of age, Muscovite, department secretary, Komsomol member, unmarried, nationality Ukrainian.

The doctor in City Hospital Number 52 looked at Konstantinov in amazement: "But I've already explained everything, comrade . . ."

"To whom?"

"The people from her institute, then of course her father. He's a very respected person, I was duty bound to tell him everything . . .

"You see, I am a friend of her husband . . ."

"Ah—the one who's abroad?"

"Yes."

"I see . . . I gather he doesn't know anything yet?"

"No."

"Well, tell him that she didn't suffer any pain—it was a sudden and complete loss of consciousness . . . A strange, idiotic death . . . Her friend said that Olga was feverish from early evening. He gave her aspirin and she fell asleep, but her temperature stayed high . . . He remembered that she had had a cough for about a week, but she ignored it, played tennis—silly, of course . . . In the morning he called the ambulance . . . We tried everything we could, but apparently there was a collapse of the lungs—which we can't do anything to stop."

"Why 'apparently'?"

The doctor didn't understand. He looked questioningly at Konstantinov.

"The post-mortem would, surely, give an exact answer," the other explained, "rather than your present approximate one, as to why a healthy young woman should die so suddenly."

"But there was no post-mortem—excuse me, what is your name?"

"Konstantin Ivanovich."

"Pleased to meet you. And I am Archil Mikhailovich. So there we are: Viktor Lvovich asked us not to open her up, and his word is law around here—such a great surgeon, Moscow's women simply worship him and rightly so . . ."

"Archil Mikhailovich, could you tell me, please, in more detail, how this all happened?"

"Well, I suppose I can . . . I was on duty. In the morning, about eight o'clock, a man telephoned . . ."

"Her friend?"

"No. Sergei Dmitrievich only appeared later, he came with me in the resuscitation unit . . . The neighbour phoned, I forget his name, an old chap, a military man . . . He said that a woman was unconscious, asked us to come quickly. So we went. Olga Viktorova was not simply unconscious, I could see at once that she was in her death throes. Her pulse was nil, her eyelids bluish, the pupils hardly reacting. In the car I put her on the drip feed, and as soon as we arrived called Professor Evlampieva, and we began a blood-transfusion. We went on trying to save her for about four hours, though, to be honest, I felt from the start that it was hopeless . . ."

"But why was there no post-mortem?"

"As I explained to you—"

"No, you didn't explain, Archil Mikhailovich."

"Viktor Lvovich begged us not to . . ."

"That's no explanation. One evening a woman is

healthy, the next morning she's dead, and you don't carry out a post-mortem! What if it was some infection?''

''No, it wasn't an infection. All the signs were of a sudden and total collapse of the lungs.''

''Does it happen often?''

''I personally have never seen such a thing . . . Well, it could happen after three to six days, if the lung process was not treated.''

''So—her friend . . . What's his name?''

''Sergei Dmitrievich. It was him who told us she had been coughing for some time, that she was sick . . .''

''So, it wasn't an infection.''

''But total lung collapses are well known, they are recorded in medical practice. D'you remember the American policeman who was about to give new evidence on Kennedy's assassination? He fell ill, they put him under medical observation, and two days later he was dead, died of lung collapse.''

Konstantinov stood up suddenly. His eyes, usually smiling and pale blue in tint, now became tiny gimlets of grey.

''Quite Archil Mikhailovich. That's what happened . . .''

''It was while I was on duty, as I said.''

''That is, four days ago?''

''Exactly.''

''Could I ask you to get me a copy of the death certificate? I'll send it to her husband, that'll be more straightforward, no questions, don't you think? Especially since her friend brought her here . . . He was very upset, I expect . . .''

''Yes, we had to give him an injection . . . But after he had a good cry he was better. He has a lot of will-power. When Viktor Lvovich came—he was at a conference in Dubna, they called him back—well, he was in such a state of shock that Olga's friend took him away. Sergei Dmitrievich organised the funeral himself the same day. He really stood up well to it.''

Academician of Medicine Sergei Sergeyevich Vogulev was an old hunting friend of Konstantinov. They had made many expeditions together: to Karbadino-Balkario to see Khazhismel Sanshokov, to Akhtyri, to Astrakhan. Unlike Gmyrya, Vogulev was a hunter-photographer whose camera was as important to him as his gun. It was him who turned Konstantinov into a photographer too (though the latter preferred the real thing, a shot at a moving target, and envied one thing and one thing only in life—a good rifle in the hands of another hunter).

Vogulev cared little for trophies, happily gave away his boar's tusks, and loved above all to sit down and eat and drink in the company of other hunters. He considered that in this stressful age no sanatorium could provide the same release as boar or bear hunting.

"All these therapies," he used to say, "these new medicines—acupuncture, hypnosis, fasting—are a load of rubbish. Game's the thing, it all comes down to the knife. You see, I am a real surgeon, after all! But it's the last resort, when cancer has you in its grip. As for heart disease, ulcers—what better cure than hunting, here in the mountains where the smell of chestnut trees, musty grass and mountain springs is in the air?"

It was Vogulev who Konstantinov rang, after he had taken a brief pause for thought. During crises like this he did not take his Zhiguli out of its garage, but drove instead in the Volga with its radio—to maintain constant contact with his units. Konovalov, Panov, Proskurin, Gmyrya—all of them had now been "called up indefinitely." Their families hardly saw them, they spent their time receiving reports and breaking them up into a multiplicity of minor questions, rightly judging that the more careful their analysis of small details, the more reliable would be the overall conclusion.

"Sergei Sergeyevich, I'd like to drop in on you, if that's all right?" Konstantinov said. "I'll be straight over."

"Come either in fifteen minutes, or later on this evening, Konstantin Ivanovich," the other replied.

"You're just beginning an operation?"

"Much worse. I've got some doctorate interviews to do."

"You couldn't put them off?"

"Has something happened?"

"Yes, it has."

Vogulev heard Konstantinov out, then lifted the telephone and dialled a number.

"Irina Fadeyeva," he said, "—I'll be an hour late. Please make sure that they leave the theses belonging to Gavrilin, Daryalova and Martirosyan until I get there— we can't let their 'well-wishers' fail them, now can we! What? . . . Well, tell them I'm held up in an emergency operation. Thank you."

He replaced the receiver, wiped his strong, though lined, face with a dry palm and rose: "Let's go," he announced. "I won't phone him first, I don't want to ask him twice about her death. Will you wait for me in the car?"

"Yes. Only I must implore you once again: Viktor Lvovich must on no account suspect what it is that is worrying you. Please bear that constantly in mind . . ."

"I worked in the same hospital as Vinter during the war, Konstantin Ivanovich. We slept under the same overcoat . . ."

"Then you misunderstand me. I haven't the slightest doubt as to his honesty, Sergei Sergeyevich."

When they were in the car, Vogulev lit a cigarette and scowled more darkly still: "I have a photograph of his daughter somewhere in my papers, she was three months old . . . We were surrounded by the enemy near Rzhev, he gave me the photo, wrote down an address and asked me, if I ever got through, to find his little Oyenka. I really lost my temper, and swore at him. He said that they would probably shoot him—being a Jew— but maybe I would be safe . . . So I shouted back that surely they'd kill a Bolshevik as quickly as a Jew—so more than likely I too would be dead. But he was frail in health even then, always coughing, so I took pity on him and kept the photograph. That kind of request is special, it's sacred, when you're entrusted with a baby only three months old . . ."

"And if he asks how you heard about the tragedy?"

"I'll say I read the obituary in the paper."

"There's been no obituary in the paper."

"Christ . . . Well then, friends told me."

"Who exactly?"

Vogulev looked at Konstantinov.

"You're holding something back, aren't you?"

"Yes, indeed I am."

"Why?"

"Because your medical orderly, say, can talk about any suspicion she might have and I don't think that would be too terrible. But I represent the Cheka. I'm not allowed to share my suspicions. I can only operate on *facts.*"

Vinter lay on the divan, a folded dressing-gown propping up his head, a rug drawn up to his chin.

"Ah, Serezhenka," he murmured, and an old man's tears at once began to stream down his cheeks. "It's good you've come . . . Would you like a drink?"

"I've got some interviews to do, Vitya. It's hard enough sober, and once you've had a nip, with my temper . . ."

"I have to take a little, you know. I can't help it. As soon as I close my eyes, I see her there in front of me . . ."

"Yes, grief is terrible, Vitya. I don't even know what to say to you. Why not *us.* Why *them,* our children?"

"Pour me a drop, eh?"

"Spirit?" Vogulev asked, pouring it into a measuring glass.

"Yes. Remember how you taught me to drink?"

"You mean, the time you got stuck in the marsh?"

"Yes."

"Last year I went back there to hunt. Silly really. Thought it would be just as wild as it was in '43. They've built a china works there, a new road, in the villages there are TV aerials . . ."

"When was the last time you saw Olga?"

"I never saw her, Vitya. After the war we all became so successful in our separate lives, we were so sure of things. It's only grief brings people together . . . I never saw her."

"Who told you about it?"

"Gnidyuk."

"Yes, yes, Mikola . . . He called me . . ."

Vinter drank, then drew the rug up under his chin, and shivered.

"I'd go after her, Serezha."

"But you've still got work to do, Vitya."

"What for? Who for? *You* can still go on working—cutting, sawing, looking for the kernel. But I'll never pick up a scalpel again. Believe me, I mean it . . ."

"Why didn't you phone me when Olga was taken to hospital, Vitya?"

"They only called me back from Dubna when it was all over."

"What about the post-mortem?"

"I wouldn't let them do one."

"Why?"

"All the signs were a collapse of the lungs. But why? I've never seen anything like it, Serezha. But I couldn't, you know, I couldn't allow it. It wasn't just her alone I buried, Serezha, I buried her child . . ."

"What?!"

Vinter sniffed back tears. He stretched out his dry, smooth, delicate hands towards the measuring-glass.

"Don't, Vitya. You're so white . . ."

"Oh, stop it, please! And pour me some more."

He drank the glass, and placed his icy fingers on Vogulev's arm.

"Do you have any grandchildren?"

"A grand-daughter."

"A grand-daughter," Vinter repeated. "That's wonderful, when it's a girl, they're so affectionate . . . I so much wanted a little more happiness in my life, just to see a little baby in the house . . ."

"Are you sure she wanted to keep the baby?"

"I didn't know anything about it at all, it was Serezha who told me everything . . ."

"Her husband, is that?"

"No, it's not, old chap—but don't worry about that! Her husband is abroad, but Serezha was the real man in her life. No, no, she had separated from her husband, she was very honest, my girl, she would never have done any-thing . . . Anyway, that's life . . . She wasn't divorced, and he works in some secret institute. It would have de-stroyed the lad's life, you know how they love to wash people's dirty linen . . . Why uncover everything and de-stroy his life too? Olyenka's gone, but he loved her, so why let him suffer? Pour me some more—please . . ."

"Why don't you come over to my flat, Vitya? For the time being, eh? Katya would love to see you, you can help out with our grand-daughter. Come now, don't cry, don't break your heart . . ."

"Thank you, no. I can't go anywhere. Serezha will soon be here, he's going to move in with me. We'll support each other, as though my little girl was with us."

"Vitya, I beg you, until this Serezha comes, let me take you with me, eh?"

Vinter shook his head. He turned his dark eyes, huge with tears towards Vogulev, and replied: "Serezha, when I die, bury me next to Olyenka, promise?"

After returning to the KGB, Konstantinov called together his unit heads.

"It's time to have a proper look at the Dubov hypothesis. We'll call him 'Woodman,' shall we? *Dub* ('oak'), wood, 'Woodman'—it seems convenient enough. It's clear that from now on we'll have to keep in constant touch by telephone. The countdown has begun, the next hours will decide the case, although—" he looked meaningfully at Proskurin, "I must remind you that any kind of haste or crudity of approach at this stage could scupper the whole thing. In the next few days we must reconstruct—preferably, minute by minute—every detail of the last hours of Olga Vinter's life. We can't interrogate anyone yet—that's plain. We've got no hard evi-dence against Dubov, so we must work with a jeweller's pre-cision. That's the first thing. Next, we've got to check on who, apart from Dubov, was present at the talks when the Nagonian Minister of the Economy came here with their gov-ernment delegation."

"The Minister of Defence was there, too," Gmyrya re-marked.

"True—only the question of deliveries was dealt with by the Economics Minister. Third. We've got to prove to the Procurator—that's my job, probably—that an exhumation and a post-mortem are vital if we are to discover the cause of Vinter's death. But it would be better, of course, if we could deploy for him some weightier arguments than we have yet.

"We've got a lot already," Proskurin remarked.

"For *us*, yes. But we need to convince *him*. After all, we'll be asking for his sanction for action, and he'll ask what evidence we have against Dubov. What do we say?"

"We'll say that it's no coincidence Luns is down in Pitsunda."

"That's no reply. You haven't yet proved to the Procurator, have you, that Luns is from the CIA? If we catch him on a mission, then that's a different matter. Today Luns remains a diplomat in everyone's eyes, with all the protocol to protect him. Try to prove the contrary, I personally wouldn't. All new incoming information, I emphasise *all*, must be on my desk, preferably in two copies. The first will go to Pyotr Georgevich as soon as I receive it.

"Well, go on," said General Fyodorov. "Let's lay out the jigsaw. Do you want to, or will you allow me?"

"I'll allow you, Pyotr Georgevich," Konstantinov smiled.

"You are very decent, I appreciate your confidence. Let's begin at the beginning."

Fyodorov glanced at the assembled company. "So—at the start of this operation Konstantinov gambled on an assumption. As a result of this gamble, which in the given instance was entirely reasonable, that is to say not harmful to society's interests, we came out with a general area which is of special concern to the CIA. This was evidenced—or rather, is evidenced—by the fact that fighting is about to break out in Nagonia and the CIA needs constantly updated information on what we know of their plans. We know something about them—but no more than that. Up to this moment we do not know the identity of the CIA agent working in Moscow, nor his contact in the Embassy. We have intercepted their radio transmissions, but we can't decode them, and, conscious of our power-lessness, we've been forced to throw a wide net. We've investigated Zotov, Vinter, Paramonov and Shargin. Twice—with Shargin and Paramonov—we were barking up the wrong tree. Paramonov was knocked out—to the count of ten, you could say. What did your men call him? 'Mac-aroni Misha'? 'Misha' I understand, but why *'Maca-roni'?''*

"Because he gave his wife so little money she could only buy macaroni. He starved her, poor woman, and then went out chasing the girls.''

"She should have gone on hunger strike, water and honey.''

"Honey's not cheap these days, at the market, you know. You couldn't exist on honey with the money he gave her, Pyotr Georgevich.''

"Funny, isn't it really . . . . Fasting has become expen-sive, eh? Well, fine. Paramonov dropped out, then Shargin was knocked out as well. Finally, there is Vinter. A strange death. A total lung collapse, you say?''

"Judging by the fact there was no post-mortem, and by how Dubov was able to pressurize old Vinter, there is indeed something strange here, Pyotr Georgevich.''

"You instituted a criminal investigation at the very be-ginning of this case, didn't you? Because of the radio transmission. So you have the basis for a legal exhuma-tion—or so it seems to me . . . But Olga's father was against the post-mortem, wasn't he? Would it be right morally to do the exhumation?''

"It would be cruel, yes. But it would be right, morally, Pyotr Georgevich.''

"What reason would you give?''

"That a CIA agent eliminated Vinter to avoid expo-sure.''

"What exposure would the CIA agent have had to fear? Who is he? What's the evidence? Why could Vinter have exposed him? What if she was an accomplice? And who can say it wasn't an accident?''

"We can exclude any accident.''

"Your facts?''

"Dubov always described himself as her lover. But no sooner had he seen her underground, than off he goes on holiday. On the very first day he takes a girl to bed, goes out on the town! Can you imagine, Pyotr Georgevich, he goes out dancing!''

"He goes dancing? The son of a bitch, eh? Hm . . . He goes dancing. And that's evidence, is it?''

"You bet it is!''

"No, I'm sorry, it isn't. I haven't heard any evidence yet. And nor have you. But another thing: have you or Slavin got sufficient facts to exclude Zotov from the list of suspects?''

"I'm used to trusting Slavin.''

"I am too, as you know. But all the same, you haven't answered me.''

"If Slavin insists Zotov is innocent, I must rely on his judgement.''

"I don't need assurances as to Zotov's innocence, I need facts proving he is not connected with the case, Konstantin Ivanovich.''

"I'll send Slavin a telegram right away. Although I had a completely different one ready—the go-ahead to return.''

"You'll have to rewrite it, then.'' General Fyodorov picked up the direct government line and dialled a number: "Hello. Good afternoon, when are you expecting Vasily Lukyanych? Oh, his flight's left . . . Fine, but who's standing in? Aha, thanks.'' He dialled another number. "Nikolai Grigorevich, hello, this is Fyodorov from the KGB. Good afternoon. Yes, all right, thanks. Nikolai Grigorevich, I have a question. Did you take part in the talks with Nagonia? Yes, that's what I mean. And who produced the documents? No, no—I mean the special deliveries. I see . . . Absolutely. From what department? Dubov? My next in command will be right over. His name is General Konstantinov, can you find the time? Ah, I see . . . Well, well! Thank you. Good-bye.''

Pyotr Georgevich replaced the receiver, took off his glasses, and stowed them in his case.

"So there we are," he said. "The documents on economic questions were prepared by Dubov. I congratulate you—Proskurin is with the ministry at this very moment. Tidy work, General, very tidy. Get ready an application, and contact the Procurator's Office. We'll exhume the body."

The diagnosis of the experts who conducted the exhumation and post-mortem on the body of Olga Vinter concluded as follows: the collapse of both lungs had been caused by the introduction of a strong-smelling substance, unknown to Soviet pharmacologists. Examination of the traces of it remaining in the body indicated that loss of consciousness could have occurred within thirty to forty seconds, though death would have resulted significantly later. The experts concluded as follows: "We, the undersigned, consider that, since the substance in question is unknown in the USSR, the actions of the doctors in casualty who dealt with OV Vinter were entirely correct. We know of no antidote which could have saved Vinter's life."

The experts also commented on the question as to whether the dead woman had been pregnant: the answer was negative. They further declared: "We must also give a negative reply to the question as to whether there were any traces of chronic lung disease in the organism. We can state firmly that the dead woman had been in perfect health until the moment when the unknown substance was administered to her."

To Slavin

Pull out all the stops to get a quick reply to our query regarding Cook & Sons. Mask carefully your interest in Dubov.

                                                          Centre

To Centre

Cook & Sons do not have an office in Lewisburg. The
two-room luxury suite No. 1096 was booked for Dubov
twelve times from March to July 1976. Cost—$95 a day.
Dubov's monthly salary in the period March-July was
$500.

Slavin

14

Glebb

"Are you alone, Andrew?"

Zotov stepped back into his hall, surprised. In the darkness of the stairwell (he rented a flat in a house where they went early to bed) stood Pilar. Her face, set in its frame of dark hair, seemed anxious, pale.

"Come in, Pilar, glad to see you. How did you find me here?"

"My dear, dear Andrew . . ."

"What's happened? Something worrying you? Please come in."

"Thank you. Can we go out onto the balcony?"

"Wherever you like. Only it's even hotter out there than inside."

"Andrew, listen carefully to me. I've come to tell you something. It's not just that I love you and want to be with you always—even in Russia, if you want. It's something else . . . Wait, Andrew, you promised to listen. You haven't seen Glebb for two days, and nor have I. He's not just a businessman, Andrew, I think he's connected with the CIA . . ."

"With who?"

"The CIA . . . And he's not here just by chance, darling Andrew. I don't know what's up with them, but Lawrence said that after what has happened, they could arrest quite a few Russians—including you."

"What is this rubbish, Pilar?! I can't understand a word of it."

"My dear old fool, you will in a moment. I would never have dared to come to you like this and confess that . . . Unless that woman . . . Andrew, Olga's dead! She's dead . . ."

"What?!"

"Yes. She died suddenly, they buried her two days ago . . ."

Zotov slumped forward on the edge of the wicker chair, placing his elbows heavily on the ironwork balcony, and wiped his forehead.

"But why hasn't anyone told me? Come on, this is madness, a stupid joke. It can't be true, Pilar!"

"Shhh, quiet. It *is* true, my dear friend, it's true."

"What's the code?" Zotov suddenly stood up. "Do you know what's the code for Paris? They say you can phone via Paris. How did you find out about Olga? What happened to her? A car accident?"

"I don't know the details. All I know is one thing—she's dead. I don't know the Paris code. If you like, I'll try to book a call to Madrid. You don't have anything to drink, do you? I'm shaking all over."

"It's over there . . . In the bar, I'll get it in a minute."

"No, I will. Don't worry. Ice for you?"

"What? Yes, with ice. No—I don't need ice. Pour me a glassfull, no ice at all."

Pilar carried in a tray with a wine glass of red wine for herself, and a large tumbler of whisky for Zotov. She gazed fixedly at him as he slowly drank it back. Then she lit him a cigarette. Her fingers were cool and soft, she stroked his face as if she was a blind woman, anxious and quivering.

"My poor darling," she continued, in a whisper. "I can feel the grief weighing down on you, I can feel it—please let me stay with you. I know it's against your rules, but I could live here. Nobody would see or recognise me. Or let me take you back to my house . . ."

"What? Hang on, Pilar, I still can't understand this at all, love. Are you quite sure we can phone Moscow, via Madrid?"

Pilar picked up the telephone—Zotov's flat seemed to

be crammed with them, there was even a pink receiver in the bathroom—and dialled the code for Madrid.

"Rosita, hello, darling. Yes, it's me. Can you help me? Yes, it's very important. It's for a person I love, I wrote to you about him, it's Zotov. Yes. Thank you. Could you telephone Moscow right away, we can't get through from here. Yes. Write down the number. What's the number, Andrew?"

"Just coming. Thanks. But where should I phone if she's . . . ? My home number is . . . Wait a minute, I've forgotten. But surely—"

"Who would you like to talk to?"

"Her father."

Pilar read out the number: "Rosita, as soon as they connect you, ring my code here, I'm at Andrew's, 803-15-48. And hold the receivers against each other. I—we're waiting. It's really important, Rosita, we're really desperate . . ."

Two hours later Pilar left the flat. In the car below Glebb was waiting for her. On the other side of the street, a supercharged Ford was parked, crammed with men in hats pulled down over their heads.

"Well?" said Glebb: "How did it go?"

"You know, I feel sorry for him."

"Me too. Anyway, did you put him to bed?"

"I'm sorry for him," Pilar repeated. "Can I have one of your cigarettes, please, mine have finished."

"Think about 'Mastermind,' *guapeña*. He's your friend, after all. This is a dirty business of ours, you have to control your feelings."

"I didn't put him to bed, John. It would have been unnatural, believe me. I'm a woman, I feel it better. Your calculations were wrong."

"I'm never wrong when I calculate about men. How did he react when you said there might be a scandal?"

"Didn't even ask about it. As though he hadn't heard. Or maybe he didn't understand."

"Good. What do you think, will he come to see you tomorrow?"

Pilar shook her head in reply: "He won't come, John. He'll be off to Moscow first thing in the morning."

"Their flight went today, there's only Friday's left this week."

"He'll take any flight."

"They can't. They only fly on their own planes. He won't be going anywhere tomorrow . . ."

"Shall we go?"

"Wait. I'm tired . . ."

"Why?"

"From the waiting, Pilar. I get so tired waiting for you, girl. I get tired when you're working. It's really heavy work—waiting . . ."

In 3 hours Glebb received the tape of Zotov's conversation with Rosita. She connected him with old man Vinter. The sound quality was abysmal, but Zotov was able to hear the awful truth—"Olyenka is dead . . ."

In 3 hours, 40 minutes Glebb arrived at the Hilton. He went straight up to the bar, where he knew Paul Dick would be sitting, drinking beer and scribbling with his felt-tip pen on paper napkins. Glebb was amazed to see that it wasn't an article Paul was working on, but a poem.

"Hello, Paul. Here you are drinking in solitary splendour, and you don't yet know about the scandal that has broken out in our corral?"

"There are too many of them already. Which one do you mean, precisely?"

"In Lawrence's department."

"Our chief spy?"

"Exactly. They've broken into his safe. If it was the opposite side, then nobody will ever know what they got. But if it was local gangsters, then we can expect demands for money for the return of the material. And then poor old Lawrence will have to pay—that kind of stuff is valuable. He was always so mysterious, was Lawrence, they must have thought he had cash in the safe. Mind you, it's funny—renting a suite in a hotel for that kind of work."

"Why is there no word about it here?"

''Because the Hilton's management are smart people. They wouldn't want to frighten off the customers, would they?''

''What's the room number? Do you know?''

''Yes—but don't quote me. 608.''

''Is Lawrence there?''

''How should I know? If he is, let me know how he reacts to your visit.''

Paul Dick laughed strangely, slipped off his stool and turned to the barman. ''I expect I'll be back in a minute. If this gentleman decides to have a drink—make him up a highball on my account.''

Glebb followed him with his eyes. Then he turned to the barman: ''Pour me a glass of orange juice,'' he said, with a mild smile. ''On my own account.''

In 3 hours, 52 minutes Robert Lawrence, having looked Paul Dick up and down in a gloomy fashion, asked: ''And who passed information of such a kind to you?''

''I don't reveal my sources, Mr. Lawrence. All I want is an answer—is it true that secret documents connected with the strategic interests of our country have gone astray?''

''I cannot comment on that question.''

''Could I then phrase it another way? Is it true that a group of unknown persons has tried to steal documents belonging to the firm for which you work?''

''Yes. That is so.''

''Then, I would like to know: is it true that you are an officer of the Central Intelligence Agency?''

''I have no connection with that organisation. I am the representative of International Telephonic.''

''What sort of interest could documents belonging to your firm have, and to whom?''

''The names of our contractors, the volume of our trade, prices—all this has a certain interest for our competitors.''

''So you are saying that the robbery was carried out by your competitors?''

''Yes, exactly. By people wishing to hinder the development of good relations between our country and Lewisburg.''

"If your firm's dealings are above board, how could this harm relations between you and Lewisburg, Mr. Lawrence?"

"Any business, however honest, can be falsified, just as any individual can be drawn through the mud. That is all I want to say, thank you."

"One last question, Mr. Lawrence."

"If it really is your last question I will answer it."

"Are you the same Robert Lawrence, employed by International Telephonic, who gave evidence to the Congressional Committee on subversion in Chile?"

"I gave evidence in the sense that we had no connection to the tragedy which occurred in Santiago. But I would prefer, sir, for your question and my answer to be off the record and not to appear in your newspaper."

"If that is your request, then I am ready to accede to it. But in that case, could you not accede to mine, and tell me what they stole, Mr. Lawrence?"

"You know the ropes, surely you realise that I cannot give you an answer to that? You must realise that it could prejudice the safety of people—good people, believe me, people who are true and trusted colleagues in our honest enterprise."

In 5 hours, 13 minutes, Director of Police Stau called Glebb, who was sitting opposite Lawrence by the telephone.

"Everything is OK," Stau reported.

Glebb carefully hung up, and sighed—deeply, with relief—before laughing: "Well, boss, now I really can have a glass of sherry—and with pleasure!"

Indeed, Glebb had good reason for his satisfaction. For the Lewisburg police, called out by Zotov's neighbours (disturbed by the sound of a broken window), had found the Russian bound and gagged, his flat turned upside down. When detectives from the criminal police searched the house, they discovered, to their great surprise, a portable radio-transmitter in the larder, and, in the bottom drawer of Zotov's desk, pages of written material in code. The coded information was exactly like the information intercepted regularly over the previous twelve months by

Soviet counter-intelligence. When Zotov came to, in hospital, he was asked by the detective about the transmitter, but refused to reply. The Soviet Consul was summoned by the police, who put the same question to him. All Zotov would say, however, was that it was a provocation, and that he would like to be flown back to Moscow.

"That will be decided by the Court, Mr. Zotov," the police detective told him. "Objects whose import into this country is forbidden were found in your flat. Obviously, his Excellency the Consul realises that I cannot break the law of my country. Until we can establish how you brought the transmitter into Lewisburg, what you have been transmitting, to whom and about what, we have no right to allow your departure. And also, from now on there will be a guard on your ward."

The evening newspapers came out with the headlines: "Russian spies at work in Lewisburg."

And only one single publication, close to the American Embassy, issued a dissenting commentary. "A transmitter—in any country which considers itself free—is not a proof of guilt," the commentary noted. "A column of figures does not have to be a code, so the arrest of a Russian engineer seems to us an unfortunate mistake, if not a crime. For as we have discovered, a certain American firm has recently suffered a similar robbery, where apparently the persons responsible were not looking for money. Whose hand is pulling the strings?"

Slavin put down the editorial and telephoned Glebb.

"John," he said: "Hello. How are you doing?"

"Hi there, my dear Vit! Glad to hear from you! How are you?"

"Fine. Where's Paul got to?"

"As far as I know, he's locked himself in his room to do some writing. He told me that he had some sensational information. Would you like to have dinner with me?"

"With pleasure. Only first I want to try to see Zotov in hospital."

"In hospital! What's the matter with him?"

"Haven't you read the newspapers?!" Slavin exclaimed. He could just imagine Glebb's triumphant face at this moment. "You're behind the times. He's been spying for somebody."

"Stop it! He's the most gentle person."

"A spy can only be a gentle person if he's an amateur, not a professional. Ring me at seven, I'll wait for you to call, OK?"

"I'll phone *you,* Vit. Give my regards to Zotov, I remembered him in the end—despite your Russian surnames, the language barrier, you know. Ask him, maybe we can help somehow?"

"Thanks. Definitely, John. That's very kind of you."

15

Tempo

"Dear Friend, We are pleased to pass on to you greeting from your charming friend 'P.' She asked us to say that your affairs are going well and that the shares which she bought from your salary have been well invested so you can expect a twelve to thirteen per cent return on them. Your pay to date is now $32,772.12. However, you requested us to send you medicine and some gold and silver articles, so we have deducted $641.03 from the total, leaving $32,131.09 to be paid. We must re-emphasize that your information is of extraordinary interest. Our leader considers that you are making an enormous contribution to the liberation of Nagonia from Communist tyranny. We would ask you to continue sending information regularly. The most sensitive question at this stage is the same old one: does Moscow know about our aid to the opposition groups? And if they know, then what exactly do they know? Should we expect them to step up their assistance to the Griso regime? As always, we value highly your information on the ground as to when and from what ports transport convoys are sailing. In the next few days we will send you new recommendations regarding the points you raised in your last message. We would like to congratulate you—all your fears can now be laid to rest. We have introduced the person you know into the 'cover operation,' and all possible suspicions will be directed at him—at least for the next few months. Meanwhile, we will probably limit our radio contact for a while, and start looking at new forms of collaboration. With all best wishes, your friends 'L' and 'D.' ''

To the Central Intelligence Agency

We would be most grateful if you could send us the latest information on the Nagonia situation. Our Embassy is concerned that Ogano's statements regarding his sympathies towards Peking are completely unqualified. The opinion of our own observers is that this job has been done in a somewhat slapdash manner, for Africa remains convinced that Ogano's forces are being trained by CIA advisers, and that his radicalism is sanctioned by Washington. Are Ogano's contacts sufficiently well controlled? We await an unambiguous answer to this question, for your proposed actions on the African continent must be linked to our overall strategy in the international arena.

Research Section, State Department

To CIA Station Officer Robert Lawrence in Lewisburg

Correct Ogano's public statements. They repeat Peking's analysis too obviously, while at the same time—according to the State Department—his contacts with us are clear to all and sundry. This contradiction is likely to make the Africans increasingly suspicious of his sincerity. The opinion expressed by the State Department corresponds to our information coming from agent "Mastermind" in Moscow. Tell Ogano to dissociate himself even more clearly from "imperialism," and to turn his fire on the passivity of the State Department and the "over-cautious restrain" of its pro-Kremlin elements.

CIA Deputy Director Michael Welsh

From a Speech by the US Special Envoy:

When my country is charged with supporting separatists and is called an ally of Mr. Ogano, I never cease to be amazed by the dishonesty of such accusers. The speeches of Mr. Ogano are permeated with the spirit of radicalism, and his criticisms of my country leave impartial observers in no doubt that this person is far from the ideals which we profess. My government can bear no responsibility for the actions of Mr. Ogano. To tie him in somehow with the aims and methods of our foreign policy means to slander my country and its government . . .

To the Ministry of Foreign Affairs, Peking

Ogano has informed me of the fruitful discussions he had with Lawrence—whom you already know. During the negotiations Ogano was promised a new consignment of helicopters and thirty light tanks. Clearly, these new supplies will be decisive in the events due to unfold here very shortly.

> Du Li, Chinese Ambassador to Nagonia

Paul Dick

This report is filed by your correspondent Paul Dick. I am standing in the African jungle, which comes right down to the sea shore, near the headquarters of General Ogano, leader of the Nagonian nationalists.

"Mr. Ogano, whom are you relying on in your struggle?"

"I rely on the people of Nagonia—*all* the people, from great to small. They hate George Griso, who is nothing but a pseudo-intellectual, and alien to every aspiration of our nation."

"What are the aspirations of the Nagonian nation?"

"Freedom and independence."

"General, some people call you a stooge of Peking. Could you please comment on that view?"

"They also call me an agent of the CIA. These are

nothing but hired hacks, bought by Moscow and Havana, trying to smear my reputation. I hate American imperialism, which is the stronghold of world reaction. Mao's ideas are of course an attraction, but that doesn't mean I am connected to Peking. My struggle is paid for by our own people, with donations from all the tribes. We are armed not so much with machine-guns, as with the support of the nation.''

''Griso has repeated twice already that he is ready to sit down at the negotiating table with you, and to resolve all the issues between you peacefully. How do you respond to such suggestions?''

''I don't believe a word of it. He responds to one thing and one thing only—force. So I am going to speak with the language of force—such is the will of the nation, and I am only expressing the views of my fellow tribesmen. The rest means no more to me than a shred of paper.''

Those were the words of General Mario Ogano, spoken to me, your correspondent Paul Dick, here in the blazing heat, with a light breeze coming off the ocean, among the reed thickets. Ogano's army lives by night, while in the daytime life stops for fear of unprovoked attack from the Nagonian armed forces. Mario Ogano is tall, well-built, dressed in a khaki jacket, Colt pistol at his side. He moves purposefully and quickly, a general who sleeps in a tent and eats the same food as his people—coconuts and cheese.

''General, how do you see Washington's position?''

''In general, or as it applies to the problem of Nagonia?''

''Both.''

''I will not try to hide my negative view of the Washington administration. How could it be otherwise—you are ruled by capitalists, by the octopus tentacles of big business. All the same, in my struggle against Griso—or in other words, against Moscow—I am quite ready to talk, even with Washington. As regards the US attitude to Griso, I would like to note that a half-hearted approach has never yet brought positive results. Your Administration to this day maintains diplomatic relations with Griso. Your Administration to this day refuses to recognise my movement as the single representative of our people. Your Administration to this day has not replied to my request for the purchase of arms. Congress seems to me to be more interested in the possible reaction of the Kremlin than in the cause of peace and democracy on the African continent.''

''Is it true that your army is being trained by advisers from Peking?''

''That is a ridiculous lie, which does not have a grain of truth in it.''

''Is it true that you maintain contact with CIA?''

''If you were not a journalist, I would hit you—in our country we do not forgive insults like that! How could I consort with the CIA when the cause I serve is National Patriotism?''

''Could you please explain to our readers and listeners how you define the concept of National Patriotism?''

''For one, this is not just a concept—it is life itself. Nationalism is the highest form of Patriotism. I dream that one day Nagonia will have its own aeroplanes—on *our* planes, I am sure I'll never crash! The meaning of Patriotism is in its individualism, based on our national consciousness. I deliberately gave you a crude example of what I mean—you Americans are a businesslike people, one can talk frankly with you. Yes, I do *not* feel absolutely safe when I fly on a French or British airline. Only when a person flies on a plane belonging to his own country does he experience true confidence and ease. Don't you agree with me?''

''I usually fly on SAS, General. Maybe I'm a bad American, but I don't like flying Pan-Am, sometimes I feel like saying prayers before take-off . . .''

''Well, as a citizen of a highly developed country, you may perhaps permit yourself not to feel nationalistic, or to poke fun at it. But for us nationalism is a weapon, any retreat from which we consider treachery and which we punish by the rules of wartime.''

''Reports have appeared in the press, saying that you intend to advance on Griso in the near future. Is that so?

''We have no plans to attack Griso, that's a lie. We will go into Nagonia on the day and hour when the people call on us to do so.

Investigation No. 8

To Centre

A shop assistant at the Rome branch of Cook & Sons, after looking at a photograph of the earrings, thinks that they were sold last summer to a foreigner who spoke Spanish well, though his native language was probably English.

Rybin

To Slavin

We need details immediately about what flight Dubov returned on to the USSR, and where he lived in Lewisburg.

Centre

To Centre

Dubov stayed in a house for Soviet specialists in Lewisburg. He returned via Rome in July, 1977. He spent three days in Rome, obtaining a seventy-two-hour transit visa at the airport. From conversations with Glebb, I got the impression that he is very concerned by the assault on Zotov and his arrest. But his concern is a little too transparent and obvious.

Slavin

After putting together all these facts, Konstantinov ordered Captain Nikodimov to arrange a meeting with Dubov. He liked the thirty-year-old captain, he had the special *edge* so vital in a counter-intelligence officer. He was not afraid to turn upside down his own assumptions, to demolish conclusions which hitherto had seemed unarguable. Some accused Nikodimov of excessive haste. However, Konstantinov rated the captain's flexibility higher. He always held up the need for a thinking person to doubt himself. There was nothing more tedious than a constant conviction of one's own infallibility.

Captain Nikodimov's good friend Igor Kutsenko worked in the same department as Dubov. From Kutsenko, Captain Nikodimov learned that Dubov had arrived back in Moscow by plane that night, and that in the morning, according to his Saturday custom, would be going to the Sanduny Baths.

"We have instituted a criminal enquiry into this matter," Konstantinov said. "That means we now have the right to employ our usual methods of investigation. The time for action has come."

"Serezha, let me introduce you to my friend, we were at school together."

"Nikodimov."

"Dubov."

"So you prefer steam to sauna?" Nikodimov asked. "Or is it your doctor's advice?"

"No, I'm afraid I don't pay much attention to doctors. I am a fatalist—whatever is written down in your stars at birth, you can't escape it."

Kutensko laughed: "That's defeatism, Serge."

"As you know, one can obey one's doctor to the letter, and then kick the bucket, all because of a drunken driver. Isn't that so?" Dubov turned to Nikodimov. "Excuse me, what is your name?"

"Anton Petrovich."

"Almost Pavolovich," Dubov remarked. "Anyway, AP is still quite Chekhovian*. Trivial, but nice. Where do you work?"

"The KGB. And you?"

"I have a lot of respect for your firm. I've got a friend there, d'you know Major Gromov?"

"What section is he from?"

"I can't reveal other people's secrets," Dubov winked. "Shhh . . . The enemy is listening, aren't you afraid?"

Nikodimov smiled: "The only peaceful place left in Moscow is the baths, here you can unburden your heart. Anyone who doesn't want Czech beer—raise your hands."

"I'm afraid I'll have to refuse," said Dubov. "Painful though it is to lift up my hand. I'm fasting today. I do it once a week, like the yogas."

"Really, does it make you feel light?" Nikodimov asked.

"It really does. Yogas are the discovery of our age, Anton Petrovich. Have you ever been abroad yet?"

"No."

"If they send you, buy some books on yoga. Honestly, I advise you. Would you like me to give you a little demonstration?"

"I'd love it."

Dubov took the cigarette out of his mouth, and applied its glowing end to the skin near his elbow. He looked at Nikodimov and Kutsenko with quick and—so it seemed to the Captain—laughing eyes.

"You see? I don't react to pain. Yoga lets you turn off your senses without any loss to the psyche. You asked where I work—it's the same place as Igor, didn't he tell you?"

"He didn't ask, Serge."

"The new generation," Dubov grinned, throwing off his sheet. "Trustfullness and conviction. Shall we try the steam?"

He waved Kutsenko and Nikodimov ahead, walked with them almost to the door into the bath section, then suddenly turned back.

"Go on, I'll catch you up."

Kutsenko would have waited, but Nikodimov pushed him on.

"Let's go, he'll catch us up, probably he has something to do."

Dubov returned to the changing-room. There he poured some beer into Nikodimov's glass, took a quick gulp, and ran back to the steamroom.

Dubov bathed as he worked—methodically, comprehensively. He scraped himself with the soap-dish until his skin turned purple, then rinsed off in the shower, chanting: "What joy, eh?! What joy!"

Nikodimov smiled back, but saw in his mind's eye the

swollen body of Olga Vinter the night they took her from the coffin in the Troyekuroysky Cemetery to the country hospital for post-mortem. They had not found one Moscow clinic they dared let into the conspiracy: one word to old man Vinter and Dubov would know everything . . . But could he really be the CIA agent?

As they waited in the small galvanized shed of the district morgue, Proskurin had asked Konstantinov: "Do you still have any doubt that Dubov really is our 'dear friend'?"

"When and if we catch him red-handed, then I'll be sure."

After the three men had finished their first bout in the steamroom, Dubov wrapped himself in two sheets and went off to the pedicure.

As soon as he had gone, Nikodimov handed in their suits to be ironed.

However, Dubov had miscalculated. His place in the queue had already passed, so he returned to the dressing-room. Nikodimov was still doling out beer to Kutsenko—it seemed his briefcase was bottomless.

"Hey! Where's my suit?" called Dubov, without even looking at the clothes rack. It was as though no detail could escape him.

"I gave it in to be ironed—Igor's, yours, and mine."

"You shouldn't have, Anton Petrovich. I don't iron my clothes at the baths, I can do it myself. Well, anyway, OK . . . It's good steam, eh?"

"A great steam," agreed Nikodimov. "We should bring some salt next time."

"What for?" Kutsenko was surprised.

"What kind of bath-goers are you?!" Nikodimov laughed. "Didn't you know, in the old days they used to scrub their bodies with honey—now it's salt—to get the sweat flowing. Off with those unwanted kilograms! I've tested the method myself—it's amazingly successful."

"We'll come armed then, next time," Dubov said, and closing his eyes beatifically, he leaned back on the bench.

When the bath attendant brought the suits back from the ironing-room, Dubov at once touched the pocket of his jacket, as if inadvertently. The keys were there. His anxiety subsided.

Retired Sub-Lieutenant Sidorenko, Dubov's next door neighbour, took an old-fashioned pair of metal-framed spectacles out of his case, hoisted them onto his fleshy nose, looked quizzically at Konstantinov, and asked: "Aren't we making the mistakes of '37, General? Falling into that same suspicion syndrome?"

"No, Comrade Sidorenko, there's no danger of that."

"You're sure?"

"I cannot reveal all the facts to you. I can only share some suspicions."

"If you would."

"Imagine the situation where a person is invited to start a doctorate. He refuses—"

"If you mean Sergei Dmitrievich, then he *is* writing a doctorate, without taking leave from his professional employment."

"I would like to be convinced of that. And can you really be sure? But let us imagine further, that this person is offered a job in an organisation paying a hundred roubles a month more, and with much greater responsibility—"

"If you mean Dubov, then he's devoid of mercenary considerations. He lives very modestly."

"But when a person, turning down all other offers, makes every effort to get into a secret department which is the object of attention from other intelligence services— how would you see *that?*"

"It's a relapse of the sickness of '37, Comrade General," Sidorenko rejoined, conviction in his voice. "That way you can haul in anyone as a spy."

"Good. I must say, I'm glad that you are so keen to defend him. Only there's one thing you can't do—you must not talk to your neighbour about this conversation."

"That I can promise you."

"How well did you know Olga Vinter?"

"She was a wonderful person. Wonderful."

"Did Dubov love her?"

"He was very fond of her."

"Did he have other women?"

"We live in a time when people look on that kind of thing differently. And then, I'm against accusing someone of the seven mortal sins, just because of some affair, a chance liaison."

"I'm against that, too—believe me! I'm just interested—from the human point of view—to know your opinion: did he love her, or not?"

"In my opinion, he did. He's a strong person, independent, he had set himself the aim of rising high at work, so obviously there were times when he was short with her. But not because she was a burden, I think. And then she was very . . . How should I say . . . democratic. . . . She was able to understand the needs of an intelligent young man . . ."

"Did she love him?"

"Very much. That's why she accepted him fully for what he was."

"Accepted him fully, eh?"

"Definitely."

"Did Dubov tell you that Olga Vinter died of inflammation of the lungs?"

"I saw it myself, Comrade General."

"Then please have a look at this—it's the medical diagnosis."

Sidotrnko was the bearer of three Orders of the Red Banner. Here was a man who had lost his dear wife Ira at Breslau by a Vlasovite bullet, when she was only nineteen years old, a Sister of Mercy and three months pregnant, and who, left alone, had for the next thirty years tried to seek out death. Sidorenko had worked in criminal investigations, fighting the bandit gangs, had been under fire many times without suffering a scratch. When they finished with the bandits, he flew off to the Arctic, landed in the taiga wilderness, put up his tent, and became a builder. For his work in Tyumen he received the Badge of Honour, after which he suffered a heart attack, was given a room in Moscow, and retired. His answer to the question why he had never joined the Party, seemed strange at first glance: "Because I never saved my wife and baby, they got the bullets that were meant for me." Once only did he elaborate on this, remarking: "Academician Tupolev got it right at a meeting when he said it's possible not to belong to the Party, and still love your country."

"Do you think that Dubov poisoned Olga?" Sidorenko asked, after a long, tense pause.

"Believe me, I hope I'm wrong. And it's for that reason I need you to agree to go with our comrades, so you can sit down at a table and try to reconstruct Dubov's life— day by day—since he came home from abroad."

In Dubov's room there was absolute, almost monkish order. A desk. On top of the desk—the high-powered Panasonic radio. A big lamp, made of bronze and bone. Strangely contrasting with these two objects—a long Chinese torch: three roubles twenty kopecks, usually sold in the Army Stores, very useful for hunting and fishing.

The books on the shelf were well-worn, mostly classics, sorted carefully by size and colour of their binding. Tucked in a volume of Dickens the agents found three thousand roubles in crisp new hundred-rouble notes.

Twenty-four hours earlier, they had interviewed a nephew of Dubov, who said how "peculiar" his Uncle Serezha was in money matters: "He borrowed 100 roubles from me, he's forever short of cash, but he gave it me back in three months, thirty roubles from every month's salary, right on time."

The same order reigned on the desk. Light and gas bills pinned together. No letters in the drawers, no addresses or telephones. It was as if this was a man who knew that he might have visitors, and had prepared in advance for the visit: "Please look!" the room said, "it's all in the open. Here I am for all to see."

In Dubov's flat there was nothing to get hold of, let alone anything that could count as a real clue. Three grand, hidden in a book? That was a *nuance*, not a clue.

Upon his return from the Sanduny Baths, "Woodman" fixed a second lock (which he had bought on the way) to his front door, then went down to the courtyard where he got into a Volga car, number plate 27-21, and drove onto the Garden Ring. Near Park of Culture Metro Station he did a U-turn and, leaving the car outside the Institute of International Relations, boarded the Metro and went to Lenin Library where he chose the exit for Kalinin Prospect. Here he made no contact with anybody, but proceeded as far as the shop *Melodiya,* and stopped, looking at his watch. At 17.20 hours he was approached by a young woman, short of stature, with dark eyes and brown hair, dressed in a blue jean suit. "Woodman" walked with her to Arbatskaya Metro Station and returned to his car at 17.59 hours. Together with "Brunette," "Woodman" went to the Rus Restaurant where they ordered dinner—four portions of soft caviar, fresh green salad, toasted black bread and butter, filet of beef with mushrooms in red wine sauce, and coffee with ice-cream. From the wine list "Woodman" ordered a hundred grammes of KV Cognac, which he gave to "Brunette," not drinking anything himself. At 21.45 hours "Woodman" returned home with the girl, where they stayed the night . . .

Tempo

Dear Friend, We are still interested in any new information which Moscow has about the situation on the borders of Nagonia, or about Ogano's group or his plans. Your information on shipments to Nagonia was very helpful in allowing us to carry out a variety of responses. Do you know a man called Vitaly Slavin? And if so, what do you know about him? We would like to ask you to make contact with us at least four times a month, rather than the usual two. The information we received from you the day before yesterday has been given to the "highest leader." He was most impressed by it. Sending you our very best wishes,

Your Friends "D" and "L."

To the Assistant to the Minister of Defence, the Pentagon

"Operation Torch" is set for next Saturday. By this time nine submarines and an aircraft carrier should be located at Point X, making possible a massive rocket and bomber strike on the capital of Nagonia.

S Perseman
Assistant to the Director of the CIA

To the Research and Development Section,
State Department

In answer to your request, we enclose for you several documents connected with the Nagonian problem. These documents are among the most secret held by the CIA, and therefore we beg you to return them to us today. Please limit their reading to your most senior colleagues, and also the office of the Special Envoy. With best wishes,

Michael M Welsh, Deputy Director of the CIA

From a Speech by the Special Envoy:

The growth of Russian aid to Nagonia fills with alarm the hearts of all Africans, indeed of concerned people the world over. We are convinced that the Griso government, installed in the palace at bayonet-point, will be unable to control the country in the event of a prolonged crisis. We are convinced that a regime which does not represent the interests of the country, will disappear into the past, yielding to the true representatives of the people, chosen as a result of broad and democratic elections. We are convinced that justice will sooner or later triumph.

My country, however, maintains a strict and consistent policy of neutrality in Africa. We may not like Mr. Griso, but as long as he is President, we will deal with him and with no one else. We may sympathise with General Ogano, but he is in exile, and we maintain diplomatic relations with the regime which sentenced him to exile. For this reason I would like to repeat formally that all accusations made against us on the grounds that we are supposedly supporting Mr. Ogano, are devoid of any foundation whatsoever.''

To Centre

I request permission to speak to Glebb.

Slavin

To Slavin

Permission refused.

Centre

To Centre

I repeat my request for permission to speak to Glebb. We can squeeze him on the scandal in Hong Kong, and on the other information we have collected about him. I am convinced that after the success of the Moscow operation we can force Glebb to cooperate in bringing about the immediate release of Zotov.

Slavin

To Slavin

We agree to the meeting with Glebb, only arrange it in such a way as to give the impression that we now believe Zotov to have been Lawrence's agent.

Centre

Stepanov

Opposite me sits a tall African. He is handsome in a special kind of way—his face has the *gleam* of a person at that moment when, after prolonged hesitation and despite the threat of death, he has taken a decision which is irrevocable and for life.

My interviewee's name is Octavio Guveita. Until yesterday he was in one of Ogano's bands. Tonight he crossed over the border, under machine-gun fire from both sides.

"You see," Octavio says, "I simply couldn't stay there any longer. I just couldn't, and that's it. Like most of my people, I can't read or write. Probably that's why we all love the old folk tales so much. We used to sit around the fire in our village, and the old men told us tales, and for us young ones it was the greatest pleasure there was. Words are like dance; it's in dance and song we express ourselves, after all songs are words, aren't they? And so, when Ogano's agitators came along and began to tell us about how in the towns instead of the old whites there were new whites from Russia, of course we got very angry—although I realise now that not all white people are the same. When I joined Ogano, I saw some special whites, though they didn't let us see them much. They live in a separate camp, far away from ours. There are a lot of old men, healthy though, about fifty years old, and they have a funny way of greeting each other—raising their right arm and calling out: Heil Hitler! That's what they shout, but we've heard who Hitler was, Griso's partisans told us when they came through the village during the war of independence.

"But I only began thinking about all this one night after the officers took us out onto the road, and we shot up a convoy of lorries. We had knifed all the guards and broken open the boxes, and then one of our soldiers—an old man, about forty-five, who went to a missionary school—said that the boxes were marked 'vaccine,' that is, they were medicine. Whereas what they told us before was that the crates really concealed Russian soldiers with guns, ready to burst into the village and take away our women. When someone told the officers what the old man had said to us young soldiers about the vaccine, they just shot him, and explained to us that he was a spy. What sort of a spy could he have been—he was from the next village?! He has a mother, a wife and five children—how can someone like that be a spy?"

Every once in a while Octavio Guveita presses his enormous fists to his strong, almost violet-coloured chest, and there are tears in his eyes.

"And then," he continues, "the officers chose the strongest from among us. They forced us to dance around a spear, a dance which the gods demand you do naked. Anyway, they saw which of us were the most skilful and strong, and took us off to the other camp, where Zepp's people live—he's their commander in chief, he often flies over to see them—and showed us a line of scarecrows in the uniform of George Griso's army. Then they said that the Germans would teach us the art of 'silent combat' with the enemy, and began to show us how to leap on a man from behind, how to cut his throat, put out his eyes and break his back.

"They tell us *we* are savages—what a lie! Yes, we love our war-dances, our songs of battle. Our forefathers had to fight continually, just to keep their families alive, but I have never been able to understand how these people, Zepp's Nazis (we all call them that), could laugh so happily while they skinned alive a goat they had caught in a trap . . . They didn't kill it, you see, they just tied it up and began to take off the skin. And the goat cried, my God, how terribly it cried, I can still hear the screams in my ears . . ."

Guveita lights a cigarette. He sucks on it clumsily, wheezes, and then coughs deeply, his whole body convulsed. It is obvious that the lad has hardly ever held a cigarette in his hand before.

"And as for Mario Ogano! They told us he was the 'leader of the nation', that he shared all the hardships of life in the jungle along with his soldiers. But I saw how he went into a small tent where a soldier's blanket was laid out on palm leaves, but later after the torches were put out, he crept over into the forbidden zone where his advisers live, and there they were entertained by prostitutes. Nobody ever saw the girls again. They say that once he's had his way with them, they're given to the guards, and after the guards have finished with them, they throw them in the river, so there aren't any witnesses.

''I was horrified, and it suddenly made me think: 'Surely people like this can't be struggling for freedom? Wild animals can't suddenly turn into lambs, can they?'

''Yesterday we were woken by the alarm and taken out onto the road. A convoy of Russian lorries was going by. They told us that there were bombs and machine guns in the crates, and that we should blow up the whole lot, so that Griso's army wouldn't get it. Last night I found I couldn't shoot any more. But I saw our boys shooting and stabbing, just as Zepp's Nazis had trained them to do. And I saw with my own eyes a girl translator with the convoy shouting, as they grabbed her: 'It's all for your children! It's for children!'

''They cut the throats of the drivers, raped the girl and then shot her to pieces with machine guns. But when they began to break open the boxes, they found that they contained rolls of bandage, children's scales—to weigh newborn babies—and sets of doctors' instruments. So I said to myself, 'that's it, I'm off.' And I left, though I knew I didn't have much chance of getting through the posts, because now there are even more of them along the frontier than before. The officers had told us that in the next few days we would be moving forward, to finish Griso off. So I wanted to be on the other side of the line, so that if you trust me with a rifle, I can shoot at our so-called 'liberators,' because freedom shouldn't be so bloody. You should not kill women and laugh, and cut up a live goat.''

Octavio Guveita went silent, his hands hanging numbly by his side.

''If I write a story about a deserter from Ogano's army,'' I said, ''without giving his name, nobody will believe me. Would you allow me to name you? Or would you be afraid, Octavio?''

''Do you mean, what would happen to my family?'' Octavio asked. ''Yes. If they found them, then of course they would kill them all. But I only have one brother and my grandfather, and they are rarely in the village, they catch fish and sell it to the white captains in the port. So you can give my name. And if you like, take my photograph. After all, a man can't always be afraid, sooner or later you've got to get cured of terror. I am ready to die for my freedom. I don't want to go on feeling like an animal, living by stealth and seeing in every face an enemy."

The Western press assures us that Ogano is not preparing an invasion. I would like to add the evidence of Octavio Guveita, from the village of Juveira, to the "black file" on the aggression that is being prepared.

Dmitri Stepanov, Special Correspondent

16

Slavin

Pilar held out a glass.

"Do you know what we call gin?"

"Who do you mean by 'we'," said Slavin, glancing at Glebb. "Where you work, or where you live?"

"I mean we Spanish."

"You call gin *ginebra,* am I right?"

"Vit speaks Spanish beautifully," said Glebb. "Like all intelligence agents, he has a superb grasp of foreign languages."

"John should know even better, you can't work anywhere without languages. Try to live in Hong Kong without Chinese—you'd come a cropper in no time! You've never lived in Hong Kong, have you, Pilar?"

"What about you?" Glebb asked, laughing a little too loudly. "You've lived everywhere, haven't you, Vit?"

"No, they wouldn't let me in, refused me a visa. I said I was going there to investigate a man called Shantz. I think he worked in the business community, but Peking put pressure on the local authorities, and they wouldn't let me in."

Pilar glanced quickly at Glebb. Her expression remained smiling and pleasant, but there was alarm in her eyes. The pupils were dilated, and it made her seem short-sighted, as though at any moment she would reach into her leather bag, and pull out some glasses in thin gold frames.

"How interesting," said Glebb. "I suppose you wrote up this expedition of yours in the Russian press?"

"No, the story wasn't right for the papers. Really, it suits a novel more—do you like adventure novels, Pilar?"

"I love adventure novels," the woman slowly replied, and again looked at Glebb.

"She loves films, James Bond films especially," Glebb came to her aid. "About Russian spies who are always on the point of victory, but lose in the end because we are stronger."

"*We?*" Slavin laughed again. "I didn't know that your firm was connected with British intelligence. You know, if I was a director, I would make a film. Or not so much make as finish one off. Take *From Russia With Love*—all I would add is just one more shot! I would put it in just after Bond carried off our coding girl in triumph to London. Just a single line on the screen—'Operation Implant successful. Over to you, Katya Ivanova' . . ."

"Paul Dick will be here in a minute, sell *him* the idea. But don't let him beat you down, Vit, the price has got to be a thousand dollars, don't take a cent less!"

Pilar took a sip of her rosé wine. Gazing steadily into Slavin's eyes, she observed: "You're sometimes a poor businessman, John. A plot like that—from what little I know of the art world—would cost a hundred thousand, at the very least. Paid in cash. On the table."

"Pay up then!" Slavin exclaimed. "*I'm* not arguing."

"Maybe in the States they would pay more," Glebb said. He had stopped laughing. "I'm talking seriously, I could call up Hollywood right now, the line is good enough."

"Are you sure that your recommendation is enough?" asked Slavin.

"Absolutely."

"Why? Surely you're not a script-writer in your spare time?"

Glebb roared with laughter. He bent over, slapped his thighs and showed elaborately how funny he thought the joke was. And then he turned abruptly back into his same old, straightforward, cheerful self.

"To hell with you, Vit! You shouldn't make fun of us poor businessmen, uninitiated in the arts!"

"Vitaly is a very beautiful name," said Pilar. "Like Vittore in Italian."

"It's like the German Wilhelm," Slavin remarked. "Although they have different meanings."

"By the way, I met that Shantz in Hong Kong, Vit. A grey-haired man with a purplish nose, yeah?"

"His nose went purple in old age. When he was thirty, it was very respectable, he wasn't allowed to drink. He worked in the Gestapo, they didn't tolerate drunkards there—no nonsense in *that* firm . . ."

Paul Dick arrived sober. He shook hands gloomily with the two men, allowed Pilar to kiss him, and refused whisky.

"I won't. That is, today and tomorrow I won't."

"What's that?" enquired Salvin.

"I'm preparing an attack on you lot, Vit—and it's a good one!"

"Is it worth it?"

"Sure it's worth it, but you have to play clean."

"I agree," said Slavin. "I agree absolutely. By the way, I have collected some interesting stories, connected with dirty tricks. I could sell them to you . . ."

"No money left. Gone on drink. But I could owe you."

"That's fine, I can wait. Well, let's start—I was just beginning to tell a story about Hong Kong, about the local Mafia there—"

"No, no!" Glebb interrupted. "Sell Paul the Bond idea, it's much better! You can't imagine, Paul, what a wicked, clever idea Vit had! I so much admire him. It's about *From Russia With Love*. Just imagine, the film ends with the girl whom Bond carried off—you remember that KGB agent— sending back to Centre a coded message from London: 'Operation Implant successful,' that is, 'I am legal now, I can proceed to carry out my official duties.' Great, eh?!"

"We use that phrase 'official duties,'" Slavin remarked, "when a person has died carrying out their duty . . ."

Dick looked gloomily at Slavin: "A nasty twist, I'd say. A bit too close to the truth."

"It wasn't *us* who invented Bond, to shoot all our people, Paul. *We* didn't make him a hero—that great slayer of Russians."

"OK, tell me your idea."

"No, how much would you pay for the Bond one? John offered me one *hundred* thousand."

Pilar interjected: "It was me who offered one hundred thousand, Vit, you're wrong."

For the first time in the whole conversation, Paul Dick smiled. "Show me a producer generous like that," he said, "and I'll earn ten million a week! And you can have seventy per cent, OK? No, tell me your idea. But it would be better if it had a Lewisburg, as well as a Hong Kong angle. I tell you, I'm as worried about Zotov as you are. First one Russian bites the dust, then another. Isn't it rather too much for one week?"

"Maybe there'll be a third?" Slavin looked questioningly at Glebb. "Anyway—here we go. Do you remember, at Nuremburg, one of the SS cases concerned a certain Wilhelm Shantz?"

"Can't say I do," said Paul.

"We Americans are a nation without a memory," Glebb remarked. "A good memory gets in the way, like a rotten scab on a wound . . ."

"If we had lost twenty million, our memory would be like theirs," said Paul. "I don't remember Shantz, probably he was one of the lower echelons of butchers, eh?"

"Yes. An executioner. We proved his part in forty-seven liquidations—"

"What's a liquidation?" Pilar interrupted. "No, if it's too horrible, don't tell me, Vit. There's too much horror anyway in the world . . ."

"By liquidation they used to mean the complete annihilation of the inhabitants of a village or town—babies, invalids, the lot . . ."

"Was that during the partisan war?" Glebb asked.

"So what?! Does that justify it?" Slavin pushed his

glass across to Pilar, and she immediately refilled it with gin.

"Do you mind fingers for the ice?" she asked.

"Not at all," Slavin replied, still staring into Glebb's eyes. "So what do you think, John? Does the partisan war justify that kind of liquidation?"

"No, of course not, Vit! I was just getting it clear. The Nazis' butchery was disgusting."

"So anyway, we exposed this Shantz. He was living in Canada, but they wouldn't give him up to us, and he went underground. Then he turned up in Hong Kong, with an American passport . . ."

"No, come now!" Glebb winced. "Surely, as I remember, he went around with some kind of a Nicaraguan or Haitian passport . . . ? I'm sure he never became a US citizen."

"Yes? Well, maybe . . . That's good . . . Anyway, about ten years ago there was a scandal in Hong Kong. They picked up a group of Chinese Mafiosi, with heroin at the airport. This same Shantz helped some Portuguese or Spanish woman—I think her name was Carmen—to get out of town. She was a real beauty, like our Pilar here. Shantz also killed the man who played scapegoat for the gang. He did that with Mr. Lao—eh, John?"

"Why are you asking *me?*"

"Well, you worked there, didn't you?" Paul shrugged his shoulders. "That's why he's asking."

"I was in and out of town, several weeks at a time. Like a commercial traveller, you know."

"Oh, I see then," said Slavin. "And of course, you wouldn't have known the CIA officer there—he was implicated in the scandal. They hushed it up, the scandal I mean, but the coals are still smouldering, John, the coals are smouldering. Paul, how would you like to fan those coals a bit?"

"I dunno . . . There's *something* there—but not enough connection with the present scandal."

Glebb again laughed loudly, though his face, Slavin noticed, was strained to breaking point.

Paul went on: "In our country, Vit, what people want

to read is *super*scandals. What you're talking about is humdrum, a boring parody of *The Godfather.*''

"What's a *super*scandal, then?" asked Slavin.

"When the wife is an alcoholic," Paul recounted, "—when the husband is a homosexual and pimps his sister out to wealthy clients, when a millionaire's son joins the Communist Party, when a bribe tops 100,000 bucks—*then* you've got something! Best of all, of course, is something to show the President in bed with the corporations—that does fine, his rivals love it, especially the serious rivals.''

"There's a wife, anyway," said Slavin, turning to John. "The story has a wife. A drug addict. A blood relation to her husband—his niece, no less. A Nazi's daughter. She was in the business too . . . D'you like it?''

"Give me the names," said Dick. "I can write it up so as to reveal all. But the story is no good for money, this is a story to make a *name* for yourself. I'm afraid they've forgotten me, forgotten all of us who fought the Nazis. These days they prefer the peddlers of that kind of immorality you were talking about before. OK, let's do business—no messing about!''

Slavin put his arm around Glebb's shoulder and whispered to him: "What do you say, John? Shall we bargain a bit—or show *some* of our cards?''

Pilar swallowed a large gulp of wine. "If I were you, I'd bargain a bit," she replied.

"All right. Now it's Paul's turn—what does he know about Zotov? They wouldn't let *me* into the hospital, refused to let me see him. Come on, Paul, let's hear your reason, and then I'll comment on it, eh?''

"Listen, Vit. Nothing's yet clear about this Russian. I—''

Slavin interrupted: *"This Russian,"* he said, "—that's unforgiveable of you.''

"What do you call it? 'Great-power chauvinism'?'' Paul smiled. "Don't be cross, it's just I find it hard to pronounce Russian names.''

"Never admit it then, Paul. You'll be accused of unprofessionalism. A newspaperman should know the name of his adversaries—even if they're unpronounceable. We remember very well the names of our enemies.''

"I don't regard Zotov as an adversary," said Pilar. "He was just doing his job."

"Where's the proof?" Glebb shrugged his shoulders. "We don't live in a totalitarian system, you have to prove his guilt with evidence. A transmitter is not evidence. It could easily have been planted."

"True," agreed Slavin. "Today's *News* wrote as much, in almost the same terms."

"Yes?" Glebb was surprised. "Well done, then! I must admit I didn't see it."

"What's *that*, then?" Paul nodded to a copy of the *News* lying in front of them on the table. The article about Zotov had been underlined in red pencil.

"That was me," said Pilar. "I was so upset by Zotov's arrest. I'd do anything to help him."

"But how?" asked Glebb. "I'd like to help too. But how?"

"It's very easy," Slavin answered. "Find the people who broke into his flat."

"And find the people who bust open Lawrence's safe," Paul Dick laughed.

"Paul!" Glebb exclaimed reproachfully. "That's not gentlemanly."

"It *is* gentlemanly, because Lawrence agreed to talk to me, and I've already sent off the story to my papers. It's called 'Beauty—a Symbol of Security.' I thought of the title when I saw the work of a group of gangsters in the suite belonging to International Telephonic. They were hunting for names of 'true friends' of the firm—the same firm that built a bridge of true friendship between the United States and Pinochet's gang. I mean, before Pinochet became a dictator, when he used to take parades standing next to Dr. Allende."

"I'll buy it," said Slavin. "You've crowned my story, Paul."

"Russians usually have a problem with convertible currency," Glebb put in. "Are you an exception, Vit?"

"It's just that I have a balanced diet, and I fast one day a week. Amazing how it helps you economize."

Pilar and Glebb exchanged glances.

"Do you practise yoga?" Pilar asked, "I could give you some literature on it, I have lots of books in Russian."

"Yes, I do practise yoga. Thank you for the books, I'll take them with pleasure. By the way, Paul, do you know whether it is the same Lawrence who refused to answer a number of questions to Congress about the coup in Santiago?"

"Yes, he's the same one."

"CIA Station Officer?"

"You can ask *me* that one, you guys," said Glebb. "After all, I've known him for years. He's as much the CIA's man as I am an agent of the Gestapo."

"Ah, well . . . Now, that *would* be interesting," said Slavin, thoughtfully sipping his gin, "—if Paul could get hold of documents showing a CIA officer linked with the Nazis—old Nazis and new Nazis. How would that go down in the press?"

"When the press was at war with the CIA," Paul replied, "we dreamed of getting hold of something like that. It's a knockout, but . . ."

"I used to box, so I know about knockouts. I could teach you how . . ."

"So this is how they corrupt our gullible free press." Glebb once more burst out laughing. His eyes had thinned to narrow chinks.

"Vit, I want to show you my pride and joy," said Pilar. "Let's go upstairs."

"So you don't want to show *me* your pride and joy, *guapeña?*" said Paul.

"When you have something you're really proud of," said Glebb, "you show it in private."

"Well said!" Slavin approved. "Spoken like a man accustomed to be a winner."

Pilar took his hand and led him up the spiral staircase to the first floor. It was a studio room with a glass roof. In the middle of the floor stood a large ottoman covered with a tiger skin. The walls were covered with ikons, all of them restored: a lot of gold, and faces with carefully delineated eyes.

"Well?" Pilar said. "Not bad, eh? Seventeenth century, northern Russia, with its outlet to the sea, that is, to freedom . . .''

"Where were they restored? Here?''

"No.''

"Shall I upset you, or is it better to lie?''

"I've always preferred to hear the truth, Vit. Always, the whole truth. Then I can tell it back.''

"The *whole* truth?''

"It depends on you.''

"Only on me?''

"I'm not a wife and I'm not a secretary. I have my own affairs, Vit, so I can enjoy the best thing there is in life—my independence. And I know how to appreciate it, because I came to it from out of the gutter, step by slippery step . . . Tell me the truth.''

"Good. Well, it's very easy to tell a seventeenth-century ikon. It's not so much the method of painting as the shape of the board. The board has to be bow-shaped, curving, made of three planks. So only one of your ikons is an original—all the others are fakes. I'm sorry, you said you wanted the truth. But I won't tell anyone, I can keep a secret.''

"You didn't keep other people's secrets very well, when you were talking about Shantz.''

"That wasn't someone's secret, was it?''

"Vit, what are you trying to get at?''

"The truth.''

"That's a real Russian answer. Whereas I've become an American. I've got used to pointed questions, concrete tasks, the price of the merchandise, the length and terms of the guarantee.''

Slavin took Pilar by her hand, and kissed it: "Do you hold an American diplomatic passport these days,'' he asked, "or do you still use one of your old ones?''

"Vit, you haven't answered my question . . .''

"Probably, the question as to who is the 'trusted friend' of Lawrence's firm would be better put to Paul, wouldn't it?''

"But that was *your* question.''

"Repeat what I said word by word, Pilar, and you'll

agree that I never asked such a question. I'm a dreamer, you see. Anyone who practises journalism is bound to be a dreamer.''

''If I answer you that question, will you agree not to answer Paul's questions?''

''No, but I can see how you love adventure novels, Pilar. I'm afraid for you. I wouldn't want you to experience any unease when climbing that staircase of yours. In general, a gentleman should always be beside a woman during such an ascent, don't you think? A man with strong muscles and a mind that thinks American-style: guarantees, precision, business.''

''Good, I'll call John now,'' said Pilar.

''I'm here already, babe,'' Glebb laughed.

He was standing next to a blank wall, a concealed door closing slowly behind him.

''I'd like to hear Mr. Slavin's Hong Kong story one more time,'' he said, ''in more detail, eye to eye.''

17

Konstantinov

Konstantinov and Lieutenant Dronov were sitting in the block opposite Dubov's, across from the window where Sergei Dmitrievich and "Live Olga" (Konstantinov's rather harsh private nickname for her) were deep in conversation. Dubov's face was fully visible to the two men—a powerful, resolute face with well-hewn features. Konstantinov tried to imagine what the girl was laughing at so merrily—for Dubov spoke rarely. Here was a mature man, an academic, a politician; a handsome man who paid careful attention to his clothes; who drove a car beautifully, wearing kid gloves to feel the wheel better; who always ordered KV cognac, or at least Georgian ("they're Aryans, their love of beauty is pure, they're not mercantile like other peoples"); who quickly and skilfully translated songs from English, Spanish and Portuguese; who made love almost tiredly, very softly—not like those boys, always so scared and with no sense at all; who listened gracefully to toasts made in his honour by friends in Pitsunda and Sukhumi; who said *"alaverdi"** unhurriedly, imitating slightly the manner of an old Georgian.

"Good old Alyabrik," Konstantinov suddenly said to himself, remembering the barman in Pitsunda. "The boy had good intuition."

When the KGB had questioned him—unhurriedly, methodically, just as they interviewed everyone that Dubov had met—Alyabrik used two rather strange phrases. He

250

said that Dubov was too obvious about how he "wets his horns," and "hangs his aiglets on the branches." When the officers asked him what "wetting horns" meant, he replied: "Don't you know? It's an expression used by Kara Leone's Abkhasians, it means to puff yourself up. You can translate it as to fight, but to fight badly, for show, without taking any risks. And you hang aiglets on the branches like tinsel to scare the birds, so they don't peck at them."

Konstantinov was surprised when Proskurin, after reading the lines he had marked in the report of the Abkhasian KGB, laughed dismissively.

"But I suppose I have no right to be angry with Proskurin," he mused. "I don't have Proskurin's qualities at all—the ability to put your head down and push forward. I'm not used to relying just on logic, but also my feelings. That's very strong in women—who have to correct their instincts, and they're so emotional, it often leads to disaster. And it's a long way back, for without self-respect you're a broken person. And you can't do without people like Proskurin, either. You hammer out the line as you move forward. The process of *yawing*—the constant deviation from a straight course—is what distinguishes the movement of a plane from a steamer. Isn't that the principle behind an *autopilot*—if there aren't mistakes, what's there to correct?"

"Where's he off to?" Lieutenant Dronov asked in a whisper.

Konstantinov laughed: "You're across the street from him. Why the whisper?"

"To practise caution, Comrade General."

"That's not how to practise. Caution means to talk normally when necessary, and to whisper silently when circumstances demand. But the way you're going, you'll end up a bag of nerves—constant tension in your eyes, your movements constricted, your answers not spontaneous. The CIA will recognise you a mile off, and doff their cap to you . . . Who's watching his car today? Looks like he's taking Olga—"

"It's odd, Comrade General. She's been staying here the last few nights, she goes out in the morning to get his *kefir**. But he's lent his car to Kurolev and Pshenichnikov to drive . . . You're right, look, they're going out!''

The moment Dubov and Olga left the flat, the telephone rang.

"It's probably Konovalov," said Konstantinov. "Tell them to keep us informed. Now look here, Lieutenant . . . In your report you say that there were no notebooks in Dubov's desk, no manuscripts, nothing typed, nothing that might resemble in some way a dissertation?''

"Nothing, Comrade General.''

"There were no photographs either?''

"None, Comrade General.''

"Listen, where does he keep his Volga?''

"In the courtyard, I showed it on the plan.''

"What about in winter?''

"I don't know.''

"Hasn't he got a garage?''

"I haven't checked.''

"Then he doesn't pay bills for a cooperative garage?''

"Should I look through them again?''

"No, don't. Too dangerous—you said yourself how carefully he checks the room when he comes back.''

"Just like a wolf, Comrade General. Stands by the door and just *looks, looks, looks*, turning his head like an eagle in the 'World of Animals.'*''

Konstantinov reached for a cigar, slowly tore off the cellophane, and lit up, "A good description," he remarked, "—'like an eagle in the "World of Animals.' '' You talk freely, with imagination, but as for your reports— when I read them, I want to lie down and go to sleep, like they've got ennoctin in them.''

"What?'' Dronov was lost.

"It's a sleeping-pill, ennoctin they call it . . .''

The telephone rang loudly again. A report came through, precisely, quickly: " 'Woodman' has dropped off 'Brunette,' did a U-turn and drove off at high speed in the opposite direction. Now he's going along the Sadovaya. Opposite the American Embassy he braked. Switched on the left indicator.''

"Log the time," said Konstantinov quickly. "All right, number two?"

"Yes, fine."

"Number one, come in please! Which way is he going, what speed?"

"He's picked up speed again . . . Now he's stopping, braking sharply—"

"Don't go past him!" Konstantinov could not restrain himself, although he knew very well how faithfully Konovalov's men would carry out the minute instructions which Proskurin had given them. "Your object is very careful. Better to lose him than reveal yourself even in the slightest."

"We've overtaken him," the reply came back, in a somewhat hurt tone. "He's got out of the car."

"Opened the bonnet," a new voice from the second car took up the commentary. "He's checking something, pulling the wires—"

"By the way, what wires does he use?" Konstantinov asked the Lieutenant. "Bosch ones?"

"Sorry, what?" Dronov didn't understand.

"Multi-coloured ones—that means they're Bosch."

"That's it! They're multi-coloured, Comrade General."

"Thank God, Paramonov's out," Konstantinov said to himself. "If it wasn't for Grechaev, we'd have to check that. These chains are ghastly. I suppose it's true, suspiciousness *is* a form of sickness. The only cure is a sense of humour, multiplied into knowledge. Or rather, not multiplied, but a sense of humour based on knowledge, that's more like it."

" 'Woodman' has driven off. Now he's turning off the Sadovaya towards the SEV* building . . . He's parking outside his block."

(The report on Dubov's actions as he mounted the stairs would be given to Konstantinov the next morning. It would have been passed to him that day, had there been time to type it out. Of course, in emergencies the information would be given to him straight away, in whatever form necessary.)

Dubov entered his room, turned on the light, and immediately froze there, on the doorstep.

"Yes, he really is like a wolf," said Konstantinov to himself. "Or a vulture. Look how he inspects it all—to see whether anything has been moved, whether anyone has paid him a visit."

"But what's *that* he's got?" he suddenly asked out loud. He couldn't quite make out the small object which Dubov had picked up from the window-sill.

"By it's shape, I'd say it was a tin such as they use for processed peas, Comrade General."

"Why isn't it mentioned in the report?"

"I didn't think . . . It's a tin, slightly dented. It was empty.

"And what if he puts his reports in there?"

"There are hundreds of tins like that lying around. If you put a message in it, the *dvornik** would throw it in the dustbin . . ."

"True, I suppose," agreed Konstantinov. "But in our business no detail can be left out. What time was it when he braked by the American Embassy? Twelve exactly?"

"Yes, exactly, Comrade General . . ."

"Get me Konovalov, I think he should be reporting about now."

Colonel Konovalov had been watching the movements of CIA personnel in the US Embassy. His reply came through pat, as though he had been expecting Konstantinov's call.

"We're waiting, Comrade Ivanov. Everything's in order here."

"I take it, everything's in order means nobody has come out of the Embassy, or their apartment block."

"That's exactly what I mean."

"Except that somehow I *don't* feel that everything's in order. I'd love to be wrong, but . . ."

"Well, I hope not."

"Your nerves letting you down?"

"It's been three weeks, after all . . ." .

Dronov suddenly said: "Comrade General, you *were* right! There *was* a bill in his desk—not the Housing Cooperative, and not Auto-Enthusiast, but something with initials like SK.''

"Have Nikodimov find the address tomorrow. See whether Dubov has a box in his garage . . . I'm sure he wouldn't let any of his friends keep his stuff. He's a vulture, a solitary bloody vulture!''

The phone rang abruptly.

"Ivanov here,'' Konstantinov grabbed the receiver. It flashed through his mind that he had picked it up wrong—bad practice for a teacher, the young lieutenant had probably noticed. The more complex or tense the situation, the calmer should be your words, more so—your movements.

"Luns has left his flat on Leninsky Prospekt. He's heading for Kutuzovsky Prospekt, going past the University.''

"Keep on the line,'' said Konstantinov, and, pressing the receiver into his ear with his shoulder, slowly re-lit his cigar—though he didn't feel in the least like smoking, his mouth was dry. "I'm just going to find out where 'Woodman' is.''

The answer came promptly from the other receiver. "It's hard going, keeping up with him, Comrade Ivanov. First he boarded a No. 2 trolley bus, went five stops, then got out opposite the *Panorama,* walked twenty metres down the road, and boarded a No. 89 bus. He keeps looking round him all the time.''

"Tying his laces, eh?''

"No. He works very professionally.''

"What's he got in his hands?''

"A folded up newspaper.''

"Nothing in it?''

"No, there's *something* there. Now 'Woodman' has got off the bus, Comrade Ivanov. He's crossed the Mozhaisk Highway, gone into Victory Park. There's no one about. Shall we maintain observation?''

Konstantinov pressed a button on the second telephone—his link with Konovalov: "Well, what's up with you? Report more often.''

"I was waiting for you to call. Our object is accelerating away from our cars at great speed. What shall we do?''

"In what direction is he going?''

"Towards Victory Park."

Konstantinov glanced at Dronov, to whom the voices over the phone were clearly audible.

"Here we go, damn it," whispered the Lieutenant: "A wolf! a real wolf, Comrade General . . ."

"Well, what shall we do?" asked Konovalov thoughtfully.

"What d'you mean, *what?* Get them!" said Dronov without thinking.

"Who?"

"Both of them!"

Konstantinov sighed, then spoke into the receiver to Konovalov: "Let him go. Block the area, log the place and time he comes out."

He pressed the button of the other telephone: "Can 'Woodman' see our people?"

"Well, it's completely dark, no passers-by at all. He's creeping along, checking around him all the time. Sometimes he pretends to do exercises, then he jogs a bit . . ."

"Block all the exits from the park, keep watch carefully—a car may come through. Get a fix on where it brakes or stops . . ."

"Good, we'll try, Comrade Ivanov."

Konoyalov was back on the line. "Our object has turned off the highway at great speed, into a narrow road leading from the Blizhnyaya Dacha to the Triumphal Arch. He braked and looked around, but we had dropped him on the highway. Then I think he turned and went slowly down the road. The park is sealed."

"Can you see anything from the Mozhaisk Highway?"

"I'll tell them to try. One minute—I'm getting a message that a car belonging to Jack Karpovich has left the Embassy, proceeding along Kutuzovsky Prospekt in the direction of Victory Park."

"Where are your men? Do you have anyone on Mozhaisk Highway?

"Yes, two cars by the exit from the park and two moving slowly towards Triumphal Arch—trying to get a fix on Luns. Luns's car is moving very slowly."

Konstantinov had to make a decision—a precise decision, and the right one. He had only a few seconds in which to do it. Were his officers to arrest Luns and Dubov, and not find any evidence, the whole operation would be blown. The agent would have carried out his task—if indeed Dubov *was* the agent, and not someone caught up in a series of coincidences (something which would have to be proved). The CIA agent would resume his activities, and the Embassy would issue a note of protest. In fact it would be only right and proper for them to do so.

The question boiled down to this: *what* was the CIA's plan? If indeed there was a plan, and this was not just some chance coincidence.

Who had to pass the information?

Dubov?

Or the opposite—was the CIA sending its agent new instructions?

Or was it a dummy run, for both the spy and the CIA officers?

But *why* then was this second car from the Embassy proceeding in the very same direction?

Were they taking out insurance?

So it wasn't a practice run, but an operation?

Konstantinov pressed the button of the telephone connecting him to Konovalov: "Can you remember when 'Woodman' left his car by MGIMO*, on Crimea Street—did any of your suspects go past it? That was the day before yesterday, at five o'clock. You see what I mean?"

"You think the car is a kind of sign? A password—or a signal, rather?"

"You can't remember anything?" Konstantinov repeated, slowly. "Or didn't you log it?"

"We weren't looking for anything like that."

"So then," Konstantinov reasoned furiously to himself, "—if we assume that Dubov left his car by MGIMO* and went off to meet Olga, so that one of the CIA men could *read the signal* as he went over Crimea Bridge (it's a common route for them, nothing to arouse suspicion, you don't even need to brake, just keep looking out on all sides), then that means the exchange of information takes place quite often, maybe four times a month. If I'm right . . ."

"Take your men off the second car," he spoke abruptly. "Get them off the highway, out of sight. That's all."

Konstantinov put down both receivers. He felt the sweat spring to his forehead.

In fifteen minutes his officers were back on the line: " 'Woodman' has arrived back at the bus stop. He's still got the newspaper in his hand, but it looks like the parcel is no longer in it."

"We've got to get Luns," Dronov groaned. "He's got it all!"

"And he'll throw the parcel out of the window and say we're abusing his immunity."

"Oh yes! I saw his mother with that bloody immunity!"

"You leave his mother out of it . . ."

Luns drove out of Victory Park near Triumphal Arch. He proceeded at top speed back to the Embassy. It was half past one in the morning.

Dubov went back on the last bus, again taking his time on the doorstep of his flat to look carefully around the room. Then he threw his newspaper on the floor, went to the desk and, taking a small tree branch from his pocket, opened it and took out a battery.

"Well, now!" exclaimed Konstantinov to Lieutenant Dronov. "How do you like that—a container!"

"I think it's a No. 437 battery, Comrade General. The shops are full of them . . ."

Dubov was sitting at the desk and unscrewing the bottom of the battery. It was a simple battery for a pocket torch—the kind you really could buy in the shops, these ones and these only, the rest—only in the *Beryozka** shops. It was a brilliant touch, Konstantinov thought appreciatively. The CIA had done it again! Foreseen everything—well, that's what they were legendary for!

Dubov took a roll of film out of the battery, placed it on the desk, took a deep breath, got up slowly, and shuffled over to the bookshelf. He took his glasses from the bottom shelf, returned to the desk, and pulled at the film with a habitual gesture. He began to read it, slowly, his lips moving slightly.

"Nobody looked properly at his glasses," Konstantinov realised. "Those aren't glasses—they're special magnifying lenses!"

Dubov was a long time reading the instructions that had just been passed to him by Luns. Finally, however, he replaced them in the battery. He pushed the battery into the Chinese torch, which was still lying on the desk, and checked whether it worked (it did). Then he took a piece of paper out of the desk, drew something on it, and burned it. He rubbed the ash in his hand, burned another sheet of paper, then a third. He was writing in ball-point pen, and he obviously feared that it might leave an imprint. Dubov rose and went slowly to the door. A minute later he was back, sitting at the desk, his head propped in his hands.

"A spy's life, when all is said and done, is like stale bread." Konstantinov turned to Dronov. "One could make a sculpture of it—*Terror and Despair* . . ."

At 7.30 hours, "Woodman" left his house in a tracksuit and spent forty minutes jogging to Victory Park and back. In Victory Park he spoke to no one, ran around the obelisk, and returned home. At 8.45 hours, he went down to his car and drove off to work.

At 9.10 hours authorisation was received from the Procurator's Office. At 9.40 hours Nikodimov's group opened a secret compartment hidden in the battery.

There were three sets of instructions inside. The first one read as follows:.

"We are sending you a new *location*. Come out of Sportivnaya Metro Station (the exit nearest to Luzhniki), walk along the right side of Frunzensky Emankment parallel to the railway line, in the direction of the Novodevichy Cemetery. As you approach the river, you will see a large railway bridge. There is a pedestrian walkway along this bridge, reached by a path and steps on either side and at both ends of the bridge. On the bridge there are four towers, two on each side. Go up the steps leading to the bridge from Frunzensky Embankment, opposite the petrol station, that is, on the side closest to the centre of town.

As you begin to cross the river, the walkway which you are on will pass one of the towers. Our packet will be inside the tower on the sill of a deep-set stone window, to the left of you, and about 30-40 centimetres from the edge. It will be disguised as a piece of grey sock, approximately 15 X 20 centimetres in size. Your pick-up signal is to leave a squashed-up milk carton: put a weight inside to prevent the wind carrying it off. If you want to send us any information, put it in the same carton. Be sure to place this weighted milk carton on the edge of the sill, in the place where you found our packet for you. Then continue your walk across the bridge and go down the steps to the embankment at the Kiev Station side of the river. There is usually a policeman standing on this side of the river, near the traffic lights. However, when you cross the river and approach the hiding-place, you are invisible to him. The policeman usually goes off duty between 22.30 and 23.30 hours. Our packet will be in place at 23.00 hours. You must pick it up at 23.15 hours, leaving in its place your pick-up signal, that is, the squashed empty milk carton, weighed down and containing the information for us. If you leave a packet for us, we will leave a squashed milk carton for you by the bus shelter on Brezhkovskaya Embankment. This time the pick-up signal will be a battered old tin of peas. It will be inside, on the side nearest to the street. You will be able to see this pick-up signal at 24.00 hours. Listen to our radio transmissions as usual at the same time. The new decoding key is the novel by Beecher-Stow, *Dead Geese*, 1965, page 82, which we gave you during our last contact. Just in case, we will repeat our transmissions from 7.00-7.30 hours when you are doing exercises before you run to Victory Park. Please persevere with the jogging. We need to see you regularly in case something important comes up.''

The second set of instructions contained the following directions:

''Dear Friend, We thank you for the photographs of the documents you sent last time, though their quality left a little to be desired. It seems that you are holding the handle of your camera not strictly vertical, but tilted slightly to the left. Please make sure that the handle is at right angles to the papers with their vital information. Our experts are presently working on another model for you, with a wider lens. But the new camera will take a month to reach you, unless we can give it to you here in the West when you come on work business.

"In the next container we will send you the extra capsules you wanted. We send them reluctantly. We are convinced that you are absolutely safe, especially after we began our cover operation here, which is going well.

"We are also sending you your salary in roubles for two months, and the jewellery items you marked in the catalogue.

"We would like to be completely frank with you regarding our views on your future. We understand your desire to come here on business and most appreciate your devotion to the ideals of Western Democracy. However, your work in Moscow is absolutely invaluable to our cause, and therefore we would ask you to consider delaying your departure for a year. By the end of this time we calculate that you will have accumulated $57,721.52—quite enough to give you a start in business.

"Regarding the cooperative flat. Although we are sending you, in addition to your salary, the sum of four thousand roubles as a deposit—calling it a 'safe house' for the purposes of our budget—nonetheless, we must express our fear lest an acquisition of this kind raise eyebrows among your friends and neighbours and ruin the story you have been using up till now—that is, 'extremely limited financial means, economy in everything.' Your relatives will be the first to express surprise on this score. We are studying urgently how to equip your present room—as you asked— with a special alarm system in case anyone enters it while you are out. To help us, we will need in our next exchange of information a full and exhaustive description of your radio set, which we will make into the command centre of the system, connected with our people on Tchaikovsky Street. This 'fail-safe' system will allow you to leave your notes at home without anxiety, cutting out the garage.

"Please send us full details of your new friend, including her finger-prints, and also the maiden name of her mother and grandmother. The tragic end to your relationship with your previous friend, who found out your secret, is a salutary lesson for you, and even more for us. We allowed our guard to fall; on no account should we have taken such a room as a meeting-place. In future we will have to rent a flat in a private house, where instead of the hotel radio system we could easily install a good stereo to give the same atmosphere as the Hilton's luxury suites.

"We send you greetings from your charming friend 'P.' She is still very much looking forward to seeing you again. Her and your financial affairs are going well, and she has promised to prepare you very soon a report on her investments and the expected dividends."

The third set of instructions said:

"Dear Friend, We would very much like to ask you to photograph all the secret documents passing through your hands, and not selectively as you have been doing to date. We have no doubts at all as to your competence, but nonetheless we would like to study *all* the angles, nuances and points contained in them. We are sure that your pen-camera will allow you to photograph 20–40 pages a day. Please could you also send us your tapes of the conversations you had with the top officials you met during your holidays in Pitsunda. Try if you can to keep to the question-list which we gave you. It eases analysis of the information for reports to the head of our government. As usual, devote the maximum attention to Nagonia, because in the very near future you will read in the newspapers about the triumph of the cause both you and we are proud to serve. Our plan has been approved at the highest level, and everything will now be decided in days, not months. Once the operation into which we all have put so much effort is concluded, it would make sense for you to have a rest. We are ready to put you 'on ice' for three months, during which time you can build up your mental reserves again and have a nice summer, and then we will re-establish contact with you, just like we did six months ago. We remind you that the next meeting is set for the day after tomorrow at 23.30 hours at object 'Park' in the usual place. The password signal is from 18.00–18.30 hours by your Volga's parking-place at object 'Parkplatz.' Your information will be in the 'branch.' Your Friends.''

Lieutenant-General Fyodorov read carefully the documents which Konstantinov had brought him. For a while, he paced up and down his office. Then he stopped beside the window.

"What does Dubov keep in the garage?"

"Diaries, letters, photographs," replied Konstantinov. "I haven't yet finished them. The photocopies they did are drying out."

"Thinking of playing him around a bit?"

"He would go along with it, Pyotr Georgevich."

"Somewhere in my war archives, there is an interesting table. It shows that of all the Abwehr agents whom we caught using the radio, the majority agreed immediately to play along with us . . . But in this instance, do we have the right to play that game? The information which he is passing hand over fist to Langley is the real stuff. The target is Nagonia. The time of the coup is weeks or rather days. We simply haven't got the time to prepare suitably credible information. They'll tumble our game and bring forward the date—hit us sooner! But right now *we* are the ones in the saddle. In fact we would be quite justified in going public with this." Pyotr Georgevich poked a finger at the heap of photocopies on the table. "Surely *that* would send shock waves in the right direction? Washington would be forced to back off."

"They'll deny it all, Pyotr Georgevich. Unless we catch one of their local CIA agents red-handed, they'll deny it."

"Where are you going to pick up Dubov?"

"At home. Straight after work, today. We can't afford to delay—he'll burn the instructions, then we'll be left naked."

"Yes, of course. Better not to be caught naked here. What's the phrase—*'they wouldn't understand us,'* eh? They wouldn't understand us, if we were left with no evidence. Well, I wouldn't understand you, for a start! What news from Slavin?''

"He hasn't been on the line yet today."

"Did you ask for him again?"

"Nobody knows where he is, Pyotr Georgevich."

18

Slavin

"Listen to me," Glebb repeated wearily. "If they didn't believe *our* journalists, what chance in hell is there they'll believe *your* newspaper revelations? We don't react to your exposés, nor you—to ours."

"Mr. Glebb, revelations like the ones I have hinted at—and it was you who suggested that we bargain—will definitely produce a reaction. There is no way that the Admiral will want to keep on his books a man connected by birth to notorious Nazis, and a woman who is on the run from Interpol and living on a false passport. Let's go downstairs. It's impolite, Paul's there waiting for us . . ."

"I set up Paul with another interview with Mr. Lawrence. He's gone off, so we're alone, don't worry. Pilar, would you mind getting us a cocktail, *guapeña?*"

"Of course not. What would our friend like?"

"Anything that you won't die of," Slavin smiled. "If *you* taste it first."

"Who's been reading adventure novels now?" the woman shrugged her shoulders. "I think it's you, not me."

She descended the staircase, and a moment later Slavin heard the front door close softly behind her. They were alone in the house.

"The papers which incriminate you aren't kept in my room," Slavin observed. "They're in a safe place."

"You mean there's no point in me liquidating you? My

God, you're pretty damn suspicious, Vit! Good, let's have it straight, OK?''

"OK."

"Well, it would be unpleasant for me if everything which you broadly hinted at to Paul, can really be backed up in print—with names, photographs, facts. But the scandal you mentioned is a different matter—it's just a load of gossip, with far more invention than truth. But I still don't like it. Your conditions?''

"Like Paul, I'm interested in the names of 'good friends' of Mr. Lawrence's firm, nothing else.''

"What nationality?"

"Ours—that goes without saying.''

"What good will it do you?''

"The same as Paul, it'll be a sensation.''

"I can give you the names. But can you, for your part, give me the papers related to Hong Kong?''

"And the ones about the Nazis? About the woman living on a false passport—aren't you worried about them, too?''

"By Hong Kong I mean the sum total of your information.''

"Good. Shall we carry this meeting over till tomorrow?''

"But it's already tomorrow.''

Slavin looked at his watch. It was 2:30 in the morning. "What do you suggest?''

"You write down the names of the people involved in the Hong Kong business for me, and I'll write down the names of those friends of Lawrence who are known to me.''

"Fine, that's agreed. Where can I sit? Downstairs? Or do you have guests there?''

"No, of course not. Let's go down.''

In the hall, when Slavin and Glebb came down, there was only Pilar. She was standing by a huge window extending the length of the wall, pressing her forehead to the glass.

"I've done a deal with Mr. Slavin, *guapeña,*" said Glebb. "You can congratulate us.''

Pilar turned round. Her face was pale.

"But it's so horrible," she said. "After all, you and I

may have little problems, but in the end we'll survive. But what of that poor Russian in hospital, if they take him back to Moscow?''

"You mean Zotov?" Slavin asked, moving forward. He feigned eager surprise.

"I don't know his name. I've never met him, I just read the papers . . ."

John Glebb glanced sharply at Slavin and laughed his wooden laugh. Slavin thought to himself that they didn't work badly in harness, the two of them, after all. She brought in the emotional side, so "natural" for a woman—as if she couldn't help it, poor thing. While he played severity and anger—Slavin already knew the style almost by heart—as if not to believe in Zotov's treachery was just absurd.

"Can Zotov really be your man?" Slavin followed the cue again.

"You believe a woman so easily? Well, I suppose it's your right to believe her and disbelieve me, and not to write down about Hong Kong." He looked again at Pilar. "But we agreed an exchange as gentlemen."

"I'll write it down, don't worry, John. But Pilar only mentioned *one* name, and you said twice it would be *names.*"

"Well, the second name is hardly relevant now. She's got nothing to fear."

"*She?* Why *she?* Why nothing to fear?" Slavin immediately saw the point of the question and he responded exactly as he was supposed to—he could see that from Pilar's eyes. "Why? Or wasn't she such a good friend of Lawrence, then, as Zotov?"

"She was a very good friend," John replied. "Only she's not around any more, so you can't do anything with her. She's dead, Vit."

"Oh I see! You mean Zotov's wife?"

"Yes," said Pilar, and she held out a tumbler of gin towards Slavin. "Do you want me to taste it first?"

"But you only drink red wine, *guapeña,*" said Slavin. "By the way, why *guapeña?*"

"Her family comes from Galicia," Glebb explained.

"Where the diminutive of *guappa*—'beautiful woman'— is *guapeña*. I just like the sound of it more."

"So they think that with their cover operation they have fully insured themselves," Slavin said to himself, as he sipped his gin. "They didn't do badly, I thought it would turn out clumsier. They've given me Vinter, who's dead, and Zotov—who's been compromised by them. And they think we'll fall for it. Very good. That suits me, oh, how it suits me! The only thing that doesn't suit me, not at all, is that you have Zotov under police guard—poor old, kind old Zotov. That doesn't suit me at all, Glebb, and you will make them set him free, I swear on my honour, you'll make them set him free."

"Well," he began, "since you have given me the names of your fr—"

"Mr. Lawrence's friends," Glebb interrupted him. "He and I are different things. I fight for my own people and my own business. He has his own aims, Vit."

"Good, I get you. That's a fair position . . . I just wanted to say that since you have given me your names out loud, I won't write mine down. I'll just tell you the ones I know. Is that all right?"

John glanced at Pilar. She nodded.

"Well—Mr. Lao, Mr. Lim, Miss Fernandez, Herr Shantz, the late secretary to Mr. Lao, Mr. Zhui, the British customs officer. You see, I have given you far more names than you gave me. Isn't that like a true gentleman?"

"Yes," said Glebb. "Sure is."

"Why are you in such a hurry?" Slavin thought, worriedly. "I didn't give you the names you must have expected—surely your memory isn't that bad? Or is the important thing to plant *your* names on me? Well, plant them—can't you see how impatiently I'm waiting?"

"No," Pilar said quietly. "There's one name you didn't say."

Glebb chuckled again. He came straight back. "Nobody will believe *her,* she's out of her mind."

"You're talking about Emma?" Slavin asked. "Eh, Pilar?"

"Yes."

"Is there anyone else I've missed?"

"No," said Pilar.

Slavin drank the last of his gin, placed the glass on the marble mantlepiece, and smiled. "And what about you?" he asked.

To Centre

I couldn't contact you because I was busy talking to Glebb. The special friend called "P" is in my opinion Pilar Suarez, the same woman as Fernandez. Glebb and Pilar named Vinter and Zotov as Lawrence's "friends" in exchange for my information about Hong Kong. I think I managed to convince him that I believed Zotov had betrayed us. Glebb is convinced that, having "given" us Vinter and Zotov, he has successfully completed his cover operation. He is counting on a restrained reaction from Langley in the event of any sensational revelations about himself and Pilar getting into the press. What he doesn't realise is that I have in my possession photographs of Pilar and Zotov on Zotov's balcony, taken on the night before the break-in.

Slavin

Investigation No. 9 (Trukhin, Proskurin)

At noon Dubov appeared in the office of his department head.

"Good morning, Fyodor Andreyevich, I have something to ask you."

"Go on."

"Could you let me go today, between two and three o'clock?"

"Have you finished work on the Nagonia material?"

"By one o'clock it'll be done. I may have to miss lunch, but I'll be finished. I want to go down to the Marriage Bureau."

"Oho! So *that's* it, eh?! May I congratulate you, from the bottom of my heart! Who's your lady-love?"

"A very nice girl, comes from a working-class family. I don't think there'll be any problems with the formalities. Have you put in the request for my visa yet?"

"We're waiting for it now."

"There's still time, of course. So you'll let me go, eh?"

"Of course, Sergei Dmitrievich."

Dubov returned to his place, glancing in at the secret department on the way. He laid out on the desk the Nagonia files, and reached for his pen. Then he began to read intently, this time holding the pen strictly vertical above the pages, following the CIA instructions. The pictures had been coming in cut off at the bottom and the top, and in Langley they valued every line, every comma . . .

At two o'clock he went down to the car park, got the Volga, and drove off to meet Olga.

"Hello, darling," he said. "Got your passport with you?"

"Yes. What is the matter?"

"Nothing. I want to give you a surprise."

He stopped the car by the Marriage Bureau and went up with the girl to the first floor. Olga hung on his arm, pressed herself onto him, kissed him in the ear.

"No need to make such a show," Dubov hissed. "Control your emotions, please."

"But if they can't be controlled?"

"That's impossible. There's nothing more important than self-control. You really want to be a wife?"

"Really."

"Why d'you want to get married so much, eh?"

"Because we're in love, I suppose."

Dubov laughed. "And what is love? Can you define it? Sorry, that's just philosophy—fill in the form, darling. In a couple of months you can come with me to the West, and there we'll sort out this philosophical problem. Do you want to come with me, eh? To work and work, to beat the bourgeoisie on its ground—d'you want to?"

"Serezha, you're so clever and strong! I love being with

you!'' Dubov filled in his form quickly and helped Olga with hers, listening with half an ear to the words of the bureau clerk as he intoned: "We heartily congratulate you on your joint decision. We expect you for the ceremony in three months. You can order a car on the ground floor. For your engagement rings go to Room 8, they'll explain it all there.''

"As regards the rings and the car, thank you," said Dubov. "But three months is no good for us at all. We're just about to go abroad, on business. I wonder whether you could help us to speed up the marriage papers—I can do all the necessary applications, if that's OK?''

Afterwards, Dubov drove Olga back to work. This time he allowed her to kiss him.

"Only not on my ear, please, it's ticklish.''

At five o'clock he handed in his files at the department, checked that the secretary had noted the time precisely, and went to a trade-union meeting.

Unlike many of his colleagues, Dubov was a particularly observant meeting-goer. When a speaker raised a contentious issue, he exchanged glances with the members of the presidium, and tailored his own reactions to suit theirs. His expression changed like an actor putting on in turn the classical masks—pleasure, indulgence, interest, puzzlement, alarm . . .

After the meeting Dubov set off home. He took the lift up to the fourth floor, pushed open the door, and immediately felt hands placed heavily on his two shoulders. On either side of him stood Proskurin and Gmyrya. By the door there were three more Chekists, as well as three witnesses—two women and a man with a strange beard (Dubov noted automatically how it was almost checked in colour—greying below, then clumps of black hair, then patches shot through with red around the ears).

"What's up, comrades?'' asked Dubov, feeling his face turn purple. His throat was choking him, a thick lump blocking his breath.

"We'll come inside with you, then we can explain,'' said Gmyrya. "Open the flat door with your own key.''

Dubov's hand had been seized by an uncontrollable trembling. The key just wouldn't go into the hole.

"Someone's b-b-been in here," he stammered to himself. "I'm sure, someone's been in here . . ."

Once in the room, the men searched Dubov, then commanded him to sit down. His face went pale, and darker patches at once appeared under his eyes.

"Here, you can look at the search warrant," said Gmyrya.

Dubov could make nothing out on the paper at all, the lines all seemed double.

"You can search the place, only what's it for?" he said. "I th-think that there must be some m-mistake. Otherwise, you're b-breaking the l-laws of socialist legality."

The detective, Captain Agibalov, pulled over a chair and sat down opposite Dubov: "Would you like to confess everything, openly and honestly?" he asked.

"Confess what?"

"Think it over. An honest confession is always taken into account."

"B-b-but what should I c-confess?" Dubov protested, stammering badly.

"You made a mess—now you can help us clear it up, Dubov," said Gmyrya.

"I've got nothing to confess And your men won't find anything in my car."

Proskurin glanced at Gmyrya. Indeed, a group of officers were already driving off in the car—it was vital to check straight away for secret caches in it.

"Well, then, you'd better start the search," said detective Agibalov. "And we'll sit here meanwhile . . ."

As he watched the Chekists begin their search, Agibalov absent-mindedly took up the torch lying on the table, and pulled out the batteries. Two of them he put down, the third he began to twiddle abstractedly in his hands.

Dubov's eyes were glued to the detective's fingers. His face turned red once more, his tongue went dry—it felt incredibly heavy.

The detective put down the battery, lit a cigarette, and pulled over an ash-tray. He carefully placed his burnt-out match in it, then looked up at Dubov. The latter was sitting bolt upright, his head thrown back slightly, his lips quivering, whiteish.

Agibalov once more picked up the battery. This time he opened the bottom, and tipped out the little roll of film. He looked at Dubov.

"That m-means you know . . ."

"We know," Agibalov replied, and from his briefcase produced a cobblestone. Or at least it looked like a cobblestone, except its weight was far too light, and when the captain pressed an invisible button on its surface, it opened. This secret container had just been discovered in the garage . . .

Dubov looked round at Gmyrya and Proskurin, who were sitting beside him, one on each arm of the chair, to prevent him from standing up. Finally he transferred his gaze back to Agibalov.

"If you want to use me for your work, tell your people to return my car at once to the place where it was. Every parking spot is controlled by the people from the Embassy. Otherwise you'll spoil the next contact . . ."

Proskurin got up and went out of the room. His place was taken by Trukhin.

"But the car is not the only thing," Dubov went on. "I myself am under continuous observation by the people from the Embassy, consequently my life has a commodity value. Do you guarantee my life? If you do, then we can do everything in the best way."

"As regards your life, the court will decide, Dubov," answered Gmyrya.

"Can't we do without a court?"

"No," said Agibalov, "I'm afraid not."

"That's a p-pity . . . I could g-give you an awful l-lot. Things that nobody else can . . ."

"Well, then give us them," said Gmyrya. "We're listening."

"It would be b-better to write . . . D-do you want me to?"

He stood up languidly, drew a pen out of the pocket of

his jacket, which was hanging over another chair, and bent over a pile of paper that was standing by the lamp.

"I, Sergei Dmitrievich Dubov," he wrote in a bold hand, "consider it my duty to declare the following, in regard to my work for the CIA . . ."

For a moment he paused in thought, deliberately raised the pen to his mouth, then suddenly jerked his head, and bit off its end with his teeth. Gmyrya had no time to intervene. Dubov slumped to the floor, his face already gone blue. The ambulance, called from Sklifosovsky Hospital, diagnosed collapse of the lungs, after which the doctors struggled for three hours to save his life. He died at ten o'clock that evening. The post-mortem revealed that Dubov, the CIA's agent "Mastermind," had perished by the very same poison as Olga Vinter. The doctor who opened his body had the misfortune to inhale a whiff of it, and collapsed unconscious. The replacement team wore gasmasks.

Konstantinov

Konstantinov looked round the men gathered in his office, cleared his throat, but found no words with which to begin. Slowly he lit his cigar, inhaled and blew out a thin light blue stream of smoke straight in front of him, as if to drive away the last, meanest and most irksome mosquitoes on an autumn hunting trip.

"Well then," he said, after finally clearing his throat, "What can we offer the boss?"

"A corpse," Gmyrya sighed heavily. "A complete and utter failure, what else can you say?"

"I wouldn't put it as harshly as that," Proskurin observed. "In the final analysis, we identified their agent, stopped the flow of information, and the CIA's instructions are in our hands. That isn't so bad, is it?"

"Why kid yourself?" Konovalov shrugged his shoulders, then stopped to listen to the sound of the clock chiming two in the morning. "What the Lieutenant-Colonel says is quite correct, of course, but we failed in our most important task. We failed to catch their agents red-handed.''

''True,'' Konstantinov agreed. ''Another failure. But we must still expose them.''

''But how can we do that now, without Dubov?'' Proskurin asked. ''There's no point in deluding ourselves, we should be satisfied with what we've got.''

''Let's analyse what we've got then,'' said Konstantinov. ''You begin, Comrade Gmyrya.''

The latter rose to his feet.

''We have very little,'' he began. ''First, we have the instructions: the day after tomorrow Dubov was due to meet an unknown agent, probably Luns or Karpovich. The all-clear sign for Dubov's car is the parking spot on 'Parkplatz.' Where this spot is, we don't know. Nor do we know the precise meeting-place in the park, and Victory Park is huge. If we want the CIA officers to go to their meeting with Duboy at location 'Park,' we have to figure out where 'Parkplatz' is. That's all I can think of for the moment . . .''

''And you?'' Konstantinov turned to Proskurin.

''I agree with Gmyrya.''

''Comrade Konovalov . . .''

''If we want to keep Dubov's appointment in the park the day after tomorrow, we'll have to think up a story for his sudden disappearance. Their agents keep an eye on him too, not just the car.''

''Is that all?'' Konstantinov checked around the room. ''Thank you. So—first, Comrade Gmyra's unit will work out and put into operation a cover-story about Dubov being sent on an urgent assignment to the Far East, to a conference on problems of the Pacific Ocean Zone. Second, Proskurin's unit will continue carefully interviewing everyone who knew Dubov—we need in particular to know his most frequent routes, the times, the places he parked. Third, Konovalov's unit will bring together all our data on the routes taken by known CIA officers—to see whether their paths crossed with Dubov so they could read signals from his parking places. I am thinking of the one at MGIMO. Most likely that was an all-clear sign, arranged probably in a previous set of instructions. Remember, he left the car there just over half an hour, met Olga, and the next day had his meeting at Victory Park."

"But how do we figure out 'Parkplatz'?" Proskurin groaned. "He gave no clues at all . . ."

"Tell Olga Vronskaya to come and see me at nine o'clock this morning," said Konstantinov. "I'll try to have a talk with her. And ask Paramonov to drop in too, after all he did Dubov's repairs."

At four o'clock the same morning Konstantinov sent off the following message to Slavin:

"Ask Glebb to help you persuade them to let you take Zotov back to the USSR. Let him see that you are being forced into this, that way you will confirm his opinion that the cover operation was a success. On no account show him Pilar's photograph at this stage. We'll leave that document for a time when it may be necessary."

At five o'clock Konstantinov approved the model of Victory Park which they had been making all day. He had to think carefully where to deploy his forces, for without any precise description of the meeting place in the instructions there was an enormous area to cover. He had just one day in which to decide his positions, to install special cameras and infra-red equipment, and to plan the arrest of the CIA agent.

At nine o'clock Olga Vronskaya knocked on the door of Konstantinov's office. As she entered she smiled brightly. There was no trace of anxiety in her face, she looked totally at ease.

"Hello, they told me to take the fourth entrance—"

"Hello. Sit down, please. Did you have time to eat breakfast?"

"No, but anyway today I'm not eating anything—only cold water."

"You have slimming days?"

"This is only the third time in my life."

"Have you spoken to your doctor? They say it isn't good for everyone."

"My friend is an expert at yoga, he swears by his fasting days." Olga glanced at the clock.

"Already a bit hungry?" Konstantinov enquired. "Waiting for evening?"

"No, I have to phone in to work."

"Why do you think you were asked to come in here?"

"Probably, it's connected with going abroad."

"You're planning to go abroad?"

"Yes. With Serezha . . . My future husband," she explained.

"I see . . . No, I asked you in for something else, although . . . I would like to ask you: how would you react to a person we suspected of spying?"

"Just the same as you," Olga answered readily. "To be a spy is disgusting."

"Why?" Konstantinov enquired. "It's just another job, after all . . . Some people are carpenters, some are pilots, some are spies . . ."

Olga burst out laughing: "A fine sort of a job!"

"And highly paid. These days a spy is well paid for his damage to society."

"I remember my mum used to read us a poem when I was small—'Hired by hostile bands, there crossed the border our enemies, their spies and saboteurs.' After that I was afraid to walk in the forest with my granny, I saw spies and saboteurs behind every bush."

"Do you love your grandmother?"

"I adore her."

"More than your mum?"

"That's an unfair question . . ."

"Why?"

"Because the answer would have to be hurtful, or untruthful—and I don't want to be either."

"Of course. Olga, I'm sorry for being so direct, but—do you love Sergei Dmitrievich?"

"Very, very much."

"So you don't just love him, but *very, very much?*"

"Yes."

"Do you like your work?"

"No."

"Why?"

"It's boring. I know I can give more, but nobody seems to want it."

"Have you offered?"

"What?"

"To give more and better?"

"It would be embarrassing . . . Like pushing yourself forward."

"Pushing yourself forward is when you ask for something, offering something is quite different . . . Which writers do you like best?"

"Well . . . Lots, really . . . Gorky . . . Mayakovsky, of course . . ."

"And what d'you like best of Mayakovsky?"

"That's easy! 'Lines on a Soviet Passport.' "

"And Gorky?"

"The 'Song of The Storm-Petrel.' "

Konstantinov smiled faintly, and sighed: "Sergei Dmitrievich hasn't yet given you a taste for medical literature?"

"He told me about yoga. It's very interesting."

"And fasting—that was him, too?"

"Of course."

"Well, I can see how he might need to, but with your figure, why bother? It's a bit premature, surely?"

"Serezha says you should prepare for old age right from when you're young. Let yourself go now, and later it will be much more difficult to get back into trim."

"That's true, I suppose. One more question: what was it that made you fall in love with Sergei Dmitrievich?"

"He's so clever and strong. My generation is often attracted to forty-year-olds, our own age-group are so feeble—mummy's boys. But why are you asking me this?"

"You yourself gave me the reason why I asked you here. Have you known Sergei Dmitrievich long?"

"No. Although it seems like ages now. When I'm at work, I'm always looking out of the window, just so that nothing can stop me from imagining his face. The girls I work with just fade into the distance, just fade away . . .''

"When did you meet him?''

"It was totally by chance. I lost my friend—we had arranged to go on holiday together, but she never arrived. And he asked me to spend the day with him, and we had such a lovely breakfast, I never knew breakfast could be as interesting as dinner—so solemn, meaningful . . .''

"So you fell in love with him over breakfast?''

"You wouldn't understand, though I know why you're asking . . . Well, and then there was the sea, and the sun . . .''

"The sea and the sun are one thing, love is quite another.''

"Maybe . . .''

"But why do your own age group seem so feeble to you?''

"I don't know, really . . . It's hard to explain. They're somehow lazy, they never give you flowers, they've got nothing interesting to say. When they tell you they love you, it's so timid—you can tell straight away from their eyes what they really want.''

"Are they really so lazy?''

"Oh, they are! Ask any man of my age whether he can iron his trousers or wash a shirt, just ask him! He'll tell you: 'Why should I, what's my mum for?' ''

"Probably you've just been unlucky, Olga.''

"Nothing of the sort, I've tried to find a good one . . .''

"Depends where you look. Anyway, fine—I haven't much time to spare. You'll agree to help us in this business?''

"Of course.''

"You don't want to ask what it is exactly?''

"No, I trust you. You wouldn't ask me to do something bad.''

"We want you to help us uncover a spy.''

"Of course I'll help.''

"Do you want to think about it first?''

"There's nothing to think about, it's my duty. What do I have to do?''

"The first thing is, you have to remember all the places

where you drove with Sergei Dmitrievich, where you stopped, where you walked—''

"Then you should ask *him*, he'll know much better than me . . .''

"I will, definitely. But first you try to remember everything, all right?''

"All right. Well, then . . . We went to the Lenin Hills, stopped there, and Serezha and I went for a walk . . . Then we went to Victory Park."

"For a couples of hours, no more, eh?''

"No, half an hour at the most.''

"Did he complain that his car was losing power, something wrong with the wiring?''

"Yes, that happened several times. But he gets out and pulls the wires a bit, and everything is fine.''

"That often happens, I have terrible trouble with my wiring too. Listen, Olga—what if we both get into my car and you show me the places where you go, eh?''

"I don't understand. Why don't you ask Serezha about this?''

"After we've checked all the places, Olga, we're going to take you to the airport, and one of our comrades will take you down to Adler. You can have a little holiday in Pitsunda—rest, sunbathe, go swimming . . .''

"Oh, that would be tremendous! Only I should phone Serezha and my mum, to tell them. Oh yes, and what about my work?''

"We've already cleared it with work, you don't have to phone there. What do you want to tell your mum?''

"Nothing really—just so she knows where I've gone,'' Olga sighed. "She always wants to know.''

Konstantinov nodded to his external line: "Phone, then.''

Olga dialled a number. Konstantinov noted that she first rang Dubov at work.

"Can I have Sergei Dmitrievich? His friend, Olga Vronskaya. What do you mean, what flight—?'' She glanced in consternation at Konstantinov. "Where? And when will he be back? Thank you . . .''

Olga put down the telephone.

"He's left Moscow on urgent business," she told Konstantinov, in a voice full of surprise. "He probably phoned, but I was here with you. How terrible, what will he think?" She quickly dialled her home number.

"Ma, has Serezha called? Oh, he phoned, did he? What did he say? Hmm . . . And when did he say he'd be back?"

"Well done, Gmyrya," Konstantinov muttered to himself, "You thought of that, too. Well done!"

"Ma, listen, I'm going off today . . . By plane . . . No, not with him. I'll tell you afterwards . . ."

Konstantinov prompted her, in a whisper: "When you get back . . ."

"When I get back," Olga repeated. "It's on office business. No, mum, please! . . . How can you think that? Well, goodbye, kiss Granny from me."

She replaced the receiver and looked over at Konstantinov, as if to ask, had she said what she was supposed to?

For a moment he weighed up whether he should tell her everything. But then he decided to wait a little, even though he was now completely certain that Olga knew nothing about the real Dubov. She had lied clumsily to her mother; she answered questions readily, without premeditation; her thoughts showed no special depth; her mind worked naively, in stock responses and predetermined formulae. But still something whispered in Konstantinov's ear: wait, you've got to wait.

He came out of the office with Olga and, depositing her for a minute in the lobby, glanced into a room where Mikhail Mikhailovich Paramonov was sitting. Seeing the General, Paramonov jumped up, straightened himself, and moved forward expectantly.

"My colleague here will have a word with you in a minute," Konstantinov said.

He nodded at Gmyrya.

"I won't have time," he explained to the Colonel. "I think it would be more sensible for me to drive her around myself, all right?"

"Much more sensible," Gmyrya agreed. "So shall I take Mikhail Mikhailovich?"

"Let him remember first. You, Paramonov—you've often driven around with Vinter and Dubov in their cars, haven't you?"

"Yes, sir!"

"No need to play the soldier, we know you're exempt from military service, so just tell us plainly. When you were driving, why did you stop—we want to help people in your situation, is that clear? And you're on no account to speak about this conversation to anyone, understood?"

Sitting Olga down in the car beside him, Konstantinov recalled the CIA's third letter of instruction: "Send us details of your new friend, including the maiden names of her mother and grandmother." But why hadn't they asked him to send her photograph? he wondered. Had they taken it themselves? Where? When?

"Olga, by the way—does your mother have a different surname?"

"Yes. She took my father's surname, her maiden name was Shvetsova."

"I see. Well, let's try to remember . . . Where shall we start? We only have about two hours for all of this. Did you go to the bridge over the Moskva River. The one near Luzhniki?"

"No, never. Do you want me to show you where we drove in Victory Park? We can start there."

"And you'll show me the place where he left you on your own, and the men and women were so friendly and took photographs of you?"

She laughed: "How did you know that? Only it was just a man who photographed me, when Serezha had gone to buy tickets for the circus."

"When was that? The day you came back?"

"No, the morning after . . ."

On returning from his tour around Moscow, Konstantinov handed Olga over to Senior-Lieutenant Kryukova, and set off for Dubov's flat. Here he looked through the book collection, and quickly found the volume he wanted: the *Hil-*

ton Hotels' Guidebook. He flicked through the pages until he came to one which had been bent back. He read:

"Two-bedroom suites at the Hilton are specially luxurious: colour TV, radio, music programmes on the hotel's own broadcasting network, a splendid bathroom with sea-water, a refrigerator and china tea-set for six persons. Cost—$95.00 per day. Rooms must be vacated by 14.00 hours."

Konstantinov cautiously closed the book, wrapped it in paper, and asked the officer who was on duty in the flat in case of visitors: "What do you think, can you get fingerprints off glossy paper?"

But he didn't need the answer. For it was now only too clear why Dubov had eliminated Olga Vinter: when the first rush of love passes, then questions are asked of a partner and they require to be answered—and what answer could he give about the luxury suite in the Hilton?

It was a tragedy of a weak and dishonest man, who found himself sharing his life with an honest woman, Konstantinov said to himself. Naturally Olga asked him about the Hilton, when they were alone, and Dubov lied clumsily. After all, she was cleverer than him. She put two and two together, and took his earrings off to her friends—she was afraid to hear what she thought the valuers would say. Even a strong person postpones the moment of truth, for truth demands action. And as someone who had worked abroad and knew the ropes, she had only one option—to come to us. And he realised this. What lie could he tell her? Say a different price? Possible. None of our people would have the faintest idea of the cost of a hotel room like that. They would know it was out of their league, pride would forbid them to ask how much. Of course, when she was in love, over there in Lewisburg, and back here for a period of time, she didn't think about those damn ninety-five dollars for love in a luxury suite. Money and love are alien to each other. So *why* did she decide to find out now? Did she guess about this other face? But how? Previously she had defended him to everybody, for Dubov was by no means universally loved—they said he was too high and mighty, called him a "Zarathustra."

Most likely, she guessed that day at Niyazmetova's flat, when he poured the wine over her and took her into the bathroom—begged her, most likely, not to say anything in front of her friend. And this offended her very nature. So she had the earrings valued. And was horrified. And went to get the Hilton guide. And finally came back to him. Confronted him with everything. And he was overcome by horror—he realised he was a dead man.

And suddenly Konstantinov caught himself thinking that he pitied Dubov. He didn't at once understand this emotion—pity towards a traitor, such a thing wasn't possible, was it?

Probably it's explicable, Konstantinov reasoned. After all, he wasn't a traitor when he went out there. How did they break him? He must be an anomaly. But there were plenty of people around, weren't there, who had some deviation from the norm. Maybe I was wrong when I argued with Stepanov? No, I was right. It's impossible to distrust *everyone* who deviates from the norm—that way lies spy-mania, which in the final analysis produces only terror, which plays into the enemy's hands. How many of our people are working abroad these days? Tens of thousands, I would think. And life goes on, anything can happen, anything can befall a person—by chance, perhaps, or through stupidity or ignorance . . . But our enemies are canny, they know how to assess a person, to demoralize and corrupt him. Conceit, greed, drunkenness—yes, these are the tools they have always used, and will always do. But surely anyone with common sense wouldn't allow themselves to be recruited and become a spy, just because they had spent a night on top of some Pilar . . . ? So it's an anomaly after all? But one anomaly is different from the next, where do you draw the line? And what is it, this mysterious line? Having identified and measured it out, we can save a person from the fall. We can save them by belief in them. Each one of us should know that people believe in us, for this gives you strength. Only a person with a pathological disorder of the moral sense can become a spy, said Konstantinov to himself, now finally convinced. And that's what Dubov was, and that's why the various factors combined to make him do what he did—the influence of Pilar, his greed, his boundless, Nietzchean pride.

Konstantinov went into his study, took three tablets of ascorbin. They said it was a tonic, and he hadn't slept the night before, not one wink. He took off his jacket and put on a woollen smock which was hanging in the cupboard. He felt shivery, although the day promised to be warm, the rain had stopped, and the streets smelt of lime blossom.

Strange, Konstantinov thought, the limes have already shed their blossom. Maybe I want to smell that scent, that summer scent, so full of joy and hope? Who was it who wrote: "The main thing is to desire wholeheartedly, only then will your wishes come true." Naive, of course, but sincere, you could feel the author's youth.

He wiped his forehead, eyelids, temples, then pulled Dubov's exercise books towards him and leafed through several pages. His attention was caught by the following lines:

"That which is holy is *strange* to me. If other people's property wasn't holy to me, and if I looked on it as my own, I would take possession of it."

"Man stands above every separate individual."

"The moral person comes inevitably to the conclusion that he has no enemy except the immoral person. And the reverse."

"The egoist, who seems to terrify decent people so much, is as much a phantom as the devil. This monster exists only in their imagination."

"If you don't label people sinners and egoists, you won't find them so! Look at yourself as more powerful than they say you are, and you will have more power! Look on yourself as greater, and you will have more! . . ."

"Comrade General, can I come in?" A voice interrupted him.

"Yes," replied Konstantinov, wondering where he had read these questions before. Was it Stirner, the founder of anarchistic individualism? Stirner had been a favourite of

Hitler—arguing for the right to exclusiveness, to seek overweening power, to see yourself as a superman.

He waited until his colleagues, summoned by the aide, had seated themselves round the table. Then he spoke:

"It seems to me that the all-clear signal 'Parkplatz' is the parking-place outside Dubov's work. He always left his car in exactly the same spot, facing the *Gastronom* shop, Olga never once saw it parked in any other position, and he usually sat her in the car at 18.30 hours—according to the instructions, the very time when the CIA should be recording the all-clear signal 'Car.' But was the signal with him *in* the car, or not? That is the problem! Or perhaps they both had to be in it—Dubov *and* Olga? Yes, yes, I mean either Vinter or Vronskaya . . ."

19

Glebb

Lawrence telephoned Glebb in the evening, after dinner:
"John, it would be great if you could spare me half an hour."

"Has anything happened, boss?"

"I just want to look at you. You fire me with optimism."

When Glebb arrived, Lawrence was sitting in front of the television, listening to a report from the left-wing journalist Alvarez, who had recently been commenting rather frequently and severely on the question of Ogano's forces stationed on the borders of Lewisburg.

"Listen to this guy, he knows where to stick it in," said Lawrence.

Alvarez was concluding his report:

"Unfortunately, we failed to translate an article by the Russian journalist Dmitri Stepanov, who is presently in Nagonia, using material given to him by Premier Griso. Documents are only documents when they are supported by photographs, quotations, official statements. Stepanov quoted a statement by General Ogano, which I will repeat, since up till now Ogano has not dissociated himself from it; clearly he would find that difficult. Ogano said: 'I will not discipline my lads if they string up the Russian invaders of Nagonia on posts. I'm a soldier, and I understand the feeling of hatred.' Four hundred Russian experts are now working in Nagonia. They include 100 doctors, 40 agricultural specialists, 15 university teachers, 90 geologists, 60 epidemiologists. Yes, they have sent many different experts there, that is true.

"Stepanov then relates how Ogano told a *Chronicle* correspondent a month ago: 'My people are ready for the final conflict. My people know how to shoot from the hip and how to stick a knife in your neck, so we know how to win. We have learned how to use the latest equipment, we have a strong backer in Lewisburg—all that makes us confident of the outcome of the battle.'

"I would like to turn the attention of our government to General Ogano's words regarding the 'strong backer' in Lewisburg. Surely our President does not imagine that the flames of war, having burst out just seventy kilometres from our capital, will blow in only one direction? The wind of war is unruly, it can spread in a direction not planned by general staffs and intelligence agencies. Thank you for your attention, ladies and gentlemen . . .''

Lawrence turned off the television and looked questioningly at Glebb.

"How do you like that!" he exclaimed.

"Does it scare you?"

"No. I think these days I only get *scared* when my grandchildren fall sick. No, it was something else that surprised me. I've already read Alvarez's report, I was given it by the Director-General of the television authority. And he said that the government was discussing whether to broadcast the report. That means, has the point of view of the moderates prevailed, if we're now hearing Alvarez on the box? Couldn't you be relying too much on just one force? Over-estimating the capabilities of Stau?"

"You mean *we*, Robert," Glebb interposed. "We've both put our money on Stau."

Lawrence made a wry face.

"Don't get yourself hung up on pronouns. I, we—what's the difference, in the end? We're in the same business, and we have to do it properly. No, it's just that the Consul is vacillating. He thinks it's not yet time to hand over the helicopters to Ogano, he reckons he's got enough equipment already. And as you know, the Consul has special contacts in the Pentagon.''

''Then send a telegram to Langley, tell them to call off 'Operation Torch'—and have done with it, Robert!''

''What's the matter with you? Why are you so sensitive, John? I called you in not as your superior, but as a friend. I wanted both of us to think through all the possible variations in the operation. Fighting one's own side is a drag, but it's a game that has to be played unless you want to risk the whole thing.''

''True.''

''Maybe we should alter our line just a little?''

''How do you mean?''

''John, I think I understand the Russians fairly well. After all, I got to know them at a time when we had friendly contacts with them—before Dulles started that operation with the Nazis in Switzerland. I'm only afraid of one thing, that the bastards here may get the wind up. They could still scupper us from behind.''

''Go on, then.''

''Don't be angry. Everyone knows that 'Operation Torch' is your brainchild. We all know what store the Admiral and his supporters have put on it. But my job is to develop our political line, and at the end of the day—as you so often remind me—I am the *boss,* and if the Russians manage to put the squeeze on the State Department over this affair, the brass hats will come down heavy on both of us—you and me.''

Glebb laughed. But his lips hardly parted—it was with him a sign of anger.

''Well, let them! I'm not afraid of big-wigs or brass hats, I'm used to them. But I still think that Stau, whom you seem to have given up on, will carry out my instructions, and that it will push the moderates here and their President in the right direction.''

''I'm coming to that, John. Is it worth provoking the Russians so openly like this? Maybe it would be more sensible to put our real money on a little subterfuge. Maybe we should edit a little the statements of our Metterniches*, temper them with a little *restraint?''

"That's your business, Robert, do what ever you think necessary. All I want is one day to get in that helicopter sent to carry me back to Nagonia . . ."

"Excuse my question, John . . . There was a mention somewhere that you had personal interests in Nagonia. That you lost some money there—something along those lines . . . I've got no objections to a personal interest as long as it's linked with our common global one. But I'd like to know—is it true?"

"No, it's rubbish. Where did you hear all this? From the Russians? And do you believe *them?*"

"No, I don't believe them. Actually, it came up somewhere else—in Europe."

"You have it on paper?"

"I will do."

"You wouldn't like to reveal your sources?"

"Give me the chance to check this source properly, and in a couple of days I'll be ready for a proper talk about it. And of course you're right to count on my support. I can't believe, John, that you could overstep in the slightest the limits of the law, and confuse your own affairs and those of our country for the sake of personal gain. I would like the world to think of us as true fighters for democracy— above board, with clean hands, legal."

"Thanks for the kind words, Robert. Only I have a question: are you sure that if we observe the letter of the law our plans will come off?"

"I assume that is precisely what we are doing, John. Or that is what I would like to think. We must play according to the rules—even with the Russians. When we protect 'Mastermind,' we are acting legally, protecting an agent. Isn't that so?"

"Who are you trying to kid, Robert? Yourself or me?"

"I don't quite understand you, John . . ."

Glebb rose. On his face there was a broad smile, which turned into a peal of laughter.

"Boss, I get you. Let me toss it over in my head, and then I'll bring you back a plan of action to cover the problems. Believe me, I respect and live by the law as much as you."

After leaving Lawrence's room, Glebb looked at his watch. There was an hour left before Pilar's cocktail party. He got into his car and drove to the Embassy. There he went up to a suite guarded by the marines—the code room.

"Send me urgently any information on persons who have published material about my business interests in Nagonia. A Russian hand is possible here. Glebb."

The coded message was addressed to the Federal Republic of Germany, to a man who had once worked as an aide to Glebb in Hong Kong. They were tied not only by friendship, but by a common interest in the operation.

Inside the Military Industrial Complex

This time Nelson Green had arranged dinner in the Department. His office there was very small and modest—the only luxury were pictures by Chagall, Picasso and Salvador Dali, in thin white frames. However, next to it there was a larger hall with eighteenth-century furniture under stained glass windows originating in Italian monasteries, and big bunches of flowers sprouting from some tall clay pitchers—a present from King Farouk of Egypt.

There was only one guest behind the huge table—Michael Welsh.

"I asked my wife for permission to serve some Caspian caviar," said Green. "Try some, it's marvellous. It came by the morning flight from Teheran."

"Then ask them to toast some black bread," said Welsh. "In Paris there's a little restaurant called Black Caviar, where they don't serve white toast—only black. They buy it from the Russians."

"I buy mine from the Russians, too. You can't beat Russian black bread. Well Michael, what news have you got?"

"A week from now you'll be able to send your experts to Nagonia."

"Don't forget to touch wood."

"What's my head for? As I always say, it's the best kind."

"No, the best kind is Ford's head, because when he was a kid, he played football without a helmet. But I have some news—and not pleasant news at all."

"I'll have it with the black caviar," Welsh smiled. "Caviar can make any news positive."

"According to my information, the banks in Zürich and London have decided that Griso's regime suits their interests best. Someone—we don't yet know who exactly—has invested about fifty million marks in the reconstruction of Nagonia. I know that's kid's stuff, but it's a significant move, Michael. Europe is beginning to show its teeth."

"Let it!"

"It's not as simple as that. In Chile I still have to work covertly to this day, Michael, and it's no good for business."

"I know."

The head waiter came in—a tall, silent Malaysian in a tailcoat and white gloves. He placed in front of Welsh a menu in a heavy red binder.

"I recommend the pheasant soup and the sturgeon, they do them very well here," said Green.

"I'm sorry, sir," the head waiter interposed, "but I wouldn't suggest the sturgeon today. I looked at the fish they delivered from Tabriz, they had none of the fat that makes them a delicacy. I would recommend *sukiyaki**— imported from Tokyo. The meat is really of the highest standard, in my opinion."

"Standards are always the same," Green grinned, "otherwise they wouldn't be standards. But if you think *sukiyaki* is better, then let's eat *sukiyaki*."

"Sorry, Nelson," Welsh said apologetically, "but I can't eat veal, I feel sorry for the calves . . . You know, on my farm I feed them milk from a bottle and teat. I can look at them for hours."

"Then, sir," said the head waiter, bearing down on Welsh, "I would recommend *angulas**. They're full of nourishment and our Pablo makes them as good as you'd find, even in Santiago de Compostella.''

"Fine, *angulas* would be great. I can still remember how they used to taste in Chile. They have a wonderful fish market there in Puerto-Monte, and the way they serve *angulas!*''

The head waiter retired, his footsteps inaudible over the thick white carpet, as careful as a hunter stalking his prey.

"The situation in Nagonia is different from Chile, Nelson,'' Welsh continued, gazing thoughtfully at the straight back of the Malaysian. "Ian Smith's men have prepared some fantastic photographic material on African atrocities committed against the white minority—it's very impressive. We already have tapes of interviews with the victims, beautifully organised. Nobody would dare to question the authenticity, it's so well done. So our raid on Nagonia will be seen as entirely humane and necessary, do you see? Added to that, I'm looking at a number of interesting possibilities. Mr. Ogano—''

"Who's that?''

"What world do you live in, Nelson?''

"Our fallen world, of course.''

"Ogano is the leader of the nationalists. He's ready to march into Nagonia, we've been working with him for three years now . . . Anyway, this Ogano will make some bitter accusations against us, d'you see?''

"No, I don't! We surely get enough of that already, all round the world. I can tell you, I'm fed up with it!''

"Nelson, in the matter of tactics, please rely on me. If we had done a proper job on Pinochet, and if we had then had a man in Moscow like we do now, then Allende's overthrow could have been carried out under the banner of national revolution and the struggle for democracy and efficiency. What Pinochet *should* have done was round on the US for our economic blockade, saying things like: 'You bloody Yankees, why didn't you give Allende the cars and spares he needed?! You bloody Yankees, why didn't you give us our mining equipment?! It's you who caused economic chaos and destroyed our most honoured son—Dr.

Allende!' And then we would have had to send cars and equipment over there—not covertly like now, Nelson. But we've learned our lesson. In Nagonia our plan is much more subtle.''

''Don't you fear that by allowing them to slander us, we might get short-term dividends, but we could be building up problems for the future?''

''What do *you* think?''

''Here's your pheasant soup.''

Welsh glanced round. Behind his back stood two waiters; beside him, like a sphinx, was the head waiter.

When the bowls had been placed before them by the waiters (their movements were balletic, super-rehearsed) Green attacked the soup with an eagerness that suggested he hadn't eaten for days.

''You have to eat pheasant hot,'' he explained. ''Pheasant soup is specially health-giving, it protects you from diseases of the pancreas.''

Finishing his soup, he pushed away the bowl and slumped forward, his chest against the table. Watching him, Welsh thought to himself: ''You can still see the Mid-West farmer. Thank God the *nouveaux riches* around here have taught him nothing. The way he handles his plate is just like one of my cowboys!''

''Michael, the Pentagon will do what you asked me, but it'll be at the last moment. They like to pretend to be independent, you know how it is with the younger ministers. The helicopters have already been transferred to the fleet, but they won't give them to . . . What d'you call him?''

''Ogano.''

''Yes, that's it. The Pentagon wants you to press them as hard as you can, d'you see? I think they feel a bit offended: you're giving them a piece of the pie, but you keep the recipe for yourself. At least let them see the overall plan of the operation. Appeal to their ambitions—that's my advice. It won't kill you, will it? Now, here's a second problem. How will Europe react? Have you got *that* situation under control? If only Bonn and Paris can be made to keep quiet—that'll be enough, considering their special relations with Moscow. Europe must support us.''

"You're asking a lot, Nelson. Paris knows that in the Congo alone our corporations have investments worth almost thirty billion dollars. Two billion of those are yours personally. Whereas Europe has no more than seven billion in total. And you want them to applaud our triumph unanimously?''

"Degenerate nations, damn them! Surely it isn't so difficult to see that if the blacks win in Nagonia, they'll kick out the Europeans like drunken sailors out of a harbourside whorehouse?! Our only hope is to hold the south of Africa, the south at least. So, supporting Gagano—''

"Ogano.''

"What's the difference . . .''

"Well, anyway, I think Europe's attitude will be ambiguous, but to our advantage.''

Nelson reached for a toothpick, covered his mouth with a hand, and dug at a molar. "Ambiguous?'' he grunted. "Despite the fact that this Ogano of yours is favoured by Peking?''

"Oho! I see your private intelligence network hasn't let you down!''

"What do you expect? You think I'd just let you do what you like . . .''

"Apart from me, only one person knows about our contacts with Peking: that's you, Nelson.''

"Not me. Besides me, your man Lawrence knows about it, and Lawrence is connected with the Dutch firm Shell. And my impression is that he's on the side of 'commonsense' Europe, that is, the Europe which is prepared to live in Moscow's embrace.''

"Is that just your impression? Or are you sure?''

"If it's my impression, that means I'm sure, Michael . . . The last thing is—how will Moscow react?''

"Judging by our man's reports they're ready to send military assistance. That's why it's vital we complete the coup in the space of half an hour. If we do, then we'll turn up trumps: Moscow observes international treaties . . .''

"Come on, now!''

"Nelson, you spend too much time watching TV. Don't listen to that propaganda garbage. They observe international treaties, believe me, they do. And that, alas, is their strength."

<u>20</u>

Slavin

He had been sitting in the car for eight hours. Twice he had seen observation cars change shift. First there was a black Mercedes alongside his Fiat, then a light blue Chevrolet took its place. His minders no longer stood on ceremony, the game was out in the open now. Slavin kept his gaze directed at the window of the ward where Zotov lay. The window was covered with a slatted aluminum shutter, but sometimes through the slits he could see the figure of a man—probably a policeman who had come up to it to get a breath of the fresh ocean breeze. During the last few days it had begun to blow, and the foliage of the palms had become needle-like, elongated. Slavin caught himself comparing their lancet-shaped leaves with medieval Japanese paintings. They had the same tempestuous quality, the only difference was that one was bamboo, the other huge shaggy palms.

Paul Dick drove up in a taxi. He caught sight of Slavin, waved a hand as if to beckon him to come in too. But Slavin responded negatively with a shake of the head.

"Why not?" Paul called back. "General Stau will be here in a moment."

"They won't let me in," Slavin replied. "They won't let you in, either."

"Don't worry about me!"

"When they chase you out, come back to me and I'll

cool you off with my air-conditioning. It sometimes works.''

Five minutes later, a huge Cadillac drew up. It belonged to General Stau, the Police High Commissioner.

They wouldn't let their own journalists near him, Slavin said to himself, but they let in poor old Paul. They're counting on us two talking—and I suppose they're right, really.

Accompanied by three heavies, Stau went into the hospital. He moved quickly, his head bent slightly forward. He wore his white suit with elan, the cuts of the jacket making his movements light and flowing, as though at any moment he could take off and soar away.

Slavin found himself marvelling once again at the elasticity of the people. No white man he had ever met could move like Africans, they were surely the most graceful people in the world. How much was this man Stau raking off from every bribe? About five percent? And every single beat policeman, every single station, took bribes. Stau was a prosperous man indeed . . .

''Mr. Zotov, can you hear me?''

''Yes.''

''I'm Stau, the Police High Commissioner.''

''Your people,'' Zotov said, parting his lips with difficulty, ''won't let me sleep. They are deliberately stamping their boots.''

''I'll tell them to walk quietly. Please accept my apologies. I would like to ask you a few questions, if you don't mind.''

''Not at all.''

''Mr. Zotov, do you still insist that the radio was planted on you by unknown persons?''

''Yes.''

''And the coded tapes, too?''

''Yes.''

''Mr. Zotov, in that case how do you explain the fact that your fingerprints have been found on the tapes?

''I don't know.''

''That isn't an answer you can give in court under oath,

Mr. Zotov. However, if we decode the tapes and find military secrets on them, you will be handed over to a tribunal.''

"What do you want from me?''

"If you admit to working for US intelligence, then we'll put you on a plane out of here as soon as your health permits.''

"And if I don't confess?'' Zotov spoke slowly, almost inaudibly. His eyes stared up lifelessly at some point on the ceiling.

"So you are a radio ham?''

"No.''

"Then where did the radio come from?''

"It was planted.''

"Who by?''

"I don't know.''

"Why did they plant it on you?''

"You find out.''

Stau leaned over Zotov. "I *have* found out,'' he whispered. "The pro-American papers here—and I know who pays whom, and how much—have started a campaign to defend you, Mr. Zotov. I brought the papers with me. Or are you afraid of your own countrymen? Two Russian cars are parked all day every day outside the hospital, they're even here at this moment.''

"Why don't you let them in?'' Zotov whispered.

"Because you're under investigation. And they don't seem that eager to see you. Maybe they're afraid that your friends will try to set you free.''

"I fought in—''

Stau leaned still lower over Zotov, afraid to miss one single word he spoke. Zotov's words came out even more slowly, and faintly now.

"Go on, talk, I'm here . . .'' Stau said.

"I know you're here . . . I fought in the war. I was shot. I was taken prisoner. And escaped. And all that time I never . . . Do you understand? Why do I have to lie now?''

"What's that?''

"Why do I have to become an animal now?''

"I don't quite understand you, Mr. Zotov. Either that, or you have misheard me. If you confess, we will not take you to court. Intelligence is serious work, I have a lot of respect for your profession. We will give you back to your friends. Straight away. Do you understand? Perhaps you would like to see Señor Lawrence?"

"Who's that?"

"The representative of International Telephonic."

"I don't know him."

Stau took a photograph out of his pocket. It showed Zotov shaking Lawrence's hand.

"Look at this. See, this is Lawrence."

"I don't know that man."

"Mr. Zotov, in Moscow they can easily check as to whether the photograph is genuine or fake. What will you tell them if it turns out to be true?"

Without waiting for a reply, Stau pressed a button in the inside pocket of his jacket. At once several voices were heard—Lawrence, then Zotov, then Glebb.

"Lawrence: Do you want to copy the data on the deliveries on the Xerox?

Zotov: Our Xerox is bloody awful, but I'll have to do a photocopy.

Glebb: Did you get the stuff yesterday that you wanted from us? Did they print it OK?

Zotov: Thanks, John, I'm indebted to you, really.

Glebb: It's us who are indebted to you, Andrew, with debts of friendship.

Lawrence: What do you think, Mr. Zotov—will your government send military aid to Nagonia, if hostilities break out?

Zotov: No question about it.

Stau turned off his pocket recorder. It went quiet in the ward, a quiet only underlined by the tedious buzzing of flies against the window-pane.

"Well?" asked Stau. "How do you explain it? You don't have to explain anything to Washington, but what about Moscow, Mr. Zotov? If I was in the KGB's place, I wouldn't believe one word you said. You should realise that the documents that were stolen from Señor Lawrence, are in safe hands, in very safe hands.''

"I would like to speak to the press.''

"Of course you can! I'll just write a request for you. There are American reporters here already.''

"No, I don't want any of them in here.''

"They will only be allowed in when you write a statement, and your real friends can openly give you the help you need.''

"Listen, I just want to die peacefully. So just go away, OK?''

"If you will not give me a positive answer, Mr. Zotov, I will be forced to give the press all the material recovered by my officers. The material reveals you as an American agent, and a court case will be inevitable—you won't be able to avoid it.''

Zotov closed his eyes. Sweat poured down his face. His nose had become more prominent in these last days, his forehead and cheeks were an earthy colour, his eyelids bluish-black.

"I'll come back tomorrow,'' said Stau. "Rest and try not to worry. We won't do anything to make your position worse. Only I can't understand you: it seems you've played a game and lost, surely you should admit defeat? Especially as the defeat is not really a defeat—after all, you get freedom instead of lifelong slavery.''

"I heard about that,'' Zotov whispered. "Somebody has already told me about that. Only it was a different voice . . .''

"Have some consideration for me, Mr. Zotov. This affair puts me in a difficult position: I am duty bound to prove your guilt, and I *will* prove it—unless you can show a little commonsense.''

The department containing Zotov's ward was blocked off. In the corridor, by the glass doors, there stood two detectives in white coats. As soon as Stau came out, he was besieged by Paul Dick.

"Mr. Stau, I am Paul Dick from the *Post*. What is the present physical state of the Russian?''

"That is a question you should put to the doctors. I'm a policeman, not a surgeon," Stau replied as he kept walking.

"Is the Russian definitely a spy?"

"Yes."

"Who was he working for?"

"Only the courts can give you a reply to that question."

"When can I have a few words with the Russian?"

"I think you should ask your own legal people: when has a man accused of espionage ever had the legal right to give interviews to journalists?"

"Can you comment on the report in the *Lewisburg News* that your officers have contravened procedures, and that there is no proof of Mr. Zotov's guilt?"

"It is a complex game, sir," Stau laughed, then ran his tongue over his lips. "But we aren't players, we're servants of the law. That's my comment on your question."

"Is the *News*, in your opinion, a mouthpiece for the CIA?"

"Did I say anything of the sort? You must be joking! We policemen also have a right to freedom of speech . . . That's all. Goodbye, Mr. Dick."

Paul got into Slavin's car, then hawked lengthily and spat out of the window. Shutting the window, he said: "Well, you promised air-conditioning?"

"Hang on," Slavin replied, and pressed a black button on the dashboard. The car immediately filled up with cool air smelling slightly of petrol.

"Can you make anything of all this, Vit?"

"Yes, I think so. And you?"

"No, I can't understand it at all. That time we were at Pilar's, as soon as I said goodbye to you, Lawrence phoned—you know, the one from the secret service, so-called 'International Telephonic.' He said that Zotov was a friend of his. So that means he's one of ours, wouldn't you agree? So why the hell are they keeping him under guard?"

"You'd better ask Lawrence."

"You think I didn't?"

"Look how tactful I am, I don't even ask what he replied."

"I've already written a story on it, so you don't have to bend my fingers back! The story is open, it's public information. Lawrence reckons that Baillieu and Zotov are links in the same chain. But he's a cunning fellow, he won't say anything definite. 'I'm just an ordinary businessman,' he said, 'and I have friends in every walk of life. It really hurts when people I like get into a stew, just because we were born at different ends of the globe from one another.' "

"But what do you expect? He couldn't say, could he, that they've got Zotov, the spy who has been passing him information? Do you expect such a confession from him?" Slavin laughed, meanwhile thinking to himself: "Sorry, Paul, I can't tell you the truth, I have to support Lawrence's version. I just can't afford to do anything else, old chap, even though you're really an honest, naive and tremendous guy—that's why you drink."

"But why are you hanging around here, Vit?"

"Why are *you?*"

"That's a good answer," Paul sighed.

"Only I just can't see why they're in such a hurry," Slavin murmured softly to himself, knowing that Paul Dick would not fail to discuss his reaction with Glebb. Slavin was absolutely sure that Glebb would be all over Paul, as his old friend.

"What hurry?"

"Well, Stau comes along, the newspapers make a hullaballoo . . . Surely it would suit them more to drag it all out, wait till Zotov's a little better, keep all the interested parties in the dark. The strongest card in their sort of politics is to keep everyone in the dark. Confuse the opposition, while they—"

"But your people are pretty frightened, aren't they? Look how the Consul swept down here, like a hawk—"

"Hang on, what have we got to be frightened of now, Paul? It's too late to be frightened now," Slavin slapped his hat, "we should have thought before! . . . Shall we go and have some beer?"

"But, Vit, why are you so interested in this case, eh?"

"When *you're* interested, it's all OK, freedom of information and so on. But if it's us Russians, it's spying and trying to snatch back a traitor. Is that justice, Paul?"

Slavin turned on the ignition and the car moved off, a black Mercedes immediately taking up its position on his tail—the light blue Chevrolet had gone to lunch, the heavies had a strict timetable. No point getting an ulcer through over-strain, the police here didn't need ulcers, they had enough problems as it was.

"Well it looks like they really do follow you everywhere," said Paul Dick. "I'm going to send back the material on your spy, then fly over to see Ogano, have a look at liberated Nagonia, and then fuck off back to the States. My nerves are going from all this confusion . . ."

"Now, now! By the way, do you find it easy to give up drink?"

"Pure torture. Nightmares, splitting headaches, a feeling of wasted time, self-pity and sorrow for humanity— whose son for some reason I still consider myself."

"Listen, Paul, I've got an idea."

"What is it?"

"What if we go and see Lawrence, the two of us?"

"Put the squeeze on him, you mean? 'The CIA caught in the crossfire: an agent of despised Capital and an agent of World Communism take out the man from International Telephonic, now moved from Chile to Lewisburg.' A good headline, eh? A fine idea, Vit! Let's go!"

"You're not afraid of any trouble?"

"Of course I am."

"Is it worth the risk, then?"

"Life without risk is like meat without mustard. Let's go."

Paul rang Lawrence's apartment from below, in the lobby of the Hilton: "Hello, Mr. Lawrence, this is Paul Dick, we would like to pay you a visit . . . Two of us, myself and a Russian, Mr. Slavin. Just a few words, that's all . . .''

The reply came back, audible to Slavin: "Come up then, please." Then there were short pips.

"There's someone with him. That wasn't him. Anyway, damn it, let's go!"

By the lift a hotel boy called out to Paul Dick: "Sir, you were wanted on the telephone three times. They sent me to look for you, it's something very urgent."

"You go up, Vit—I'll be along in a moment."

Slavin went up to the fifteenth floor and knocked on Lawrence's door. He could hear music in the apartment, but no one came to the door. Slavin knocked again. It was party music, black jazz from New Orleans. But the door remained shut.

Slavin shrugged his shoulders and went back downstairs to the press room—the teletype and direct international lines were here. Paul Dick was nowhere to be seen.

"Where's my friend?" Slavin asked the boy who had just met them in the lobby.

"He telephoned someone and then went straight out. I think he was going to the Embassy."

"Did he say so?"

"No, it was just my impression, sir."

"You should cross yourself, when you get impressions like that," Slavin remarked.

"Very well, sir. I shall certainly start using the sign of the cross."

Slavin grinned and glanced over the latest press releases. There was nothing new. It felt like the lull before the storm.

Returning to the lobby for his room key, Slavin felt something uncomfortable in his spine. Someone was standing behind him and staring at the back of his head.

Slavin turned round. John Glebb continued staring at him, no trace of a smile on his face, his features heavy now, almost wooden.

"What's happened, John?"

"Nothing in particular," Glebb replied slowly, "—if you don't count that Lawrence has just been killed."

21

Konstantinov

At three in the afternoon Konstantinov went down into the lecture-room, where the participants in the forthcoming operation had gathered together. In the middle, on a large table, Gmyrya had set up the model of Victory Park.

"Comrades," Konstantinov began. "The operation which we are carrying out is an unusual one. Upon its success depends the fate not only of an innocent Soviet person—Zotov, who as you know is in serious trouble—but also to some extent the future of a friendly government. I would like you to bear this constantly in mind."

Gmyrya rose.

"Please have a look at the model, comrades. We anticipate that the American agent will come from the direction of Leninsky Prospekt, from the Embassy flats and past the University. Before the exit to Mozaisk Highway, he will then turn right into a narrow roadway, which leads through the park. Near the new monument, he will brake, stop for a split-second and throw something out. Or he could put it down on the ground, that would be ideal—probably a secret container shaped like a small branch. We want to pick him up with this container still in his hand. So we will have to exercise maximum caution, no radios—it's quite likely that there is a second, back-up Embassy car equipped with electronic eavesdropping devices. In an hour's time we will start blocking off the area. The distance between you should be not more than twenty metres, at night the park is pitch-black, the only lights are along the road. So I repeat: you must be very careful.''

"The essence of the matter, comrades,'' Konstantinov observed, ''is that we have not discovered the exact place where the secret containers are exchanged. There are two theories, each of which has it own logic. The first is that the branch is dropped as the car turns into the narrow road, while the car is invisible for a moment in a small hollow. Or it could slow down by the obelisk, a very natural manoeuvre—the driver admiring the view of a new Moscow building development. For this reason we have to block off an enormous area, so that nothing is left to chance. That's why Colonel Gmyrya asked you to observe maximum caution. Are there any questions?''

"Comrade General, is tonight our only chance?'' asked Junior-Lieutenant Zhokhova.

Konstantinov reached for a cigarette. He answered heavily: ''Yes, as far as we can tell, it's our last one.''

At six o'clock Konovalov called in: ''Comrade Ivanov, five cars have left the Embassy. Luns isn't among them. They are proceeding along the Garden Ring in the direction of Crimea Bridge.''

"Who from the CIA?''

"Jacobs and Karpovich.''

"What are they doing?''

"Nothing much . . . No, Jacobs has pulled out suddenly into the left-hand lane. Probably he wants to read the signal from the Volga.''

"Is Karpovich backing him up?''

"No, he's going along quietly in the third lane . . . Not looking right or left . . . Jacobs has read the signal, turned back quickly into the right-hand lane. He's made a circle, gone down to the embankment, come out on the embankment . . . He's gone past Dubov's block . . . Looking at his usual parking place . . .''

"Maybe the signal 'Parkplatz' is the parking place by the block of flats?'' Konstantinov suggested thoughtfully, looking questioningly at Gmyrya and Proskurin, sitting next to him. "Otherwise, why did he drive past Dubov's house, eh?"

"He's going up the lane," Konovalov continued meanwhile. "He has stopped beside the Embassy . . . he's running into the courtyard, didn't lock the car-door . . . Come out again . . . Holding a heap of newspapers . . . He's got into the car . . . Comes out on the Ring . . . Driving in the middle lane. Turns suddenly into the left outside lane, looks around him."

"Can he see you?"

"I don't know."

"That's not good enough," said Konstantinov.

"He's gone back into the second lane, going towards Crimea Bridge."

"Who's that speaking? Number Two?"

"No, this is Number One. He's still in our field of vision."

"Good. Carry on."

"Yes, sir."

At a quarter to seven, Jacobs parked his car beside the block of flats where the Embassy staff lived, and went up to his flat.

At seven o'clock, Konstantinov left for Victory Park.

At one o'clock Konovalov's men were told to go home. It was raining, everyone was wet to the bone. The CIA hadn't shown up. Failure again.

Slavin

My darling Vitaly,

I have thought of a philosophical formula, it's beautiful: hypocrisy sways like a curtain fixed between two iron bars, with a triumphant petty-bourgeois in the middle! Our neighbour Valery Nikolaevich met me by the lift yesterday and asked me: "Is it hard for a beautiful young woman to endure prolonged loneliness, or does free love guard her from this feeling?" I wanted to tell him he was just a nosy old parker, but you have taught me self-restraint, and I answered him with an almost parliamentary tact.

Anyway.

How I miss you, Vitaly! Not because I'm a young lady so weak she needs the protection of a man with biceps. Not because I was made from your rib and I'm proud that you're my lord and master. No, it's that the world, for all its richness, is still rather short on talents, and the fact that you are talented is perfectly obvious to me.

Oh yes, by the way, the Ilyins have bought an incredible puppy, one month old. But can you imagine—it doesn't piss in the house or whine at the door! It looks like a bear and is incredibly friendly . . . What if I buy a puppy like that for your return? I hope you will be returning, sooner or later!

Anyway, back to your talents. Do you know what I have realised? I've realised that what attracts a woman to talent is its individuality. And every individuality is outside the law, which added to its rareness makes it very interesting to a woman. This is well illustrated by the fact of Eve's fornication with Adam, and if you try to prove to me that Adam forced her to do it, then I will burst out laughing. By the way, where shall we go for our holiday? The writer's union has opened a new home in Pitsunda—the bars are open till twelve, which is amazing in itself, for holiday-makers are supposed to be in bed in deep sleep by eleven, so as to be ready to greet the new day to the accompaniment of the "Good Morning" programme! The rooms there are luxurious, with balconies. What do you think? I would happily give someone from "Lit Fund" an X-ray reaching to their core, but they have their own beautiful polyclinic. So consequently I'm not *defitsit**, they don't need my services!

Anyway. Have a think! Or shall we go to the fishing hut? But then I won't be able to wear my long skirt. I made it out of linen, you'd like it very much.

Come home as soon as you can. Tomorrow I'm going to a fortune-teller. We have an amazing blind woman here. She tells fortunes and cures lupus by a kind of exorcism.

Anyway.

Actually, in my opinion, the human heart isn't strong enough to influence the mind. The heart is softer. I have become bad-tempered. One can get rid of that habit—hide a yawn, listen to stupidity—comfort Lilya. The only thing you can't teach yourself is to get used to waiting.

But some people can. Whereas, even as a child, I couldn't—my constant bloody impatience! Probably you find it hard to bear, eh? How lovely it would be to have a woman who was calm as a heifer, and, just as *unfidgety*. Well, what word would *you* call it?

Do you understand what I'm on about all the time? I know I distract you from your work, but I want you to get angry with me, then you'll be able to think better! I should present a candidate's thesis on the "Theory of Distraction from Work by the Irritant of Love." My women friends would tear me to pieces!

Some news. I had a phone call from Konst.Iv. and Lida. Both spoke very cheerfully about how you were doing so well and would be back any day, that your mission was unusually straight-forward, almost a holiday—from which I gathered they were trying to soothe me. So I said so. Konst.Iv. laughed and admitted I was more or less right, but said there were no serious grounds for worry.

Nadya Stepanova phoned. Though they're apart now, she still asked about Dima. She doesn't waste words with me: after all, I'm not a wife, just a friend, and you have to beware of these friends—a bad example can be catching.

I told her that you were away, and so I didn't know anything about Dima, I only read his reports in the newspapers. I'm sending you his letter in this envelope, I really wanted to open it, but if a woman ever looks at a letter addressed to her husband, or at his notebook, that means their love is finished. The attrition stage has begun, it's time to divorce. Funny isn't it: people divorce when they still love each other, but when love is finished they cling onto each other, refuse a divorce, have big rows and make all kinds of complaints to the authorities.

The weather is strange here: cold, then hot. We have a lot of hypertonic crisis cases. Do you remember, Kholodov advised heart-sufferers to move into the cellar during months of uncertain sunshine? Maybe he was right, eh?

Darling, yesterday on my way home from the clinic I saw two doves fighting in the square. I would never have thought that doves could fight. Picasso, symbol of peace, and so on. And then I realised that they were fighting because of love. But can you call that *fighting?*

Please see if you can buy me a book by Eyres on trau-matology in children. We seem to get a lot of breaks, especially with girls, falling out of windows. Helping with the housework, when mum or granny aren't at home. First they open the bottom bolt (correct logic) and reach round easily, then when they've washed the bottom, they open the top and fall out. When I was a girl, they never let the parents into the hospital, but now we let the mums and grannies in, and they sit there all day. We're getting soft. Though the situation with nurses is very bad. They're all taking cleaners' jobs, working in two places. That way they get 180 roubles in their hand, you can't argue. As a radiologist on 160 roubles, I look up to them.

I really wanted to order an oak picture-frame for your study, it's one I know you'd like. But I discovered that "our planet is poorly equipped for pleasure"—Mayakov-sky is right as usual! They told me it would take a *year* at least for the order . . . To hell with them, don't you agree? Only come back as soon as you can, and let's try to spend the first Saturday and Sunday together when you come. And even better—Friday night as well.

All love and kisses,

                                                    Irina

Dear Vitaly,

They gave me your note. I have begun to unravel the Glebb business. I'm waiting for a reply from Bonn, where something very interesting seems to be shaping up. Well done for putting me onto the story! It turns out—though I'm still at the stage of getting more details—that Zepp Shantz is a shareholder in certain companies which were connected with Nagonia. Because of this, he is helping to send out cut-throats from his storm-troopers as mercenaries to Ogano.

I have a friend, Kurt Geshke, a very useful fellow, used to work with *Der Spiegel,* a friend of Valraffe, who's interested in the story. Some time ago I gave him my material on Mao's people in West Berlin, so I think he'll help me with Zepp Shantz. For the time being, as Kurt wrote me, at least one thing is clear: Zepp's cut-throats aren't flying to Lewisburg on Lufthansa, they'll be brought in secretly on American military transport planes, which is— according to Pentagon rules—strictly forbidden. They're afraid of disclosure, and so on. Kurt is covering himself, but he knows how to wait so that publication of the story will have maximum effect, and how to force people to ask the question: who gave permission for the transports? And what if the Pentagon is playing a dirty game, letting Shantz arrange it all, to mask their role? Kurt thinks that the scandal will be devastating. He is also, by the way, checking out the local CIA officer, digging up something on him. He thinks he may have burned his fingers somewhere, though he doesn't say much about this. Overall, the boy is doing fine. I sent him a telex, and within five hours he had replied with a telegram—obviously, he didn't want the wrong people to read the contents. And there are a lot of ''wrong people'' about.

So that's how things are, old chap. How's Moscow? Anything good to report? It's hot here—in both the literal and metaphorical sense. I have to fight my corner a bit. Luckily the Consul is a clever fellow, he realises that the sensitivity of a writer is different from that of the other professions (which is not elitism, simply a statement of fact). For this reason, he supports my reports, though others complain that I mix my colours too richly. But I'm not exaggerating at all. We journalists are a corporate lot, and both *their* journalists and *ours* all agree that the battle is about to begin. Ogano has taken hysteria to the absolute pitch when there is nothing left to do except start shooting. At night there is machine-gun fire on the streets, armoured patrols move up and down, otherwise terror would grip the city. Griso has refused to impose a curfew, which to be honest, worried me—I was in Chile on the eve of the putsch. True, I couldn't say that the revolution here is not arming itself—they have taken up arms and they've learnt how to fight for it. Defending the revolution is as difficult as making it. Though I think Lenin said that to defend it is *more* difficult.

Yesterday a comrade was criticizing me. He objected that there was too much dialogue in my reports: a book is one thing, journalism—another. I explained to him why I love dialogue: it's precisely dialogue that allows you to approach or to veer away from a subject, to widen the frame of an issue or to narrow it; to drop a problem or to return to it, and most important—to get the reader on your side. After all, everyone's fed up with direct exhortations. Dialogue allows you to bring forward a character, give him your thoughts, or the opposite, use his words to defend yourself, italicize them, work on them. It's a game of the intellect, isn't it?

But they objected: "It's not in the tradition of Russian journalism."

To which I said: "The best and most talented poet of our epoch perished for just that reason—that he was outside the poetic tradition. But I have no intention of shooting myself, though I couldn't anyway compare myself with Mayakovsky."

So let's return to our sheep. In general, I probably seem like the kind of writer who defends his ideas with arguments that seem at first glance to contradict them. Why is this? Because the best proof of the power of good in the world is a good, sharp description of the ravages of evil. Some people are confused by this, they want just one colour, but it won't work, people won't believe it. The public is too clever now, after all, where has there been a cultural revolution if not in our country, for all our idiocies? What do I mean by this purple passage? This is what I mean— that you should read me carefully if you want to catch my connections. I write less in words than in blocks, in other words, in ideas. Take off your hat, boss, I'm so modest!

Ergo: Kurt offered to bring together all the information

on Uncle Shantz, a Nazi *we*'re looking for, together with the uncle's nephew—whom *he* is interested in. And to publish it all together. And further, Kurt is hinting that the kinship of these two sons of bitches extends to some third equally nasty type. Who this is, he doesn't reveal. Which means, I conclude, that he is unearthing something very interesting.

Tomorrow they've promised to drop me on the border in the area where Ogano's bands are stationed. Do you know what that fellow has done? He ordered a portrait of Griso as a shooting target—and was himself the first to shoot it through. Curiously enough, it seems that the target was printed in the States—they discovered the stamp on it—but the picture of George Griso was done by a Chinese. They always seem to draw Africans or Europeans with some of their own national features. I hope you won't accuse me of nationalism here?

In the press bar here I latched onto this Englishman, who proceeded to lecture me: "We told you about the yellow peril in '45, but you sent trucks to Peking, when your own people were living in dug-outs."

I was furious. "I loaded those wagons," I said to him, "with my own hands. And they went through Byelorussia where it's true, the people were living in dug-outs. But we were right, because I know the so-called 'yellow peril,' I know the Chinese and I love them, because I've lived with them, eaten with them from the same plate. Mao and Hua will pass (I wanted to put it differently, but the Englishman would not have understood, how could he appreciate the subleties of the Russian language?), but the Chinese, like the great nation they are, will remain, and they will remember, they are *bound* to remember who helped them, and at what time and at what sacrifice to their own people. They cannot but remember—I think I'd even put it this way—"It's a poor politician who thinks only in terms of today." You should think ahead. A politician is a builder, and if, by the way, there was even just one builder in western politics, and not just lawyers one after the other, they would immediately understand what we want. After all, it's easy to work out what we are building and what we want to build. Though perhaps they do understand, and that's why they are trying to ruin us with this rearmament. And in general, they say they distrust Chinese expansionism, but I don't believe it. Nobody ever understood us better than that high intellectual, Blok: "Yes, we are Scythians, yes we are Asiatics, with slit and greedy eyes." The "Scythians" is a far better hymn to Russia than all the folksiness of our bast-slipper merchants. Why bast shoes, anyway? If I were involved in industrial cooperatives, I'd make some gold out of the bast-slipper industry—there's no more comfortable and hygenic shoe, but the bourgeoisie has beaten us to it! They sell rope shoes everywhere, somewhat modernised, to be sure. Seriously, this is not one of my complaints in the series "Russia— the country of idiots." It's business.

My time is up, old boy. I've already gossiped on too long. You have that special quality—you can listen. And I find myself under your hypnotic spell even here, in Nagonia.

Salut, Camarada! Venceremos!

Hug Irina, there you have a real comrade. I envy men who have women friends, there aren't many of them. So you have to take care of them, without spoiling them. *Domostroy** wasn't a bad book, was it?

All the best, old man. Hug all our friends, tell them I miss them very much.

Dmitri Stepanov

However, Slavin never received this letter. He had been arrested by General Stau's officers.

22

Glebb

The plane was due to take off for its border destination in the jungle at 10:00 P.M., when the darkness was already impenetrable. Nonetheless, on his way to the military aerodrome, Glebb took a false beard and moustache out of his briefcase and swiftly pasted them to his face. In this disguise he was immediately unrecognisable.

Forty minutes later the helicopter landed on the seashore. Ogano was waiting by the strip, his teeth glinting in a big smile.

"Glad to see you, John," he said, clasping Glebb's cold hand in his own giant, soft palm. "How much time do you have? About two hours, no more?"

"If anything, less, Mario."

"Let's go. They've cooked shark's fins for us. We can talk over dinner."

"It's ages since I tasted shark," Glebb drew in his breath. "I just love it. Who's your cook? My friend Van?"

"Yes, Van really is a good cook. I must thank you for recommending him."

"I never recommend anyone whom I don't know. Van used to indulge me in Hong Kong—like no one else!"

The meal was laid on a wooden tressle under a palm-tree. Torches burned around three chairs, their light plucking out of the darkness the watchful figures of guards armed with light Israeli machine-guns—small enough to be toys.

"Where's Lao?"

"Here I am," out of the night came Lao's voice. "Darkness is my element."

Glebb turned round. Military adviser Lao, once Peking's representative in Hong Kong, stepped out of the dark towards the table. His face was pale. Since the time he had operated from Mr. Lim's banking corporation, he had become thinner, older, and his face was lined with deep creases.

"Feeling ill?" Glebb inquired, shaking his hand. "Or is it nerves before the fight?"

"Neither—I have no right to be ill or nervous."

"Are those your orders? Or conviction in our victory?"

"Both."

Glebb swung round to face Ogano: "There are too many people here, Mario. Our talk is too important."

"My guards don't know English, not one damn word. They're good warriors, but that's all."

"All the same, John is right," said Lao. "Why don't we take a walk along the shore, and build up an appetite for the shark?"

He took Glebb by the arm: "What I'm most afraid of is that Langley will take it into their head to send us a new Station Officer."

"Ten days before 'Torch'?! They'd be idiots!" Glebb laughed.

"Well, do you think that they're geniuses? Of course, they'd be idiots, but I'm still very afraid about it."

"Maybe I should send the Admiral a telegram?" Ogano asked, "In my own code."

Lao laughed: "And what would it say?"

"Just that I have established a good working relationship with Mr. Glebb, and so I ask—"

Lao shrugged his shoulders in annoyance, breaking in: "—and so I ask you not to send a new Officer, otherwise my people will have to shoot another Yankee. Is that it?"

"You'll have to sacrifice one or two of your men," Glebb remarked. "Leave the bodies somewhere, and we'll release a report to the press that during a shoot-out two terrorists from the Red Action Army were killed . . ."

"No way!" Lao objected. "I'm amazed at you, John. The Red Action Army will lead people straight to us. Whereas our—*and your*—story is that Lawrence was killed by leftists. The Russians or Cubans. My men are working on the link between his killers and Nagonia. It's coming on fine. All it needs is a little polishing and we'll release it to the papers. But what I wanted you for, John, wasn't just this. We are busy carrying out your orders, but in return we find that you are letting us down."

"How?"

"Two weeks ago you promised to send us another consignment of helicopters. Where are they?"

"D'you think it's that easy to clear all this gear with the Pentagon?"

"Look, I don't complain about clearing my side with *my* Minister of Defence, do I? You send me an alarm signal, and in two hours my men eliminate Baillieu. You ask me to take out Lawrence: in two hours we have a plan, and we eliminate him. How I do it, and what I tell Peking, is my affair—nothing to do with you, is it? So why should I be interested in your relations with the Pentagon?"

"The helicopters will be here," said Glebb. "I give you my word."

"When?"

"I need to take away with me the finalised plan of action, with the corrections which I sent for you to look at. Once they have that, I can demand that the navy releases them immediately."

"Good. Thank you. We very much hope so, John. Now—the second thing. You promised that the Russian supplies to Nagonia would be stopped. But, on the contrary, they're increasing."

"I think that if you can produce some stuff on Lawrence's killing, and it's really good, we'll be able to drive the Russians into a corner. The newspapers will start demanding that the ports be closed to their ships. So I need that material from you."

"D'you really trust that Stau?"

"Yes, I do."

"Are you paying him?"

"He's a good friend," Glebb smiled. "He's a man I trust."

"Who is going to deal with the Russian you set up for Lawrence's murder?"

"Stau. But we need a dead body. Or a couple of them. And a leak, saying that a Russian by the name of Slavin was in contact with us and financing the Red Action Army which carried out this foul crime against an American businessman. And so on."

"John, our commando groups are going to need some drugs before we fly to Nagonia. They need a little tonic."

"I wouldn't advise that, Mario."

"The guys are going in there to a certain death. I doubt whether any of them will make it through . . ."

Lao put in: "We can regulate it, John. If they start smoking again after the operation is completed, we'll shoot a couple of dozen of them in front of the troops. That'll sober them up."

"I still wouldn't recommend it," Glebb repeated. "But if you both insist, I'll hand out forty grammes tomorrow. No more."

"Don't be so tight, John," said Lao. "If you need a new lot of heroin, I'll support your request. Shantz can get some good stuff in Hong Kong. I've never refused you in this, have I?"

"Exaggeration is the deceit of an honest man," Glebb sighed. "You're always holding your hand on your Adam's apple, Lao. Would you agree with me, Mario?"

"No, not at all," the latter said, and burst out laughing. "I always support Lao. We're both coloured people and you're a bloody Yankee, and you hate coloured people . . ."

Lao took Glebb by the arm and led him to the table.

"John, don't you get the impression that someone in Washington is against giving us the help we need? . . ."

"Yes, I do. 'Realistic politicians,' the sons of bitches, peace-lovers! The Kennedy idea haunts them—Kennedy, and especially Roosevelt."

"But will the Admiral stand firm? He won't back down to your realists?"

"No. I don't think so. Only we must act quickly, Lao. When Mario strikes, when his commandos go into Nagonia, we'll all have to get stuck in. We have to get the planes and paratroopers in straight away. We've got to start as soon as possible."

"What do you think about starting three days ahead of schedule?"

"I couldn't say right now . . . We're waiting for the latest information . . ."

"From whom?"

"From our loyal friend."

"As a rule, information is given by disloyal people, John."

"Every rule has an exception."

"What kind of information will he give you?"

"We're waiting for an unambiguous answer—will the Russians intervene or not if Mario goes into Nagonia?"

"They won't have time, John," Ogano replied. "Three hours after we begin, the Russians won't be able to budge. They'll have to deal with *our* government. Now please sit down, gentlemen. Let's not let the shark overcook for the waiting."

"Where is the plan of attack, Mario?" asked Glebb. "I mean the final one, with corrections?"

"Here," said Ogano touching with a finger the breast pocket of his field jacket.

"Mario hasn't sent anything to Langley in his code?" Glebb asked.

"Why should he?" Lao shrugged his shoulders. "We want *you* to become Station Officer. What sense is there in going over your head? We have drawn up a plan, and we will follow the plan, John. Now, the last thing—can you help us with your contacts in Moscow?

Glebb spread a napkin on his knees, twisted his tumbler in his hand. He looked at Ogano.

"Would you like whisky? Or gin?" the latter inquired.

"I'd prefer Russian vodka."

"I'm waiting for a reply, John, said Lao.

"You won't get one."

"John, we've been friends for ten years. I dragged you

out of the mire in Hong Kong. I've raised you up here, got rid of Lawrence for you. Don't stop me going up the staircase myself.''

''I'll answer you as soon as Mario's in Nagonia, Lao, OK?''

Lao shook his head: ''Don't spoil your own career, John. I don't want the names and code-names of your agents. I don't need them yet. But judging by your actions, which are as clever as ever, I would say that you have someone in Moscow. I'm prepared, in return for your information from Moscow, to help that person in their work. For you. I mean, are you sure your agents are properly covered? That there's no threat of exposure?''

Glebb drank the vodka which Ogano had poured him, sighed noisily and replied: ''Don't you worry about our people, Lao. They're so well covered, they have nothing to fear for six months at least.''

''Look, then. I thought it was my duty as a friend to share my anxiety with you. In the last war, the Germans lost because they had too high an opinion of themselves, and too low an opinion of their enemies. Don't repeat the mistakes of your forefathers, or it will cost you your head. I am not convinced that you will get anywhere with Zotov. Duplicity is no method in politics—and it seems you are determined to move from being a big-shot behind the scenes into the league of politicians. In fact, that's almost too obvious . . .''

''My dear Lao, I value your friendship, I really do. But you're looking at this too obviously. Zotov will have to clear himself, do you see? He will have to prove his innocence, and that will take many months, and we both of us know very well that an agent cannot work productively for more than a year. At any rate, I don't count on more. All I need is for my loyal people in Moscow to be insured against disaster for the period of a year. After that the flood can come for all I care. Mario will make me his adviser on economics and finance, I don't ask for anything more. Give me the corrected plan, Mario, it's time I went . . .''

To the Central Intelligence Agency
Department of Strategic Planning

Top Secret

28/01-45-78

The plan of "Operation Torch" has been redefined to take account of the points raised by the Director. In its final form it is as follows:

1. "X"-Day is Saturday, 7:00 A.M.

2. The Presidential Palace will be taken not only by the armoured column of commandos, but also from the air, by twenty helicopters which are arriving the day after tomorrow at Point "S."

3. George Griso will be offered the chance to address the nation to tell them of his freely taken decision to hand over power to General Ogano.

4. If he refuses, he will commit suicide.

5. George Griso's funeral will be organised by the Ogano Government, which will announce a period of national mourning.

6. Ogano will turn for aid not to us, but to Peking. Furthermore, in his speech, a final version of which is attached, he will condemn the intervention of US Marines.

Acting CIA Station Officer, John Glebb

Text of Speech by General Ogano to the people of Nagonia

My dear Countrymen,

I sincerely congratulate you on your liberation. The uprising against foreign oppression has been crowned with victory. You have called me, and I have come to you, to offer myself to the service of my nation.

We mourn the tragic death of George Griso, who proved unequal to the task which fate allotted him. But that is not his fault, rather it is the ill fortune of all our nation, which only recently threw off the chains of colonial slavery.

I think that our victorious national movement will be accepted with joy by our friends the world over.

I should say that the hand of fraternal aid has already been extended to us by Peking.

I must in no uncertain terms condemn the landing of a group of US Marines.

I want to repeat that I will always serve the cause of our national revolution!

God and Victory are with us!

23

Konstantinov

Film director Ukhov telephoned Konstantinov every day. The actors' auditions for his new film were over, but his regular consultant had not yet even seen the script, and the Artistic Commission refused to give the final go-ahead until they had the opinion of an expert.

"Good, what if I came about ten o'clock?" Konstantinov asked. "Would that be possible?"

"Come at twelve if you like!" Ukhov began to seethe. "There'll be you, the director Zhenya Karlov—he said he knows you—and myself! There's no problem, come at one in the morning if you like!"

"Can I bring my wife?" Konstantinov asked.

"You're welcome, I'd be most glad."

Konstantinov left the studio phone number with an aide, saying that in case of emergency it was only ten to fifteen minutes' drive to Mosfilm. Then he called Lida and asked her to meet him at the entrance at 9:55 P.M.

"Couldn't you say five to ten?" Lida smiled to herself.

"I could. But it sounds somehow less positive to me," Konstantinov replied.

It was stuffy in the viewing-room, the air-conditioning was out of order. Lida looked anxiously at her husband's face—he had lost weight. But he was talking merrily enough with Ukhov and Karlov, joking with the film editor Masha, lamenting about the lunacy of the weather—there had been

324

no summer at all, just non-stop rain. Then he told a funny story, asked permission to take off his jacket, and finally suggested: "If you don't object, shall we begin, eh?"

It was a film about the Cheka, and at the very start of work Konstantinov had spent almost two weeks looking at the script. He had dotted the text with so many notes that Ukhov groaned when he saw it.

"Konstantin Ivanovich, do you realise that this script has already been approved?"

"So why do you need me?"

"You know why! You're a professional, you're supposed to check its accuracy from the point of view of content."

"That's what I was doing. But if the author writes 'puzzle yourself with a question,' how can I avoid correcting his style? It's rubbish."

"It's not rubbish. The phrase is quite widely-used, you hear it all the time."

"And more's the pity. Barkhudarov treats the verb as meaning 'put in a cul-de-sac.' And I don't want our Chekists speaking bad Russian!"

"Does it really mean that?" Ukhov was surprised. "Damn it! Thanks, I'll have to look that one over."

"Look it over, please," Konstantinov repeated, grinning. "Anyway, let's get on. My main impression of the film is that it contains a lot of half-truths. Of course, the author has the best intentions, he wants to soften the image of the KGB. So we have the officer's wife waiting for her husband at home at night, we have the young captain falling in love with the restaurant singer who is linked to the black-marketeers, and we have the general who knows everything about his enemy well in advance . . . What we want is the *truth*, and if the author doesn't know it, then he should sit down and talk to us—we'll help him with pleasure! And another thing: you've got spies all over the place, and that's untrue. A spy is a rarity these days. A serious spy is a highly complex foreign policy act by our enemies. To recruit a Soviet citizen these days is a very complicated task, the very essence of our society contradicts it. A person who willingly or under pressure denies what our life has given him, is an anomaly.''

Ukhov wrung his hands and swore that he wouldn't change anything else in the script; the thing was done, it was too late to change the whole structure of it.

"I'm not demanding anything, you realise,'' Konstantinov remarked. "I'm just saying what I *have* to say. It's your right to disagree with me and ask for another consultant.''

In the film world there are two categories of directors: the "stoics,'' who spurn any correction even from a colleague, and the "schemers,'' who fearlessly dismantle an idea if they see sense in the opinions of their comrades. Ukhov was a bit of both. In the early stages, before the production order was signed for a film, he was magnanimity itself, accepting any sensible suggestions quite graciously. However, as soon as the money was released for the film and the cash meter began running, he changed from schemer into stoic. A new Ukhov appeared, dictator and tribune, spurning any word of criticism, replying to all suggestions: "But *I* think different.'' And that was it.

When Konstantinov mentioned inviting in another consultant, Ukhov calmed down, began philosophizing about the vulnerability of the artist, made a speech in praise of the Cheka, and finally accepted Konstantinov's criticisms.

The first sequence was a landscape: an actor walked along the bank of a river, then broke into a run, then signalled from the bank, with a fine gesture. Konstantinov suddenly could actually taste water in his mouth—dark, warm, sweet.

"I want to see how he moves,'' Ukhov explained. "It's very important—an actor's plasticity of movement.''

"Try to remember how Dubov moved,'' Konstantinov said to himself, automatically. "He avoided the camera. Why? On their instructions? But that wasn't so clever—a person who is always afraid of something is a deviation from the norm, and we immediately note the deviation down in our list of clues.''

"Now, look carefully at this bit,'' whispered Ukhov.

"We chose Bronevoy for the main positive role, we're going to have a fight with the Artistic Committee over it!"

"Why on earth?" Konstantinov was surprised.

"Stereotypes of thinking. They're afraid you'll see Muller in him."

"How silly! An actor is a mimic, the greater his gift of reincarnation, the higher his talent."

"Ah! If only you were a member of the Artistic Committee," said the editor Evgeny Karlov. "Then our life would be easier!"

Bronevoy was good and sound, but something was constricting him, making him tentative. Konstantinov realised that the actor didn't like his lines. In truth, there were three dimensions here: first, the script, then the film-editor's work, and finally the third personality—His Highness the Actor. Bronevoy was reading a text he did not like: it was as though some invisible filter was restricting him. Where in the script an exclamation mark had been placed, he passed by in a whisper. Where there was a meaningful question, he spoke it with a laugh. In brief, he was trying to help the script-writer, but it wasn't coming off. The basis of cinema is dialogue: if the cues that carry its main theme are right, the film will get by. If not, nothing will help, not even the most resourceful editing.

In the next sequence the actor tried the role of spy. Konstantinov immediately reacted against his hunted look: from the very first shot he conveyed terror and hatred.

"It would be no fun at all chasing *him,*" he observed. "You could see him a mile off!"

"So what? Do you want us to make the enemy heroic?" Ukhov exclaimed. "They'd have my head!"

"Who?" Lida asked, placing her hand on her husband's cold fingers. "Who would have your head?"

"I'm afraid it would be your husband, first and foremost."

"Nonsense," Konstantinov's face puckered. "If you remember, right through the film I've kept emphasizing that your enemies seem naive and stupid. Whereas they have intelligence and talent—that's right, talent!"

"Can I quote you, when I speak to the Artistic Committee?"

"Don't bother, I can say it myself. I feel sorry, not so much for the audience as for a talented actor. It's humiliating to be forced to speak a lie, while making out it's the truth."

The rest of the scenes Konstantinov sat through in silence. He felt he was being looked at from two sides—by Ukhov, tensely, expectantly, and by Lida, affectionately, somehow sadly.

In the moment before they switched on the lights, Lida took her hand off his palm and moved away slightly.

Ukhov lit a cigarette, wiped his hands, and said with a poor attempt at jollity: "Well, let's have it straight!"

"Do you really want it *straight?*" Konstantinov asked.

Karlov laughed: "We don't need everything. Give the director a chance, Konstantin Ivanovich."

"Well, I didn't like it very much," said Konstantinov. "But please don't be cross."

"You have a favourite word, Konstantin Ivanovich—justification. What's your justification here?"

"You see, it's all a bit sloppy. There's no thought. But the work of the KGB is, above all, about thinking. And thought is the opposite of cliché. That's what I mean. My boss, General Fyodorov, during the war was head of a department catching German spies. He told me a very instructive story. They had a double agent, who sent the Abwehr a telegram, to Canaris, asking for men, arms and another radio set. The situation was similar to the one in Bogomolov's great story *August 1944.* So, you see, failure was just inconceivable here, we *had* to win. But soon after he sent the telegram, the double agent suddenly went and died of a heart attack. And then, damn it, a coded message arrives from Canaris's people telling him to specify what parts he needed. And every agent has his own radio 'handwriting,' it's almost impossible to copy, or to deceive the enemy. So what were we to do? They sent a reply: 'I'm transmitting with my left hand, because my right hand got injured in the bombing.' At once the question comes back: 'How is Igor feeling?' This was the alarm signal, the agent had told us before. So we reply soothingly: 'Igor's left the infirmary, he's gone to Kharkov to Auntie Lyuda.' But that didn't satisfy Canaris. They sent a coded message to yet another agent, instructing him to come back across the front line, after first meeting the man who had died to check that his hand really was wounded. What could we do? What would you have done?''

"Don't know, I'm sure," said Ukhov.

"Have a think. No hurry. By the way, the agent whom they summoned had been in prison under Fyodorov's supervision. So what would you have done?''

"I'd have said that I couldn't get through the front line."

"Canaris wouldn't take that for an answer."

Karlov spoke: "If that's not an answer, then the operation had failed."

"That's not an answer either. The operation—we already agreed—*had* to succeed. If it had failed at that stage, Fyodorov wouldn't be my boss now."

"Well, don't torment us!" said Karlov.

"Fyodoroy spent a week with the agent who Canaris had summoned. He was Russian. He had been taken prisoner, had broken, and gone off to join Vlasov's rebels, where they put him to work for the Abwehr. Fyodorov as good as lived in this man's room, looking at him from every angle, certain that even in an enemy you could find a human being. And all the time the Chekists were looking for his relatives—almost impossible, given the mass evacuations. And they found his young brother. They found him at the front. And brought him back by plane to Moscow. Fyodorov arranged for the two brothers to meet and go out on the town. They came back the next evening, and a week later the agent was on a plane to Canaris, and later came back, so the operation was successful. Now, isn't that a story? Letting an enemy go back? Quite a challenge for a writer—to describe Fyodorov's feelings as he waited for the messages to start coming again to the man who was supposedly wounded in the hand?''

"A good plot for a film," said Karlov.

"But what shall I do with my own script-writer?" Ukhov groaned. "Strangle him? He just doesn't cut it, does he?''

"Employ a dialogue specialist," Konstantinov advised.

"In the West they have clever people working in films. You look how often they use writers to do dialogues—good ones, I mean . . ."

"A good writer costs good money," said Ukhov.

"And also: your actor's method is sound, but it doesn't gel, does it, really?"

Ukhov turned to the film-editor Masha: "Show us some photos of other actors. Averkin looks much the same—do we have him on tape?"

"Yes we do."

"In fact he's almost a double, only he moves badly," Ukhov explained.

The projector began to whirr, and Konstantinov actually shuddered—the actor they were looking at now was indeed the split image of the man who had played the spy so dimly before.

"What! Have you made him up like that?" he asked.

"Yes. Rimmochka here is a genius," Karlov replied. "She can get a hundred per cent likeness."

"Incredible!" said Konstantinov, feeling a strange inexplicable excitement, "completely incredible!"

"Cinema is a synthesis of the incredible," Karlov suddenly chuckled. "I had an actor die on me recently, he was the star part, and we still had three scenes to shoot with him, you understand? We couldn't re-do the whole film—that would have been impossible, nobody would have paid for it. Then I found someone who was a double from behind, and somehow managed to film him in profile for the last three scenes. Nobody, not even the professionals, noticed the substitution!"

Konstantinov laughed, then rose abruptly, put on his jacket and reached automatically for his cigars.

"Comrades, excuse me, I must go."

On his return to the KGB, Konstantinov didn't wait for the lift. He ran up the stairs to the fifth floor and called Gmyrya and Proskurin.

"We need a double, we need one today, so tomorrow he can drive Dubov's car. We have to find someone who can get into Dubov's car every morning, and drive to work along the embankment, park his car, go into the Institute by the front entrance—and come straight out of the back entrance to us! And then, at six o'clock, take the car and pick up Olga and go back to Dubov's house. It's the only way. We'll bring Olga into it, once we have the double.''

"She won't do it," Proskurin objected, "she's in love with him."

"I'll try to persuade her," Konstantinov answered. "First we've got to find the double. I've got a feeling that if we can just do this, we might lure the CIA out to make contact. Most likely they've gone off the air because they can't *see* Dubov. After all, they said they watch him all the time . . ."

"What if they spot the double?" said Gmyrya. "It's not impossible. That would mean utter failure, they'd never come out."

"It depends how we handle the double," said Konstantinov. "We'll arrange him properly, get his movements right. Now, look . . . I've analysed the control signals which the CIA gave Dubov. And it seems that they took him by the following routes: the Garden Ring, Park of Culture, Leninsky Prospekt. That's one route. The second one is: across Dorogomilovsky Bridge, along the embankment, past Mosfilm, up Universitetsky to Leninsky Prospekt. Right? And the third route is: Mozhaisk Highway, turn onto the small ring-road, past Victory Park, across Vernadsky, Leninsky Prospekt."

"Right," Gmyrya grunted.

"Olga told me that usually they stopped by the park on Universitetsky Prospekt. After that, by the columns at Gorky Park. He always picked her up at the same place, by the Institute, which we can assume is signal 'Parkplatz.' They came to both these places at the very same time—from half past six to seven o'clock. The CIA cars went past them at that time."

Gmyrya and Proskurin hung on to their superior's words.

"Olga remembers that on Tuesdays they went to the colonnade, and on Fridays—to the park on Universitetsky. Today is Monday . . ."

"But who are we going to put in the car?" Proskurin

sighed. "We don't have a double, do we, Konstantin Ivanovich? Why delude ourselves?"

He looked fixedly at Konstantinov's cigar, calculating that as soon as the general began to puff out his dry blue smoke, he too could light a cigarette.

"Go on, smoke!" Konstantinov guessed Proskurin's thoughts. "You get in a bad mood when you don't smoke. By the way, where is Gavrikov?"

Proskurin and Gmyrya exchanged glances.

"Hm, I see," grunted Gmyrya. "He *is* a bit like him. Only he moves too quickly, too abruptly, whereas Dubov was so *solid*—he knew his bosses would like him better that way!"

"As it happens, I like my subordinates solid too," Proskurin put in. "But that doesn't mean that everyone solid is a spy!"

"Just the same as speed and a sharp tongue are the determining characteristics of a gossip and chatterbox," said Gmyrya. "But Gavrikov really does look like Dubov—the trouble is, he's at the hospital, Comrade General."

Konstantinov set off for the hospital, where Senior-Lieutenant Dmitri Gavrikov's father—Vasily Feofanovich Gavrikov, a steelworker (like most of Dmitri's male relatives) at the Hammer and Sickle factory—lay dying. The old man could hardly move his huge, calloused, workingman's hands. He was unconscious for long periods, but when he came to, opening his eyes slowly, he would invariable whisper straight away: "Dimka, where are you?"

To this Dima would reply: "I'm here, dad."

Then the old man would take his son's hand in his own icy-cold fingers and place it on his chest. Then he was still again, a faint smile lingering on his face. Dmitri thought of the security he had always felt in his father's hands—what could be more beautiful in life than the security of a father's support? Whereas now the old man reached out for Dmitri's hand, and was only content when he touched his fingers.

While his father was resting, Dima went out into the

corridor for a break, lit a cigarette, and wept. He had forbidden himself to cry, so that his father, who noticed everything (wasn't that what being a father meant?) wouldn't see his red eyes and say: "Why are you crying, son?" For what could he reply? It was three weeks now since he began telling the old man that the operation had gone well and that he would soon be discharged and back at home, and his father still gratefully accepted the lie, and only kept reaching for his son's fingers.

It was here in the corridor that Konstantinov found Gavrikov. The lieutenant was standing by the window, his forehead pressed against the cold metal frame, gazing out at the green and luxuriant park below, and thinking with horror of how he would take his father from this place, through the flower-beds and bushes, how he would carry his dead weight down to Vagankovo, and how the undertakers would hammer down the nails in unseemly haste, looking at their watches just as they did two years ago when they buried his mother, so coldly businesslike in their manner with the whiff of vodka and onions on their breath, and false sympathy in their voices . . .

"Hello, Dima," said Konstantinov quietly, placing his hand on Gavrikov's shoulder. "Sorry, I know it's the wrong time to come."

Dmitri turned. He seemed not over-surprised at the General's appearance. He wiped his eyes.

"He's still hanging on," he answered.

"Dima, I've come here with a request. I'm sorry I have to ask it of you but there's nobody else. If I could have avoided coming here, if there was any other way I could think of, believe me, I would have left you in peace."

"Has something happened?"

"Yes. Can I tell you?"

"Of course."

Konstantinov took Gavrikov to the make-up room at Mosfilm. Gmyrya was already waiting for them. He had been sitting there for forty minutes, beside him—a suitcase with two of Dubov's suits and all his shirts and ties.

Ukhov had gone off set. So it was Director Karlov who introduced Gavrikov to Rimma Neustroyeva.

"Rimmochka, dear," he said. "Make this handsome young man into somebody else. Have you ever been in the films, Dima? Watch out for the girls from the make-up department, they can turn a man's head! Where's the photograph?"

Gmyrya took from his wallet a portrait of Dubov and showed it to the woman.

"Well I never! I was on holiday with him in Pitsunda!" Rimma bellowed. "A very nice man, only I forget his name."

"Igor," said Gmyrya, looking in dismay at Konstantinov. Surely their whole cover-story was not about to fall apart? "Igor Pavolovich."

"No, it isn't," Rimma replied. "Not Igor, surely? Hang on, I'll remember in a minute. First names I find hard, I remember surnames much easier. That's it—Dubov!"

"No, you're wrong," said Konstantinov. "I'm afraid you're wrong there, this man's surname is Lesnikov. Igor Lesnikov."

"That's strange," the woman remarked, as she placed Gavrikov's head against the back of the chair. "Never mind, good luck to him . . . Please relax, young man, and close your eyes. Why are you so tense?"

Konstantinov looked at Karlov entreatingly. The director understood. "Rimma," he said, "darling, we need this done as quickly as possible."

"If you want it quickly, then you won't get Lesnikov, that's all! Look at your eyes!" she turned back to Gavrikov, "they're so swollen! Overdid it a bit last night, eh?"

"He doesn't drink," Konstantinov cut in. "He's got personal problems—that's all, Rimmochka."

"Well, how can he go on set, then? You can't hide grief from the camera. I remember I once did Lyubov Petrovna—"

"She means Orlova," Karlov put in: "Lyubov Petrovna Orlova."

"That's it," Rimma continued, applying colour to Gavrikov's face. "She was in such pain, it was the last stage of cancer. And the thing she most worried about—she was *such* a great woman, a real artist—was that the audience might sense her suffering on the screen. We girls are terrible, we can't hide our feelings, least of all pain! We always say that you men can't stand pain, whereas that's what you're good at—bearing pain and concealing your feelings. I hate women, honestly, I hate them! Now then, laugh please," she said to Gavrikov. "Laugh, give us a laugh . . ."

"Can't we make do without laughter, Rimmochka?" Konstantinov put in.

"Absolutely impossible! It's laughter that lays a face bare. Without that, how can I really work?"

Gavrikov wrenched his face into a smile.

Konstantinov unwrapped a cigar, puffed out some blue smoke, and looked at the lieutenant in the mirror. "You can hardly tell them apart now, Dima and Lesnikov. What do you think, Rimmochka?"

"I haven't started yet! I've got to do some false hair, or shall I make his hair stand up with a drier?"

"What's quicker?"

"What's quicker is what's best. More haste, less speed, as they say. Who are you anyway? Evgeny Paylovich's new assistant?"

"Consultant," Karlov answered. "He's my consultant."

Neustroyeva turned again to Gavrikov. "You're no actor!" she said to him, applying some light grey tone to his eyebrows. "You're so tensed up, you're going to find it hard on set."

"Damn you!" Konstantinov said to himself in anguish. "And I can't say anything! She's breaking the lad's heart."

"Rimma love," Karlov came in, apparently he had again sensed Konstantinov's alarm. "Being the genius of reincarnation that you are, can you remake Dima for us in about ten minutes, OK?"

"No, Zhenya, ten minutes is utopian. When you're a servant of the Muse, you can't cut corners . . . Listen, it's funny, but that Dubov, who's so like your Lesnikov—you know, I rather liked him. His face was well organised. But now, when I think of it, I'm surprised, there's a flaw in that face . . .''

"Why do you say that?" Konstantinov asked.

"I can't explain. Physiognomystics is like everything else inexplicable—a false science. But there's . . . I can't explain, it's just a feeling.''

"He has a very slack mouth.'' Gmyrya grunted. "A man's mouth should be firm, but this one has a slackness.''

"That's true,'' Rimma agreed. "And his eyes are strange . . . When you look closely into a person's eyes, you see their true self, you just have to learn how to look for it. There's a point between the pupil and the white, everything is expressed there, every little trait . . .''

Konstantinov glanced at his watch. Olga was already back in Moscow, they would have to hurry to prepare her. These were the last minutes, everything was beginning to slip through his fingers, it was always like that. Only you had not to panic, just do everything in order, keep going and work steadily. "We'll set the bait and catch them!'' he muttered to himself. "If only Rimma can finish Dima's face first without breaking his heart!''

Retired Lieutenant-Colonel Sidorenko returned from the sanatorium to his flat, and opening the door of the lift, saw Gavrikov in Dubov's suit, standing in the passageway with Konstantinov and Gmyrya.

"Hello, Serezha,'' he said. "How did you—?''

"This isn't Serezha,'' Konstantinov announced. "Good day, Lieutenant-Colonel, thank you for returning so promptly. This isn't Dubov,'' he repeated to the thunder-struck Sidorenko. "It's one of our colleagues, I'll introduce you in a minute.''

Gavrikov glanced questioningly at Konstantinov: should he tell the man his surname?

"Senior-Lieutenant Gavrikov,'' Gmyrya did so for him. "From counter-intelligence.''

"But where is . . . ?'' Sidorenko began. Then he stepped into the passageway, and led the three men into his flat. His rooms were furnished in an almost feminine style, with a lot of fine china and lace cushions.

Lieutenant-Colonel, Konstantinov began. We would like you to help Comrade Gavrikov, by telling us how Dubov walks, how he stands up from the chair, how he lights a cigarette. Maybe you can also remember other characteristic movements of his . . . Character is like age, my opinion is that you tell it clearest not by how a person eats, lies down or walks—but more by how they sit down on a chair or get up from it.''

"Age—yes, but character—I wonder . . . Serezha is very conscious of his movements, the way he speaks.''

"Comrade General,'' Gavrikov whispered. "Would it be all right if I telephoned the hospital?''

"Sorry, Dima. Of course you can.''

When Gavrikov had gone out into the passage, Sidorenko asked, "Have you arrested Dubov?''

"Yes.''

"Then why can't you show the original to his understudy?'' Konstantinov unwrapped a cigar, puffing out some light blue smoke.

"Your neighbour committed suicide as we were arresting him,'' he replied. "And *no one,* except you and us, yet knows about that. But I can't lie to you, Lieutenant-Colonel. I just can't.''

"Serezha—Dubov was more thick-set. You'll have to feed up your understudy a bit,'' Sidorenko observed. "Although he does look very like him.''

Gavrikov came back in, sat down on the edge of the chair: "May I smoke, Comrade General?'' he asked.

"Please do, Dima. How's your dad?''

"Asking where I am . . .''

"In four hours you'll be back there.''

"I'm ready now, Comrade General.''

"What's up with your father?'' Sidorenko asked.

"Cancer of the stomach . . . Well, shall I begin by walking, standing up, and smoking? And then you correct me, all right?'' said Gavrikov.

"Serezha—or rather, Dubov—had a very particular way of lighting a cigarette,'' said Sidorenko. "He shook it very accurately out of the packet, took it in two fingers, and put it in his mouth—always in the left corner of the mouth. And his first drag was always a deep one.''

"What cigarettes did he smoke?'' Gmyrya enquired.

"Apollo-Soyuz.''

"Try to find *them!*'' Gmyrya exclaimed, to Konstantinov's questioning look. "They're in the *Beryozka* shops, but nowhere else.''

"Then get some in a *Beryozka,*'' said Konstantinov. "And double-quick. Thanks.''

Gmyrya drove off, and Gavrikoy attempted shaking a cigarette out of the packet, poking it into the left corner of his month, lighting it, and taking a deep breath of smoke.

"Not bad,'' commented Sidorenko, "quite close.''

"That's how the sheriffs smoke in Westerns,'' Gavrikov said. "We used to copy it when we were at school. Another thing is, when he gets up from the chair, he should lean with both hands on his thighs . . .''

"That's it, exactly,'' Sidorenko cried. "You've got him to a tee!

"Hello, Olga,'' said Konstantinov, ushering the young woman into his office. "I'd like you to meet someone.''

Olga stared at Gavrikov in amazement. However, it was sunny in the office—not semi-darkness as in the hallway outside Sidorenko's—and with a woman's trained eye, she immediately spotted the make-up.

"Serezha?'' she said in a strange voice. "No, it's not Serezha. He never said he had a twin.''

"That's because he doesn't, Olga . . . Can you tell me, though, where—in what exact place, on what street—Dubov's engine stalled the last time? I'd like you to try to remember one more time.''

"What's that?'' The young woman evidently had not caught the question. She was still staring at Gavrikov. "What are you talking about?''

"Listen. You remember you said that his engine stalled, and you sat in the driver's seat and turned on the ignition while he fiddled with the wires, and then you went for a drive.''

"Yes, that's right."

"And you remember exactly how last Tuesday the car got clogged up by the colonnade at the Park of Culture?''

"Yes, yes, *that*'s where it was! The engine stalled there twice. He even joked about it, saying it was 'the umpteenth bloody time in the same place' or something like that. But where *is* Serezha?''

"He has been arrested."

"What?!'' The young woman winced and her hands flew up to her face.

"He's a spy, this Serezha of yours."

"No!"

"Did he ever tell you about Olga?''

"About *who?* Who's she?''

"She's a woman whom he killed when she guessed about him. And the day after her funeral he invited you out dancing. Yes, yes, down in Pitsunda. I know you realise we don't say such things lightly. We are counting on your help, Olga . . .''

"That means you weren't counting on it before? You didn't trust me before, but now you've decided to?''

"If we didn't trust you, if we had any doubts, I wouldn't be talking to you like this!''

"I'm glad you trust me,'' the woman said curtly, and her eyes narrowed and went cold. "I'm very grateful for your trust. But, you see, I just don't trust *you.*''

Konstantinov glanced at his watch. There was an hour left before they would have to leave for the colonnade. Gavrikov still had to try out Dubov's car. The boy had a licence, but he'd only ever driven as a learner, he had no real experience.

"What would make you trust us?'' Gavrikov asked in a quiet voice.

"Let me see Dubov. So I can ask him about this and hear what he has to say. Then I'll do anything you ask.''

"I like your attitude, Olga,'' said Konstantinov. "You're right to be angry. You're fighting for yourself now, aren't you? For your right to love him?''

"It's not important, what I'm fighting for. That's my affair. I said what my conditions were—and that's all."

"Let's go down to the car," said Gavrikov. "You'll see we're telling the truth. In just an hour, you'll see the proof of it."

"What, they'll bring Serezha to the car?! In chains, I suppose?" Olga asked, and something akin to a bitter smile appeared briefly on her lips.

"No, it's just you'll see *why* Dubov asked you to sit in his seat by the colonnade," said Gavrikov.

"Why's that?"

"You'll see for yourself in an hour," Konstantinov said. "When between 6:30 and 7 o'clock a car with a diplomatic number-plate goes past you, very slowly."

"But you can see cars with diplomatic number-plates all over Moscow."

"But I've told you the exact time when such a car will come past you, Olga. It's no coincidence, it's a system. And when Dubov took you with him, you were just a puppet."

"I wasn't a puppet!"

"Olga," said Konstantinov, and reached for a cigar. "If you refuse to do this for us, you will be ashamed to look people in the face. So please go out now with Comrade Gavrikov, to the colonnade and back. We're not asking you to do anything else."

"I won't go."

"What is the question you want to ask Dubov?"

"I just want to look him in the eyes and ask: 'Is it true, Serezha?' That's all. And he'll tell me it's all lies."

"And you would believe his words more than our proof?"

"It depends on what kind of proof you have."

"Radio messages from a spy centre, for example."

"Show me."

Konstantinov took from his desk the file containing the radio messages, and found among the decoded ones the message in which Dubov was asked to send Olga's biographical details. He offered her the sheet of paper: "This one is about you. I think the question about your mother and grandmother's maiden names was put to you first by Dubov, not me. Only his method was more subtle—he took you to the Registry Office.''

At 18.30 hours, as ''Dubov'' fiddled with his Volga's engine wires alongside the colonnade at Gorky Park, Luns drove past. Olga looked slowly at her watch, then at the number-plate—and burst into tears. Her body and face remained still. The tears were childlike, as large as peas. They poured from her eyes and ran down her face.

On Tuesday morning at 7.15 hours the CIA intelligence centre came on the air. The coded message addressed to ''Mastermind'' read as follows:

''Dear friends, We were reassured to see you at the appointed place, which means that everything is all right. However, we did not go to object 'Park,' because we didn't see your car at ''Parkplatz,'' and also because we suspected that we could be observed at 'Park.' I have set our exchange of information for Thursday at the usual time at object 'Bridge.' We would like to read your signal, conveying your readiness for the meeting, by control point 'Children.' The signal is a stripe of lipstick on the post, from 18.30–19.00 hours. Your friend 'D.' ''

Konstantinov raised his eyes to Gmyrya: ''We have thrown them the bait,'' he said, ''and they've taken it! But where the hell is object 'Children'?!''

Olga Vronskaya could offer no answer to this question. She was still being driven around Moscow by Gavrikov.

''If we can't work out this blasted object tonight or tomorrow,'' said Konstantinov, at a midnight meeting with all his officers, ''then all our efforts come to nothing. We'll have sent Zotov to his destruction, and as for Vitaly . . .''

24

Slavin

"It's about sixty hours, I reckon, since they came for me," he said to himself, lying on the narrow couch in the dark cell. "So in twelve hours' time they'll *have* to start interrogating me, one way or another. They couldn't hold me any longer, there would be too much of a scandal."

He moved his fingers slightly. There was still sensation there, although the handcuffs were sharp and tight, and cut into his skin.

"Glebb has gone too far," Slavin thought unhurriedly. "This is the second time he has gone too far. Once with Zotov, when they planted not just a radio, but also the code tables in his house. The second time with me, picking me up for the murder of Lawrence. But can Paul Dick *really* be hand-in-glove with him? I suppose it's possible, anything is possible. The man is drinking himself to death, and people in that state quickly lose their sense of what is right and wrong—only a genius can hold out and avoid becoming an animal, and Paul isn't a genius. Or have they worked on him . . . ? Well, that's enough of him . . . If only things go right in Moscow! Then it'll be fine, they'll get such a shock, they'll be reeling! Obviously, they used Pilar to catch Dubov. She's good, very good. Relaxes a man, wraps him around her little finger. And she's clever, she should be on the stage. But you can't make a living on the stage here, the poverty is too great . . . Lawrence was eliminated by him, too—by Glebb. He wants all the glory for himself. And to have Dubov to himself, too. No, he isn't really that clever, is he? A professional, careful, and bold enough with it, but he oversteps himself. Like their advertisements: constant overkill. But he's no slouch, he *acts*—I think they're made like that, 100 years has made people dynamic. I wonder what they'll offer me, they're bound to offer me something, aren't they? To become a double-agent? Too naive. Their evidence that I killed Lawrence? But they haven't got any. Hang on . . . Did I stop and stand outside his door? Yes . . . Did I knock? Yes . . . But my fingerprints aren't on the handle. Though Glebb could have switched door-handles—and put the one from my room onto Lawrence's suite. I wonder who'll pay for my room?" Slavin laughed out loud at the idea. "I'll send the bill to Glebb, let the CIA pay for it! I'll let their newspapermen get onto it . . . I wonder what effect the photograph of Pilar and Zotov would have on Glebb? He'd be frightened, he'd worry that I might have taped the whole of their conversation, though he searched Zotov's flat twice when he planted the equipment there. But they won't release Zotov until the whole thing is tied up in Moscow. If only our men can catch the CIA red-handed, they'll be dashing around like squirrels! We've just got to hold on . . . All this is terrible, but at least Zotov is still pretty ill. If he was better, they'd have set up some show, I don't think he realises the kind of thing they can do. They'd have played him back our conversation about how he's the only one who knew about the deliveries—and what could he say? I don't know what he'd do. But what are they cooking up? *Why* don't they take me for questioning?"

Slavin wasn't called for interrogation. Instead Stau came to his cell.

"Mr. Slavin, I want to talk to you as a fellow-professional."

"What does *that* mean?"

"It means that you understand things as well as anyone. Your game is up."

"What game?"

"Your one," Stau insisted.

"Look, I'm not going to talk to you. I'll only talk if you bring our Consul in here."

"Are you sure you're doing the right thing?"

"Absolutely."

"Good, the Consul is waiting in the interview-room. Let's go. But I'll ask you one last time: is there anything you'd like me to give you? I can guarantee to grant you whatever you request. My friends tell me you're a very serious person, and one should always take good care of serious people, don't you think?"

"Yes, that's true. But let's go."

The prison corridors were brightly lit, so brightly that Slavin's eyes hurt after his long confinement in the darkened cell.

"This arrest means the end of your career," said Stau. "You realise that, don't you?"

"Why so? For a writer, prison is a very useful way of spending the time, you know. It gives you something to think about when you're free again."

"Mr. Slavin, your career is finished. We know very well what the KGB does with people once they have been detained by us . . . ."

"What does it do, then?"

"You handle yourself well, I must admit. For that reason, let me suggest once more that we don't talk to the Consul, but to some other highly intelligent and efficient friends of yours."

"How much will they offer for me?"

"I beg your pardon?"

"How much money will they offer for a statement from me?"

"Well, for one, you don't yet know what statement they want from you. The evidence against you is overwhelming, Mr. Slavin, and we would prefer you to keep silent. Do you understand? The more silent you keep, the easier it is for us to do what we want to do. It's going to be difficult to take you out of this game. It'll cost you your memory, Mr. Slavin, but afterwards your friends will take you with them and *give* you, as you put it, an amount appropriate for such a significant service.''

"Approximately what? A hundred thousand?''

"Can I take that as a statement of your conditions?''

"Mr. Stau, I don't know whether you're taping all of this, but if you are, don't be in too much of a hurry to take it as my conditions—you could come off the worse.''

"How's that?''

"That's all I'm prepared to say.''

The Consul was not alone in the interview-room. Next to him sat a representative of the Prosecutor's office and an official from the Ministry of Foreign Affairs.

"Good afternoon, Vitaly Vsevolodovich,'' said the Consul. "We have already lodged a protest at your unlawful detention here. The Ministry of Foreign Affairs authorised this meeting on condition that someone from the Prosecutor's Office was present. What can you say about what has happened?''

"I haven't got anything to say, yet.''

"How's that?!'' the Consul was taken aback.

"Slow down, friend, slow down,'' Slavin mentally told the consul. "Don't push me, don't force your own ideas forward. Try to memorize what I say, then we'll get something for both of us.''

"I consider my arrest to be unlawful,'' Slavin replied, slowly.

"Some of the local papers, particularly the *Post,* have printed stories alleging that the police have evidence of your complicity in some kind of a Soviet spying. What can you say to that?''

"Let them prove it.''

The Prosecutor's officer looked at the man from the ministry, lit a cigarette, and stretched out his legs. In a heavy voice he asked: "Then don't you want to make a protest regarding your arrest?''

"Well, nobody has yet showed me an order for it. I was told I was being held. But arrest is a different matter. Where is your evidence? Do you have witnesses? Could one of them be US Citizen Paul Dick? Or John Glebb?''

"We don't want to go into details of your case,'' the

Prosecutor's officer cut him short. "You are accused of breaking our laws, espionage, and of other crimes—that's enough."

"It depends for what. I still don't quite see what the police want to get out of this business. In any case I can't think that their interest coincides with the interests of other government departments—your Ministry of Foreign Affairs, for instance."

"We are moving away from the point," the Prosecutor's official again cut him short. "Your Consul wanted a meeting with you, and he has got it. You haven't been beaten. Anyone can see you have been treated humanely."

"Well, except for the chains," the Consul observed.

"They are handcuffs," Stau corrected him.

"In any case, I think we will bring this meeting to a close," said the Prosecutor's official. "The charge against you will be made during the next five days."

"It should have been quicker," Slavin thought. "Why have they put it off for so long? If they want a big scandal, they should charge me straight away and start expelling our people. Perhaps someone in the government isn't too keen for Ogano's attack to begin right now . . ."

"Mr. Prosecutor," he said, rising from the stool fixed to the floor in the middle of the meeting room. "When can I give your people my own evidence? Because I do have evidence, stored in a secure place. And I think it will shed a somewhat different light on this whole business. Every case should be examined down to the last details, Mr. Prosecutor, even a provocation. But your foreign . . .—I mean, your friends—have left a lot of loose ends. And in as much as my case is linked inextricably with Zotov's one, I would like you to look at the whole problem together. Don't you find it all a bit tendentious and one-sided? That's all that I wanted to add . . ."

"That'll keep them busy for a while," thought Slavin, as the cell door banged shut behind him. "Let them sit down and mull over what I really meant. It all helps to win time. And I hope it ruffles a few feathers in the Ministry—after all, *they* are the ones who have to announce the decisions being taken for them by Glebb, and not everyone likes being a monkey pulling chestnuts out of the fire. So let them mull it over. Good—I'm glad we managed to force them to have that meeting. This whole business will be decided in Moscow, let's hope it has *already* been decided . . .''

That evening the *Post* ran an article which went: "How long are we going to tolerate this Russian espionage blitz? How long will Russian agents be allowed to stand guard over the injured engineer Zotov? Why hasn't the press yet disclosed the details of the case against Slavin—who many consider to be one of the organisers of the murder of the American businessman Lawrence? Who is going to answer these questions? Why doesn't the Government issue a plain and unambiguous warning to the Comrades from the Kremlin: 'Either you have absolute respect for our sovereignty, or you take your people out of here, because we cannot tolerate those who break our laws.' ''

That same night Paul Dick appeared on television. His face was ashen, his voice cracking: "I would just like to know," he began, "what charge has been dredged up against Vitaly Slavin.

"I would like everyone to know the truth. It was I who told Slavin to go to Lawrence's rooms. It was I who telephoned Lawrence. In fact, I should have gone up with Slavin to meet the dead man.

"However, I was called over to the telex by a boy who has since disappeared. When I got there, the duty officer passed me a telephone message from the Embassy which said that the Ambassador wanted to see me on urgent business.

"I rushed over to the Embassy, where I found that the Ambassador had not called for me, nor was there any urgent matter to deal with.

"I must stress that somebody needed Slavin to go upstairs to the room occupied by the late Robert Lawrence. I must stress that Slavin has no connection at all with the matter about which he has been charged.

"I do not agree with the ideology expounded by Mr.

Slavin, nor have I ever agreed with it. When I say 'ever,' I mean ever since the war, for in 1945 he and I were wartime allies. However, I must stress that even in our present state of opposition to each other certain rules of the game must be observed. There is no other way, unless we want to break our heads on the sides of tanks. This is Special Correspondent Paul Dick speaking, and declaring my readiness to repeat this evidence under oath.''

Early the next morning Glebb came to his room.

"Paul, don't get mad with me," he said, dispensing with the usual greetings: "There's been a shoot-out. Two young guys from Nagonia were killed. They were on their way to meet Slavin with some secret documents. They were his agents. I still don't know the details, but it looks like they were carrying a report on the material stolen from Lawrence. It's all well and good you saying what you said last night—freedom of the press and all that—but surely there's no question now of testifying under oath?''

25

Stepanov

"Several days ago officers from the Nagonian National Police arrested three workers from the city's electric power station—two technicians and one fitter.

"This evening the arrested men were taken to the Procurator's Office, where a press-conference was held with three representaives of the press: Jimmy Reeves from New York, Khaleb Ar-Raud from Morocco, and myself.

"After the press-conference, we went to the Continental Hotel and transmitted our three reports simultaneously. The story filed by Khaleb Ar-Raud was published with some minor abbreviations. However, the report by Jimmy Reeves, as he expected, was cut to ten lines and put in small print on page 15, under the heading: 'Nagonia— Arrests Continue of Opponents of Griso Regime.' For that reason I consider it my duty to present a full account of the press-conference which we attended.

Reeves: Why were you arrested?

Velasco (fitter): Because I was in contact with a man called Hans Kruger.

Christoforo (technician): I was arrested while listening to a transmission from the CIA office in Lewisburg.

Dias (technician): I was arrested for contacting Mr. Ho In Ya, the press attaché at the Chinese Embassy.

Ar-Raud: What sort of contacts did you have with Ho In Ya?

Dias: I was arrested while passing him information on the country's energy resources.

Stepanov: Who told you to collect that information?

Dias: Ho In Ya. He was interested in how long we could keep going without Russian aid.

Reeves: How long have you known Ho In Ya?

Dias: About two months.

Reeves: Did he pay you?

Dias: I refuse to answer that question.

Ar-Raud: Mr. Christoforo, what information were you passing to the CIA's Lewisburg headquarters?

Christoforo: I hadn't yet told them anything. They asked me questions about the equipment used in the power station, the TV Centre and the army barracks.

Reeves: Why were the CIA interested in this?

Christoforo: I don't know.

Stepanov: When were you recruited?

Christoforo: I was working for them before the present regime took over. They helped me to get my education. They gave me a free ticket to Baltimore, where I trained for a year at a power station run by the firm Worlds Diamonds.

Ar-Raud: Who was it who recruited you?

Christoforo: I was recruited in Lewisburg by John Glebb. He was a shareholder in our electrical company here before the present regime took over. I knew him when he used to come to Nagonia on business for the firm. He brought some planners with him—he wanted to invest some money in another power station designed exclusively to run the diamond mines. Worlds Diamonds wanted to continue prospecting for diamonds along the border with Lewisburg, and Glebb took their engineers and planners out there with him. I went along as their guide.

Reeves: Did Mr. Glebb force you to collaborate with the CIA?

Christoforo: No, he just asked me to help him. He said he would return the favour by helping me to further my training.

Stepanov: I would like to ask the technician Velasco: do you know who Mr. Kruger is?

Velasco: He's an engineer.

Stepanov: What else do you know about him?

Velasco: He said he was a representative here of Zepp Shantz, and that Shantz's men were going to free our country.

Ar-Raud: Who is Zepp Shantz?

Velasco: A man who is sending Mario Ogano legionaries from Europe. According to Kruger, this man Zepp is friendly with the CIA. He told me "Shantz is a powerful man, he has a relative, an American, who is a big shot in the CIA and is coming over here very soon."

Stepanov: Do you know the surname of Zepp Shantz's relative?

Dias: Kruger never told me his name.

Stepanov: But does *he* know it?

Dias: I don't know.

Reeves: Who did Kruger recruit you to work for?

Dias: My younger brother works in the Worlds Diamonds factory in Munich, they have a branch there. Kruger said that my brother had been accused of raping a white woman. He said that if I wanted to save my brother, I would have to start collecting information.

Ar-Raud: What information?

Dias: Kruger was interested in anything connected with military airfields or army vehicles. He also told me to find out who was designing the plans for the new naval port, and the exact location of the electric power lines there.

Reeves: Did you have any other tasks, apart from collecting information?

Dias: He said that I should be ready for action.

Reeves: What kind of action was that?

Dias: The last time we met, Kruger said that in two days' time three men would be coming to me from Ogano with some dynamite. I was supposed to hide them at my house. He never gave me personally any instructions connected with sabotage or terrorist attacks. I categorically denied this accusation at the preliminary investigation.

Ar-Raud: During the investigation, were you tortured?

Dias: No.

Reeves: Why have you confessed your guilt?

Dias: What else could I do? They found Kruger's instructions in my pocket.

Stepanov: How long were you supposed to hide Ogano's men at your house?

Dias: I don't know. Kruger said it was not for long. "Just for a few days"—that's all he said.

Reeves: Did you receive any money from Kruger?

Dias: Yes.

Reeves: How much?

Dias: When I was arrested the police took 300 marks away from me. I didn't even have time to check the money, it was still in the envelope.

"And so, not one American newspaper could be found to print Jimmy Reeves's report.

"Why?

"Because, of course, this information shows absolutely clearly the steadily growing activity of the CIA against Nagonia.

"Let us look at this man Zepp Shantz. Yes, he really does have an American relative, a man called John Glebb. Detailed information on this mysterious association has been collected by an American journalist, and will appear very soon—if not in the USA, then in whichever European country is willing to risk the publication of the truth about the links between a CIA officer and a neo-Nazi.

"The US Press Office in Nagonia has issued a statement declaring that reports about the help given to Ogano's bands by the CIA and Peking are a Russian and Cuban invention.

"How is it possible to square the evidence of the three arrested agents on the one hand, and the official statement of the US Embassy Press Office, on the other?

"The CIA is trying to turn the African continent into a

battlefield. They are inventing new means for the conduct of a 'Cold War.' They are arming Ogano's men. They are preparing terrorist acts. But as they say: 'He who sows the wind, will gather the whirlwind.' "

Dmitri Stepanov, Special Correspondent

Inside the Military-Industrial Complex

Simon Chou knew that besides being Vice-President of the corporation PLB, Harold Weekly was also an old friend of Michael Welsh. The two men had fought together in Korea, then Weekly went into business while Welsh stayed behind to work with Dulles.

So when he received an invitation from Weekly to cocktails, it only took Simon Chou—a lawyer and the unofficial leader of the Chinese lobby—a few telephone calls to discover, in general terms, what the likely theme of their conversation would be.

And he was not mistaken.

The guests quickly split up into groups linked by common interests: builders went off with financiers and architects; aviation chiefs—with military men and diplomats; farmers with futurologists and people close to government circles. As soon as Weekly had greeted all his guests and the party was properly launched, he took Chou by the arm and led him off to the summer-house at the bottom of the garden. Weekly's New York residence was opposite Central Park. He was most proud of the fact that it had a garden twice the size of Harrison Salisbury's.

"Listen, Simon, you wouldn't like to make a quick trip to the mainland?" Weekly began.

"Depends on what I can offer them . . ."

"Whatever you say, national character always shows through," Weekly laughed. "We always take the bull by the horns, whereas you are caution incarnate."

"Who is *we*, Harold?"

"We Americans."

"*And you?*"

"You Chinese, Simon. You Chinese."

"I feel I must correct you," Chou remarked. "I would put it differently: we *American citizens of Chinese origin.*"

"Well, that's for the press, Simon. You and I are practical men, we don't have to tie on ribbons to show where we came from. I'm talking about Nagonia, about the position of your fellow-countrymen there."

"All our lives, my father and I have tried to become American, but you still keep on reproaching us for where we came from. It's offensive, Harold."

"I'm sorry . . . You can criticize someone because he's drunk or takes LSD, but you can't do so because of their nationality, surely? One just states that as a fact."

"So what can I take to Peking," Chou resumed, smiling strangely. "That is, assuming there is some advantage here to my firm."

"Thank you. Your delicacy is appreciated and is no more than I have come to expect. Yes, there will be something in it for your firm, and in the near future. I'm talking about Peking's position on Nagonia—in the broadest sense. Ranging from their reaction to press reports that some of those fighting in Nagonia were recruited by a guy with Nazi connections, to the recent speech by your UN Ambassador on the possibility of clashes on the border with Lewisburg."

"I guess what really interests you is the first point, Harold. Zepp Shantz is the one you're talking about, I think. And he really is a revolting character, and that will go down badly in Europe, where a lot of people still remember Hitler . . . As regards the speech by the Ambassador of the Chinese People's Republic in the UN, well, I think that we already have channels to discuss this kind of thing with Peking."

"Well, I couldn't ask for a better answer than that. You certainly do your homework, Simon."

"Thanks, Harold. So what can I take to Peking? I mean, I need some formal business proposal."

"Is that really necessary?" Weekly laughed. "I thought you could pop over there any time you wanted. My friends swear you always keep one foot in the door."

"A foot is a foot, but I still have to find the money to pay my staff their wages."

"That's more like an American! Fine. You see I *would* like you to take Peking a contract. It's advanced optics, vital for your northern border, the Russians will raise a stink straight away."

"When can I meet your people to go over the small print in detail?"

"It's all in the file, and the file is right here in my safe, along with an air ticket. The plane leaves tonight, Simon. We'll sort out the details when you get back. There's a percentage on the deal set aside for you, though in principle I should have taken two percent myself, because Peking will give you whatever you want anyway. We've worked the whole thing out carefully."

Twenty-three hours later Simon Chou landed in Peking. At the airport a black Mercedes belonging to the Vice-Minister of External Trade Ho Liu Bo was waiting for him. The Vice-Minister was a general in the intelligence service and a leading light in the policy strategy team considering ways of increasing China's influence in the Western hemisphere.

After listening to Chou, General Ho lit a mentholated cigarette and shrugged his shoulders:

"They're really making a mess of every move. Why did they have to drag Weekly into it, of all people? He's a bastard, fought in Korea, we've already exposed some of the things he did there. So why ask *him* to do a deal with you over Zepp? Sometimes I'm amazed at Welsh—a clever chap, but he makes mistakes like a novice . . ."

General Ho sent the file with the contract off to the experts, and asked Simon Chou to record on dictaphone everything new or important that he had heard in the USA since his last visit to Peking. The general was concerned above all to detect emerging policy. It was this that interested him more than the nitty-gritty of facts; that was what the lower rungs of intelligence and the press analysts were employed to dissect. Putting off a lunchtime meeting with a representative of British Petroleum, Ho drove to the Cen-

tral Committee, warning the Defence Minister beforehand
about the purport of their discussion. The latter was a
loyal follower of the Great Helmsman, a close ally of President Hua, and an outstanding strategist and soldier.

That same evening the Press Department of the Central
Committee summoned the editors of all Peking's leading
newspapers, as well as the directors of radio and television.

The instructions conveyed to them were sharp and to
the point.

"We demand an answer from the USA's European allies
as to whether the freedom-fighters led by Comrade Mario
Ogano are indeed being supported by neo-Nazi elements.
If no proof can be found to substantiate such allegations—
and at the present time an unequivocal substantiation seems
unlikely—we will have the opportunity to launch an attack
on Moscow and Havana for their slandering of the leaders
of the national liberation movement and of Comrade
Ogano, a true fighter against colonialism and the hegemonism of certain superpowers. Meanwhile, we must collect all available material on Zepp Shantz and his men, so
that when the time comes it can be used as a stick to beat
the Washington administration. That time will be the moment when we are able to kick the Yankees and their European stooges out of Africa, and to raise the flag of the
Great Helmsman over the Dark Continent. Are there any
questions?"

Simon Chou flew back to the States that night via Ja-
pan—luckily there was a connecting flight. General Ho
saw him off at the airport. He was still puffing at his Sal-
ems, and talking away with an irritation that could not be
concealed.

"We've got to find out once and for all who is behind
these politicians and businessmen who are always scaring
the Americans with their talk of our mythical unreliability
and of possible Chinese hegemonism in the not-too-distant
future. Who is it? We need names—individuals, corporations, the mass media organisations which they control.
That is my paramount concern, Comrade Chou."

"Is that unreliability really so mythical, Comrade Ho?"

"You sound as if you weren't Chinese, Comrade Chou. I'm surprised to hear such a question from you. Watch out you don't get too integrated, it's the worst danger of all. When I worked in Paris—you know the restaurant I ran, it was a top-class establishment—I blocked off my own rooms and lived entirely in the old Chinese style."

"If I try to live Chinese-style in the USA, nobody—whether Weekly or anyone else—will ever put anything my way . . ."

"You mean that contract? We're turning it down. Tell him, please, that we already have a deal on optics . . . Only don't let on," Ho laughed, "that we bought the equipment from the same firm that finances Zepp Shantz's movement. Tell him that we can't do business with him but if he sets up another company and puts in someone else, we'd be ready to sign a contract for about 500 million dollars if he could offer us a ready-made factory for calculating equipment. Now, on our position at the UN, say that everything depends on the guarantees which have been discussed through diplomatic contacts. Explain that we haven't yet received a satisfactory answer to the query we raised—they'll understand what I mean. We are prepared to stand back, but China's interests in Africa mustn't be harmed in any way. Report this to Weekly *verbatim*. The exact nuances are important here, all right? . . . So what are you going to say? Have you got it memorized?"

"You mean two phrases: 'everything depends on the guarantees which have been discussed through diplomatic channels,' and 'we are prepared—' "

"That's right," the General cut him short. "That's all. Have a good flight."

26

Konstantinov

He just couldn't fall asleep. Nor could he take a sleeping pill—the situation was such that a crisis could arise at any minute. So he tossed and turned until dawn on the couch in his office. At four o'clock he got up and went for a walk outside.

On the streets, the silence was almost tangible. He remembered Slavin, their last conversation about peacefulness and tranquility. Now Slavin was in prison—*that* was fine tranquility for you!—and he, Konstantinov, was walking through the streets of Moscow, which he loved so dearly that it made his heart ache, and could do nothing to get Vitaly out of there. The CIA wouldn't come to "Bridge" because they wouldn't see a sign by that damned point called "Children." What the hell was "Children"? Where was it?

He walked along the Lubyanka to the Boulevard Ring. Trucks were out washing the streets and Konstantinov caught the flash of a rainbow in the puddles. Feeling a few drops of water splash in his face, he moved off the pavement into the roadway. A second truck crawled up closer to him. He winced and shuddered as the droplets of cool water, sharp as a shower, splattered on his face.

"Never mind," Konstantinov suddenly thought, "it's not the end. Even if I can't finish this business myself, and I have to go, at least the rest of the lads will be there . . . There'll be Volodya Grechaev—who came from

Bauman* and is now established with us. There's Igor Trukhin, once in the Northern fleet, now an ace, a real counter-intelligence ace. There's Streltsov, son of a Hero medal-winner, a useful chap even if he's still very young. There's Konovalov, who went into the war as a para-trooper, got riddled with bullets, but thirty years later he's still working like a young man, as keen as ever—amazing! There's Gmyrya, Nikodimov—all good people. It would be terrible to leave knowing you left nobody behind you: an artist without a school, a director without followers . . . That really would be terrible. But once you're sure there are people to pick up where you left off—then it's not so bad, then nothing can be so bad . . ."

"Comrade!" a shout jolted him.

Konstantinov's eyes blinked open. On the other side of the street stood a police Volga. A lieutenant, wiping his face with a large handkerchief, was shaking his head: "You can't stand there in the road. And with your eyes closed . . . Don't you know what pedestrian crossings are for, eh? Honestly, it's like children. I can understand children, they don't yet know the signs, but you . . ."

Konstantinov stepped back onto the pavement.

"I'm sorry . . . Thanks," he said.

"When you're knocked down, whose fault will it be?"

Konstantinov mumbled again: "I'm sorry . . ."

And suddenly his glance rested on the triangular road sign attached to a post—a boy and a girl holding hands and running across the street.

"Children," he said to himself. "The sign says 'Children.' It's fastened on a post. Couldn't *that* be the object 'Children'? But *where?*"

Konstantinov ran back to the KGB, called for a car, and drove around all three routes where Olga had said Dubov regularly stopped. He counted eight "Children" road signs.

But which one should they mark with the lipstick? And should the mark be crossways, or up and down?

"Come on, let's get back sharpish," Konstantinov told the driver, and picked up the telephone to ring Konovalov.

The voice at the other end told him that Konovalov, too, had not been sleeping.

"Get me out of the records section the photographs which Captain Grechaev did," Konstantinov said.

Konovalov spluttered. Clearly he did not understand the purpose of the command.

"Do you remember, two years ago you gave Grechaev a roasting for being over-suspicious?"

"I've done the same since—and for the opposite, too. But what is it you wanted to know?"

"He went round after Krager and Wilson . . . Don't you remember, they were taking a lot of photographs, while in transit from Tokyo. Both of them were from the CIA planning department—surely it can't have slipped your mind?"

When Konstantinov arrived at the office, the photographs were waiting for him. He laid them out on the large boardroom table in a neat, long row, and began sorting them slowly, thoughtfully, like a card-player: Red Square, the University, the Rossiya Hotel, GUM, the Manezh.

Finally, he selected three photographs from the row and put them in his file. He glanced up triumphantly at Konovalov.

"He's not so bad, after all, old Grechaev, is he? Look at the detail! He copied each and every picture taken by our visitors here! Brilliant! And what it shows is that the secret cachés and meetings with Dubov were all planned two years ago!" Konstantinov jabbed his fingers at the three photographs: one showed the bridge over the Moskva River, with its towers clearly visible, and a policeman on the embankment—the one who "usually goes off duty at 22.00 hours." The second showed the monument in Victory Park which Dubov had passed the day before, exactly at the spot where Luns had braked his car; and the third picture was of a road-sign saying "Children"—a close up of a boy and girl running: drivers beware!

Konstantinov turned the photograph over. "Krupskaya Street, crossing by sign 'Children,' " the caption read. "It fits perfectly," he commented. "Krupskaya Street is right on the route to the Embassy block on Leninsky Prospekt.''

He stretched for the telephone and dialled Proskurin's number:

''You wouldn't like to come for a little drive with me, eh?''

He walked past the post twice, up and down, as casually as possible: it was seven o'clock in the morning, a time to have a stroll and stretch your legs a little.

The first time he walked past, Konstantinov drew his finger across the post, underneath where the sign ''Children'' was fixed to it.

''No, that's not right,'' he decided. ''Passers-by would notice, I'll have to try differently.''

He went back and made another movement with his hand, this time a longer one. It looked better, more like a man messing about abstractedly as he walked along.

''That's it,'' Proskurin approved, from the car.

When Konstantinov got back inside, Proskurin shook his head, doubtful as ever: ''But why are you so sure that the lipstick should be the same colour as the one we found at Dubov's?''

''Why should it be any other?''

''Maybe that's the one Olga used. And he used a different one for the marks.''

''Olga uses lipstick, that's true. But her lips certainly aren't made of cement.'' Konstantinov took the little tube of lipstick they had found in the search out of his pocket, ''Look how scratched it is—this is definitely the one he drew with.''

''I don't know,'' Proskurin still resisted, gloomily, ''I'm not sure of anything any more.''

''It's nerves,'' Konstantinov agreed. ''Our nerves are stretched to breaking-point. But we must stay confident that we'll do it. We *must.*''

At 17.50 hours Gavrikov left Centre and drove off towards Krupskaya Street. Stopping the car outside a shop, he opened the door, shook out a cigarette from his packet of

Apollos, and lit up. All this time the dreadful fear had never left him that his father would most likely die before he got back. The drugs had stopped helping, and the old man was in constant pain, whispering over and over: "Mitka, where are you? Mitka! Oh, God . . ."

Gavrikov stepped towards the *kvas** container. Konstantinov had calculated that this would look better than a chance visit to the shop. The whole area had been under constant observation by Konovalov's team. Their failure in the park had showed the need for the strictest precautions, and Konstantinov reckoned it was quite possible that the CIA would position somebody on Krupskaya Street to watch Dubov mark the post. Gavrikov had been given a miniature radio set in case Konovalov's team identified a secret observer—especially if the observer had a camera. Then Gavrikov would have to smoke constantly—there was nothing like a cigarette in your mouth to change your features—and would have to pay special attention to imitating Dubov's cowboy stride.

By the post, Gavrikov paused for a second, then daubed a line across it with his lipstick holder. Immediately he heard a screech out behind his back. "Hey you, rub that off!"

He turned around, and found himself facing an old man in a straw hat, holding a bag of the type his father used to call an *avoska**.

"Rub it off! I said, wipe off that paint!" the old man called out again, and reached into his pocket.

At the same moment a crackling, far-away voice came out of the radio hidden in the Lieutenant's pocket.

"Number One! Move off the street immediately. Get into the Volga and go! There is a car proceeding from the Estate in your direction."

The "Estate" meant the Embassy. According to the unwritten laws of intelligence work, an agent may not see the person who reads his signal. If the two of them see one another it is an alarm signal and the meeting has to be postponed—"this bloody meeting," Gavrikov said to himself, "on which everything depends."

"Number One! Can you hear me? Come in, immediately." The old man in the straw hat had meanwhile taken a whistle from his pocket. Its shrill sound echoed along the street. Curious glances were turned towards the two of them, especially from the customers clustering around the *kvas* barrel.

"Look here, grandad, I'm just doing some measurements," Gavrikov said, for some reason in a whisper.

"Humph! I'll show you measurements!" the old man cried, and he grabbed hold of the sleeve of Gavrikov's jacket with his bony fingers.

"Number One! Number One! The car is now in Universitetsky approaching Krupskaya to read your signal. Leave the area immediately!"

"Look, dad," Gavrikov said, "I'm doing measurements for a survey. My car is just there. See, I haven't even turned the engine off."

"A private taxi!" the old man screeched. "I know you! Private taxis don't do surveys!"

"The car is our engineer's, not mine, dad. Wait a minute, I'll just turn off the engine."

"No, you first wipe the paint off the post! *Then* you can turn off the engine."

Old man Guskov had woken up that morning in the worst of moods. The day before he had been in the House of Veterans till late evening, agreeing next year's plans, everyone bickering till they were sore in the throat. Shubin was on his high horse again about stepping up youth work, but the bastard refused to allow elections for the president of the cultural section. Guskov was sure he was keeping the post warm for Utin who was still in hospital; despite Utin's two heart attacks, they still wanted him to head the cultural section, though he simply wasn't up to it and never had been: his field was catering but he just wanted to be in charge of something and to be giving orders to Venka the artist. So old man Guskov had been in a bellicose frame of mind from the morning and had no intention of giving in.

"The main thing is a firm line," he used to say. "If you're weak and you don't drum it into their heads, young people will never see sense. They've had it all their own way too long, they're too bold!''

''Number One! Number One! What's happening? We don't understand. Number One!''

''Well, then, let's to the police station, grandad,'' said Gavrikov, and tugged the old man abruptly towards the car. ''Let's go down to the station, let *them* sort it out!''

''All right,'' the old man assented. ''But don't you drive too fast!''

Gavrikov pushed the old man into the car, dashed round to the driver's seat, crashed into gear and accelerated, veering over the centre line because he could still hear echoing in his ears the indignant voice of the officer from Konovalov's group. He pulled into a courtyard *cul-de-sac*, turned the corner, jumped out of the car, bent double— and vomited.

''A drunken driver!'' the old man shouted triumphantly, and blew hard on his whistle again.

''Police! A drunken driver!''

A policeman was close at hand. He ran up to Gavrikov and held him by the arm.

''Thank you, Guskov.'' He turned to the old man, ''you've picked up a right one this time!''

The next moment a car belonging to the Vice Consul at the American Embassy drove past the sign ''Children,'' then picked up speed—the signal had been accepted.

''Don't trail it,'' Konstantinov warned. ''Let him go now. We'll be waiting for them by the bridge.''

At 23.25 hours, a CIA agent working in the Embassy under a diplomatic passport was arrested while placing a parcel in the secret caché in the tower of the bridge over the Moskva River, and brought to the KGB's reception centre at Kuznetsky Bridge. In a closed container, together with a poison capsule, were found instructions and questions—the final decisive ones before the launch of ''Operation Torch.''

Inside the Militay Industrial Complex

It was chiming midnight when Michael Welsh finally managed to speak to the Special Envoy. Up until eleven o'clock he had been closeted with the men from the Pentagon discussing the start of "Operation Torch." It had been a fairly difficult meeting.

Welsh had booked a table at a Malaysian restaurant just around the corner from the Soviet Embassy—a detail which gave him a special frisson of pleasure.

The Envoy was there waiting for him, his splayed, boxer's nose stuck deep in the menu.

"Glad to see you, sir," said Welsh. "I'm sorry it's so late, but I was completely stuck up earlier on—this same business of ours."

The Envoy turned and surveyed the diners sitting at the neighbouring tables.

An amateur conspirator, thought Welsh, with distaste. Afraid we'll be overheard, I suppose. I wonder how he'd react if I told him that the three tables closest to us with their sedate-looking clientele were booked by us, and that all these ladies and gentlemen are employed in our section covering the "protection of negotiations."

"Here you are, sir," Welsh continued. "I've already prepared texts for the speeches of the three ambassadors in the General Assembly. The first speech will be Chile— I think his emotional rhetoric will get the Assembly going. I'll send you over a copy with an aide the day after tomorrow—the day before 'Torch' begins."

"That's not necessary, sir. Too much information can be inhibiting. I much prefer the *ex prompto* response."

"A well-prepared *ex prompto* is always best," Welsh smiled. "However, as you please. By the way, I asked them to serve us a real Malaysian meal. I hope you like their cooking?"

"Sure I do! It's a fantastic mixture of tastes."

"I'm so pleased."

Welsh leaned back in his chair, watching the waiter as he silently laid out the little dishes piled high with exotic hors d'oeuvres.

"Unfortunately, my doctor has forbidden me to take alcohol," the Envoy sighed. "Every stage of your life—after you're seventy—can be seen as a 'loss zone.'"

"With me that stage began at forty," Welsh observed, "with ulcers . . . Anyway, sir, after the Chilean Ambassador has spoken, the second blow will be struck by Israel. No emotion here, just facts. We mustn't let the Soviet bloc and the Third World grab the initiative, we must attack ourselves. After the Israeli Ambassador comes the delegate from Paraguay: 'The Russians and Cuban aggression in Africa is a threat to world peace! The cowardly position of the Carter administration is leading humanity to nuclear catastrophe. What is necessary is the immediate creation of a Pan-African peace-keeping force.' And so on. Then the South African representative will come in, demanding a stop to the bloodbath in Nagonia and declaring that sparks flying from the conflict there have already reached the territory of his country. He will present the delegates and ambassadors with photographs and evidence of refugees asking for asylum. After that, I think, it should be the turn of the Soviet bloc, to put down their resolutions . . ."

"But what about Europe? What will be the reaction of the European ambassadors?"

"I guess you mean, first and foremost, the position of West Germany?"

"Unquestionably."

"First signs are that Bonn's reaction will be negative. We are trying to take steps to avert this, but I wouldn't put too much store on them. The main thing is to stretch it out. After all, time heals all wounds, sir. I have asked the Chilean Ambassador to take as long as he can, we've got to wear out the delegates, sir. According to the scenario our guys have worked out, your own speech should come only on the second day. Yes, yes, sir, leave it till then. By that time Ogano will have carried out a spring cleaning. His men will hold all the key positions—so we reckon—and the control of the country will be in their hands. The Ambassador of Continental China will propose a resolution condemning the role of the USA in Nagonia, but the tone of his speech will be restrained. And it is only after that, we think, that *you* should speak."

"OK . . . Well, I think that's not a bad plan at all . . . What will France say?"

"Sir, I know that you are worried by Europe's position, but the key to this whole thing is the element of *surprise:* first the action, *our* action, then the talking afterwards. We've prepared some appendices for you . . ."

"Thank you. I confess I don't like plans, but—"

"No, you're quite right. But look here, we've got you fact sheets based on documents which haven't yet been disclosed either in the media or in our own press releases . . ."

"Very interesting."

"Would you mind if my assistant brought them around to you in your office tomorrow morning?"

"By all means. But hand them to me personally."

"The intention of the fact sheets is, basically, to help you show the genuinely national character of Mr. Ogano's movement. Then, after expressing your condolences to the family of George Griso, you show that the tragedy that has taken place in Nagonia is a direct consequence of the Kremlin's expansionist policies and their attempt to turn Africa into a new Vietnam and to draw the USA into an armed conflict. That is why you will propose the sending to Nagonia of a NATO peace-keeping force, made up primarily from the European countries, while agreeing at the same time to the immediate withdrawal of our fleet from Nagonia's territorial waters."

"Excellent! In that way we can force Europe to take a position! Very neat, sir! Like all diplomats, I don't exactly love your firm, but in this case I'd be happy to have a wee sip of gin to your guys, for working out such a fine scenario. Does Nelson Green already know about it?"

Welsh shook his head.

"Unlike you, I've got no money in Worlds Diamonds . . . No, I wanted to knock the plan around with you first, especially since your suspicion of my firm is so well known . . ."

The Special Envoy laughed, and placed his large, sweaty palm on Welsh's small, strong hand.

Not the Finale

In the morning the Ambassador of the United States was summoned to the Soviet Ministry of Foreign Affairs.

Next to the Soviet diplomat sat Konstantinov—his eyes sunken, dull from lack of sleep. His face, however, was as gleamingly well-shaven as ever, his tie fastened in a specially elegant knot. Over the last seven days he had lost five kilograms. His neck seemed to protrude from the collar of his shirt, which now appeared too large for him.

When the Ambassador managed to tear his eyes off the poison capsule lying on the table in front of him, the Soviet diplomat opened the file which lay next to it.

"What we have here, Mr. Ambassador, are photocopies of questions which the CIA put to its agent. These questions show that in the very next few days an act of aggression is planned to begin in Nagonia. If we give the press the information that the CIA has been passing poison to its agents, and if we release the CIA's list of questions relating to Nagonia, then . . ."

He paused. The Ambassador was quick to take his cue.

"My Government," he said, "would be duly appreciative of a decision by your Government *not* to make this matter public . . ."

"Can we hope that your Government will take appropriate steps, not only for the release of Soviet citizens Zotov and Slavin, but also to prevent any act of aggression in Nagonia, Mr. Ambassador?"

From the speech by the Special Envoy:

The loud campaign orchestrated by the countries of the Soviet bloc as to some planned aggression against Nagonia cannot be substantiated. The date set for such a plan has passed, without the silence being broken by the sound of machine-gun fire. The groups of the left-radical Ogano have now been re-deployed away from the Nagonia border, and Mr. Ogano has stated that his men were occupied there in farming communities, not in military barracks directed by any mythical CIA instructors. I would like to repeat once more from this high platform: even if we do not like the nature of a regime in this or that country, we have never interfered, nor intend to interfere in the internal affairs of other states. I think that this statement should place a full stop to this propaganda campaign whose one aim was to slander my country in the eyes of the people of Nagonia, their government and their leader.

Konstantinov had written a draft letter he would send recommending the decoration of Gmyrya, Grechaev, Dronov, Nikodimov, Konovalov, Panov, Proskurin, Streltsov and Slavin with the medal "For Military Service." He decided not to call for a car, but to walk instead. The accumulated tension of the last few days had still not subsided. On Kalinin Prospekt he boarded a bus. A young lad was sitting by the window reading the evening edition of *Izvestiya*. Around his neck there hung a small transistor: Alla Pugachova was singing her hit about the harlequin.

Konstantinov glanced over the lad's shoulder at a small column of print in the bottom right-hand corner of the paper. It read:

TASS is authorized to announce that a few days ago Soviet counter-intelligence uncovered and intercepted a CIA operation aimed against the USSR and Nagonia, which our country is tied to by a treaty of friendship and mutual assistance. Full responsibility for attempts to continue such operations, borrowed from the arsenal of the "Cold War," lies with those who are deliberately trying to hamper the development and strengthening of good-neighbourly relations between the Soviet Union and American peoples.

After his release from prison Slavin decided not to go to the hotel. Instead, he set out straight away for the hospital. His mood was one of great elation. He could already almost see in his mind's eye the fields north of Moscow, purple with cornflowers, as his Ilyushin came in to land at Sheremetevo.

However, when he arrived at the hospital, he discovered that Zotov had already been taken to the airport. The Lewisburg authorities had offered to send a doctor on the plane with him, a suggestion which the Soviet Consul had accepted, noting wryly: "The Red Cross plane will have a Soviet doctor and a full medical team on board. But I think your doctor may be able to help our medics. After all, you have all the information on his illness and treatment to date . . ."

Slavin drove to the Embassy. There he was handed a rather strange telegram from Konstantinov. It contained a single word: "Cheers."

And that was all.

Slavin laughed. He asked Dulov to book him a ticket on the first flight to Moscow, listened politely to the latter's plea that Slavin should not go back to the Hilton—anything could happen, Glebb wouldn't forgive him lightly—and set off for the hotel.

No sooner had he locked the room door behind him and headed for the bathroom, than the telephone rang.

"Hello, my old friend," Glebb's hoarse voice could be heard in the receiver, "You wouldn't like to meet an unemployed American? I'm sure we could find something of mutual interest to talk about."

"Why not?" Slavin replied. "Can Pilar do the cocktails? Or would you prefer a drop of Russian vodka?"

GLOSSARY

Abkhasia—an Autonomous Republic on the Black Sea forming part of the Republic of Georgia

Abwehr—German military intelligence

alaverdi—Georgian word meaning "your good health"

angulas—a type of fish

asau, merlusa—African fish

avoska—string shopping bag (from the word *avos* meaning "just in case")

Bandera—leader of fascist terrorist groups operating in Ukraine in 1943–47

Bauman—a Moscow educational institute

Beryozka—Soviet shops which take only foreign currency

Borzhomi, Essentuki, etc—brands of mineral water common in USSR

Butyrka—a prison in Moscow

Canaris and Muller—high-ranking Nazi Intelligence Officers in World War II

Cheka—an acronym of the Extraordinary Commission for Combatting Counter-Revolution and Sabotage (1917–22), and used to refer to the present-day KGB (see note)

Chekhov—the famous Russian writer (1860–1904). His first name and patronymic (father's name) were Anton Pavlovich

Chekist—officer of the Cheka or its successor organisations

chelovek—man or person

Chukray—well-known Soviet film producer

dacha—country cottage

defitsit—deficit, shortage

Domostroy—work of mediaeval Russian literature codifying the principles of patriarchal family life

dvornik—yard-keeper

Felix Edmundovich Derzhinsky—comrade of Lenin and founder of the Cheka

Gastronom—general grocery and food shop

gotel—hotel. Not the correct Russian word for this meaning (which is *gostinitsa)*

Ilf—Soviet humourous writer, co-author (with Petrov) of the classics *The Twelve Chairs* and *The Golden Calf*

kefir—a milk drink similar to yoghurt

KGB—Committee for State Security, dealing with intelligence and counter-intelligence matters

Komsomol—Communist Youth Organisation, for children and young people aged 15–27

kvas—a traditional Russian drink, made from black bread and yeast, slightly alcoholic

Metternich—Prince Metternich-Winneburg, head of the Austrian Government in 1809–21, an opponent of Russian influence in Europe

MGIMO—an international research institute in Moscow

MID—Ministry of Foreign Affairs

Mosfilm—Moscow Film Studios

Mtsyri—means "a saintly character," taken from *Mtsyri* ("The Novice"), a long poem by Lermontov

nataska—coaching or tutoring

NKVD—People's Commissariat of Internal Affairs

OBKhSS—State Audit Commission

okroshka—cold soup with vegetables and *kvas* (see above)

pirozhki—small meat or vegetable pies

Pugachov—leader of a peasant rebellion in 1773–75, during the reign of Catherine the Great. This period is described in Pushkin's novel *The Captain's Daughter* with its hero, the nobleman Grinyov.

putyovka—a ticket to a resort, including travel, board and lodging (plural: *putyovki)*

Raypischetorg—District Food and Catering Organisation

Rayprodtorg—District Trading Office

Rublyov and Theophanes the Greek—the most famous icon-painters of Russia's Middle Ages

Rushnichok and *Polyushko-Polye*—traditional Russian songs

samovar—traditional Russian tea-urn

SEV—Russian initials for the Council for Mutual Economic Assistance (Comecon)

Slovo o Slovakh—literally "A Word about Words'

sooshki—small ring-shaped crackers

sukhari—Russian melba toast

sukiyaki—Japanese dish with beef and noodles

sulguni—Georgian goat cheese

Thorez, Togliatti—heads of the French and Italian Communist Parties respectively after 1945

TsSKA—Central Army Sports Club

Twentieth Congress—The Congress of the Soviet Communist Party where Khrushchov denounced Stalin and ushered in an era of liberalisation in the USSR

Vlasov—former Soviet Commander A. Vlasov, who led armed units which fought on the side of Nazi Germany in World War II

Vlasovite—follower of Vlasov (see above)

Zhiguli—Soviet car, marketed in the West under the name Lada

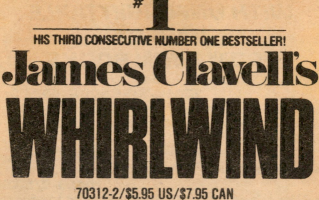